T0323897

Praise for Abbie Williams

"Williams populates her historical fiction with people nearly broken by their experiences."

— *Foreword Reviews INDIES Finalist (Soul of a Crow)*

* Gold Medalist - 2015

— *Independent Publishers Awards (Heart of a Dove)*

"Perfect for romantic mystery lovers ... a sweet, clever quickstep with characters who feel like longtime friends." — *Foreword Reviews (Wild Flower)*

"Set just after the U.S. Civil War, this passionate opening volume of a projected series successfully melds historical narrative, women's issues, and breathless romance with horsewomanship, trailside deer-gutting, and alluring smidgeons of Celtic ESP."

— *Publishers Weekly (Heart of a Dove)*

"There is a lot I liked about this book. It didn't pull punches, it feels period, it was filled with memorable characters and at times lovely descriptions and language. Even though there is a sequel coming, this book feels complete."

— *Dear Author (Heart of a Dove)*

"With a sweet romance, good natured camaraderie, and a very real element of danger, this book is hard to put down."

— *San Francisco Book Review (Heart of a Dove)*

Also By Abbie Williams

The Way Back

a SHORE LEAVE CAFE *novel*

Abbie Williams

central
avenue
publishing

2018

Published by Central Avenue Publishing, an imprint of Central Avenue Marketing Ltd.
www.centralavenuepublishing.com

THE WAY BACK

978-1-77168-127-8 (pbk)
978-1-77168-128-5 (epub)
978-1-77168-129-2 (mobi)

Published in Canada

Printed in United States of America

1. FICTION / Romance   2. FICTION / Family Life

TO THOSE OF YOU WHO HAVE FOUND THE WAY BACK,
AND THOSE OF YOU WHO CONTINUE TO SEARCH...

Prologue

Jalesville, Montana - February, 2014

THE IMAGE OF HER IN MY HEAD WAS SO CLEAR I BATTLED the urge to reach outward, even as my hands were frantic with motion, saddling my horse, stowing gear. I breathed clouds of exertion into the cold night air inside the barn, pausing only to lean my forehead against Arrow's familiar hide, trying desperately to keep level. I would help no one if I lost all control right now; deep inside, my heart shrieked at me to hurry.

I would tear myself inside out to have her returned to me. To see Ruthann enter the barn from the freezing winter's night and tell me I had been worried for no reason. I gritted my teeth at the pain of this thought, at the longing for her that spiked in my blood. My father's barn, the barn in which I'd spent thousands of hours learning the way of horses, cleaning tack, shoveling shit and forking hay, was dark with nightfall, bitter with cold. My mind stalled, rebelling against the absolute fucking agony of being separated from her, pulling me from the hell of this February night and tossing me backward to the first time I'd taught her to saddle a horse.

As though echoing my thoughts, Banjo, her mare, gave a low-pitched whinny from her stall, stamping her hooves. Arrow whickered in response; the two of them were accustomed to riding together and attuned to one another's moods. The sun had been setting as I showed Ruthann the steps that summer evening, bathing her in its radiance, and the familiar process (which I could have performed blindfolded since age five) were all but lost as I studied the woman who owned me, heart and soul. Did she know how much I loved her, how that love filled me every single moment, day or night, waking or sleeping; filled me whole.

I am coming for you, angel. I will not give up until I find you, this I swear on my life.

"Goddammit," I muttered, throat raw. I bumped my forehead against Arrow's neck, despising myself for provoking the fight that led to Ruthann leaving our apartment only yesterday.

Don't think about that. If you fucking think about that, you'll only panic and lose precious time.

The memory of the way her eyes looked when I told her to go was a blade jammed in my heart. Arrow nickered and stamped his hooves, and I pressed my palms to the warmth of my horse's hide, gaining strength. The lyrics to "Yesterday," the beautiful old Beatles song I had drummed countless times while my brothers played guitars, flooded unbidden through my brain and a sharp jab of fear caught me off guard, fear as primal as any instinct. I longed for the impossible; I longed for yesterday. If I could only go back to that moment when I told Ruthann to go and bite back the jealous, angry words.

The sickness of regret threatened to cave my chest.

Oh God, let me find her. Don't let it be too late.

"I need you, old friend," I told Arrow. He was saddled, the leather gear bags at his haunches bursting with the supplies I'd had time to gather from my childhood home. I could not consider what I would do if it didn't work – if what I was riding toward this early morning, an hour before sunrise, was not possible. It had to be possible; I would will it so. I whispered to Arrow, low and insistent, "I need you more than ever right now. Don't let me down. You hear me? Don't let me down now."

I thought for only seconds of what would happen here, in Jalesville, in the aftermath of my sudden disappearance in the wake of Ruthann's. Tish and Case knew where I was going; they had agreed to explain things to Dad and my brothers, and to Ruthann's family back in Minnesota, if we hadn't reappeared within a week. Good fortune willing, we would be back even before then. I turned up the collar of my down jacket, settled my hat lower over my head, and mounted my horse. Within seconds we'd cleared the yard, headed due west, toward the site of my family's old homestead, founded well over a century ago by my many-times-great grandfather, Grant Rawley.

I used my teeth to free my right hand from its thick leather glove and reached inside my pocket to touch the folded papers I'd placed there. A chill made my spine jerk and Arrow sidestepped, neighing in irritation. I closed my eyes and saw Ruthann's face, her golden-green eyes that saw to the deepest part of me and from which I could hide nothing. I pictured the fullness of her mouth, her thick, dark curls in which I had buried my face and hands so many times now, the soft silkiness of her belly, her graceful arms and legs, and the strength with which they wrapped around me. The sweet scent of her freckled skin, the way she fit so exactly against my body, how I fit so exactly within her, made for her alone.

Longing for her clenched me so hard in its grip that I groaned, the sound lost in the accelerating wind. Arrow's hooves crunched the thickly-packed snow. Determination overrode the icy numbness of my hands and feet.

"I'm coming, Ruthie, I promise you," I vowed to the snowy dawn, concentrating on the thousands of images of her I held sacred in my heart. "I love you more than I could ever love anyone in this world and I am coming for you."

I knew she had disappeared into the past.

I would find her, or I would die trying.

Chapter One

Smothering.

Unable to breathe, I floundered, ripping at my face to tear away the blanket covering it, only to encounter nothing but emptiness. I screamed so hard my throat was shredded, I tasted blood, but no sound met my ears. There was only a pulsing pressure that threatened to shatter the curved boundaries of my skull, the sound of an unforgiving January wind streaking across the frozen surface of a shrouded lake.

Though the words were incomplete in my mind, the sense of them hovered somewhere near –

Help me!

I was insubstantial, not so much a physical body as a rush of air. I hurtled motionlessly through open space, the way you would feel as a stationary passenger in a fast-moving airplane, a soap bubble, a husk, as fragile as an eggshell emptied of its liquid contents.

Dear God, help me!

I clung to the one name that had brought me back twice before, had pulled me from the brink of this empty, echoing terror. Need for him was stronger than my fear; need inundated my hollow body.

Marshall! Please hear me, Marshall!

But this time, I was not returned.

I became conscious in splintered fragments. Sharp points of light darted into my mind and then away, carrying bits of awareness. For a time I fought full consciousness. At last I could no longer resist and squinted at the blinding brilliance. Sunlight stuck fingers down my eye sockets.

Pain.

I attempted to sit; it didn't take long to understand I was incapable.

"Help...please, *help me...*"

The words rasped against my paper-dry throat. My tongue felt three times its usual size, a flopping cartoon tongue. Instinct led me to curl around the pain in an attempt to center it; this motion sent agony exploding like small, powerful firecrackers attached to my nerves. Tears stung the rims of my eyes. My shaking hands encountered the source before my brain stumbled to the same conclusion – broken ribs. I whimpered, unable to help it.

I let my eyelids sink, not caring in that moment if I died.

Night was a cloak anchoring my body to the earth. I lay with shoulder blades flat against the ground, unable to shift to another position. For an unknown reason – or maybe *many* unknown reasons, I couldn't begin to guess, not just now – I was outside and all sensory evidence suggested it was not in fact wintertime, even though the last memory I was able to conjure through the vice grip of physical pain involved heaping snow, and ice, *and sadness –*

"No," I begged, shying away from whatever the memory contained.

I was an unchained prisoner, trapped on the ground, surrounded by empty land and chilly night air, hearing what seemed like every cricket within fifty miles sawing a tuneless, repetitive chorus. My skin rippled with goosebumps and was blistered by mosquito bites, my limbs jittering with cold. I had no idea where I was. My body hurt so much I was certain I would be dead before morning and still it didn't come close to rivaling the gouging ache in my heart.

Just go, I begged the memory. *Please, just go...*

A deep, gruff voice demanded, "What in God's name?"

Heavy rumbling and the clinking of metal links invaded my ears, sounds I could not place into context. But then there was the unmistakable *whoosh* of a horse exhaling through its nostrils. Seconds after that I heard stomping hooves.

It was daylight once again.

A second voice, younger than the first, exclaimed, "Why, it's a woman!"

"Jump down, boy, quick!"

"A woman, lying right here in the grass!"

"Quit flapping your jaws and get to her. Is the poor thing dead?"

Running footsteps approached and I sensed someone kneeling near my head. I heard the dry crackle of grass stalks and a shadow fell over my face, at once blocking the hammer of midday sun. The smell of an unwashed body hit my nose with enough force that I cringed away, groaning. The man connected to the voice and the smell placed his fingertips on my neck, gently probing for a pulse. He called, "She's alive!"

His voice was immediately closer to my face. "Miss? Can you hear me?" When I couldn't manage to respond or open my eyes, he persisted, "Miss! You're hurt. Can you hear me?"

My head rolled weakly to one side and I felt a hard-textured palm cup my forehead; the touch was light and gentle but brought the strong odor of him closer to my nose. I gagged.

Another person knelt on the ground, with considerable grunting, and addressed me. "Here now, little lady, you'll be right as the rain." This second voice, though low and rough, was reassuring.

My eyelids cracked to a slit and I saw the two shapes silhouetted against a fiery-blue sky. One was an enormous, hulking figure, the second a much leaner man; both wore hats with wide brims. Had either meant me harm, there wasn't a thing I could have done in my present state. My eyelids sank; I was too exhausted to keep them open.

"Miss, I'll help you take water," the younger voice instructed. He cradled the back of my head and brought the rim of something to my mouth; even though I couldn't see him, his gentle touch conveyed sincere concern. Water dribbled between my lips, wetting my swollen tongue. I was so grateful that tears burned my closed eyes. I coughed and choked, but a trickle of lukewarm liquid slid down my throat.

"There now," he murmured. "Take a little more, if you can."

He waited until I had swallowed another mouthful before lowering my head; he kept his hand beneath it as a buffer against the hard ground.

The other man, the one with the gruff voice, spoke up. "You don't feel fevered, little lady, but your forehead's been struck bloody and you're bruised something terrible. I won't hurt you, I'm just gonna feel along your side."

I groaned, even though his touch along my ribs was lighter than powder. Pleading sounds rolled from my ragged throat.

"She's hurt real bad," he muttered to the younger man. "Miss, me and the boy'll lift you into our wagon and get you somewheres safe. Will you let us do that?"

I managed one jerking bob of my chin as affirmation. Together they lifted me from the ground and if I hadn't been so dehydrated I would have sobbed; as it was, I could only manage pitiful little huffs of breath. They carried me with great care, I was aware of this, but it was still almost unbearable; finally they deposited me in the open back of a wagon, onto rough wooden boards that scraped against my torn clothes and elbows.

"You rest, miss," the younger one said, climbing in the wagon, careful not to jostle the cramped space. He situated himself on my left side, settling beside my prone body. "You're a bit sunburnt but I'll make sure you don't get no more sun."

I wanted to thank him, I really did. But I could not make my tongue work.

"My name is Axton Douglas, miss, and that there is my uncle, Branch Douglas, right over there." He spoke companionably, as if we were old friends. "We'll take care of you, don't you worry." He shifted, wagon boards creaking. "Here, you need more water."

He helped me again to drink and his touch was tender. He smelled terrible; I could only guess that he hadn't bathed in weeks, but he and his uncle had saved me from the likelihood of a slow, painful death on the ground, and therefore I was in no position to complain. The wagon jerked and clanked as the uncle climbed aboard in order to drive the horses. I groaned, aware of things in spotty patches. We lurched forward.

Axton said, "There's lots of bumps on the trail, miss, I'm sorry," and so saying he edged closer, aligning his leg with my left side, resting one hand on my forehead in order to keep it as still as possible.

"*Gidd*-up," the man named Branch commanded and the wagon began rolling along.

"Careful," Axton cautioned.

"I can't smooth the way none," Branch said, with clear apology.

"I know," Axton allowed. I sensed a natural curiosity mingling with his concern. He asked quietly, "What's your name?"

But I slipped beneath a blanket of unconsciousness.

"Wake up, miss, you need more water," someone murmured.

His body odor was smothering and I could not move away from it – though, oddly, his breath, which I could feel on my eyelids as he bent near, wasn't unpleasant. Even so, I tried to breathe through my mouth rather than my nose so his lack of deodorant and soap wasn't so potent. My torso ached and my temples were squeezed by a throbbing headband, but I was not as thirsty. My tongue felt normal-sized again. I remained flat on my spine.

It was sunset and we were rumbling over bumps along uneven ground. As I opened my eyes I beheld a wide expanse of sky, all the blue heat of earlier washed away and now tinted a creamy violet. The air felt dry and cool. The younger man riding in the back of the wagon with me – he had told me his name but I could not remember it – was still bracing my body with an outstretched leg, studying me in the gathering dusk. I guessed him to be somewhere in his late teens. His hair was shaggy against the backdrop of the sky; he'd shed his hat.

"How're you feeling?" he asked, bending toward me. "You been asleep all afternoon. We'll be into town in less than an hour, now."

"A little better," I mumbled. "What's your name again? I don't remember..."

"Axton Douglas." He sounded cheerful; his teeth flashed in a grin. "And that's my uncle, Branch Douglas."

"Thank you," I whispered.

"What's your name?" He was clearly eager to learn. "What happened to you? How'd you come to be alone by the trail, with no wagon or horses about? I been wondering about you all this long afternoon."

"Boy, let her be!" his uncle commanded; from my supine position I couldn't see anything but the older man's head and bulky shoulders. Branch sounded affectionately irritated, a tone I knew well. A tone I had heard many, many times before. Wasn't that how…

Wasn't that just exactly how…

Oh God.

What's wrong?

Something is so wrong…

My mind, half-deranged with exhausted pain, would not assemble together well enough to finish this thought.

"But what's *your* name, miss?" Axton pressed.

I wanted to answer this question. I knew my name – it was there, somewhere, I knew it was. Tears blurred my vision along with frustration and fear. I struggled through a muddy mental swamp of sounds and images, unable to pull forth the right answer.

"I don't know," I whispered miserably.

"She's been hurt bad," Branch was telling someone. "Poor little thing soiled herself, too."

I had, and was sick with embarrassment over this fact, but there was nothing to be done. Branch had halted the wagon only a minute ago, before lifting me into his huge arms and climbing wide steps to enter a building; he carried me like a baby, my head cradled against his massive chest, and the smell of his leather garments was so strong I could hardly bear to inhale. I heard the sounds of conversation, laughter, and clinking glasses from somewhere nearby; I was too embarrassed to open my eyes.

"Lord above, take her upstairs," a woman ordered. Her voice was low-pitched and rough, like a heavy smoker's. "I can only just imagine the story behind this one." There was a pause before she purred, "Axton

Douglas, just *look* at you. You get any more handsome and my girls'll skin them britches right off of you. You best watch yourself in here." She laughed, her tone full of crude suggestion.

"Dammit, Rilla, leave him be," Branch ordered. "He's just a boy."

"He ain't a boy. He's a man, you old blind turkey." I felt the woman's touch on my cheek. Her wrist smelled of musky perfume.

"Ax, go fetch Doc Turn," Branch said.

"Doc's drunk," Axton replied, and I imagined him shrugging. "I seen him outside The Forked Hoof as we came down Main."

The woman chimed in again, rife with impatience. "Go and fetch him anyway! Celia, come with me. Where in the name of Jezebel did you find this beat-up gal, Branch?"

"A dozen or so miles from town, near the creek bottom. Damn near rolled the wagon over her. She was lying beside the trail." Branch spoke as he carried me up a flight of stairs; I cringed at the clunky motion. My pants were wet with urine but Branch held me securely. The quality of the light on my eyelids changed, becoming soft; the lights downstairs must have been brighter. Up here, it was dim.

Open your eyes, I thought, but instead they rolled backward into my skull.

Somehow, the pain had been erased.

I hovered just a few inches from the ceiling, suspended effortlessly, watching events unfold in the little room just below. I saw my naked body lying on a narrow bed; a nightstand was positioned nearby, on top of which was a small, brown-glass bottle. Two women worked over me, dipping rags in a basin of water between them, washing my skin. One of my legs was bent, the bottom of my foot touching the inside of the opposite knee. My head was limp, tilted to the side so that I could only see one of my closed eyes, unpleasantly cast in gray shadows. My hands lay lax, the undersides of my wrists pale in the candlelight, streaked with blue veins. My hair was tangled and scattered across the pillow.

I looked dead.

Who you suppose beat these bruises into her? One of the women skimmed her fingers over my forehead and downward along my ribcage.

She ain't been beat, the other disagreed. *Looks like a fall.*

The one touching me let her fingertips glide across my belly, a gentle caress. The touch provoked images that blazed through my mind with all the force of a beating – but I welcomed these sensations as I had never welcomed anything.

C'mere, angel, and let me kiss your lips. His husky, loving voice poured over me with the sweetness of honey; hovering there near the ceiling, I jolted to life. My desperate gaze flew around the room, seeking the man attached to that voice.

Which lips, exactly? I heard my teasing response, my easy laughter, and felt him beneath my hands, the warm strength of his naked body as I fit myself against its length.

You tell me which, he murmured, kissing my neck, caressing my breasts with knowing fingers.

Both, of course. I shivered with heated delight.

I love you, Ruthann, oh God, I love you. I can't do without you. Tell me you know that, angel.

I know it, sweetheart. I could taste his kisses, could feel them all the way to my center. *I love you, too. I love you with all my heart. Don't go –*

Desperation slammed my senses. He was dissolving from my grasp. My arms were clutched around nothing.

No! Oh God, no, please don't leave me here!

But he was already gone.

The next time I became conscious I was in the bed rather than hovering over it. A curtain of mist hazed my vision, as though someone had applied cellophane to my eyeballs. Two women hovered behind a man sitting on the mattress near my left hip. The man was elderly and bearded; he wore little round glasses and smelled like a nasty barroom floor. He cleared his throat and ordered, *Every hour or so, another dose.*

We'll need a fresh bottle in that case, one of the women said.

It ain't for you. Give it to this here girl. There was open disgust in his tone.

I just had me a taste, the woman replied, sounding sullen.

He muttered, *Whores'll be whores.*

I had no desire to be here so I closed my eyes and floated away.

Day and night seemed to swirl together; I was reminded of cake batter being stirred, a continuous incorporation of the liquids into the powders, a creamy whirl of flowing time. When the twirling sensation finally ebbed I could smell the sweetness of vanilla extract and melting sugar grains; I stood quietly, watching as an older woman with plump, freckled arms and a long, gray braid hanging over her shoulder used a whisk in a yellow bowl. She smiled down at me with love, resting a hand on my cheek.

She said, *Just a taste now, little Ruthie.*

On the other side of wide windows, a blue lake gleamed under bright midday sunshine.

Two curly-haired girls, both older than me, caught my hands in theirs, swinging me over each crack in a well-used parking lot. They made a game of it, laughing and exclaiming, lifting me as high as they were able. I studied their faces with awe. Their eyes seemed to glow, one with a shimmering golden-green light, the other such a dazzling blue I could hardly look straight at her.

I stumbled, losing my grasp as though my hands had suddenly melted, and fell to the ground. Blood seeped from my knees. Bits of gravel grew sticky with blood, clinging to the gashes in my skin.

I cried at the sight, tears hot on my cheeks.

It's all right. The blue-eyed girl spoke soothingly, crouching to put her beautiful face near mine. Gentle hands stroked my hair. *You'll be all right, Ruthie.*

You'll be all right.

Gray eyes appeared next, intense gray eyes like a storm front coming across the lake, inescapable and dangerous. But I had no fear. I wanted those eyes close to me. I knew them. Need rose inside me as swiftly as a river flooding its banks.

I'm coming for you.

I will find you, Ruthann, I swear to you I will find you.

His voice was severe with the desire for me to acknowledge the truth of what he spoke, and even suspended as I was in a spider's web of unreality I struggled toward it. I moaned and cried for him, feeling my legs jerk and my arms twitch.

Another voice, one I did not know, sliced through my awareness with a sharp demand *—Where's that goddamn bottle? It's wearing off!*

Try as I might, I wasn't strong enough to shove away the woman who loomed near and forced me to drink from a small bottle.

"Leave off that laudanum, Jesus Christ," someone muttered. I thought it might be Branch Douglas. And then I could smell him, and knew for sure. "It's been past a week now. She's frail as a newborn. She don't need no more of it."

"She ain't your responsibility," the low-voiced woman replied. "Nor mine. I been losing money on this room, I'll have you know."

"I do know it, and I have a coin for you." Branch sighed. "I feel responsible. I feel I oughta look out for her. No one knows a thing about her. The boy and me been asking everyone. No people, no nothin'."

"She's an awfully pretty little thing." The woman's words were loaded with insinuation.

"Jesus *Christ*. That never crossed my mind. She's but a young girl!"

"I got plenty younger than her working for me. You plan to marry her?"

"I ain't the marrying kind," Branch responded crisply. His tone suggested he may have literally shuddered at the thought. "Leave me be. I have a wish to speak with her."

"She ain't even awake."

"She's flutterin'," he said, and my eyelids were doing that very thing.

"I'll not be ordered from my own room," the woman muttered, but moments later I heard the click of a door closing. I opened my eyes all the way.

Branch sat on a chair he'd dragged near the bed. By the unforgiving light of mid-morning, he was a sorry sight. He was a big man, round as a barrel through the middle, thick-shouldered, huge hands curled around the tops of his widespread knees. I couldn't make sense of his outfit, which seemed to be made of old leather, dirty and stained, shiny at the kneecaps. His face and hands were tanned a deep brown. A long red scar sliced across one cheek and he was as bearded as a sheepdog, with shaggy, graying hair. His eyes were full of kindness.

"Good morning," he said, with a nod. "Glad to see you looking alive, little lady."

I managed a weak smile. For whatever reason, I liked him.

"You feeling any better this morn?" Despite his ragged appearance, he asked this question like a gentleman.

"I am." At the rough quality of my voice he jolted to motion, reaching for a cup near the bedside. He passed it to my hands and I rose to one elbow to accept it. I drank the lukewarm, metallic-tasting water and tried for a deep breath. The pain holding me prisoner had eased.

"You're looking better," he observed. "I don't want to trouble you none but I am sore curious about you. Where's your people? How'd you come to be alone way out here in the territory?"

"Where?" I whispered, easing back against a pillow. It was sweat-soaked and smelled terrible. And I wasn't any better; I couldn't recall the last time I'd bathed. My scalp itched, my skin itched, and my teeth felt mossy. I closed my eyes and tried to focus on one thing at a time.

"Montana Territory, miss. Ain't a place for a lady on her own." He rubbed his palms briskly over his thighs. "Axton and me came from Tennessee, once upon a time ago. Axton's pa, my older brother, was killed in the War, and his mama died not long later. I raised him up from a sprout, soon as I got home from the fighting. We been on the move a long time now. We get by as we can. We've done some mining in these parts and staked a little claim north of town. Now that I think on it, we've been here near to five years. Don't seem so long as that."

My head swam and Branch saw something wrong in my expression; concern bunched his features and his bushy eyebrows lifted. "What's troubling you, little lady? I would truly like to know."

"What is the year today?" I sounded so stupid to my own ears. But I needed to know.

Branch's eyebrows now drew together. "The year?"

"Yes," I whispered. I tried not to appear as desperate as I felt. "What is the year, today?"

"It is the eleventh of July, year of our Lord 1881," he answered politely.

I squinted; my heart jerked and lurched, gaining speed until it battered my insides. I swallowed hard. The water in the tin cup had left a bad taste in my mouth.

"They've been plying you with laudanum, pretty regular," Branch explained. "I figure that's making you forget things. You're a bit hazy yet. Doc thinks you got a cracked rib or two, honey, and you're awful bruised up. Can't splint a cracked rib. Ain't nothing but time and rest can heal it. He thinks you fell from a horse. Do you recollect?"

I shook my head, numb with growing fear. I had no recollection of anything beyond waking on the ground and being found by Branch and Axton.

Branch held my gaze, his expression both earnest and kind. "I aim to look after you. The boy and me ain't got but a shanty to live in, so I can't rightly bring you out there. But Rilla said she might be able to find work for you, to earn your bed here." He rumbled a laugh, clarifying hastily, "Not as a whore, mind you, though them gals are all good girls. But perhaps Rilla's got other work you can do, until we find your people. For now, you rest."

"Thank you," I whispered. I was so confused and scared it seemed a wad of coals had caught fire behind my breastbone. But I didn't let Branch see this, not when he was trying his best to help me.

"Do you recall your name?" he asked. "I feel we ain't been introduced proper-like. My name is Brandon Charles Douglas, after my daddy, but I been called 'Branch' since I was a sprout."

"Ruthann," I whispered, as though plucking the name from thin air. But it was mine, I somehow knew this truth. Tears prickled my eyes as I said with quiet certainty, "Rawley. My name is Ruthann Rawley."

"That's a fine name." Branch smiled broadly, relieved I had remembered something. One of his front teeth was brownish with rot. He spoke with fondness. "Ruth was my mama's name, God rest her. And Rawley, you say? That's inneresting. I wonder if you're related to the marshal. He has kin in these parts."

At the word *marshal*, my heart jolted. I put my hand over it to still its frantic thrusting.

Branch continued explaining. "Though, Rawley ain't been in these parts in a good three months. He has a vast amount of territory to cover but he'll be back this way before autumn. He deputized Alvin Furlough to keep an eye on the town in the meantime, but everyone knows Alvin ain't a threat to no criminal. At least, not when he's drunk, and he's drunk most of the time." Branch stopped his musing and held out his right hand. He grinned. "I'm right pleased to meet you, Miss Ruthann."

"I'm pleased to meet you, too." I slipped my palm against his and his grin stretched wider, exposing more rotten teeth, as he pumped our hands two times.

"Pleased as a peacock," he said amiably. "You hungry, honey?"

"I am," I whispered.

Chapter Two

Axton came to sit with me that very evening.

I had sipped tea and beef broth intermittently since morning, all I could manage to stomach just now, and was currently wrapped in a worn shawl and stationed in a rocking chair on a narrow back porch, which faced west. I felt like an invalid, even though I had tried rather hard not to feel anything at all through this endless day. Terror crouched at the back of my mind, waiting for me to openly acknowledge its presence.

"It's pretty out, ain't it?" Axton asked. He sat to my right, rocking in a languid, unhurried fashion as he studied the setting sun.

I kept my own chair still, too unsteady to rock, both bare feet pressed to the floorboards of the porch. In my hands I clutched a tin cup of tea. It was warm against my palms, for which I was grateful – despite the shawl tucked around my shoulders, the rest of my body was chilled. I'd battled bouts of trembling all day.

"Ain't it?" Axton encouraged softly, hoping to elicit a response.

"It is," I agreed, and this was true; the view was a pretty one. The town, such as it was, sprawled in the opposite direction, leaving the western view unimpeded. The land was wild, rangy prairie, studded with scrub brush. To the north, a ridge of foothills broke the otherwise straight line of the horizon. The air was still and dry, tinted a brilliant purple as the sun sank. A fire seemed to be burning in the sky just beyond our view; thin clouds blazed in a bright variety of orange hues. Behind us, in the saloon, lanterns were being lit, sending slices of golden light into the gathering darkness.

"Uncle Branch and me do some mining, yonder, beyond our claim,"

Axton said, gesturing northward. "There's plenty of gold in the hills, if you're lucky enough to find it. We ain't expecting to get rich, but that would be a fine thing indeed."

"Indeed," I echoed. Piano music from the main room of the saloon came tinkling through the back door, propped open to the pleasant evening with a corked gallon jug. Someone was playing a fiddle. Tears wet my eyes.

"We'll look out for you, don't worry none," Axton assured me, as he had three times already; he'd spied my tears. "Miss Rilla said she'll let you help with the wash. She won't make you work as a whore, Uncle Branch made certain."

Hysterical laughter threatened at his words but I bit into my tongue. Axton used the word 'whore' very matter-of-factly; it didn't sound like an insult in that particular tone, simply a job description. And though I didn't know him well, I couldn't imagine Axton speaking cruelly about anyone. I found it in my heart to be grateful I was under no expectations to work as a whore at the saloon; had that been the case, I felt empty enough to disappear into the open prairie. This time, I'd be sure I wasn't found before I died.

"It's like we're in a movie," I whispered.

Axton tilted his head to look my way and I sensed his confusion. "Like we're in a what?"

I shook my head, not sure exactly what I meant either. Strange images had troubled me erratically throughout the day; I tried to blame the laudanum. I muttered, "Never mind."

I'd learned many things about Axton in the past hour. His shyness faded the longer we sat together on the porch, replaced by an earnest curiosity; he was also kind and intuitive, recognizing my inability to answer personal questions, eagerly filling the void with his own stories. His parents had been named Charles and Mary Douglas but he didn't remember anything else about them, or his former home in Tennessee; his father was killed in action during the War Between the States without ever setting eyes upon Axton, and his mother died before he was a year old. Both were buried in a small Tennessee town called Suttonville.

"My birthday passed last month. I'm just a year shy of a full score, now," Axton said.

I thought for a minute. "You're nineteen?"

He nodded, looking over at me from his rocking chair. There was a sense of openness about him I found reassuring, despite everything; I wanted to beg him not to leave, as he would surely do any moment. The sun had already vanished. He'd placed his hat on the faded gray porch boards and sat with both boots braced on the rickety railing, like a kid. The lantern light spilling from Rilla's back windows fell across the half of Axton's face turned toward me; he offered a bashful grin. Lowering his voice, he admitted, "I've never been with any of the girls here. They tease me something fierce about it but Uncle Branch says I oughtn't to. 'Course, he thinks of me as a boy. I figure he always will."

I had been briefly introduced to several of the women employed in Rilla's saloon earlier today. I couldn't conjure up any names but their faces loomed in my memory. I said, "Some of them don't seem much older than you." I hesitated, not sure if he would be embarrassed at my next question; it didn't take a genius to observe that Axton was lonely. "Are any of them your friends?"

Axton seemed surprised I would ask, replacing his booted feet onto the floor and leaning forward. "Naw. They're busy and they'd expect me to pay them for their time, anyhow."

I studied him for a few silent seconds. Maybe I was every bit as lonely, or maybe I was searching for familiarity in his face, desperate to forge a connection. Axton didn't fidget under my gaze – I recognized he was just as inquisitive about me. His hair was uncombed and shaggy, waving back from his forehead and falling along his temples; in the glow of multiple candle lanterns it took on a burnished, red-gold hue. He was much taller than me, wide through the shoulder but otherwise slim as a heron. His eyes were a deep, mossy green. Even when not smiling, his suntanned face retained a sense of easy humor. I had to admit that beneath the multiple layers of dirt and grime, Axton was really good-looking. He, however, seemed completely unaware of this fact.

According to our earlier conversation, the business establishment in which I'd been offered a place to live in exchange for helping with the daily washing, as per a tentative agreement struck between its owner and operator, Rilla Jaymes, and me, was well-respected and well-visited; known as Rilla's Place, it was one of five local saloons. The town was built around a small spring, near which the railroad depot was stationed. A round wooden water tank, girded by bands of steel, was visible from the second-floor window of Rilla's and bore the name of the town in stenciled white letters – *Howardsville*. There was a general store, which housed a post office, adjacent to Rilla's, and in the alley between her building and another saloon stood a small wooden shack with a canvas door, which she had referred to as 'the laundry.' I had yet to see inside this space.

"Miss Ruthann, you must be tired," Axton said, changing the subject. "You ain't fully recovered. Though, you look a fair amount better than when we found you."

"I feel a little better." It wasn't a complete lie. Physically, at least, my state of being had improved. I hadn't eaten anything solid and my stomach was growling. "Do you think there's any real food around here?"

Rilla gave me the distinct impression that she would put up with me for now, but not completely willingly, and I was hesitant to ask direct questions of her. She was a tough-looking woman far too old for the sort of make-up she plastered on her face, including sticky reddish lipstick used to enlarge her lips. But she had allowed me, a stranger in every way, to remain in a room in her saloon, had offered me a job and provided me with soap, clothing, and a small tin of smelly green salve for my peeling, sunburned face and arms; therefore, I couldn't be too harsh in my opinion of her. But it didn't change the fact that her eyes were flat and unfriendly.

Axton jumped to his feet, then immediately bent to retrieve his hat. "Of course! I'll be back directly. You wait here."

As though I had anywhere to go.

Left alone with his rocking chair, which continued rocking even without him, ghost-like, I listened to the sounds trickling from the saloon, chattering voices and laughter, the clink of glasses and bottles. The piano music was rollicking now. Somehow these were all sounds I knew and recognized; the real answers I needed seemed only to mock me, hovering just beyond my consciousness. I could neither coax nor demand them forth.

Who are you? How can you know your name but not who you are?

What are you doing here?

There has to be someone, some family, looking for you. You don't belong here.

Oh God, I should know these things.

How can I not know these things?

At least I knew my name, and clung to it with all my heart.

"It *is* like a movie," I whispered. I knew this word but not *why* I knew it, and tears washed over my cheeks. I watched a single star glint to existence in the darker sky above the fading tatters of sunset.

"First star I see tonight," I was compelled to whisper, and then covered my face with both hands, sick with confusion. My stomach, so recently hungry, curdled like sour milk.

"Miss Ruthann! C'mon!" Though he had disappeared inside the building, Axton now popped around the far side of the porch and jogged up the steps. "You gotta see the moon!"

He helped me to my feet and down the steps, leading me to the front of the saloon. I gasped, I could not help it, as we cleared the structure and the eastern sky came into full view – where a spectacular full moon floated an inch above the horizon, gleaming-white and otherworldly.

"Oh wow," I whispered, clutching the shawl together between my breasts, and Axton chuckled.

"Wow is right," he agreed, holding my elbow to his side, patting my forearm. He treated me with such tenderness I could almost excuse his awful body odor. It seemed no one here was bothered by one another's bad smells except for me. Even the women who worked in the saloon, who'd spent a long time dressing and preparing for the evening, were stinky. Their fancy dresses had yellow, sweat-stained armpits.

"Axton, I'm so scared." The statement leaped from my mouth and I felt his body twitch in response, as though surprised by such an admission.

"Well…" He spoke slowly, gathering his words. "I figure I would feel just the same. There ain't anyone you know from Adam, anywhere in sight."

"See, that's just what's so crazy," I whispered, watching the moon. Its outline blurred with fresh tears and I lifted my free hand, pressing my thumb to the corners of each eye in turn. I tried to explain, sensing him listening intently. "I know when you say 'Adam' you're talking about a religious story. I've heard of that story, right? But I can't remember my mother's name. I don't even know if I *have* a mother." I choked down a sob and Axton patted my arm again, probably just wishing I would shut the hell up. "See, the thing is…I think I have a husband. *A family.*" I heaved with the force of a sob, tipping forward.

Axton made a clucking sound of concern and shifted so I was sheltered in his embrace. I buried my face in both hands and wept, shaking with sadness, digging my fingertips against my eyelids. There seemed to be people murmuring in the background, people out and about on this beautiful summer night to marvel at the enormous moon, but I didn't care what anyone thought, overwhelmed by my own pain.

"Where do you think they are?" Axton asked after I had quieted, rubbing his palm over my back in a slow, continuous circle. He kept me close to his chest, where it was warm and I could cling to a shred of comfort.

A squeezing fist clutched my heart at his gentle question. My eyes remained closed but the moonlight was brilliant enough I was aware of its pale glow. I whispered, "I'm so afraid. I'm af – " The word broke around a cry. I bit down on the urge to lose complete control and finished, "I'm afraid they might be…dead." I could barely speak this word.

I felt him flinch, though he must have been anticipating this response based on my reaction. "You don't know, for certain?"

I shook my head, feeling raw and weak. I wanted to collapse. "I'm so sad. There's so much sadness inside of me. Where did it come from?"

"We'll figure it out." Axton drew back but kept hold of my upper arms. "We'll figure it out together, Miss Ruthann, I swear. Me and Uncle Branch ain't gonna let anything happen to you."

Tears fell again, beyond my control; I was so grateful I could hardly speak. At last I whispered, "Thank you. I can't thank you enough, Axton."

He offered a sweet smile, shrugging as if to suggest offering one's time and help to a stranger was nothing out of the ordinary. The moon had lifted another few inches into the black heavens. I hadn't seen it glide upward and yet it had moved, literally before our eyes.

"The world's a pretty interesting place, ain't it?" Axton whispered, unconsciously echoing my thoughts. There was a hush in the air around our bodies, despite the sounds of escalating revelry from nearby buildings.

I had to agree.

The room in which I'd spent the week recuperating at Rilla's was now to be mine for the foreseeable future. It was located at the end of a creaky, uncarpeted hallway, one of six closed doors. Axton escorted me inside the saloon, cheerfully suffering the subsequent teasing from both the women circulating the floor and several of the men elbowed up to Rilla's bar. As much as I longed to avoid attention, not to mention interaction, Axton and I seemed to draw it; I was shocked at the comments men and women alike felt free to direct our way. Rilla Jaymes, packed into a dress so pink it hurt the eyes, stood at the end of the bar smoking a skinny black cigarette; she appeared deep in conversation with two men, her free hand resting on her hip, a wreath of silver smoke hovering over their heads like a raincloud.

"Hoo-*hee!*" shouted a man at one of the gaming tables, lifting his glass in a sloppy salute. "Young feller's finally getting a taste of a woman! Don't nobody tell his pappy!"

"She's a pretty one, too. Got them sweet curves what makes for a good ride."

"Looks like she got all her teeth, too. Watch out for bite marks, young feller!"

One of the women sidled into our path, forcing us to halt, her impressive cleavage showcased in a tight-fitting bodice. She hooked a finger between two buttons on the front of Axton's shirt and stroked his chest. "Darlin', I told you I'd take care of you the first time."

Axton's cheeks heated to broiling but he only tipped his hat brim in a polite gesture. "I ain't taking advantage of Miss Ruthann. I'm just escorting her to the stairs, see."

"Darlin', you come up with me and take *all* the advantage you want."

She let her index finger trail down his belly toward the front of his pants but Axton's attention was diverted by yet another voice, this one from a man probably not much older than him, with a scraggly yellow beard.

"Who you got there? How long you gonna take with her, pup?" He sounded less like he was joking than the others and my stomach twisted into hard little knots.

Axton retained calm but tightened his grip on my arm, shifting us so that I was not so visible to the man. "She ain't working the floor."

"Why the hell not?" the man demanded, but Axton did not rise to this bait, instead leading me around the woman and toward the wide staircase which dropped from the floor above; I resisted the urge to look over my shoulder, feeling the bearded man's gaze penetrate a spot in the middle of my spine.

Axton murmured, "Don't pay no mind. He can't follow. No one's allowed upstairs unless it's with one of the girls. C'mon, let's get you a plate and then I best head for home."

I was terrified to be left alone but asking him to stay was out of the question. I tried to muster the courage to bid him goodnight, anxious sweat gathering at my hairline and beneath my arms. He led me along a short, dim hallway to the back of the saloon; I'd seen this space by daylight and knew it was a kitchen of sorts, containing a hand pump, cupboards, and pantry shelves. A single candle glowed from a wall holder and I spied a second staircase, narrow and dark. The back porch, where Axton and I had been watching the setting sun, was only steps away, the screen still propped open by the jug.

"I found some cornbread and honey when I was in here earlier," Axton said, indicating a plate on the small table in the center of the room. He found a discarded lantern and took a moment to light it from the candle on the wall. "Take these up to your room. You'll be safe there."

My heart would not slow its nervous pace. He handed me the lantern and the plate, and I was glad to have full hands so I wouldn't relent to the urge to clutch his shirtfront and beg to return home with him.

"Will you come back tomorrow, Axton?" I prayed he would say yes.

"Of course. Me and Uncle Branch aim to look out for you." He hesitated, obviously concerned. "Don't worry. I'll wait here until you're safe upstairs."

"Thank you for everything." My throat was closing and I turned away and stumbled up the steps, unwilling to cry in front of him a second time.

"Good-night, Miss Ruthann. I'll see you first thing in the morning."

I heard his footsteps retreating down the back porch steps as I hurried upstairs, the lantern swinging in my grip and throwing erratic splashes of yellow light. I retreated to my room, realizing immediately there was no lock. My gaze swept over the furniture, desperate to find something to shove against the door; despite Axton's assurance that no one could venture to the second floor without accompaniment, I was taking no chances. The bureau was too heavy, as was the bed; the chair would have to do. I wedged it beneath the knob, thankful the door swung inward. Breathing hard, I rested my forehead to the scarred wood for several heartbeats. The saloon was in full swing but the sounds were muffled by the closed door.

You are all right. It's all right.

But I wasn't. I was anything but all right.

A small oval mirror hung above the bureau, upon which I'd set the plate and the lantern; its reflective surface doubled the flickering light, snagging my gaze. Moving as slowly as someone in chest-high water I approached the mirror.

Your name is Ruthann, I thought, studying the eyes staring out at me from the rippled glass. The candle flame created patterns of light and shadow over my sunburned face. I lifted my hands and traced the outline of my chin, my nose and lips. *You have looked at yourself many times before. I know you have. You know who you are.*

As though to force recognition I became frantic, unbuttoning the layers of borrowed skirt, blouse, and underskirt, wriggling free of the small corset that left red grooves in my white, freckled skin, red grooves that appeared even more grotesque as they crisscrossed the mud-colored bruises on my torso. My ribs ached as if beaten with clubs but I didn't care in this moment, letting the garments fall to the wooden floor. I stood naked in the puddle of material around my bare ankles, cupping my breasts, gliding both hands downward over my belly as though sculpting clay, to the triangle of dark hair just below. There was a distinct quickening within me and I pressed the base of both palms to my pubic bone, sliced by a sense of deep urgency.

Who are you? Why are you here?

I tore at the braid in my hair, shaking out its length. My hair was heavy and dark, hanging nearly to my hipbones. Fear and agony blazed hot trails through my chest. There were no answers, no matter how desperately I longed for them. I shuddered with a need I could not explain, running my hands up and down my bruised, wounded body. Tears rolled down my cheeks, dripping from jaw to collarbones, wetting my chest. I rubbed my thumbs over the tear tracks, wanting to beat answers from my mind, wishing I had the ability. My eyes were stark with fear.

"Help me," I begged the empty room. Downstairs I could hear the sounds of a party in full swing. I reeled, struck by a rush of dizzy nausea, and gripped the edge of the bureau to stay upright, overwhelmed by what I knew was in my memory that I could not currently touch. Panic swelled behind my heart and I pressed one hand over it as if to contain both the panic and the gouging ache of sadness centered there. I knew these feelings would consume me if I let them and so I clung to my one defense, as I had all day.

"My name is Ruthann," I whispered, staring hard at the hazel eyes in the mirror. "My name is Ruthann *Rawley*."

Naked, I crawled onto the narrow bed; the sheets and pillowcases had not been changed since I'd lain in them the past days and nights, reeking and dirty. I supposed with the morning light I would have my work cut out for me over in the laundry shack; if I stood up and went to the window, I could have drawn aside the curtains and looked down upon it. I curled into my own arms. In the next room over I heard a door open, close, and then the sounds of muffled laughter, a woman's voice and a low-pitched response. Not a minute later a headboard began a steady, repetitive thumping against the wall behind my bureau, followed by the sound of a man groaning.

I turned my cheek to the damp, soiled pillow, closing my eyes. Over and over, as though praying, I whispered, "*Ruthann Rawley*."

Chapter Three

Two weeks passed and the patchwork of bruising on my body and the aching in my ribs diminished. The weather remained fair and I watched the moon wane until it resembled a fingernail paring, before disappearing altogether. Every evening Branch and Axton came to sit on Rilla's back porch with me, where we would admire the setting sun and they would tell me about their day. In turn, I would inform them about mine – long, repetitive days spent doing laundry. From what I'd learned, laundry meant bending over.

I either bent over a washboard to scrub undergarments or bent over a cauldron of steaming water, into which I would dip load after load of bigger items, such as bedding. And a whorehouse, I'd also learned, produced piles of soiled bedding. Using a long wooden paddle, I swirled the sheets and flannels, letting them boil clean before lifting them out. Once they'd been cranked through the drying press, a clumsy contraption I hated on sight, I hung the heavy items over clothesline ropes strung between Rilla's and the adjacent saloon. Rarely did other women from Rilla's offer their help but I preferred to work alone because it meant I didn't have to make conversation with semi-hostile strangers.

My hands grew accustomed to the heat; at night I dreamed of billowing material and brimming buckets of clothespins. It was exhausting, mind-numbing work (the thought plagued me that there *must* be an easier way – I muttered this to myself about a hundred times a day) and I was too drained by evening to do much talking; instead I creaked at a slow pace in the rocking chair and listened to Branch and Axton, who had become my dearest friends in the world of Howardsville. I counted my blessings, which were meager, that they had claimed me. If not for them, I couldn't have managed the energy required to get out of bed, especially after a night spent trying to block out the sounds of male customers being serviced, hour after unending hour.

The women at Rilla's slept until early afternoon, leaving me the only person prowling the saloon by dawn's light other than the intolerant cook. When she realized I wasn't there to disturb her – I tried my damnedest to avoid contact with almost everyone – and that in fact I hardly spoke, her attitude thawed. I recognized that physical depletion contributed to my lethargy but it ran much deeper; the emotional pain clamping my heart was the main reason I found it difficult to breathe, or manage even a small smile for Axton and Branch, who were two of the kindest men (at least I thought) I'd ever known. Overall I did my best not to feel anything all through the long days and endless nights.

I had visited their claim shanty, as they called their cabin and its acreage, for the first time yesterday afternoon, a ten-minute wagon ride from Howardsville. They owned a pair of mules to pull the wagon and two horses for riding. Axton's horse was an especially beautiful animal, a sleek, long-limbed, rust-colored gelding he called Ranger; Ax had raised him from the day of the foal's birth, five years earlier. Ranger's mother, Ruby, a solid sorrel, was Branch's horse. I was immediately drawn to the animals. After Branch helped me from the wagon seat I approached Ranger and stroked his long nose, murmuring to him.

"You've ridden before?" Axton dismounted and stood holding the reins as I rubbed Ranger's square jaws. The gelding exhaled through his nostrils and gently nosed my waist.

I peered up at Axton, shading my eyes with one hand. "I don't know, but I'd like to try. I mean, if it's all right with you."

"You'll be needing some trousers," he added, gesturing toward my thighs with the leather lead line. "You couldn't ride in them skirts."

I'd been wearing pants when they found me back in July but my old clothes had been disposed of, at least according to Rilla; she told me they were beyond repair. I knew I would prefer pants to the layers of skirts I was expected to wear, which not only flapped around my calves and dragged irritatingly in the dirt, but inhibited my every movement; I would've had to hike them thigh-high to run. Nothing fit right; I rolled the waistbands of the skirts and underskirts so they didn't fall past my anklebones.

The secondhand shoes I'd been given were too small and so I often worked barefoot, refusing to think about the weather growing cold enough to prevent this habit. I hated, with a blistering passion, the corset that latched around my midsection, but the day I'd rebelled and decided not to wear it I was far too exposed, my breasts heavy and wobbly without some sort of restraint. After catching more than one man eyeing my chest, I'd plodded back up the steps to my room and wriggled into the pinching, itchy garment.

"Maybe you have some I could borrow?" I'd asked Axton, and so this evening he brought me a pair of pants, rolled into a neat bundle tied with twine.

"I don't know that a lady oughta wear trousers," Branch said for the second time. He was trying his best to be polite, I knew, but he was really concerned. "I feel it ain't proper."

"Aw, Uncle Branch, she can't ride in a skirt." Axton was even more animated than usual, unable to keep from grinning at the prospect of a riding partner. "Why don't we take the horses out tomorrow afternoon, what do you say, Ruthie?"

I couldn't help but smile in return, admiring the joy in his green eyes. I adored Ax; since the second day I'd known him, I'd indulged in pretending he was my younger brother. This fantasy helped keep me functioning; I clung to the notion that if life at Rilla's grew too unbearable, Axton and Branch would let me live with them at the claim shanty.

"I would love to ride tomorrow afternoon."

Very few people Axton's age resided in Howardsville. Branch had explained that while more homesteaders arrived every year, this deep in the territory there weren't many women, other than those who worked in saloons. The men, overall, were a pretty rough lot, dirty and bad-mannered and best left alone, seeming to want nothing more in the evenings than shots of whiskey and the company of women, in that order. I steered deliberately clear of the main floor at Rilla's once the sun went down, hiding in my room without so much as a book to keep me occupied. Sometimes I felt like I might start screaming and not stop.

The man with the ugly yellow beard drank in Rilla's bar almost every night and eyed me more than anyone else, usually while wiping his lips with the back of his wrist. Although he hadn't addressed me since that first night I could feel the weight of his eyes if I wasn't careful to be out of sight after dusk. Once he'd grabbed his crotch while keeping his gaze pinned on me; to say he made me ill with discomfort was a gross understatement. Instinct suggested I should voice my concerns but I didn't, not wanting Axton and Branch to worry over me more than they currently did. I already owed them more than I could ever hope to repay.

After the two of them bid me farewell and rode for home I crept inside, hurrying through the darkened kitchen, intending to climb the back staircase and bury my face in my pillow; now that I was in charge of laundry, my pillowcase was relatively clean. I sniffed at my armpits and grimaced, wondering when I would muster up the energy to pump and haul the water required for a full bath. 'Full' was not an accurate de-scription; the tin washbasin was no wider than arm's length and required the bather to wash in increments. My hair was dirty and limp, tied in a customary braid; I itched all over. I had just put my right foot on the bottom step when two things caused me to freeze.

The first, which struck with a cringing horror, was that my period was going to start any day – likely tomorrow, if the dull ache across my lower belly was any indication. The second was the sudden awareness of a woman bent forward over the hand-pump sink. Though I avoided interaction as much as possible, I felt a sharp, concerned pang. Almost before I knew I'd moved, I was resting a hand on her shoulder.

"Are you all right?"

She acknowledged my presence with a small huffing sound. In the dimness of the otherwise empty kitchen I recognized Celia Baker, a plump, dark-haired woman with breasts the size of ripe watermelons; I only knew her name because she had been considerate enough to in-troduce herself more than once. She was probably about a decade older than me, pretty but somehow hardened, with observant gray eyes. Her full, sensuous lips were her best feature but she was missing four front teeth on the bottom row and seemed to spend an inordinate amount of time pressing the tip of her tongue there. She didn't answer my question.

"What's wrong?" I pressed, whispering, although I needn't have bothered keeping quiet. No one would ever hear us all the way back here what with the chatter and thumping music from the main floor. But I felt like she deserved privacy.

"I had a twinge," she muttered, remaining tipped forward. Seeming impatient, she swept hair from her face, tucking it behind her ears. She wore a gown with a low neckline edged in tiny crystal beads, which tinkled like fairy bells when she moved. She growled, "*Goddammit,*" and plucked a fake beauty mark from her face; it had fallen from her cheekbone to her bottom lip. With an angry movement, she flicked the paste decoration into the washbasin.

"Is there anything I can do?"

At this she released a throaty laugh and then drew a long breath. With a tone of quiet bitterness, she muttered, "What's been done is done, and I gotta live with it."

"What do you mean?" I asked, wondering why I was bothering. Her business was none of mine but I found I couldn't just walk away and leave her alone in the dimness. The moon was new tonight, the sky as black as charcoal. I couldn't help but feel that my soul, at present, was every bit as abandoned by the beauty of the moonlight.

"It's nothing," she insisted, but then she heaved a little, covering her lips with the back of one hand while the other rode low on her belly, and just like that, I knew.

"You're pregnant," I whispered.

"I'm caught," she snapped, and although I was not familiar with the phrase I knew it meant the same thing. I could tell she was crying and trying to hide it and so I kept quiet, my hand resting lightly on her back. At last she whispered, "I was too much a coward to get rid of it when I had the chance. And it's too late now."

I didn't know how to respond. Her dress felt slippery and my callused palm kept catching on the sleek material. She gulped, hiding her face; her voice emerged slightly muffled. "I know the poor little thing's daddy, imagine that. Not many a whore would know such a thing, but I do. I was fool enough to save myself for him when he was in town last spring. I was half in love with him, I suppose." She issued a disgusted sigh. "And me a woman who should know far better. I am a goddamn fool, many times over."

"Where is he now?"

"God only knows," she said darkly. "He visits this town on his circuit, maybe three times a year. He had his fun with me. He never figured I'd get caught by him." She grumbled, "Fuck the well-hung son of a bitch anyhow. I knew I wasn't careful enough. *Dammit. Fuck me* in a fucking potato sack."

In other circumstances her creative cursing would have made me laugh; just now I was too concerned. "What will Rilla say?"

Celia eased back and smoothed both hands over her stomach; this movement, such an instinctive maternal gesture, tore at my heart. Her enormous breasts were harnessed high in a corset, showcasing about an acre of cleavage. She smelled like stale sweat but even so I felt the urge to hug her. Despite her tough words and manner of speaking, she seemed so terribly vulnerable. She finally answered, "Rilla won't force me out. Tilda's been caught before. She sent the child back east on the train, in the company of a do-gooder mission woman."

"How can I help you?"

Celia's expression shifted as a small but genuine smile elongated her mouth, the first I'd ever seen on any of the women's faces. "You're a kind woman, Miss Ruth. I don't know heads or tails of your story but you're in despair, I can tell."

"Never mind me," I mumbled, surprised she had noticed me at all. "I will help you if I can. Just tell me what to do."

"Help me with this bellyache," she groused. "I can't hardly stand the smell of food but once I head out to the floor and grab a fella, I'll be stuck in my room 'til morning. I best eat now."

"You can't continue to work when you're pregnant!" I stared at her with true horror.

Celia rolled her eyes and replied briskly, "I can if I want to live under this roof." She studied my face, which must have registered open shock; she snorted a laugh. "Don't look so stunned, girl. I'm caught now, so at least I don't have to worry about getting caught again for a few more months anyhow. It's always a real sore worry for us girls."

I finally realized there was no point arguing.

"Silver linings," I muttered.

"You're a funny little thing," she said in return, and surprised me for the second time by kissing my forehead. Her breath smelled faintly of mint and I listened to my gut and hugged her close, for just a second. Her breath tickled my ear as she whispered, "Let's keep this a secret, for now. In another month I won't be able to hide it no more, but for now, promise me?"

I nodded, drawing away.

She lowered her chin and studied me at close range. "Your name's Rawley, ain't it?"

I nodded again.

"Huh. Well, if you're related to the marshal then you're related to his child."

"How do you mean?" I did not follow.

"Marshal Rawley is the one that got me in this state," she explained, breasts rising and falling with a deep sigh. "He's due back this way in the next month or so. Could be you'll recognize him as your kin," and I thought she sounded cautiously hopeful.

"Marshal Rawley, the lawman?" I clarified, my heart throbbing so hard I could barely hear my own voice. Branch and Axton had spoken of this man, speculating that he might know someone connected to me, someone who could explain why I was alone in Montana Territory.

"His given name is Miles and he's the marshal, yes," Celia confirmed. "He won't ever know I got caught by him, but he's the daddy all the same."

"What do you mean? You won't tell him?" I demanded.

Celia laughed, heartily this time, as though I'd just told her an unexpectedly good joke. "Of course I won't tell him. Are you half-witted, girl? *Shit.* Miles ain't a bad sort, as men go, but I know men. And no man – dirt poor or with the means to buy an empire – would trouble himself for a whore's child."

I felt hot and sweaty, more upset than the situation should warrant. "But it's *his* child, too. *Damned right* he better 'trouble' himself."

She made a clucking sound and swished out her skirts, in preparation to end our conversation and get back to work. Amusement colored her tone. "Whoever you are, you must've been raised a lady. But that ain't the attitude out here, girl. I know my place."

"You have to tell him. He should know the truth. He could help you."

Celia shook her head, polite but firm. "I'd be much obliged if you'd keep my secret, at least until I can tell Rilla."

And I had little choice but to promise I would.

Chapter Four

THE NEXT AFTERNOON I WAS WEARING HIS TROUSERS WHEN Axton rode Ranger up to Rilla's Place. Thrilled at the prospect of riding with Ax, I'd hurried through my daily work before scurrying to my room to shuck my skirt and underskirt, next tucking my blouse into my borrowed pants. I had an immediate problem, realizing after examining the strange pattern of buttons on the waistband that I required suspenders – and in a building full of women, there were no suspenders to be had. And so I improvised, journeying back to the laundry shack and digging up a length of rope, which I knotted around my waist, effectively creating a belt. I was wearing my too-small shoes and longed for the kind of hard leather boots Axton wore, knee-high and sturdy, made for fitting neatly into a stirrup.

"You look real nice, Ruthie," Axton said, half-teasing, as he halted Ranger and eyed my boyish outfit. I stood in the shade of the overhang on Rilla's front veranda and felt a smile tug at my lips, which had been his intent. This early in the evening the foot traffic to and from the saloons was light, though the elderly man who sat on a stool near the piano and played the fiddle, night after night, was already sawing out a melody. The day was fair and sunny, as usual, with little wind, and the anticipation of riding a horse created within me a small beat of real excitement.

"I really don't, but thanks all the same." I harbored no illusions about my appearance. I was surrounded daily by women who sold their bodies for a living and whose ample breasts and curving hips were constantly on display; by night, I dug my fingers in my ears to muffle the grunts and moans, the steady thumping, filtering through the thin walls. The sounds of sex made my body ache. Even when I felt like I could cry no more for what I didn't know, what I couldn't remember, when my head throbbed and my eyes stung – all the sobs I held inside throughout the day came hurtling out by night.

"You *do* look nice," Axton insisted, holding the reins in his right hand, forearms crossed at the wrist and braced on his saddle horn. Ranger snorted a loud breath and stepped delicately backward, as though anxious to keep moving. The late-afternoon sun was gorgeous on Ranger's rusty hide and picked out copper highlights in the unkempt hair visible at the back of Axton's neck, beneath the brown, wide-brimmed hat he wore. With the sun backlighting him, his shoulders appeared all the more wide and strong; I reflected again that Axton had no idea just how appealing he really was.

"You look like a cowboy," I observed, and his eyebrows lifted.

He contradicted, "I got no experience with cattle."

"Trust me."

"Here, climb on up. Uncle Branch said Ruby would be a good horse for you to ride at first, but she's at home."

So saying, he extended his left hand and helped me step into the stirrup on that side, shifting his foot and then swinging me up with easy grace. I settled just behind the saddle and caught hold of his narrow waist. My long braid hung down my back, slapping my spine as Axton heeled Ranger to a steady trot to take us beyond the town limits. I was thankful the claim shanty was to the north so we could avoid riding through the rows of dirty canvas tents where many of the railroad workers lived, south of Howardsville. They were a mobile work force, hence the temporary lodging, and most had a bad look – the yellow-bearded man among them. The type to drag a woman into an alley and feel no remorse about what happened next.

"The girls at Rilla's were laughing about how I looked," I admitted to Axton. None of them were openly hostile – since our conversation in the kitchen Celia had actually been downright friendly – but the rest of the women regarded me with either wariness or amusement. One, a woman named Lucy, commented on how much time I spent with Axton and asked if I was planning to make him into a man. If so, she said to send him her way directly after.

The first words to pop into my brain had been, *You wish, fat bitch.*

But of course I didn't say that aloud.

Instead, I vented to poor, unsuspecting Axton. "If they want to judge me for wearing men's clothes, they have another thing coming. Seriously, Ax, they all have sex with dozens of men every night. I *hear* it. There's no escaping the sounds. If I want to dress like a boy and ride a horse, they have *nothing* to say."

Axton didn't respond; it suddenly dawned on me I'd embarrassed him. This suspicion was confirmed when he finally said, "I never thought of it like that before." He cleared his throat and clarified hoarsely, "I mean, about the…sounds." I knew if I could see his face he would be as red as a raspberry.

"I'm sorry," I said at once. "I should think before I say things like that."

"Don't be sorry. I ain't a kid." He chuckled then, surprising me by adding, "It's because you're so pretty and soft, if you don't mind my saying so. Them whores are just jealous of you, is all. You look soft and they look hard, that's all there is to it."

I sat in silence behind him, absorbing his sincere words. Finally I realized I should thank him and so I did, to which he replied by shrugging one shoulder. A minute later he ordered, "Hold on," and I felt his thigh muscles tense as he tightened his knees around Ranger, sending the animal into a light canter.

The motion of the horse beneath us was familiar. I closed my eyes, willing a memory to strike the surface, to offer the smallest clue. I knew I had been on horseback before, my body knew the feel of it. I held fast to Axton, trusting him, and decided to simply enjoy the ride. It was a quick run out to the claim and I opened my eyes to watch the landscape flash past us, the rippling grasses that grew tall outside of town, changing now from green to hues of gold as the summer slipped toward autumn. There weren't many trees out here other than a few skinny cottonwoods, nothing to obscure the sunlight streaking over us.

Branch was frying bacon at the cookfire as we rode up and my mouth filled with saliva at the delicious scent; meat was rarely a part of my daily meals. I slid down from Ranger with no assistance and hurried to hug Branch, who squeezed me against his bulk and planted a smacking kiss on my temple.

"Evening, honey. Got my Ruby all saddled up for you. The old girl seems right excited."

"Same here!" I said, and Branch grinned, his grizzled face with its livid scar crinkling into wrinkles as he did so.

"It's good to see you with a smile, sweet girl. Hate to see you always looking so sad."

"You two must be on a mission to make me feel better."

"You make the whole evening better, darlin', that's God's truth," Branch said. "I'll have this bacon fried by the time you two get back. Ax, don't ride too far out or it'll be burnt to a crisp."

"We won't, Uncle Branch," Ax promised. He shifted on the saddle and his tone grew more solemn. "Lots of talk in town today. I heard tell Marshal Rawley is riding back but he's a good hundred and fifty miles north."

"I heard the same." Branch poked at the bacon. "You'll recall Cole Spicer, boy. Heard tell he was headed this way, too, from the east. We ain't seen Spicer in these parts in near four years. The marshal is likely eager to reunite with him. Boyhood friends, they are."

"Talk is that Bill Little's gang resurfaced out near Yankton. You reckon that's true, Uncle Branch?" Axton asked this question with both anxiety and awe mingling in his tone.

The mention of the marshal sent my blood churning and I pressed both hands against my heart, as though I had the power to slow its beating from the outside. It took me a moment to realize Branch's wrinkled face appeared uneasy.

"Bill Little's gang ain't been heard from in near four years," Axton continued. He had not dismounted, looking more at home astride Ranger than he did standing on the ground.

"Who's Bill Little?" I asked, looking between them.

Branch sighed before answering. "Bill Little used to lead a gang of criminals, some of which were his own brothers, before they was all shot and kilt. I heard the same about the trouble out by Yankton, boy, I hate to say. No-good trash, that's what. Back in 'seventy-six Little and his men stole a woman in these parts. Now, I ain't saying she was the first woman they stole but this particular woman was to be married to a young man named Malcolm Carter. I don't recollect her name, do you, boy?"

"Cora," Axton said at once.

I pressed harder against my heart, but it would not slow its beating.

Branch continued, "Well, they took Miss Cora, and the Carter boy took off after them. Malcolm Carter rode with Cole Spicer in them days, and Grant and Miles Rawley – the marshal, that is, but he weren't the marshal back then – and a pack of better friends you ain't ever seen. A man named Wainwright was the marshal back in them days, but he done got shot up on that journey, got kilt stone dead. Miles took up the marshal position and held it ever since."

"What of Cora?" My mouth was dry.

Branch shook his head, mouth twisting in a sad slant. "Bill Little claimed they never kilt her, but she's gone as sure as if they had."

"And now this Bill Little is back in the area?"

"No, Bill Little is dead as a coffin nail. The Carter boy kilt him and near half his gang, too."

"But how…"

"The fellas what survived ain't been heard from since, but they've kept the same old name. They're suspected in the shooting of a homesteader, three days' ride east of here." Branch scanned the horizon as though expecting a hard-riding gang to appear on that edge of the world, horses lathered and guns drawn; I restrained a cold shiver. He mused, "It's bad news, that's what. Makes me think I oughta carry a pistol at all times, like I used to."

"And you said the marshal and Cole Spicer are on their way to Howardsville?" I asked, attempting to keep up.

Branch nodded. "It's been a piece since Spicer's travelled out this way. Been in Iowa these past years, I do believe, but you know them young men with a taste of the wanderlust on their tongues. Can't say I blame

'em. I wandered a goodly amount in my own day. Getting too old now."
His gaze flickered to Axton, silhouetted against the sky on his horse,
both man and animal gazing westward. Branch didn't need to speak the
words for me to understand his meaning; he blinked, the sun striking his
eyes, and changed topics. "You two young'uns best get to riding before
it gets dark."

"Yes," I agreed, not about to let this opportunity slide.

"Let me fetch Ruby for you." Branch indicated the small fenced corral just beyond their shanty, a wooden cabin hardly big enough for two
men. The structure they referred to as their barn was not appreciably
larger. He unlatched the gate and I followed close behind, holding out
my palms to Ruby, a beautiful horse with a silky black mane and swish-
ing tail. I cupped her jaws and murmured to her, and she let me mount
with no trouble whatsoever. Minutes later Axton and I rode toward the
sunset.

"You just laughed!" Axton called over his shoulder, about ten paces
ahead.

"I did," I marveled, leaning over Ruby's neck, feeling her muscles
against the insides of my legs as we flew over the ground in a steady
canter. The mare's scent was familiar; at last, here was a strong smell that
didn't hurt my nostrils. Ruby's hooves struck the earth with a comforting, three-beat rhythm and created a subtle vibration in my body, as
though we were part of the same being.

Axton didn't pester me with questions about whether I was doing all
right, or feeling all right, and instead just kept riding. I followed, letting
him retain a slight lead. When he heeled Ranger and sent him into a
full-out gallop, I did the same with Ruby, holding fast to her reins. I
wasn't afraid as we raced over the prairie, only exhilarated. We must have
ridden a good five miles before Axton slowed our pace, decreasing from
gallop to canter; then trot to walk. His elbows jutted to the sides as he
halted Ranger, waiting for Ruby and me to catch up.

As we neared, Axton looked our way and the setting sun gilded his
outline as he sat easily in the saddle, obscuring exact details, creating a
halo around his cowboy hat, making it appear black, highlighting his

wide shoulders and lean frame. I reeled at the sight, pounded by a force I could not explain. It wasn't Axton who inspired this feeling but instead his lean, lanky, broad-shouldered shape that reminded me of...*that reminded me of...*

Oh dear God...

The sun blazed just at the crest of the earth, sending scarlet spikes across my vision.

"That's a sight, ain't it?" Axton nodded at the sunset and didn't appear to notice my keen-edged distress.

I could hear the exerted breathing of both horses, could feel Ruby's ribs lifting and falling as she drew air. I gulped down a painful storm of sobs and managed to whisper, "It is."

We watched in silence as the sun began its gradual disappearance; the light it cast was a pure, blazing copper. Bright spangles dotted my vision with each blink. It was three-quarters sunk in a river of fiery purple clouds when Axton looked my way. "You ain't remembered nothing yet, have you, Ruthie?"

I shook my head, momentarily wordless.

"I seen that sadness on your face just now. I wish it wasn't so."

"I know. I really do, Ax."

His expression was one of abject concern; worry drew his brows together, forming twin vertical creases above his nose. "Me and Uncle Branch will always watch out for you, no matter what. Even if you never find your people."

I reached and gripped his right hand, closest to me as he held the reins. "That means more to me than you could possibly know, Ax. I don't have anyone but the two of you."

He continued to study my face. "I know we ain't ever met before this summer but I feel I can tell you things, Ruthie, like maybe you're my kin, or that I've known you before now..." He floundered to silence, unsure how to make his point.

"I know what you mean," I said, and I truly did. "I trust you, too. You've never seemed like a stranger."

Relief that I understood washed over his features, restoring their usual good humor. The last of the sun created a thousand shades of green in his eyes. His lashes were as red-gold as his hair, long enough to cast spiky shadows over his cheekbones.

I confessed, "I wish you were my brother, Ax. I pretend you are."

He grinned anew, tipping his hat brim in a teasing, gentlemanly manner. "I would be honored to be your kin."

"Thank you for this," I said, indicating not only the horses but the entire sweep of the foothills – it was stunning out here in the open country. Restorative. It was exactly what I had needed tonight.

"You are most welcome." He scanned the darkening sky and decided, "We best ride back."

This time we kept to a slower pace, riding close together.

"You said there are other Rawleys in the Howardsville area?" I was terribly curious about them, especially given Celia's news. If I had a connection to the family, I would be related to her child.

"The marshal was raised in Iowa but his brother, Grantley, is a homesteader maybe a day's ride from here." Axton indicated westward. "We'll ask the marshal when he gets back to Howardsville. Him and Uncle Branch are old friends. The marshal's mama is from the same place where Uncle Branch and my own parents were raised, back in Cumberland County, in Tennessee. Maybe the marshal will have some answers for you, Ruthie."

"Maybe," I whispered, thinking of Celia at the saloon, probably already with her first customer. The idea of a woman expected to spend each night providing sex for man after unwashed man was repulsive enough on its own; it was ten times worse knowing the woman was pregnant. Celia had morning sickness. She'd told me just this afternoon how much her breasts ached and still there was no respite for her. She was forced to do her job or she would earn no money, and then she would starve.

Anger resurged in my belly, a small, intense flame. "Axton, if I tell you something, will you promise not to tell anyone?"

"A secret?" There was undeniable excitement in his tone.

"A secret," I affirmed. "It has to do with the marshal."

Axton waited expectantly, eyebrows raised. In the shadow of his hat brim his irises appeared the deep green of pine boughs.

I took a chance; Celia's secret was burning a hole in my throat. "One of the women at Rilla's told me she's pregnant with the marshal's baby."

Axton's brow creased; he didn't respond.

I assumed he was equally upset by this news and prattled on, "Celia would be mad at me for telling you but I'm worried about her. I think she should tell the marshal the truth but she won't. She doesn't think he'd do anything about it and that's wrong, in my opinion..." I trailed to silence, realizing Axton looked more puzzled than angry.

As I faltered to a halt, he muttered, "I don't...you see...I don't entirely..."

It was my turn to frown, in confusion.

Even in the gathering dusk, I saw the flush that overtook his face. "I don't know how a man, well, you see...how he would *know*, with a whore..."

I took pity on him and interrupted his stammering. "*Celia* knows. She knows the baby is the marshal's because he was the only man she was with when..." A sudden rush of embarrassment struck me into silence for the second time. After a beat of awkwardness, I squared my shoulders and continued, with determination, "You see, Ax, a woman knows her child's father because each month a woman has her period, which basically means she bleeds from between her legs for a few days..."

His face grew almost comically horrified. "Bleeds?"

I rushed to explain, "It just means a woman is fertile – able to have a baby – which is completely normal. All women have a period."

"Period?" Axton repeated weakly.

Oh for Christ's sake, Ruthann, you idiot, I scolded myself. But it was too late to turn back now.

"Yes, a period of time when you bleed. It's not too painful or anything, usually just annoying, and it's how a woman knows she isn't pregnant. Once she *is* pregnant, because a man's sperm reached her egg, then the bleeding stops and she doesn't have her period until the baby is born. Or until she's done nursing." I had no idea where all this knowledge was coming from.

Axton's expression was changing to one of tentative interest. I was suddenly sure no one had ever spoken of these things with him. He said hesitantly, "Sperm?"

"Yes, that's part of what comes out of a man when –" I almost choked, in danger of being too candid.

But he seemed to understand; he blushed even brighter and cleared his throat. When this wasn't enough, he coughed.

I had to see this conversation through now. "Anyhow, poor Celia ended up getting pregnant last spring and she knows it's the marshal's baby because she wasn't with anyone but him that month. But she doesn't want to tell him since she thinks he won't do a thing about it."

Axton sounded truly perplexed. "But what could the marshal do?"

"He could marry her and give the baby his name. He could take care of them. It's his responsibility."

Axton said quietly, "But she's a whore."

My temper rose with a heated, crackling sound. "Don't call her that! She's a woman who deserves better!"

"Marshal Rawley won't marry a whore." Ax spoke with certainty. Even as riled up as I was, I understood there wasn't a hint of cruelty in this statement; Axton was just telling the truth as he observed it.

"Then he needs to give her money, at the very least," I persisted. "I plan to tell him. When will he be in Howardsville? You guys said a hundred and fifty miles…"

Axton said firmly, "You can't tell him. It *ain't* our business."

The little shanty house popped into view on the horizon, along with the glinting orange spark of Branch's cookfire, and I found no good reason for my argument, other than self-righteous anger that a woman would be left to deal with a pregnancy which was hardly her fault alone. I felt the basic injustice of this deep in my bones.

Axton smelled bacon and said gladly, "Supper. C'mon, let's hurry!"

I spent the night at the shanty, unwilling to make Axton ride all the way to town and back just to escort me to Rilla's. Branch insisted I take his bed – a faded patchwork quilt spread over a black bear's hide in the back corner of the room, topped by a small, lumpy pillow. I was reluctant to oust Branch from his usual sleeping place but he insisted, rolling up in a blanket near the fire instead.

"I spent many a night sleepin' in hellholes, believe you me, Ruthie," Branch said. I had finally broken him of his habit of adding 'Miss' before my name. He elaborated, "Durin' the War, I done slept with one eye open, always sure the Federals was about t'attack an' cut my throat as I slept, even durin' the blackest, rainiest nights. So's sleepin' near the cookfire on a fine night like this ain't nothin', don't you worry none, honey."

Branch's Tennessee drawl became more pronounced the higher the stars rose in the sky, the longer he spoke of his younger days. The three of us sat around the fire under a full spread of twinkling stars for a long time before saying good-night. Branch told story after story of serving in the Confederate Army, tales which Axton had heard many times before, good-naturedly chiming in details as Branch allowed. I listened with a sense of fascination, so grateful for these two; so many times I'd considered begging to be allowed to stay here at the shanty with them for good, instead of returning to my miserable room at Rilla's.

But there's no space here. You have privacy at Rilla's. To a degree, anyway.

Axton, whether out of a desire to be a gentleman or simple shyness, I wasn't sure, chose to sleep alongside Branch at the fire, rather than in the cabin with me. I imagined Ax lying awake, mulling over the mysteries of women and their periods, and smiled as I curled into the quilt on the thick bear hide, not daring to remove a scrap of clothing other than my shoes, angling my right arm beneath my head. Rather than glass in the single, thick-sided window cut into the log walls, a piece of canvas was nailed in place to keep rain at bay, allowing the muted orange glow of the fire to glimmer through. I drifted to sleep studying the warmth of the firelight on the square of cloth, hearing the men snoring just a few yards away.

Perhaps it was the comforting sound of a man relaxed and sleeping well enough to snore that bumped against a hidden memory –

Three-quarters asleep, I shifted position, sweaty and restless; the quilt bunched between my legs, pressing insistently against the juncture of my thighs.

Come closer, angel. I can't sleep unless I feel you against me.

My entire body jerked at the sound of his voice. My closed eyes shifted in their sockets, searching for him.

Stay, I begged. I would rip myself inside out to make this happen. *Please stay with me.*

Always. I love you, oh God, Ruthie, I love you.

Don't let me go…

His lips were warm on the nape of my neck, his hands strong and passionate as they caressed my belly and cradled my breasts, his fingers spread wide and thumbs stroking my nipples. I shifted violently, attempting to turn so I could see his face. Desperation swelled to bursting in my chest.

Stay with me. Please, oh please, stay with me…

I thrashed, clutching at him, and came abruptly awake to the dimness of the shanty cabin. I sat up and scrambled to my knees, scrabbling through the tangled quilts. The essence of the dream washed immediately away, like water down a drain, and I fell back to the crumpled bedding and sobbed for what I didn't understand.

Chapter Five

ANOTHER WEEK DRIFTED PAST LIKE COTTONSEED ON A lazy breeze, taking us well into August. I continued my daily routine at Rilla's, living for the promise of an evening's ride with Axton. In the last month I'd learned firsthand what it meant to have your period while living in a saloon on the territory prairie, and it wasn't a pretty picture. In fact, it was outright awful. I'd grown accustomed to the unwashed state of my hair and body, to traversing the yard to reach the communal outhouse, but being forced to wrap my lower body with cotton binding which needed changing every few hours was something to which I would never acclimate.

I kept my thoughts fixed through each hot, endless day upon the moment when Ax would come riding up to Rilla's to collect me, as he did late every afternoon, and we would canter out to the claim shanty and then beyond. Branch made supper for the three of us every night, usually bacon, sometimes biscuits. We drank water and coffee, sweetened with a pinch of brown sugar; occasionally Branch sipped from a jug of whiskey. When he drank, his stories flowed with vigor. He was a born storyteller and I found a certain amount of joy in his tales, at least enough to sustain me through the next day; I felt happy sitting wrapped in a wool blanket near their fire, listening to Branch's deep, drawling voice.

I'd even managed to wash Axton's hair, a fairly monumental accomplishment. It was the tin bucket of water, sitting alongside the hand pump behind their shanty and warmed all day by the sun, that gave me the idea. I eyed the bucket, then Axton's tangled hair and unwashed face; the very next evening, I secreted away what the girls at Rilla's called a 'soap cake,' with a plan in mind.

"Ax," I murmured, as sweetly as possible without giving away my ulterior motives. Branch checked the biscuits, baking to golden perfection in a covered, cast-iron pan while Axton sat whittling a small chunk of wood near the fire. At my speaking of his name he looked up and smiled, and my heart went *twang* with love for him; I couldn't have loved him more if he was truly my little brother. Speaking offhandedly, I murmured, "Maybe I could wash your hair for you."

Both men's eyebrows lofted high, Branch's in amusement and Axton's in pure alarm. Ax said immediately, "Well, I don't much like getting wet," and Branch snorted, slapping his knee, and then chuckled.

"Boy, you oughta *be* so lucky to have a fine gal like Ruthie make an offer like that."

Axton lowered his head but his shoulders shook with laughter. Sensing my advantage, I stood in front of his bent knees, hands on hips as I made a show of perusing him.

"C'mon, Ax," I wheedled. "If you let me, I'll…" I tried to think of a suitable bartering tool. Then it hit me. "Ladies like a clean man, that much I can tell you."

Branch hooted and laughed. "Darn tootin'!"

Axton lifted both hands, palms outward. "But I –"

"No 'buts,'" I said firmly, catching hold of his wrists. "Come kneel over here by the bucket."

Axton dutifully knelt before the bucket I'd dragged closer to the fire. The auburn sun streaked across his hair, creating a gorgeous array of red and copper. With no small amount of satisfaction, I murmured, "Good."

With a rough linen towel draped along his shoulders, Ax tipped his head over the bucket. Branch provided me with a tin cup, which I used to soak Ax's hair, one dip at a time. With the first pour, he sucked a sharp breath and complained, "Aw, it's so cold…"

"Hush," I reprimanded. "It's worth it, just you wait." Once his hair was suitably wet, I lathered my hands and scrubbed his scalp. The soap cake smelled like lye and didn't exactly turn to manageable foam, but I made do, using the edges of the towel to wash his ears and instructing him to scrub his face. Once complete, I wrapped the towel about his head and demanded, "Branch, do you have a hairbrush?"

Branch, smoking his pipe and watching us with true enjoyment, shook his grizzled head. "A hairbrush? Jesus, I ain't been in possession of such a thing in my entire life, honey-love. I ain't even seen one since my dear mama's."

"*Branch,*" I complained.

Axton held the towel, gathered in a loose turban on his head, and blinked at an errant drop of water rolling down his nose.

I observed, "Well, at least you're clean. How does it feel?"

"Strange," he admitted. "And cold. But thank you kindly, Ruthie."

I positioned him near the fire and resorted to combing his tangled curls with my fingers and a small, forked stick. He shivered and shuddered, periodically murmuring, "That feels so good," as I worked.

Branch said, "Ain't no one combed your hair since you was a sprout back in Tennessee. I apologize, boy. You ain't had a woman's touch in too long."

I smiled at these words. "You really do have beautiful hair, Ax. Look at these highlights in the sun." I caught a curl between my fingers and displayed it for Branch, admiring the gold and scarlet woven into the strands of his hair.

Branch said, "Don't rightly know where that red come from. His ma and pa neither one was fair that way. You're a 'hop out of kin,' boy, that's what Granny Douglas would have said."

I ruffled Axton's hair and then bent to kiss his cheek, with pure affection. "There. All done."

Axton grinned and ducked his clean head, muttering, "Aw, Ruthie…" and then his green eyes twinkled with new delight. "Uncle Branch, I believe you're next."

"Jesus *Christ,*" Branch uttered, spewing a stream of pipe smoke. He was quick to add, "Not that I don't appreciate the offer, dear little Ruthie, but I ain't had no need to bathe since last spring. And I won't before winter, likely."

Ax grinned wickedly. "But the ladies…"

Branch flung his hands heavenward. "Well, boy, as you know, I ain't had to worry about them since far longer than last spring," and we were all laughing then, as the sun sank in a ruby sky.

The women at Rilla's teased me with increasing intensity about my relationship with Axton, until Celia made them stop. While I could have continued to ignore the snide innuendos, there was a certain amount of relief in knowing that someone else cared about me, at least enough to ensure the teasing cease. Celia carried herself with admirable fortitude and though I wouldn't have said we were friends, exactly, I felt safe around her. As though I could trust her to a certain degree. What's more, I liked her. She was strong and kind and life had dealt her a shitty hand. I sometimes lay awake envisioning how I'd help her reunite with the marshal, how I'd get them back together – or whatever the equivalent.

"What *do* you see in young Axton, if you don't mind my asking?" Celia said one early morning, when I was getting up just as she retired for the night. I stood pouring myself a tin cup of coffee from the kettle on the woodstove and jumped at the sound of her voice; I hadn't heard her enter the space. The kitchen was empty and I'd assumed, like usual, no one was awake but me.

"Good morning," I responded as Celia approached with a silk shawl drawn around her shoulders. By the early light of day she looked worse for wear and my heart thudded in sympathy, adding fuel to the flame of my anger toward the man responsible for getting her pregnant. Her dark, shining hair hung loose over one shoulder, her make-up beneath her thick lashes rather than upon them, her lipstick smudged. Her beauty mark was in place upon her cheekbone; I wondered if she'd found the one she'd flicked away, or if this was one of many. Her breasts appeared swollen and uncomfortable in her tight costume. Her irises were a rich, deep gray that exactly matched her silk shawl.

"There's a sad look in your eyes again, girl," she observed, sitting on a wooden chair at the small table near the stove. She sighed, cupping her lower belly, and then asked with a surprising amount of gentleness, "You sweet on him?"

I replaced the kettle on the stove and sat across from her. "No, not like that."

"Axton Douglas is kind, I can tell, and handsome, which ain't a usual combination." She reached and curled her right hand around my left. Her hands were soft and warm, and it felt good to be touched by a woman, so good to have a woman listening to me. I curbed the desire to snuggle into her plump arms and be comforted. "You could do far worse, believe you me. Ain't any life out here for a lady, Ruth, I know this. You'd do well to marry that sweet feller, sooner than later."

"I don't…" I despised my inability to explain what I felt. "I care for Axton very much, but I just can't…"

Celia supplied, "Do you think you're already married? Maybe a widow?"

A sharp-edged sob cut my chest from the inside, obliterating words. Even though I didn't answer, Celia's mouth softened.

"I don't know what's been in the past for you, girl, but I do know Axton Douglas would make a good husband. He's young, but so are you. Mark my words, you could do worse."

I changed the focus to her, whispering, "How are you feeling these days?"

She blew out a breath with lips pursed, before pressing her tongue against the space in her gums where she was missing teeth. "Tired, mostly. I plan to tell Rilla about my condition this afternoon. No use keeping a secret that won't improve with time."

"What will you do with the baby?" I whispered, truly concerned.

She released my hand and swept both palms over her belly. "I aim to send it back east, soon as I can make arrangements. I can't keep it."

"But it's your *baby*."

"It's trouble is what it is," she said, though not without a note of pain. She seemed to be studying my eyes for answers. "You're a softhearted girl. I saw that from the first. You must toughen up, Ruth, there ain't no other choice out here."

"There's always another choice," I said, and then as quickly wondered,

Is there?

Celia said, "Not for ladies or whores, either one."

It began raining less than an hour later, while I was busy lighting the kindling pile beneath the laundry cauldron, prepared to start the first load of sheets. I hadn't heard the sound of raindrops since my arrival in Howardsville many weeks ago and peeked out from the canvas cloth that functioned as a door to the laundry shack, surprised. The sky had been clear only a few minutes ago. The air was refreshing, cool and damp, and I stepped all the way out, lifting my palms toward the dripping heavens.

A fast-moving storm blew in from the west, broiling with tall gray clouds. I watched, unfazed, as people scurried for cover while lightning sizzled across the sky. Thunder soon made the ground tremble and the rain progressed swiftly into a downpour, but I remained standing in it, letting it soak my body and my hair. Perhaps it was nothing more than a basic instinct to be clean but I tilted my head back, scraping my long hair away from my forehead, letting the dust and grime wash away. On inspiration, I darted back inside the laundry shack and grabbed a soap cake, and then proceeded to scrub my scalp. I prayed the rain would continue until I had rinsed, and was lucky.

When Axton rode up to collect me later that afternoon, under a true-blue sky, the first thing he said was, "I didn't know your hair was so curly."

I had not braided my hair, as I usually did, because it felt so good on my back, hanging loose and clean. After the storm I'd changed into my riding clothes and finished the laundry, and now here was Axton, ready to ride.

"It's just washed," I replied, a little self-consciously.

He nodded without saying anything else, studying me with a somber expression. Since the night I'd spoken so openly about women and their periods, Axton had grown increasingly comfortable asking me questions, about anything that crossed his mind. He was possessed of a curious, intelligent nature and I enjoyed our honest talks, but an uncomfortable twinge gripped my gut as I thought of Celia's words from this morning.

What if Axton misinterpreted my attention?

No, you're only imagining that, I thought.

He shifted in the saddle and offered such an engaging grin that the twinge in my gut sharpened. His very next words were, "Me and Uncle Branch got a surprise for you."

"You do? What's that?"

Axton's grin widened. "Just down the street, yonder. Come look, Ruthie!"

With true wonderment I stepped out into the dusty street (the rain had dried up almost the moment it fell), peering in the direction he was indicating. Upon seeing nothing out of the ordinary, nothing to suggest a surprise, I looked back at Ax.

He shook his head in pretended annoyance, dismounted and handed me Ranger's lead line, then walked ten paces away, gesturing to a dun-colored mare tethered to the hitching post in front of the saloon next door. At last it dawned on me and my mouth fell open. I continued to stare in stun as he unwound the mare's reins and walked her to me.

"How?" I whispered. "When?"

Axton was so pleased by my delighted reaction it seemed his face would split with a grin. "Dang, I wish Uncle Branch could see how happy you look."

"But..." I'd been reduced to one-word utterances. I stretched out my right hand and cupped the dun's square jaw. She was shorter than Ranger by a couple of inches, the color of a wheat field. Her brown eyes were gentle and watchful, her mane and tail both a rich golden-blond. I stroked her hide and tears slid down my cheeks.

Axton explained, "Uncle Branch got her for nothing a'tall, from Doc Turn. Doc needs a new horse and planned to get rid of her."

"She's beautiful." I was crying and laughing. "She's for me?"

Axton nodded. "She ain't even got a real name. Doc always called her Girl, or Girly. You can pick a new one, if you'd like. She's fifteen years, near about, but she's a good girl. He didn't sell his saddle with her, though, so we'll have to get one for you."

I could not wait to ride my horse. *My horse,* a gift as amazing as it was unimaginable. I threw my arms around Axton, startling him; Ranger tossed his head and snorted, but my horse simply flicked her tail.

"I don't have any money," I told Ax, drawing away. "I don't have a place to keep her!"

"She can stay with us, for now," he said, still giddy. "And she didn't cost a thing, Ruthie, truly."

"Thank you, sweetheart." It seemed I could never thank him, or Branch, enough.

"What's this?" a new voice asked, and we both looked up at the porch to see Celia emerging, wearing a dress as yellow as freshly-sliced lemon cake, her beauty mark adorning the bountiful top curve of her right breast this afternoon. She looked tired and uncomfortable but her gray eyes were alight with curiosity.

Axton tipped his hat brim and acknowledged, "Ma'am."

She winked at him, angling her breasts his way, and he blushed bright as a sunset.

"Celia, this is my new horse," I said, and she smiled like a mother at me.

"Ain't that Doc Turn's old horse?"

"Ain't no more," Axton supplied cheerfully. "He was getting rid of her and Uncle Branch snapped her up. I brought her just now, for Ruthie."

"How kind," Celia murmured, looking pointedly between Axton and me.

I pretended I didn't notice her look and instead patted the horse's face, one hand on either side of her jaws. "What should I call her? I can't keep calling her Girl, can I? That's such a dumb name."

Instead of answering, Celia's animated gaze suddenly flickered down the street. In the next instant her mouth tightened, lips compressing, and her shoulders squared; she turned with a flip of her skirts and reentered Rilla's without another word. Axton didn't notice a thing. I was the only one wondering at Celia's abrupt departure.

Axton suggested, "How about you ride her first and then decide on a name?"

I craned my neck around Ax to see what had caught Celia's attention. Axton turned to peer over his shoulder, observing, "Oh, there's Marshal Rawley. I just heard he was back."

"Where?" I demanded. Of course this was why Celia had acted so strangely.

"That's him, yonder." Axton indicated with a tilt of his hat brim and I saw immediately which man he meant.

From a distance of two blocks I eyed this stranger, the marshal, as he sat horseback in the sun, with rising levels of angry disdain pumping through my blood. I knew it was not my business, I *knew* this. And yet, thinking of the expression on Celia's face just this morning as we discussed the inability to keep her baby, anger claimed the upper hand; I imagined my eyes taking on a red flame.

"Boost me up, will you?" I requested of Axton.

"Surely will," he said, doing so, but I could tell he had no idea of my actual intent.

I shifted my hips, orienting myself to the feel of an unsaddled horse – it felt different, not nearly as secure, and though I could not imagine riding this way for any length of time, the distance I intended to ride just now was short. I was thankful the mare wore a bridle and gripped the slim leather reins, one in each fist.

I looked down at Ax. "I'll be right back."

Axton made a small sound of protest but I'd already heeled the mare and was beyond hearing him; I heard only a furious buzzing in my ears.

The marshal sat astride a beautiful gelding. I had, in fact, never seen such a gorgeous horse, observing this as I rode near as though once-removed from myself. His mount was taller at the withers than mine by a good three inches and its auburn mane and tail glinted richly in the slanting afternoon sunlight; by contrast, its hide was a bright, silvered gray. At the lower joints of its legs, the color shifted to rust-red.

"Marshal Rawley?" I inquired sharply, bringing the mare to a halt just off his horse's right flank.

The marshal, with a long cigar held between his lips, had been engaged in reading a small piece of paper (I could see, now that I was close to him), his booted left foot out of the stirrup and braced casually on the iron endcap of the hitching post, and turned now to regard me with an insulting lack of urgency.

Time lurched to a halt as I studied this man I had never met. The daily sights and sounds of Howardsville snapped outward and away, as if stretched on long, taut cords. I heard only the rushing of my blood, the way it would sound if my hands were clamped over both ears.

And my heart. Furious and hot, it wanted to beat through my chest.

The marshal had a long, straight nose and a thick black mustache which obscured his top lip, leaving only the lower in sight. He was dressed in a gray leather vest, much worn, over a collared white shirt, open at the throat and with sleeves rolled back. His eyes were in the shadow of a wide-brimmed black hat but they held steady on mine with irises almost as dark as his hat.

He blinked once and seemed to draw himself together, removing the cigar from his mouth to inquire, "Whom do I have the pleasure of addressing?"

His silver horse snorted as if to contradict this polite question.

I summoned a confrontational tone. "Never mind who I am! I'm here to bring your attention to a woman who – " And then I faltered, my bravado leaking away as I second-guessed my actions. Celia would kill me. She would despise this potential scene I was causing, though no one seemed to be paying much attention.

The marshal's black eyebrows arched, but in an amused way, I could tell. He prompted, "A woman who…"

He was younger than I'd imagined him but still probably a good five years older than me. There was something maddening about him and I felt tricked, terribly disoriented, as I stared in frustration at his face. He was possessed of a capable, self-assured aura I could tell women found disarming; he was also unreasonably handsome and it was not difficult to see why Celia had been willing to save herself for him the last time he was in town, fat lot of good that did her now. His marshal's badge, attached to his gray vest, winked in the sun.

"A woman who needs you," I said at last; unfortunately, this was too indirect.

A half-smile lifted the right side of his mustache; he took a deliberate moment to tuck the paper within a vest pocket and draw on his cigar. I battled the urge to knock it out of his hand. Releasing a stream of smoke, he drawled, "Ma'am, I'm on business at the moment. But later, if you'd allow me, I'd be downright pleased to attend to your needs."

"You two-bit *asshole*," I sputtered, hardly able to choke the words past the lump of rage in my throat. I felt a small spurt of satisfaction to see the way his expression changed, registering surprise. Sensing my mood, my new horse danced sideways and I tugged her back in line, tightening my thighs around her sides. I glared at the marshal.

"A woman in men's trousers, with an unsaddled horse, calling *me* names?" he asked, retaining an air of calm, but I could sense a certain level of astonishment. He looked a little more closely and commented, "Isn't that Doc Turn's horse?" That half-smile again as his gaze flickered briefly over my breasts and hips. Returning his eyes to my face, he commented wryly, "Well, you're by far the loveliest horse thief I've ever laid eyes upon, that's God's truth. Though, you won't get far without a saddle, I feel I must tell you."

Fuming little volcanoes erupted across my midsection. Was he…did he actually think he could *flirt* with me?

"This is *my* horse. And don't change the subject!" I hissed, gripping the mare's reins. She was agitated by my rising voice and what was surely my resultant body language.

"I am not changing the subject." He appeared deeply amused, his dark eyes holding fast to mine.

I straightened my spine. "I would like to talk with you, if you have a moment."

"Regarding what, exactly?" he asked, and I found myself too flustered to respond. To my further irritation, when I continued to sit in stubborn silence he finally said, "Suit yourself," and dismounted as gracefully as a dancer, proceeding to tie his beautiful horse to the post, turning his back on me.

I leaped from the mare; she nickered and snorted, but I clutched her lead line and stalked directly to the marshal's side. He looked down at me with no small amount of surprise; he was much taller than I was, broad through the shoulder but otherwise very lean. He gave me two seconds of attention before finishing his task. He then expertly tamped out his cigar and tucked it into yet another vest pocket.

"Regarding a private matter," I said, looping my horse's reins about the hitching post.

"Ma'am, I don't believe we've ever met before this very afternoon." He stood with fists planted on hips, a large pistol strapped around his waist, but despite this masculine and rather intimidating pose, I did not step aside or away. I remained in the sunlight while he stood in the shade afforded by the overhang. I shielded my eyes with one hand and continued to glare as he said, "Forgive me for wondering just what private matter you and I may share."

"It's not about *me*." I lowered my voice. "It's about Celia Baker."

"The whore?" he asked, though not maliciously. His tone indicated he simply wanted clarification. "What about her?"

"How *dare* you call her that?"

He opened his mouth to speak but then seemed to think better, and shifted his weight to the opposite hip. He finally said, "For such a lovely little thing, you have a fair amount of fire in you. And besides, Celia *is* a whore. I'm doubtful she'd be upset with me for the saying so."

"*Men*," I raged, nearly vibrating with emotion. He probably thought I would let it drop if he piled on the compliments. I seethed, "You're all the same."

"Ma'am, I admit I'm downright confused by all of this." He offered his right hand and invited, "Why don't we begin afresh? My name is Miles William Rawley, marshal to these parts. May I have the pleasure of your name?"

Before I knew what I was doing I reached up and flicked my middle finger against his chin, as hard as I could. He yelped in surprise. I whirled away in a hurry and was planning to climb atop my horse and flee, but he grabbed my elbow and forcibly kept me from forward motion. I struggled, attempting without success to yank my elbow from his firm grasp. I whirled around, venomous, and kicked his shin.

You idiot. You didn't want to make a scene and now look.

"Dammit, would you stop?" he all but growled, releasing my arm.

Axton was suddenly there, flying from Ranger and hurrying to my side. He tucked his arm around my elbow and tipped his hat at the marshal, saying apologetically, "Marshal, please excuse Ruthann."

"*Ruthann*," the marshal repeated, with a subtle air of triumph. "Well, that's something, at least."

"Let go of me," I grumbled at Axton, from whose gentle grip I easily tugged free.

I tucked loose curls behind my ears, feeling more like an idiot (not to mention a sloppy, tangled-hair idiot) than ever, as the marshal straightened to his full height and stared right back at me; confusion and disquiet radiated from him. His chest expanded with a breath; he demanded, "Ruthann, what?"

"This is Miss Ruthann Rawley," Axton answered, and the marshal's eyebrows drew together.

"Who is your father?" he asked next. "Have you kin in this area?"

"She doesn't know," Axton, ever helpful, supplied. "She can't remember a thing but her name. She was injured real bad when Uncle Branch and me found her earlier this summer."

"Found her?" the marshal repeated. His frown deepened and a horizontal crease appeared at the bridge of his nose. "Injured?"

"Stop talking about me like I'm not standing here!"

"I'm sorry, Ruthie, I was just trying to help."

I ignored Ax for the moment and glared fiercely at Miles Rawley. "Don't bother asking because I don't have any answers."

"My brother homesteads west of town," the marshal said, as if I hadn't spoken. "Grantley Rawley is his name. The rest of our family resides in Iowa. We've no relatives in this area, that I am aware."

"You're soon to have a child in this area," I said then, a low blow. All thoughts of what Celia might think about me blathering her news flew right out of my head.

"Come again?" the marshal demanded.

"You made Celia Baker pregnant. She is going to have *your baby*, come winter."

His eyes drove heatedly into mine. "How do *you* come to know this?"

"Because she told me," I said, spurred on by angry righteousness. "And you should do right by her."

I watched him struggle for, and find, composure. He said quietly, "There's no way of knowing whose child Celia might be carrying. I shared her bed last spring, that is God's truth, but so did countless others."

"Oh, easy for you to say!" I cried, riled up all over again; I'd felt a fleeting pang of sympathy. "This way you don't have to claim a shred of responsibility, do you?"

"She is a *whore*." He appeared incensed, eyes and voice ablaze.

"She is a *woman* who is pregnant with *your* baby!" I yelled.

Poor Axton was as red as his hair. Other people in our midst sounded like nothing more than chickens, clucking with gossip.

"I'll not entertain that notion another moment." The marshal made an abrupt about-face and headed for the entrance of the building I'd failed to realize we stood near – the jailhouse.

I heard Axton murmur, "Ruthie, c'mon…" but that didn't stop me from darting after the marshal and clutching the back of his vest, curling my fingers along the bottom edge to gain a handhold on the smooth leather. His back was hard and very warm against my knuckles, even with the material of his shirt between us, and just like that my knees went weak. It took everything I had to keep my gaze steady on Miles Rawley's face as he turned with deliberate and distinctly angry movements. My hand slipped free from his vest and slid around his waist before I snatched it away.

"I'll thank you to leave me be regarding this matter." His voice was low and rough.

"That would be *so* convenient for you, wouldn't it?" I was failing miserably to disguise my agitation.

"This is absolutely *none* of your affair." He bent closer and pointed his index finger at my chest, not touching me; more to emphasize his point. And in the space of several hot, frantic heartbeats I swore I saw him in a hundred different incarnations –

But not exactly him…

What in the hell…

Clean-shaven and grinning, laughing and teasing me, making me laugh in return; his eyelids just slightly lowered, as though in extreme pleasure, his forearms braced on either side of my head and my thighs curving around his hips; my hands buried in his thick hair as he licked a hot path downward along my belly…

I blinked, gasping a hard, painful breath. I had to step away.

He reached to prevent this and caught my upper arms in an unforgiving grip. His eyes narrowed, his brows lowered – his expression could only be described as staggered. Had he also experienced the same unexpected blast of images? My heart was flaying me from the inside out. He shook me just a little, his confusion as palpable as my own.

"Let go." My words emerged as a pathetic huff of air. I shrugged free of his grip and he allowed it. I could hardly manage the steadiness required to put one foot before the other and did not look back as I unwound the reins, climbed up the hitching post fence so I was able to mount my unsaddled horse, and then heeled her; I only knew I needed to get away.

I cantered my mare far into the countryside, out into the foothills, where the air was tangy with the scent of sagebrush. I let the sun touch my face, trying desperately to recapture other touches, other sensations, unsettled to such a degree I felt ill. I halted the mare and limped down from her back, my heart aching so severely I hunched around my midsection. I crouched near the mare's front legs; she nosed the part in my loose, messy hair. I curled both arms around my head and rocked back and forth.

"Who am I?" I moaned, over and over. I shifted, sliding both hands over my belly and then lower, shuddering at the strength and urgency of my need.

"I was happy," I whispered. Agony bit into me, hard enough that my chest would not expand. I crossed my forearms over my breasts and clutched my shoulders. I felt like I might come apart if I didn't hold as tightly as I was able. "Once, I was happy."

Chapter Six

"BILL LITTLE'S BEEN DEAD A GOOD FOUR YEARS," SAID THE man leaning over Rilla's bar. "So why the hell is he being named in them killings out near Yankton? And what about the cattle rustling?"

"I asked the marshal hisself just today," said the man lounging along-side him. "Rawley said it ain't Bill Little, said he seen Little dead with his own eyes, but I dunno…"

The speculation had been rolling endlessly the last two days, ever since the marshal's return to Howardsville. Talk of criminal activity was on everyone's lips. As afternoon bled to evening, I lingered on a stool at the extreme end of the bar, believing myself all but invisible, listening to the swirling gossip, which was only heightened by the never-ending sup-ply of hard liquor. Rilla encouraged gossip; she said nervous customers were more easily persuaded to part with their money.

"Some of it's been stirred up since fancy-man Yancy sent his men to town," said someone else. "That son of a bitch and his railroad interests. You recall Yancy was the one fronting the gold for Bill Little's expenses. That was the talk, back in 'seventy-six…"

"Some said Yancy was the one who raised a posse to go after Carter, back when."

"Marshal Rawley rode with Carter then, you'll recall. Riding a fine line with the law."

"Rawley's gotta obey the rules now," said another, and they all chuckled.

I put my forehead onto my arms atop the bar, feeling lower than I had since I'd been found in the prairie outside of Howardsville. I'd been unable to surface from the trench into which I'd fallen since my confrontation with the marshal; I could not explain why, even to myself. I'd avoided Branch and Axton for two days, the longest I'd been apart from them since they'd found me.

I missed them so much it hurt; I hadn't seen my new horse in as much time but knew Axton was taking care of her. I'd lied to him earlier, telling him my head ached too much to go for our usual ride. He was so concerned; he never considered the fact that I was lying. Now, *having* lied and been subsequently left at Rilla's, I wallowed in my own depression, eavesdropping on conversations about the one man I wanted more than anything to avoid.

For the first twenty-four hours after telling Miles Rawley the news that was not mine to tell I'd walked on needle points, expecting him to stride through the swinging doors and demand an audience with Celia. I imagined Celia's subsequent and justifiable fury, but as the entire next day passed and I spied neither hide nor hair of the marshal (neither did I gather enough courage to inform Celia what I'd done), I assumed he'd decided to ignore the entire situation. And for whatever reason, this caused me to sink even further into despair. I'd hardly spoken a word to anyone since the afternoon Axton presented me with my new horse.

I wanted to be riding her over the prairie right at this very moment. I needed to pick up my sorry self and walk outside. I imagined Axton and Branch eating dinner and worrying about me, and the thought gifted me with strength to lift my head. I hadn't even thanked Branch for the horse; I was behaving like a selfish, ungrateful child. I wished with sudden fervor I'd gone with Axton this afternoon. This wish inspired a flicker of determined ambition – I realized I could walk out to their claim shanty. It wasn't more than a few minutes on horseback. I could walk out there in a quarter of an hour. Probably even less. But then doubts crept through my head.

You can't walk there alone. It's dangerous after dark.

But it's not far. No more than a couple of miles. You can spend the night. You can give Branch and Ax a hug and sit near the fire. You can see your horse.

You haven't even named her yet.

The prospect of thanking Branch in person and giving my horse a proper name filled me with a sense of purpose, scraping the sharpest edges from my sadness. I stood up and began snaking my way through the bar, jammed to full capacity as evening advanced. I recognized I needed to hurry if I wanted to reach Branch's before the full onset of night.

"Hold up, girl." He issued the words in a commanding tone, catching me off guard; I was so accustomed to slipping around and between, unnoticed. But then again, I wasn't normally on the main floor at this hour. Before I could sidestep he clamped a hand around my forearm, halting my progress, and with a sinking heart I realized it was the yellow-bearded man I tried my best to avoid. He eyed my breasts, applying pressure to my arm. "When you gonna start working the floor for Rilla? I been waiting for weeks now."

"This here girl wears trousers," the man beside him observed with obvious disgust, draining his small glass of booze and thumping it back against the scarred wooden surface of the bar. He grinned at his own statement, showcasing tobacco-stained teeth, gesturing toward my thighs.

"She ain't wearing trousers just now. I can tell she knows how to show a fella a good time." His grip tightened to a painful level. Cold fear pierced my ribs as I mutely studied his bearded face, which was slick with sweat. His eyes were a pale, watery blue, oddly intense, and my stomach jolted. He leaned closer and muttered, "You want me to squeeze them ripe titties, don't you?"

My teeth came together on their edges and I found my voice. "Let go of me, *asshole.*"

His smile disappeared as swiftly as if I'd decked him. Before I could blink he clamped a palm around the back of my neck and growled, "You don't give me orders. Ain't nobody give me orders. You need some sense beat into you, girl?" He jerked my head forward and my jaws clacked. He insisted, "Do you?"

"Jesus, leave her be, you drunk fool," the rotten-toothed man said, dragging him away from me. "Jesus *Christ,* Aemon."

The man named Aemon sneered and reclaimed his stool; he dismissed me with a strange whistling sound that emerged from between his teeth, flapping one hand through the air and draining his drink with the other.

Go upstairs, go to your room and get the hell away from here, my better judgment warned.

But longing to see Branch and Axton, and my new horse, overrode my concerns. Restless, crawling desire diluted the fear and I ducked around male bodies in my flight from the main floor, scurrying outside and down the front porch steps. Howardsville was far from quiet but the immediate sounds from Rilla's were muted, bringing me a small sense of peace. I scanned the eastern horizon in an attempt to judge remaining daylight; the sky was already indigo, growing spangled with stars, but there was enough time before full dark for me to reach the claim shanty. Branch would be upset with me for walking that distance alone, but it would be all right. They would be happy to see me, I knew.

A brief commotion down the street caught my attention and I spied the elaborate carriage that had arrived yesterday morning, by train no less, drawn by a matched pair of gorgeous black horses, their hides as glossy as onyx. Word was a wealthy businessman named Yancy had sent his men to the Territory to scout the area for a suitable building site, one upon which Yancy's son and the son's new wife would be able to stay when conducting railroad business. Gossip had been flying about the wife arriving without the company of either husband *or* father-in-law, and therefore perhaps inappropriately chaperoned, but although six grand railroad cars had rolled into Howardsville yesterday, suggesting royalty, no one seemed to have actually set eyes upon this alleged young wife.

Maybe she's in the carriage. I was interested despite everything, but when the carriage clattered past my position at the bottom of the steps I saw only men; two of them had rifles braced lengthwise across their laps. Slightly disappointed, I thought, *Or maybe not.*

The laundry shack where I spent my days was only a few paces away, in the alley between saloons, and my riding pants were folded in there; I'd forgotten to bring them up to my room earlier. I made a quick decision to change clothes. It would be so much easier to walk across the prairie, which wasn't nearly as flat as it appeared from a distance, without being hobbled by long, flapping skirts. I drew aside the canvas door and ducked within what had become a familiar space, shimmying out of both skirt and underskirt; my lower half was completely naked and would have been for only a second. I wadded up my skirt and set it aside, reaching to grab my pants – and that was when he grabbed me.

"Told you I been waiting." His mouth was on my ear. His beard brushed the side of my face and I smelled booze.

I made a sound which should have been a scream, but surprise snatched my breath and stole all the force. I struggled, jerking and twisting, and he clamped a palm around my mouth, forcing me forward, cupping the bare flesh between my legs. He grunted as his fingers made contact and plundered my flesh. I thrashed against his hold, furious and hideously disgusted by this intrusion of my body, trying to slam his nose with the back of my head. He was stronger than I would have imagined and tilted his head to the side to avoid any such attack; he ordered, "*Keep still*," and roughly bent me double.

My forehead struck the hanging cauldron on the way down and spots danced at the edges of my vision. In the dimming light he dug one hand into my hair to keep me immobile and struggled to undo his trousers with the other. Instinct ripped through the stunned horror of what was happening and I stomped on his foot with my heel, as hard as I could, hearing a dull thunk – my terror-dazed mind registered this as my shoe connecting with his boot – but then he slumped to his knees, issuing a low-pitched groan, which I could not for the life of me account for. Surely my foot hadn't knocked him out?

"*Bastard!*" a woman's voice hissed.

I tried to spin around but I was stuck in a slow-motion reel, shuffling to the side to avoid making contact with the man as he sagged to the ground. My eyes darted like frightened minnows, landing upon a woman framed in the doorway, gripping a piece of firewood in her hands.

"Is he dead?" she wondered aloud, sounding more curious than concerned, poking a shoe from beneath a long, narrow skirt to nudge his stationary form. She insisted, "If he is, we shall hire my uncle. He is a

Bostonian lawyer, a very good one, and no harm shall come to either of us." In the next breath she inquired, "Are you harmed? I observed this beast follow after you. Thank heavens I was walking the town instead of remaining cooped within that ridiculous rolling prison car."

I was naked from the waist down but so overcome by her presence and rapid speech I didn't move to cover myself.

"Forgive me, you are undoubtedly in a state of shock." She tossed aside the firewood and stooped to grab my clothing from the ground. "Please dress and then we shall report this depraved individual to the law in this town. Attacking a woman on the street is a hanging offense. Or, it *should* be so."

I held my skirt and underskirt against my belly but couldn't muster the proper movements to replace them.

"Oh, my dear, you are in a state. Here, I shall help you," she offered, and did so. Once I was fully clothed she led me out of the laundry shack. I couldn't discern her facial features in the gray gloaming light but I could tell she was young. She smelled clean and sweet, her hair tucked beneath a hat with an arrangement of flowers on the band. She extended her right hand, which I numbly shook, and said formally, "I am Patricia Biddeford." Then she giggled, explaining this by correcting herself. "Patricia Yancy, rather. I am only recently married. I've not yet grown accustomed to inserting my new surname when making introductions. May I ask your name? I regret we have been forced to meet under such circumstances. You seem pale. Truly, even in the darkness. Where is your home? Why are you here in the alley at dusk, improperly garbed and unprotected? I admit I am quite confused."

I hadn't yet spoken a single syllable. I assumed Patricia Yancy would carry on until I did so, and whispered, "I live just up there," indicating the second floor of Rilla's.

Patricia's eyes widened. "But you are so very young! Surely you cannot mean to tell me you are employed as a prostitute. I am quite aware the darker aspects of life have been deliberately kept from me, courtesy of my father's wishes, but nevertheless…"

"I'm not a prostitute," I said, interrupting her prattling, regaining a tentative handhold on my self-control now that I was reasonably safe from harm. My terror was fading and I found the ability to speak in coherent sentences. "I live at Rilla's in exchange for doing laundry."

"Where is your family?" Patricia demanded, her hands fluttering as though to straighten or tidy something, at last settling for smoothing the length of my hair. "Have you no people? What is your name?"

I drew myself up as best I could. "Ruthann Rawley."

"Are you kin to the marshal? I was introduced to him only yesterday morning, when we first arrived in Howardsville."

"No," I said, rather too tersely. Something occurred to me and I sent a question her way this time. "Why are *you* out and about alone?"

She didn't squirm but a beat of knotty silence passed before she confessed, "I rather...insistently...suggested my escorts find something to amuse themselves this evening. I assured them I would be safe as a kitten in the train car. They left Mrs. Mason with me, of course, but she is *such* a sound sleeper, you see..."

"So you snuck out."

"No, I most certainly did not! I am a grown woman, a *married* woman, and if I should *choose* to – "

The man she'd struck with the firewood, who continued to lie on the dirt floor of the laundry shack, emitted a low moan, snapping our attention his way. I shuddered at the sound and Patricia said firmly, "My situation is neither here nor there. Come, let us find the marshal and report this crime."

"No," I said again. "I haven't been hurt."

"Have you taken leave of your senses? You must accompany me and report what this man was about to do to you. Of course you have been hurt! There is a wound upon your forehead! This beast put his hands upon you. He is a criminal, an immoral ruffian."

I knew she was right but I didn't want to see the marshal. My heart took up an erratic jangling against my ribs.

"Come along," Patricia said, insistent as a buzzing bee. Once around the corner, where the lantern light bisected the darkness, she tucked my elbow against her side as if I might try to escape. "The jailhouse is but a few blocks this direction."

I let her lead me even though I knew the way all too well; it was exactly where I had last seen Miles Rawley. As we neared the jail I caught sight of his gorgeous silver horse tethered to the hitching post alongside another. Oblong patches of light spilled forth from the windows of the small wooden structure. The deep, muffled sound of men speaking reached our ears through the walls; it was clear the marshal and at least one other man were inside. My feet stalled. All I'd really wanted this evening was to visit Branch and Axton, and ride my horse. A dizzy rush blurred my vision and I clung to Patricia Yancy's arm.

Patricia spared not a second for hesitation before sweeping inside the jailhouse like she owned the place, though from what I'd learned in recent gossip her father-in-law owned most of the town. Perhaps this building was indeed her property, by default.

"Gentlemen," she greeted, with no appreciable loss of composure.

Whatever conversation we'd interrupted came to a screeching halt. I could hardly contain my writhing embarrassment as the marshal looked up in obvious surprise. He sat behind a large wooden desk, hatless and smoking a cigar, his thick black hair loose and hanging past his shoulders, his bootheels resting on the gleaming surface of the desk. An ashtray was balanced on his lap. Another man sat in an adjacent chair, holding a tin plate full of food, which he'd been busy eating. I watched as his hand, holding a fork, slowly lowered toward his lap.

The marshal recovered his power of speech. "Mistress Yancy, good evening." His eyes moved past her and then his boots hit the ground. His chair rocked backward as he stood, almost losing the ashtray in the process. "Ruthann. You've been hurt."

At these words, Patricia turned to examine my face. In the lantern-lit space of the jailhouse, which contained two barred cells, both currently empty, she affirmed, "You are bleeding."

"Miles," said the man who'd been eating, tossing a cloth napkin toward the marshal, which Miles caught as he strode around the desk.

Patricia stepped to the side; I did my best not to retreat as the marshal approached, intense eyes fixed upon me. He clasped my right shoulder, gently pressing the folded material to my forehead. When it became apparent he intended to hold it in place, I reached up to take the cloth from him, muttering, "Thank you…"

He ordered, "Come, be seated."

He led me to the only free chair in the room. I was so flustered I'd hardly taken the time to notice the second man, who set aside his plate and stood to his full height; Patricia stationed herself near the desk, hands clasped at her waist.

The marshal knelt in front of me. "What has happened?"

I felt foolish and tongue-tied as I sat holding the cloth to my bleeding forehead. Without his hat the marshal appeared younger and somewhat less imposing. His obvious concern set my blood churning. In such close proximity to him my breath was shallow and try as I might, I could not force aside the insanity of the images which had plagued me since the day we met – those of making incredible, passionate love with him, but not *exactly* him. His skin was darkly tanned, as though he spent every daylight hour outside. He appeared stern just now, frowning, his dark eyebrows pulled low. His nose was long and knife-edged, his eyes walnut-brown and fixed on mine.

As though sensing I needed her, Patricia answered. "I brought Miss Rawley here because she was attacked. A man followed her from Rilla's place and accosted her in the adjacent alley."

The marshal demanded harshly, "What man? When was this?"

"Not a quarter-hour ago," Patricia said.

"Where is he now?" asked the other man. He spoke with controlled ire, shoulders tensing; he had the look of someone who could hold his own in any fight, tall and solidly-built, sunburnt to a deep tan like the marshal. His hair was a beautiful shade of auburn, much like Axton's. A pistol was strapped in a leather gun belt around his hips. He and Miles exchanged a quick look, the kind which speaks volumes, in the way of longtime friends.

"He remains in the alley where we left him," Patricia said. "Come, I shall show you."

"I thank you for the offer but I know the place." Miles turned back to me. He rested his fingertips to my elbow in a touch both brief and gentle. "Remain here, if you would." At my nod, he stood and issued brisk orders. "Cole, keep watch. Mrs. Yancy, you will also remain here for the time being. I will return directly." And he disappeared into the night.

Patricia hurried to my side, her skirts brushing Cole's boots as she walked past him. Even though we'd just met I could tell Patricia was flustered; she drew a chair, the one Cole had vacated, closer to mine and perched on its edge, observing softly, "You're trembling. You are chilled."

Cole grabbed the jacket draped over the back of the marshal's chair and arranged it around my shoulders. At once I was inundated with the feeling of the man who owned this jacket, a man I had enough trouble keeping from my mind; Miles's jacket smelled of cigar smoke, and of him. There was no other way to describe it. My heart lurched and I felt a sudden, overwhelming desire to lift the collar to my nose, to better inhale the scent trapped in the lightweight material.

You're crazy, I told myself.

"Thank you," I said to Cole, who crouched on my opposite side so I was between him and Patricia. Though Cole looked like he could wallop anyone's ass he chose there was an aura of ease about him; I sensed he was a man accustomed to being around women.

He replied, "It's nothing."

Patricia was studying Cole; she spoke in the somber tone of someone confessing a secret. "I saw you this morning."

"I saw you as well." He shifted position, forearms to thighs. Their gazes held.

Able to find a moment of calm, I marveled in silence at Patricia's beauty, which I hadn't noticed in the past chaotic hour. She appeared, to my eyes anyway, much too young to be a married woman. There was an honesty to her face, a sense of someone unable to keep secrets well and who probably spoke her mind; I'd already had a taste of that. Her features were delicate in contrast to a voluptuous mouth; her lashes were long and charcoal-black, framing blue eyes so deep and captivating I found it difficult not to stare. Cole seemed to be experiencing a similar difficulty.

"You are the man who used to ride with the marshal." Her tone indicated she knew more about Cole than she was currently admitting.

"I am," Cole replied without hesitation, but I could tell he wondered just what she was implying, if anything.

Patricia broke the intensity of their gazes and came close to babbling as she explained to me, "My father-in-law wishes to build a house in this area. He roamed the western lands for some time before making his fortune near here, in a silver mine. I spent the past spring in Chicago listening to talk of the wild Montana Territory and its many charms. I insisted upon being allowed to visit in the summer months."

"What of your husband?" Cole asked, with an undercurrent of something I couldn't quite interpret; something dark.

Patricia busied herself fussing with a silver button on her waist; keeping her gaze lowered, she said, "Dredd has no wish to leave Chicago. He shall only venture here under duress." She braved a look at me. "By 'duress' I mean his father, of course."

"The Yancys are nothing but lowdown cowards and criminals," Cole said then, with thinly-disguised heat. My eyes darted his way. The set of his features dared Patricia to disagree.

"They are my husband's family," Patricia countered, and her chin lifted. "I shall thank you to recall this fact and apologize."

"That doesn't change a goddamn thing," Cole said, not sounding the least apologetic. "They're still criminals. Your husband's brother, Fallon, should have been at the end of a hanging rope years ago. He's too well-protected now, the weasel-faced bastard…"

A hot flush spread over Patricia's face and bloomed down the neck of her dress. Her lips dropped open and I thought she was too shocked to reply. But she squared her shoulders and snapped, "Mr. Spicer, how dare you suggest that I –"

Her angry utterance was interrupted as the jailhouse door crashed open as though kicked, slamming against the wall and subsequently emitting the marshal, clutching the man from the alley.

"Cole," the marshal said succinctly, and that was all it took for Cole to rise and lead both Patricia and me out of the way. Patricia slipped an arm around my waist and drew me closer to her; Cole positioned himself in front of us, though the sorry figure being half-dragged into the room hardly seemed a threat at this point.

"I hope you enjoy this evening's accommodations, Turnbull," Miles said conversationally, unlocking one of the small cells in the room. "I'd get used to the view from behind bars, if I was you."

Patricia kept a firm grip on my waist. Between her warmth and the marshal's jacket, my trembling had stilled. The man who'd intended to rape me was summarily tossed to his knees, his bearded face beaten to a bloody, swollen mess. The marshal relocked the door and then stepped back, his gaze seeking mine.

"Thank you," I felt compelled to say. My throat was tight and hoarse.

"Come, Ruthann, you shall stay with me this night," Patricia said, with authority.

"No, Miss Rawley will remain here," Miles responded, in a tone which brooked absolutely no argument. "I have a desire to speak with her."

"She is hurting and I shall care for her." Patricia's arm remained locked around my waist; we were almost exactly the same height.

Miles said, "I will care for her, rest assured," and my heart went into a seizure.

"I'm all right," I murmured to Patricia, touched by her concern.

Patricia turned her blue eyes to Miles and implored, "Once you have spoken, I insist Ruthann be escorted to my train car."

"Your people will be looking for you at any moment," Cole said to Patricia. "Come, I'll walk you back."

"I do not wish to leave this place, not until Ruthann is able to accompany me." Her expression dared him to deny her this request.

A grudging smile tugged at Cole's mouth. He disregarded her order and said, "Let's go," holding forth one hand in polite invitation, nodding at the door.

"I shall *not*."

"I'm just fine," I said quickly, hoping to thwart an argument. "I have a room at Rilla's, but I thank you for the offer."

Patricia was plainly torn; she was used to getting her way, I could tell. She finally said, "I shall find you first thing in the morning, does that suit you?"

"It does." I tried for a smile.

"Come along, Mrs. Yancy," Cole said, emphasizing her name just slightly.

Patricia kissed my cheek before sweeping past the men and out the door. Cole looked to Miles, the two of them exchanging a brief, wordless conversation that spoke a thousand things to which I was not privy.

Seconds later Cole followed Patricia, and Miles and I were alone.

Chapter Seven

AEMON TURNBULL, THE MAN HUNCHED IN THE JAIL CELL, issued a low, groaning grunt, and this sound temporarily drew the marshal's attention; he said quietly, "We will speak in my quarters rather than this office, Miss Rawley. If you'll accompany me?"

Though he framed this as a question, it was actually an order; I could do nothing but nod. He locked the front entrance to the jail and I allowed him to lead the way outside, where the air was chill and the sounds of the town at play in the saloons drifted to our ears. A small wooden structure, no bigger than Branch and Axton's shanty cabin, was situated a few yards beyond the jailhouse; Miles had plucked the lantern from the desk, which he now placed on a tabletop in this, his personal space.

My eyes roved anxiously from the table with three mismatched chairs to a small porcelain basin of water, a fat-bellied woodstove, and a narrow bed made of ropes stretched taut over a wooden frame, covered by a disheveled quilt. I darted my gaze at once from the place where he slept.

"Please, be seated," Miles said, withdrawing a chair. "I apologize for the unseemly location of this conversation. I am unwilling to converse before that vermin in the jail at present, and I have a wish to speak with you. I have since our first encounter."

I sat, awkward and nervous, clutching the bloody cloth, his jacket still hooked over my shoulders. Miles dragged a chair around the table, closer to me, which seemed to create a force field in my chest; it was all I could do not to scramble away, as tense as though I sat here naked. Without asking permission, he took the cloth from my hand, dipped it in the basin and then squeezed it out.

His shirtsleeves were unbuttoned, rolled back from his forearms, which were covered in dark hair. He had lean, strong, long-fingered hands, which I studied as they performed the small tasks; the dark hair continued over the backs of his wrists. I watched as though transfixed as he leaned and dabbed at the wound on my forehead.

"Turnbull struck you?" His anger at my potential response was held carefully in check.

I nodded.

"He claims you and Mrs. Yancy struck *him*," the marshal went on, placing his fingertips beneath my chin, holding me steady as he administered the damp cloth. His touch was gentle and warm at both points of contact on my skin. No more than two feet of empty air separated our faces as he cleansed my forehead; he said softly, "I hope you realize I am not going to hurt you."

I found my voice at last. "I know."

"You appear afraid of me," he justified, pausing in his ministrations to look into my eyes. His fingertips moved against my chin, not quite stroking me but not far from it. I thought he must be able to feel the strength of the pulse in my throat. He turned to rinse the cloth, tinting the water faintly red with my blood. I released a narrow breath, clutching his jacket together between my breasts.

"I'm not afraid of you," I found the wherewithal to say.

He reapplied the cloth to my forehead; he hadn't squeezed it out as well this time and a lukewarm drip of water rolled down the left side of my nose. I reached to swipe at it the same moment he did and our hands collided. Unexpectedly, he smiled. My heart throbbed in response.

He said, "Well, that's good. And I apologize."

I spoke before I thought. "No, it's me who should be apologizing." His eyebrows lifted in an obvious question and I hurried to explain, "For accosting you on the street the other day."

"About that." His focus returned to my forehead and he took a moment cleaning the last of the blood away, finally sitting back and folding the cloth over the edge of the basin. "Are you able to tell me what happened this evening?"

I gripped his jacket tighter around my body; his eyes followed the movements of my hands. "I was planning to walk out to Branch Douglas's claim shanty."

"Walk out of town?" he interrupted. "Surely you have better sense than to walk alone after dark."

"No one notices me. Usually Axton and I ride together in the evenings, and I eat supper with them – "

He interrupted for the second time to repeat my words, rather more heatedly than necessary. "No one *notices* you?"

"They really don't." He looked as though he thought I was lying and I felt a spark of temper, insisting, "I don't work as a…" The word lodged in my throat. "As a whore. Rilla offered me a place to live if I help out with the daily laundry. I don't normally hang out on the floor after customers start arriving, but still…"

"Have you no idea how vulnerable you are?" Miles was visibly upset. "A woman alone, wandering the streets of this town after dark? I wouldn't let my own mother consider such, and she could probably outshoot me on any given afternoon."

"I don't make a *habit* of it. I was only alone tonight because I told Axton I didn't feel well enough for our usual ride."

"Branch and Axton Douglas look after you? They claim to have found you earlier this summer, badly injured. What of this? How came you to be alone on the prairie outside Howardsville?"

"I wish I knew." I felt the familiar prickle of tears and used my knuckles to swipe at them; the jacket sank from my shoulders.

"Allow me," he said, drawing his jacket around my upper body. Our gazes clung. I felt as if with the slightest touch applied to any part of me, I would burst like a soap bubble. My heart beat with such agitation I could feel it to the soles of my feet.

"Thank you." My voice shook.

"Who are you?" he whispered. His hands, having accomplished the polite task, now lingered; he cupped my shoulders, with extreme care, as if I was constructed of glass. My gaze moved between his eyes and his lower lip, the top hidden by his full black mustache. My thighs began trembling.

"I don't know.".

"I do not understand." He lifted his hands and tucked hair behind my ears with movements both adept and tender, and the trembling overtook my belly. He whispered, "Your hair startled me so, when you first confronted me. It was loose and I am unused to seeing women with their hair loose, at least in the daylight hours." He seemed to realize he was behaving exceptionally boldly – certainly out of line – and he could never know I wanted right then to lean into his full embrace. I wanted this so much physical pain swelled in my chest.

"Forgive me." He leaned back, withdrawing his touch. He appeared ashen beneath his darkly-tanned skin. "I very much apologize, Miss Rawley. I am not myself this night."

I felt desperate with the need to understand. "Then who are you?"

Instead of answering, he asked, "How is it that I *know* you, when I am certain we have never met before the other day? I have felt I must be losing my mind since last I saw you."

"I've felt the same way," I whispered.

"You've been hurt and I am behaving most abominably." He sounded tortured. "Aemon Turnbull will pay, of that rest assured. I have no doubt he would have caused you greater harm if not for Mrs. Yancy happening upon you. She struck him?"

"Yes. She saw him follow me so she followed *him*. She saved me. Marshal," and a sharp pain stabbed my heart as I spoke his formal title rather than his name. "You weren't wrong. I should know better than to walk alone at night. I just wanted to see Axton and Branch, and my new horse. I missed them."

"They care for you? They look out for you?"

"They do."

"Have you no family, no one searching for you?"

"I can't remember," I said miserably. "I don't know a thing about my life."

"Rilla Jaymes allows you room and board, in exchange for laundry duties?"

I nodded.

"She treats you well in her establishment?"

I faltered, not wanting to seem ungrateful; Rilla gave me the security of a nightly bed.

"Rilla Jaymes does not strike me as a compassionate woman," he said when I didn't answer. "I dislike imagining you at her mercy. I dislike the thought of anyone mistreating you."

I said in a rush, "Celia Baker. She cares for me. And she really is pregnant. She has no reason to lie and she would kill me for having told you. She won't tell you herself."

His eyebrows drew together, forehead creasing in a combination of denial and confusion. "I cannot…how may it be possible…"

"She told me she was with you, and no others, last spring before getting pregnant. And she believes there's nothing you would do, even if she told you the truth." I hadn't intended to punish him with these words but his expression indicated I had. I said quickly, "But you can help her. You can arrange it so she won't have to send the baby away."

He clenched his forehead with one hand, as if to stop a flood of thoughts he wanted nothing to do with. "You must think me a heartless man, a man without principle."

"I truly don't. But Celia needs help."

"I cannot raise a child." He sounded horrified at the prospect. "I haven't the means. I haven't a wife."

My thoughts whirled through possibilities. "What about your brother? Isn't he married? Isn't he near here?"

"Grantley? Yes, on both counts. But he and his wife have two of their own children. I could not ask my brother to raise my bastard child…oh, dear God…"

I whispered, "You could marry Celia."

He looked even more horrified than he'd sounded moments ago. "I could *not*."

"So she's good enough to share your bed but not your *name*?" I cried. "Is it because she's a whore?!"

"It is because I do not love her. Nothing would stop me if I loved her."

His tone was deadly serious. "My father taught me two things. One, to ride a horse. Second, to marry a woman for love. He loves my mother with his whole heart and I have always listened to what my father taught me."

I felt totally out of control. "So you can have sex with her for a solid *month* but you can't stoop to *marrying her*?! What the hell would your father have to say about *that*?!"

"Dang, you two, I can hear you all the way outside," said Cole Spicer, entering the little cabin without a knock. He looked amused, eyeing me with a grin. He teased, "You seem far too ladylike for the kind of language I just heard."

I nearly bit through my bottom lip, unable to suppress an angry glare in Miles's direction; he spoke at the same moment, saying to Cole, "I'll thank you to take your sorry, eavesdropping self out of here."

"I just got here," Cole returned easily, not in the least perturbed, kicking a chair around so he could brace his forearms over the back of it. "I ain't going anywhere for a day, at least." He looked between the two of us, still grinning. "Is Rawley taking good care of you, Miss Ruthann?"

It would be unfair to act like he wasn't and so I nodded, now avoiding Miles's gaze.

"I'm glad to hear it. He's never been a true ladies' man, like myself," Cole continued, winking at me. He seemed almost giddy.

"You want a severe beating, Spicer? Right here?" Miles demanded.

"I don't see anyone who could deliver it," Cole threw back.

"Did Patricia get safely home?" I asked, breaking into their brotherly-sounding bickering.

"She did indeed," Cole said, merriment fading. He was silent, reflective, for the space of a heartbeat. "She seems intent on befriending you."

"I would like that." I wondered at his pause.

"She said she wishes to see more of you this week." Cole rested his chin on his stacked hands, which were curved over the rounded chair back; his eyes were the brown of acorns, almost devilish in their expression. I found myself speculating he'd always been the friend who got everyone else in trouble with his ideas.

"Well, I'm not going anywhere," I muttered.

"Has Miles offered you something to drink? Food of any kind?" Cole pressed.

The marshal issued a deep sigh, rubbing his fingertips over his forehead in the manner of someone with a headache. I felt a small twinge of sympathy. I told Cole, "He cleaned my wound and determined that someone is looking out for me."

"He ain't ever been much of a host. We've been friends a long time, Miss Ruthann. We don't hold nothing back when it comes to each other's business, do we, Rawley?"

"*Jesus Christ*," Miles muttered. "Would you rather spend the night in the alley? As I can arrange it."

Cole ignored this jab. "The cook in the saloon next door was friendly enough, earlier. I'll run and see if she can fix me one more plate. You must be hungry."

I was, but I said, "I don't want to trouble you."

"No trouble at all," Cole said. "Give me just a minute," and he disappeared out the door.

In Cole's absence, Miles moved to kneel near the woodstove. Without a word, he began building a fire in its belly and for a time we were silent, the tension slowly leaking away. At last, without looking my way, he said, "I should have asked if you were hungry. I apologize."

"I'm sorry, too. I shouldn't have yelled at you." I was surprised to hear myself admit, "It's just that you make me so *upset*."

Miles looked over his shoulder, his expression more serious than ever. Behind him, in the woodstove, the fire glinted to existence.

I rushed on, "I know it's not my business, I really do, but Celia is my friend. I care about her. And she's so worried." The thought of my conversation with her the first night we'd spoken intruded into my head; *I was half in love with him*, Celia had said and she meant Miles, the man kneeling before me just now.

"And you are worried for her," Miles understood.

I forced myself not to fidget under his steady gaze.

I began, "I am – " but Cole suddenly returned, bearing a plate of biscuits and sausage gravy; my stomach clenched in hunger. I'd eaten nothing since my breakfast of a boiled egg and lukewarm coffee.

"Thank you." I accepted the plate and a bundle containing both fork and butter knife.

"My pleasure." Cole settled again onto his backward chair. "Cook next door was sweet as pie to give me a second plate. It's because I've got a nice smile."

I gouged an enormous forkful from a biscuit and dragged it through the thick sausage gravy, smiling at his teasing bravado.

Cole tipped his chair on two legs, like a little boy. "Miles, this night has been unexpectedly exciting."

Miles closed the woodstove's grate and rejoined us, claiming the same chair he'd used earlier, dragging it just a little closer to mine. "It's been unexpected, that's for certain."

The quiet, dimly-lit space lent me a fleeting sense of confidence; before I could lose my nerve, I asked Cole, "Why would you say Patricia's husband's family is criminal?"

Cole righted his chair and rubbed a thumb over his jaw, plainly unsure how to respond; I was, after all, a stranger to him. Both he and Miles radiated a sense of strength and capability I found reassuring and slightly intimidating, and I hoped he would trust me with an answer. At last he said, "That's a long story, Miss Ruthann. There's plenty I could tell you to help you understand but it involves the business of my very dear friend, Malcolm Carter. I couldn't tell you the entire story without Malcolm here. Does that make sense?"

"Of course." I was touched he would take his friend into such consideration.

"I meant every word I said about the Yancys," Cole went on. "They're a treacherous, dangerous lot. Always have been."

Miles added, "Patricia's father-in-law, Thomas Yancy, was once a marshal but he was run out of Iowa City back in 'sixty-eight, when he was my family's neighbor. There were allegations at the time that he was involved in an attempted murder. He disappeared without a trace and my mama took in his sons, Fallon and Dredd. Then Fallon up and ran away. Scared my mama half to death. This was long ago, when we were just sprouts in Iowa." Miles sighed and his gaze lifted up and to the left, as one looking backward through time. "The Yancys disappeared for a long time after that. Wasn't until the mid-seventies that we heard word again, when they struck it rich with a silver vein in the mines near here. And since then they've multiplied their wealth seemingly without end, purchasing land and ore mines and investing in the market. Fallon, damn his rotten hide, has a knack for investment, so they claim, but he's as dirty as they come. A thief, a killer, many times over. He'd do anything to increase his wealth and position but he's a coward to his core. The family resides in Chicago these days. I haven't seen hide nor hair of any Yancys in a good four years and don't relish the thought of seeing any in the future."

I considered this information, disliking the notion that anyone connected to Patricia was a criminal. "Surely Patricia wasn't aware of their illegal doings when she agreed to marry into their family. She's so young. What's her husband's name again?" I only remembered thinking it had been an unusual one.

"Dredd," Miles supplied. "He's the younger of the two. He lived with us for nearly half a year and I know him better by far than his brother. My mama believed most of the bad things Dredd ever did were because Fallon pushed him."

"Patricia is eighteen," Cole added, his voice low and quiet. "I asked her on our walk. Her pa died a year ago, her ma back when she was just a little girl."

Miles glanced at his old friend; there was a winsome note in Cole's voice not present earlier.

His tone gaining strength, Cole said, "And a halfwit could see she ain't happy."

"Spicer…" Miles spoke with a subtle note of concern, enough to bring Cole's gaze back to his; Cole pressed his lips together in a stubborn manner, briefly closing his eyes.

"Your family is still in Iowa?" I asked Miles, redirecting the conversation, curious to learn more about these people with whom I shared a last name. "Axton has told me some."

"They are." Miles's voice softened with fondness. "My parents reside in the same farmhouse in which my brothers and I were raised, along with Willie, my youngest brother. Cole's family settled on the adjacent acreage in the summer of 1868, around the time Fallon ran away."

"And you believe Fallon is worse than Dredd?"

Miles nodded. "He is by far the worst. I've hated him since our boyhoods. I don't rightly know how to explain him, except to say he is dangerous. He cares for nothing and no one, except himself."

Cole interjected, "Fallon needs hanging. I vow to see that bastard at the end of a hanging rope before I die." He paused. "I hope you don't think me a terrible man for the saying so, Miss Ruthann."

"I don't. If you say he's dangerous, I believe you." For whatever reason, I trusted their opinions.

Miles said, "Though we haven't seen the son of a bitch in nearly four years, I could not agree more." Immediately he apologized. "Excuse my cursing."

"It's all right," I murmured and Miles reached and curved one hand around the back of my chair, his long arm making a V between us. I ignored the way my heart thrust at this simple, protective gesture, remembering something else. "There was speculation at Rilla's just tonight that Thomas Yancy funded Bill Little's gang once upon a time."

Both men nodded seriously.

Miles said, "The Little brothers fought alongside Thomas Yancy in The War Between the States."

Cole picked up the story Miles had started. "My pa, Henry Spicer, and Miles's pa were both soldiers in those days, too. My pa bought a farm neighboring the Rawleys' place in the autumn of 'sixty-eight, like Miles said. We'd intended to reach Montana Territory but decided to settle in Iowa. My youngest brother and sister were desperate ill, you see. It's only been since last winter that my folks have decided to finish the journey they originally started."

"Will they settle in this area?" I asked.

Cole nodded affirmation. "They plan to undertake the journey next

March, or thereabouts. I spent the past month visiting them in Iowa and made good time on the ride here, what with the fair weather. Pa, Mama, and my brother Charles are readying to move, while my sister May and her scalawag of a husband – "

"Who is *my* brother, Quinlan," Miles interjected, with the slightest smile.

"May and Quinlan married this past spring and will stay behind and farm our old land, in Iowa," Cole explained. He bumped a fist against Miles's shoulder. "Them two lovebirds. Quin is already to be a father."

I observed the subtle way these words affected Miles, striking him with a deeper significance – a married brother could acknowledge and welcome a child.

"What are your plans here?" I asked Cole.

"To visit this ingrate." He nodded at Miles, with a grin. "And to scout the land near Grant's homestead, to report back to Pa. They'd like to settle near Grant and Birdie if they are able."

"And also to give me unimaginable grief and trouble," Miles said.

"*Shit*," Cole scoffed, with a laugh. "What else are friends for?" He looked my way. "Patricia asked me to remind you she'll call on you in the morning."

"Good," I murmured. I admitted, "I like her very much."

"She likes you, too." Cole's eyes moved upward but he was not seeing the rafters. Hushed and reverent, he muttered, "Those *eyes*. I expect she saw straight through to my soul."

Miles said, without challenge, "No good can come of that, my friend."

Cole's chest expanded with a deep breath; he rose, all at once restless, and rooted around in the single cupboard like a dog after a bone, at last extracting a corked brown bottle. "Thanks be to Jesus you keep a supply, Rawley. You got three drinking glasses?"

"None for me," I said, eyeing the whiskey the way I would a dead skunk on the side of the road.

Cole returned to the table with two small glasses, each with a three-quarters pour of clear amber liquid. As he took his seat, he asked Miles, "You think it might be true, what they're saying about Little's gang? That

Vole might be alive and running the show?"

"We have to assume it's possible. You'd think Bill Little himself rose from the dead to hear the talk around these parts the past few days," Miles said, downing a sip of his whiskey.

I'd finished my biscuits and gravy, wishing there was something to drink that wasn't eighty-proof. I watched Miles as he considered this new serious issue; his posture had changed, growing both threatening and defensive. He kept his hand on the back of my chair.

"If it's Vole riding this way, we'd best be ready," Cole said, draining his glass in a neat gulp.

"I agree. Though I doubt he would chance approaching us, not after all these years. He's named after a varmint and it suits him. He went to ground years ago. I wasn't a lawman back then, didn't have the legitimacy to shoot him on sight, as I would now."

"If it's him and he wants a fight, he'll provoke it." Cole leaned over the table. "He's too much a chickenshit to come after us. He wants us to come after *him*. That might explain the killings and cattle rustlings. He'd recognize you'd have to investigate such matters."

"He is not an intelligent man, though intelligent enough to evade a hanging, thus far. But he must realize another marshal would control the territory that far east of here."

"Howardsville is the eastern-most of your range, ain't it?"

"It is. Besides, if Vole rides this far he'll skirt the town," Miles said. "He always hated towns, if you'll recall."

"We shoulda run down that rat-faced bastard and killed him four years back, regardless," Cole said, with fire. "I knew it then. He's goddamn slippery. And as Miss Ruthann just mentioned, he's connected to the Yancys. Vole did Fallon's dirty work once upon a time, and likely still does."

"Excuse us," Miles said. "We are being unpardonably rude, speaking of matters unknown to you. We speak most freely with each other."

"It's fine," I insisted. "I feel safe with you two, like I can trust you. Maybe it's crazy…"

Cole spared me a warm grin. "It ain't crazy."

Miles agreed, "It is not the slightest crazy. You may surely trust us," and I experienced the sudden urge to collect his hand from the back of my chair and braid our fingers together.

"Thank you, marshal." I dared to meet his eyes; he was not as close as he had been touching my face and my hair, but enough that I could have counted each of his numerous eyelashes. There was a hint of happiness in his expression, I was not imagining it.

And yet the trench of sadness in my heart was deeper than ever.

Chapter Eight

MILES ESCORTED ME BACK TO RILLA'S NO MORE THAN FIF-
teen minutes later, gently buffering my elbow with his hand; the lantern
light pouring out from the lively saloons and their many temptations
intermittently gilded us as we walked along. I hadn't removed his jacket
and he made no comment.

"What's your horse's name?" I'd paused outside the jailhouse to admire the animal, taking a moment to pat its neck, and the horse whickered in response.

"Blade," Miles replied. "I've had him from the day he was born."

We walked past yet another saloon and Miles's long nose and black
mustache were momentarily highlighted in spun gold. He'd donned his
hat, leaving his eyes in shadow.

"I haven't named my horse yet." I kept my gaze away from him in
hopes of calming my hard-pounding heart. "Axton brought her to show
me a few days ago but they keep her out at their claim shanty. He and
Branch are so good to me."

"I am most happy to know this. Despite your earlier anger with me."

"My anger? It's not *my* anger you should be concerned about."

"It is your opinion that concerns me." He spoke in such a solemn
tone. "I would rather you thought well of me."

"You should talk to Celia when we get there," I insisted.

"She will be engaged in…other ways, currently."

Though I wanted to, I didn't think now was an opportune moment
to remind him Celia was definitely 'engaged' right now, with his child
growing inside of her. I persisted, "Tomorrow, then."

"I will, however, speak to Rilla Jaymes of what happened to you this night," he declared, changing the subject with as little subtlety as any man. "I would have her know Aemon Turnbull will never be allowed near you again."

"Thank you for your help." It seemed like a paltry offering after everything he'd done for me this evening, but I was uncertain how else to frame my gratitude.

"You are most welcome. You will take care not to walk alone after dark?" I could feel the strength of his gaze even though I kept mine averted. "Especially now I am fearful one of the worst men with whom I have ever dealt may be roaming the countryside again."

I thought of the things he and Cole had discussed – the man named Vole, killings and cattle rustlings, the continued threat of the Yancys – as I promised, "I'll take care."

We were nearing Rilla's front entrance and my eyes roved to the alley where the laundry shack was located, where I'd been introduced to Patricia only hours ago. Miles surprised me by pausing in the glow of the lanterns adorning Rilla's windows and turning to face me.

He whispered, "May I?" and gently grasped my chin. I could not prevent a small intake of breath; his fingers were warm and the ever-present aching in my heart only intensified. "Your forehead is wounded. That bastard Turnbull hurt you and I would like to destroy him."

He sounded so dead-serious I envisioned him stalking back to the jailhouse and repeatedly smashing the man's face against the iron bars, and he'd already beat the shit out of Aemon Turnbull earlier tonight. I grabbed his elbow and ordered, "No! Please don't do such a thing."

"Ruthann Rawley," he murmured, not seeming to recall what he'd just said about destroying a man, his eyes tracking all over my face, as if there would be a test later and he must memorize every detail. His thumb swept slowly back and forth beneath my lower lip; I had the distinct impression he didn't realize he was stroking my skin this way.

He wondered aloud, "How come you to have my name?"

"It's my name, too." A lump swelled in my throat. "It's the only thing I know for sure."

"You will take care of yourself?" He framed the question differently this time. "I dislike the thought of you being alone here. I dislike it very much."

"I will," I whispered, knowing I should go inside but unwilling to part ways. Who knew when I would get the chance to see him again? I wanted to speak his name. I wanted him to keep touching me. But then, like icy water striking my flesh, I thought of Celia, and felt cold and sick with shame. I mumbled, "Good-night," and shrugged from his jacket, shoving it into his hands and fleeing up the steps before I relented to the urge to touch his handsome, serious face.

Left alone in the spill of light, I knew he watched me go.

Morning arrived, along with Patricia Yancy, who was dressed in a fashionable narrow skirt and matching jacket of periwinkle blue, the jacket fitted at the waist, the material falling in graceful pleats to the back hem. The collar of her ivory blouse was high, almost severe; her honey-brown hair arranged in a series of intricate topknots, with soft, curly bangs adorning her forehead. Her eyes were the shade of morning glory blossoms, bluer by far than her clothing, and her cheeks were flushed with excitement.

"It's what Mrs. Mason calls the 'lunatic fringe,'" she said gaily, indicating her bangs. "It is the absolute *latest* in hairstyling. We shall trim one for you, if you wish, though your hair is already so curly. You needn't the hot irons to make ringlets. Lucky girl." Fingertips hovering near my right temple, she whispered, "Are you feeling well? Your poor forehead. It is so bruised this morning."

I couldn't help but smile at her chatter. I stood on the front porch, prepared to start the laundry, but paused to speak with her, setting aside both the bundle of dirty linen and the basket of clothes pins. Patricia looked so different than the women I was accustomed to seeing on a daily basis – she was tidy and proper, clean and beautiful. Her hands were slim and delicate, the left adorned by an ample diamond that threw multicolored sparkles in the sunlight. My left thumb moved almost instinctively, reaching to caress my third finger as if expecting to encounter a ring; of course it was bare.

Though the day was hot, I shivered.

"Did you speak long with Marshal Rawley last night? What of the man Turnbull, who attacked you?"

"He's still in the jail, as far as I know." My eyes flickered in that direction; unfortunately Miles and Blade were nowhere in view on the dusty morning street. I did, however, catch sight of a most welcome horse and rider.

"Ruthann, what's happened? Marshal Rawley rode out to our claim last night and told us you'd been hurt." Axton dismounted Ranger and scooped me into an embrace. I hugged him hard in return, patting his back, noticing as if removed from myself that his hair still smelled clean. Patricia, ever helpful, caught up the reins Axton had dropped in his haste to hug me.

"I ain't to let you out of my sight after dark, Marshal Rawley said." Axton held me by each shoulder as he studied my bruised face with his brows drawn inward. "He's leaving Howardsville tomorrow and ordered me to look after you."

"Tomorrow?" I repeated dumbly.

"Aemon Turnbull did this to you?" Axton continued, low-voiced with anger. "I'll kill him myself."

I put aside all thoughts of Miles leaving town and spoke firmly. "Ax, don't worry, really. I'm all right. I was lucky enough that Patricia Yancy intervened. I'd like you to meet her."

Patricia, close behind him, offered a glimmering smile as Axton turned. And just as quickly, all anger fell from his face. He froze, then blinked in slow motion, clearly as beguiled by her beauty as everyone who met her. In fact, he was so comically speechless I had to step in and make an introduction for him.

"Patricia, this is Axton Douglas, my dear friend." I sent her a smile acknowledging his fluster.

"I am most pleased to meet any friend of Ruthann's." Patricia offered her right hand, clutching Ranger's lead line in the other. Axton's throat bobbed as he swallowed; he wiped his palms briskly over his thighs, finally taking her proffered hand between both of his, cradling rather than shaking it.

Oh, buddy, I thought sympathetically, now biting the insides of my cheeks to keep from giggling.

Patricia was amused, and touched, I could tell, discreetly withdrawing her hand and passing Ranger's reins back to Axton. She commented, "Your horse is a beautiful animal. What is his name, Mr. Douglas?"

"Please, do call me Axton." He gained partial control and cleared his throat, squaring his shoulders and saying more calmly, "Ranger is his name. I've raised him from a foal."

"When I was a girl my father stabled two riding horses for our personal use. Mine was a roan mare named Dancer and I loved her dearly. I was inconsolable when she died."

Axton was so lost in Patricia's eyes it took him a second to realize he wasn't entirely certain what 'inconsolable' meant. At last he murmured, "I am sorry to hear that. Have you a horse now?"

"Not one of my own, unfortunately."

Axton rallied, to my amusement, offering Patricia a sweet but unmistakably flirtatious smile. "If you'd ever like to ride Ranger, I'd be honored."

"How very thoughtful of you. I may take you up on that offer, Mr. Douglas."

Axton abruptly lost his cool, cheekbones taking on heat as Patricia beamed afresh.

I jumped in to save him. "Ax, please tell Branch not to worry. I'm just fine here in town."

Axton refocused on me with visible effort. "I'm to bring you to dinner tonight, Ruthie. Cole Spicer is coming, too. Uncle Branch said he'd pay good coin to hear some of Cole's fiddle music before they head west." He added, with a wistful note, "Wish I was heading west."

"Who's going west?" I demanded; Ax had said 'they,' after all. Immediately I realized, *Miles and Cole, of course*.

"Marshal Rawley," Axton replied, and my heart sank. "That's why I'm to look after you this week, as he'll be away."

Patricia shaded her eyes with one hand. "I was to accompany my father-in-law's men this very day, westward as well, when they leave to scout land. However, Mrs. Mason has determined just this morning that the wild countryside does not suit her and she shall remain in Howardsville until Thomas's men return. I am *most* disappointed. I cannot hope to accompany the men without a proper chaperone." She sighed. "At times I *detest* being a woman."

"But isn't that why you came here in the first place, to see the land?" I asked.

"It is, yes. Perhaps you shall let me call upon you this week instead, Ruthann, and assist you with your daily tasks?"

Axton and I eyed her with similar skepticism; my forehead crinkled as I envisioned this delicate, well-dressed flower of a girl stirring laundry in the huge, cast-iron kettle, braced over the steaming cauldron with the heavy wooden paddle in hand.

"I am stronger than I look," she insisted, reading our faces, and I smiled. Axton flushed anew and looked away, at the ground, down the street, and then back to Patricia, unable to keep his eyes from her.

"Won't you be bored? It's not enjoyable work," I pointed out.

"Heavens, no. You shall keep me company. I find your company *most* pleasurable. Mrs. Mason cares not for how I spend my day, and Thomas's men shall depart by the noon hour. They long to be rid of the responsibility of me, see if I am wrong." She surprised me by murmuring softly, "Cole said…"

Her voice faded away and her lips compressed; it was improper to use his first name like that, I figured, but I saw the way her longing gaze roved down the street in the direction of the jailhouse, just as mine had earlier. Not spying Cole, she said, "Last night when he escorted me home, Mr. Spicer informed me that his family originally set out for the Territory when he was but a young boy. They were forced by circumstance to reside in Iowa but have long wished to complete their original journey."

"The Spicers are moving here next spring," I added. "Miles and Cole were talking about it last night."

Patricia searched my eyes. "Did you speak long with them after I retired?"

"Not too long," I assured her, hearing the sincere and barely-contained envy.

Axton said, with great apology, "Ruthie, I must get on, but you'll come out to the claim this evening, won't you? We've missed you so." His gaze returned to Patricia. "And please do join us as well, if you've a mind to. Cole and the marshal have already agreed."

Patricia brightened like a sunrise. "Why, thank you, Mr. Douglas."

I promised, "Wild horses couldn't keep me away."

Patricia said, "I shall be there even if I have to smother Mrs. Mason."

"She's just kidding." I giggled as Axton's eyebrows lifted in mild alarm.

Watching Axton ride away, as gracefully as though he'd been born to a saddle, Patricia murmured, "He is delightful, however gullible." She eyed the laundry I'd set aside and offered brightly, "Well, shall we get to work?"

I bit my lip to keep from smiling.

"I am insistent." She flipped her narrow skirts.

"You'll get dirty," I warned, leaning to retrieve the small basket of clothes pins.

"No matter!"

By the noon hour both of us were dirty, drenched in slick sweat. August had grown hotter with each subsequent day; other than the rainfall that occurred the morning Miles Rawley returned to town, there hadn't been a cloud to mar the sky or block the radiance of the prairie sun. Patricia had long since shed her jacket and rolled up her sleeves; her delicate ivory blouse was wrinkled, damp with exertion, her hair drifting downward from its collection of pins. Before daring to unbutton her limp collar, she confessed in a hushed voice, "But I feel so scandalous!"

Because it was just the two of us working side-by-side in the laundry shack I was amused she felt the need to whisper. We'd propped open the canvas doorway to gain access to what little breeze the day allowed and could hear the activity of Howardsville on the nearby street. None of the girls from Rilla's had interrupted our work. I thought of Celia; I hadn't yet admitted I'd spilled her secret to the marshal, and felt like a lowdown coward. I would have to tell her soon; I owed her that much.

A traitorous part of me rejoiced, *You'll see Miles again! Tonight!*

Stop it, Ruthann. Jesus Christ.

"No one here cares if you unbutton your collar," I assured Patricia, pausing in my work to roll my aching shoulders. I stepped out into the sun so I had room to lift my elbows above my head and fully stretch, just in time to spy a rider dismounting at the hitching rail in front of Rilla's; his red-gold hair gleamed in the dazzle of the noontime sun.

I'd just opened my mouth to inform Patricia we had company when Cole caught a glimpse of me and called, "Good morning!"

I saw Patricia twitch inside the laundry shack, her attention darting toward the sound of his voice. Immediately she began rolling down her sleeves and tucking up her wayward hair, but it was too late; Cole had already walked the few paces required to reach us. My gaze leapfrogged over Cole's shoulder; it wasn't as though I actually *hoped* Miles might be with him...

Cole stood with self-assured ease, hands on hips, addressing me with cheer. "Ruthann. You're looking well." He caught sight of Patricia hiding out in the laundry shack and his eyes took on an undeniable glint of happiness despite all the very good reasons he shouldn't dare. Adopting a more formal tone, he acknowledged, "Mrs. Yancy," and then could not resist needling her. "You've been hard at work this morning, I see."

"As I imagine you have not," she threw back at him, joining us.

Cole's eyes detoured to the unbuttoned neckline of her blouse and his grin deepened.

"I've a long ride to make, starting first thing tomorrow," he returned, with typical good nature. "Can't hardly blame a man for taking it easy this morning." His amused gaze ate up her disheveled hair and sweat-stained dress, though I heard only sincerity in his voice as he said, "Might I observe how *absolutely* lovely you look today, Mrs. Yancy."

Patricia grew so flushed she appeared sunburned, even though she kept her expression just slightly haughty.

"Miles sent Aemon Turnbull packing before dawn," Cole informed me before Patricia could formulate a response. "Told the bastard if he ever rode back into Howardsville it would be for the last time."

I was not sure how to respond to this news.

"That was very good of the marshal," Patricia said, finding her voice. She wiped her hands on the apron I'd lent her and untied it from her slim waist.

"It was indeed," Cole agreed. He was an exceptionally good-looking man but I could tell he knew it. I imagined a thousand scenarios, fair or not, in which he used those good looks and sexy, knowing eyes to his considerable advantage; it was difficult to imagine any woman speaking the word 'no' in his presence.

Patricia shaded her gaze and asked, with an excess of innuendo dripping from her words, "And what brings you here this noon, Mr. Spicer? It is a bit early in the day to indulge in the many charms of a saloon, *is it not?*"

He winked and replied without missing a beat, "Never too early for that," and Patricia's cheeks blazed all over again. Cole continued, "Has Branch's nephew been around to invite you to dinner? Miles asked me to make certain."

"He has," I said. "Will we see you there, as well?"

"You can count on it." He left seconds later, bidding us a polite farewell.

Patricia watched until he was out of sight, only then muttering adamantly, "That *man*."

I peeked at her from where I stood hanging clothes on the line. Admittedly egging her on a little, I observed, "He's really cute, isn't he?"

She whirled to face me, gorgeous eyes wide. She demanded, "'Cute?' What word is this to describe a grown man? I have never heard of such a thing. He is *incorrigible*." She lowered her left hand, which had been shading her gaze, and a sunbeam got stuck in her wedding ring, sending a dazzle of prismatic light into my eyes.

I spoke before I thought. "What about your husband?"

We'd discussed many things this morning, including Patricia's privileged upbringing as an only child in Boston and her sorrow over her father's death only a year past, but not yet of the topic of marriage. I felt I had an unfair advantage after the conversation with Miles and Cole last night and hadn't intended to imply any sort of incrimination with this remark, but the expression upon her face altered, growing wary.

Her tone was guarded. "What of him?"

I felt like a jerk but I wanted to hear Patricia's opinion on the matter. "I only meant you must miss him."

Her lips twisted and she remained silent. Her hands drifted to her hips, latching there with slow movements.

I reached for another clean, damp garment, fastening two pins over it before guessing quietly, "You aren't happy with him." In the wake of this observation the sounds of the town, horses and halter chains, the rumble of wagon wheels and the occasional man's voice raised in conversation, receded to the distance.

Patricia smoothed both palms over her waist. Without challenge, she asked, "Is it that obvious?"

I considered lying, attempting to visualize this husband, picturing him as a sniveling weakling at the Yancy family home in Chicago, wealthy and entitled, ordering a servant to cut up his steak at dinner; Dredd Yancy was a man who probably hated to be out of an air-conditioned environment.

Wait – a what? My mind struggled to make sense of what I'd just thought.

"Dredd and I have more in common than I would have guessed, at first," Patricia said before I could answer, moving to help me hang laundry. "He has been without a mother from a young age, as have I. He is well educated and articulate, the product of many expensive tutors. And he is possessed of an absurd and, as time has proven, unattainable desire to please his father, just as I was."

"Was he cruel to you?" I asked, praying she would say no.

"My father, or Dredd?"

"Dredd," I clarified. "What a strange name."

"It was his mother's surname," Patricia explained. "And no, Dredd has not been cruel to me. Perhaps 'indifferent' is a better word. My father and Thomas Yancy sustained a friendship and Father wished for me to be wed to Thomas's eldest son, Fallon, at first…" A sudden shudder overtook her spine and my senses snapped alert at this mention of Fallon, the man Miles and Cole had said, without hesitation, should be hung.

Patricia continued, "Though I remain ever so grateful Fallon had no wish to marry *me*. Being related by marriage is unfortunate enough. I have never beheld such hollow eyes as that man possesses. My only consolation would have been that Fallon travels extensively for his business dealings. His sustained presence in Chicago is something of a rarity." She stared into space for several seconds. "Fortunately, Father settled for an alliance with Dredd. It eased Father's passing, knowing I was secured in marriage to one of Thomas's sons. Other than my mother's elder brother, my father was the last of my family."

"Do you think Fallon is a criminal?" I asked, debating whether to tell her what Cole and Miles had said last night, at the risk of offending her.

Patricia closed her eyes and inhaled through her nostrils. She whispered, "I am sure of it." She opened her eyes and the blue of them was almost shocking. She caught my wrist in one hand and implored, "You shan't breathe a word of anything I have told you."

"What is this?" a woman demanded before I could respond, in a hoarse, commanding voice I knew all too well. And then Rilla was upon us, flapping across the dusty alley with her breasts leading the way. She was dressed as respectably as she could manage, which wasn't saying much, her face with its usual pinched and irritated expression, lipstick red as death. "Why in God's name is Mr. Thomas Yancy's daughter-in-law hanging laundry in my alley like a common servant? Ruthann, is this your doing, you lazy little – "

Patricia cut her off, administering a tone I was certain had sent many an actual servant scurrying. "How *dare* you speak to either me or Ruthann in such an insolent manner? I do as I please!"

"Not here you don't, you impertinent young hussy!" Rilla glared at us with concentrated venom. She threatened, "You want the town speculating that you've taken up work at a whorehouse?" Rilla chuckled at her own cruel words. "How would your husband's daddy feel about receiving such news secondhand?"

Patricia's lips compressed and her face went suddenly bloodless, though with alarm or anger, I wasn't entirely certain.

Rilla turned her annoyance on me. "Ain't it enough I lose one of my best customers because of your idiocy, girl? And now Marshal Rawley, that self-righteous son of a bitch, is telling me who I can and cannot allow into *my* establishment."

"You will shut your *despicable and unworthy mouth*," Patricia ordered, with real fire.

Ouch. Anger it was, then.

Rilla's eyes bulged out of her mascara-streaked face. She had probably just rolled from bed. No stranger to confrontation, she reached a thick-fingered hand, grasping Patricia by the hair. She hissed, "Speak to me that way again and you'll be more than sorry, missy."

With no appreciable loss of composure, Patricia yanked free and stepped away, crisply informing Rilla, "*You* would be the sorry party in such a situation, mark my very words. I shall go, and take Ruthann with me. No longer shall she remain in this squalid den of vice and corruption."

Shit, shit, shit. My stomach flapped with increasing panic.

Rilla tugged at the tight bodice of her gown and lifted her chin with the imperious nature afforded those who feel they are being unfairly judged. She nearly growled, "Just like a little rich, spoiled hussy to look down on others."

"Come, Ruthann," Patricia ordered. "Let us collect your belongings."

I stood frozen in a state of semi-stupefaction. "But this is where I live."

Rilla was furious. She spat, "No longer, you worthless bitch! I want the both of you gone."

"But I…" I faltered, truly fearful now. That this had come to pass in the last thirty seconds was beyond me. I was quite suddenly homeless, a concept Patricia could not possibly comprehend.

"Get," Rilla seethed. "You have exactly *five minutes* to get out of my sight for good."

I spent those five minutes frantically packing everything I owned in the world, all of which had been donated to me (two skirts with ragged hems, two blouses, an underskirt petticoat, two pairs of stockings, and a thick wad of cotton binding), wrapping these items in one of the skirts and tying it with a length of rope. Patricia followed me upstairs to assist, contrite now, though I couldn't make sense of her consoling words, terrified as I was by this turn of events.

I shed my skirt and tugged on the riding trousers Axton had lent me, trembling so hard I struggled to tuck my blouse in the waistband, let alone cinch it with the length of rope I'd been using for that purpose. I'd grown unpleasantly skinny in the past weeks. Though my ribs had healed and no longer ached, they were visible in rows along my sides; my collarbones were prominent knobs beneath my skin. Often I ate nothing more in a day than bacon around Branch's evening cookfire. I grimaced as I caught an unwitting glimpse of my reflection in the mirror, taking a moment to glance around the space which had been mine for the past summer. I had no memories of anything before this room.

"Come," Patricia murmured, resting her hands on my shoulders. "All shall be well, Ruthann, I promise."

A shadow darkened the doorway and Celia was suddenly there, wrapped in her silk shawl. Her face was free of cosmetics, gray eyes wide with concern. She guessed quietly, "Rilla has ordered you out."

I flew to her arms and Celia hugged me close. She smelled of stale sweat, musky perfume, and tobacco, but I clung to her, letting her comfort me. She whispered against my hair, "Where will you go, sweet little Ruth? I am sore worried about you."

"I told Miles Rawley about the baby." I drew back enough to see her face. No beauty mark in sight; she looked younger and more vulnerable without her customary layer of make-up. Her steady gaze betrayed no errant emotion at this news.

"You did," she said, not a question. She curled her plump hands around my forearms. "What possessed you to do such a thing?" But there was no anger in her tone, only a sense of resignation.

"Because he deserves to know." Tears washed over my face. I gulped and it cost me to say it, but I knew I must. "And because maybe he can help you. He could marry you."

Celia smiled sadly as she regarded my face, no doubt acknowledging what she considered my complete idiocy; she smoothed both hands over my hair. She whispered, "Well, I can't rightly be angry at you then, can I? Where will you go?"

"With me," Patricia said decisively, at my shoulder. "Ruthann shall come with me."

"You take care of her, young miss, you hear?" Celia ordered, releasing me and drawing her shawl around her torso. "Ruth is a dear little thing and I care a great deal for her."

"Please, you take care of yourself, too," I begged, my throat dry. "I will check in on you, Celia, I promise I will."

Celia's expression changed, wonder lifting her eyebrows. She caught my right hand between both of hers and placed it upon the swollen curve of her lower belly. There, beneath my palm, a small bump thrust outward. She whispered, "He's moving so much today."

"I promise," I vowed, feeling Miles's baby pressing back against my palm.

Outside under the blistering sun I floundered, growing dizzy as we descended the porch steps. I was clutching the bundle of my belongings to my stomach and stumbled over the bottom stair. Patricia kept a firm grip on my elbow, just as she had last night. She said in my ear, "It is all right. Come, I am certain you have not yet had a proper meal today. We shall retire to my train car."

I allowed Patricia to guide me across the street and together we angled south and east, out toward the railroad depot and its subsequent tracks. I was aware of very little until we reached our destination, hearing a buzzing in my head, letting Patricia lead me to six railroad cars strung in a line along an offshoot of the main track, two painted dark red, four flat black, all adorned with white script that read *Redd Line RRC, Chicago,*

Illinois. She climbed three metal steps with a sense of familiarity, entering the first red car, and we were enveloped by cool dimness. I blinked in the shadowy interior space as Patricia helped me to sit on a velvet loveseat. I dropped the unraveling bundle of my clothes to the floor.

She knelt and grasped my hands. "You are in distress and I am deeply sorry. But please do not worry. You shall accompany me back to Chicago and live in my home. I would be delighted if you should agree to this. Rilla's was an unsuitable place for you to reside, as you realize. Dredd shall take out an advertisement in every paper east of the Mississippi, Ruthann, and find your people. What say you?"

I found the energy to squeeze her hands. "Thank you."

"You rest now," she invited, managing a charming smile. "We have a dinner engagement this night. And we shall worry about tomorrow, tomorrow."

Chapter Nine

I WAS UNAWARE HOW MUCH TIME HAD PASSED WHEN A sharp knocking sounded on the door of the train car, about ten paces from where I lay beneath a cerulean satin comforter. I blinked to consciousness, hazy and disoriented, eyes darting in confusion until I recognized Patricia's personal compartment. I was tucked in her feather bed, wearing nothing more than a borrowed chemise, a long, blouse-like garment Patricia had lent me, fancier by far than anything I possessed, made of soft white cotton and edged in fragile lace. It left my arms, neck, and calves bare.

Earlier I'd bathed in the small washtub Patricia filled with water, kindly taking this task upon herself. The water was cold but her soap was lilac-scented and her monogrammed ivory towels the softest linen imaginable. After cleansing every inch of my skin, I collapsed atop her bed. The tiny sleeping chamber was windowless, allowing no clue as to the time of day, and I wanted to ignore the knocking, praying that whoever was out there would just go away. Where was Patricia? I was groggy and irritable; she'd been here when I went to sleep but had since disappeared.

"Ruthann? Are you there? It's Marshal Rawley," he called from right outside.

"Just a second!" My throat was raspy but he must have heard because he quit knocking.

I scrambled from beneath the covers and searched for my blouses, seeing neither in sight. I did spy one of my ragged skirts and hurried to button it over the chemise, my hair swinging loose and tangled. Embarrassed that I was taking too much time to answer, I swept my hair forward to cover my breasts; I was not wearing a corset. As further safeguarding, I crossed my arms and stumbled barefoot through the bedroom and adjacent sitting room, in which the shades were drawn, to answer the door. I opened it and immediately squinted at the brilliant punch of afternoon sunshine. Just as quickly, I re-crossed my arms over my breasts.

"I have awoken you." Miles sounded apologetic. Right on cue, he added, "I apologize. I was most anxious to see you after hearing you were ordered from Rilla Jaymes's place this morning. What has happened this day? Rilla would tell me nothing and I did not know where you had disappeared until just minutes ago. I have been deeply worried."

I found myself unable to do a thing but stare up at him, backlit as he was by the sunlight. He appeared just as concerned as he claimed, studying my face as if to search for any additional signs of harm. He wore a collared shirt, open at the throat, his gray vest with its marshal star, and dark trousers. His sleeves were rolled back, as they had been last night. Again I noticed the black hair on his forearms and the backs of his wrists; I could see evidence of hair on his chest, his shirt open past his collarbones. He held the door with one hand, his hat in the other. His forehead bore a faint sheen of sweat and I felt hot and tight all along my thighs and upward into my belly.

How is that I know you, he'd said last night.

At last I found my voice. "You needn't worry."

His eyes were intent upon mine. He was no more than two steps away and my heart was pounding like someone attacking a set of drums. As though thinking aloud, he observed, "Your hair is down."

My nipples pressed against the backsides of my crossed arms, almost through the thin material of the chemise. I was so confused, so powerfully drawn to him – a man who was, in all truth, a stranger to me – shocked by the urge to move forward the mere inches it would take to tuck my face against his bare neck. I said stupidly, "It is."

His chest expanded with a slow, deliberate breath, the way someone would inhale in order to decrease tension, to get level. On the exhale, he repeated, "I have been deeply worried this day."

"I touched your baby," I whispered, thinking of Celia, alone back at Rilla's. I would *not* acknowledge what felt suspiciously like a broiling, burning lump of jealousy wedged behind my breastbone, nor would I think about Miles making love time and again to Celia last spring, enough to get her pregnant. No, I would *not* think of that...

His eyebrows drew together, creating the horizontal crease above his nose; all I seemed to do was trouble and confuse him. In a tone indicating he demanded understanding, he asked, "What do you mean?"

"The baby moved inside of Celia." The blazing coals in my chest swelled to encompass my throat. I whispered, "Have you talked to her?"

"I spoke with her this very day, but minutes ago. She asked me never to return to Rilla's. She was the one who finally told me you had left with Mrs. Yancy."

"You can't listen to her. She needs your help. She needs *you*."

He shook his head and I hated how my voice had broken on that last word. I felt a sensation of coming undone, of being lost within the expression in his eyes, and further, I felt like a traitor. Miles was not my man, and yet...*and yet*...

"Is Ruthann awake?" I heard Patricia's voice from outside, moving closer, and the marshal stepped to the side, passing a hand over his face. He appeared agonized. Patricia hurried up the metal steps, which chimed under her heeled shoes. She swept past Miles and enveloped me in a hug. Over her shoulder, I saw Axton sitting on the seat of his flatbed wagon, drawn by Ranger and my own nameless horse.

Patricia said decorously, "Marshal Rawley, how good of you to call. Mr. Douglas is here to escort us to dinner at his home as soon as I inform Mrs. Mason." And then, in a scandalized undertone, "*Ruthann*, you are in a state of undress. Gentlemen, please excuse us!"

So saying, she tugged me inside and closed the door. I felt like a tornado had just blown through the train car. Patricia perused my outfit and decided, "I shall lend you proper clothing."

Mostly to be contrary, I asked, "Who the hell is Mrs. Mason, anyway?"

Patricia smiled at my cursing. "My ladies' maid. Dredd hired her for me, back in Chicago. Hers is the other red car. I could not ask for a better chaperone. She refuses to travel without her laudanum supply, which keeps her quite perfectly dazed at all times."

I thought back to my early days at Rilla's, and could relate.

Miles waited the few minutes it took for me to braid my hair, locate my corset, and dress in a clean blouse and skirt, both in shades of sky-blue, Patricia's preferred hue. He was mounted on Blade, chatting with Axton, and both men looked our way when the door opened; Patricia offered a radiant smile while I concentrated on not hooking the toes of my shoes on the metal stairs and therefore falling to my face. Miles dismounted to help us aboard the wagon but I stopped to greet my horse, letting Patricia go first.

"Hi, girl," I murmured, stroking her jaws, then her neck. She blew a breath from both nostrils, right between my breasts, and I planted a kiss on her velvet nose. "I've missed you."

"She's been missing you too, Ruthie," Axton said, taking Patricia's hand to assist her as she settled beside him on the wagon seat. I saw how pleased he was to extend this courtesy; Ax was a goner for her already, it was obvious.

"I know," I said, with mild guilt pangs, resting my cheek against the mare's neck, overcome by everything that had happened in the last twelve hours. My horse smelled familiar and her very presence was a comfort. She was calm, flicking her tail as I lavished a little love on her. Miles, having assisted Patricia, joined me near my horse's nose. He reached and scratched beneath her chin. I spoke to the mare, murmuring, "I haven't even named you yet."

"She already has a name," Miles said. "Doc Turn always called her Girl." The horse gave a quiet whicker, as though acknowledging this truth, and Miles patted her neck. "See, that's right, isn't it, Girl?"

"But that's a stupid name," I said, peering up at the man standing beside me. He had replaced his hat and it created a shadow over his eyes, but I could still detect the hint of good humor in their depths.

"You look as pretty as a prairie spring," Axton was saying to Patricia.

"You flatter me," Patricia said, beaming. "But thank you all the same, Mr. Douglas."

"May I?" Miles asked, offering his arm.

He rested one hand on the small of my back, cupping the other around my right elbow, to help me atop the wagon. I faltered, not having lifted my skirt high enough to compensate for such a big step up, but he kept me steady. His hands were warm and strong, and I tried to pretend I didn't feel those brief, very proper touches at other points on my body.

Patricia hauled me alongside her, scooting closer to Axton and tucking her hand beneath his right arm. Even with the space between us, I could sense his heated flush of pride at this action; I thought of how Ax and I had been discussing labor during our last talk, the kind which happened when women gave birth. He'd been very concerned about the amount of pain women were expected to suffer through in order to deliver a child. And not long before that conversation he'd asked me, with considerable blushing, how a man made sure a woman enjoyed lovemaking. Or, as Ax referred to it, 'the marriage act.'

You make it sound like something that has to pass through Congress, I'd teased him.

I've heard stories, he confessed, and earnestness replaced his fluster. *But I know you'll tell me true. I want to make sure I know how to please a woman. A woman oughta be pleased during the marriage act.*

You are one-hundred percent correct, I'd said.

It was so damn easy to love Axton.

Miles mounted Blade with graceful movements. He held the reins and sat the saddle as though both were second nature to him, and rode on the right side of the wagon, closest to where I was sitting, though maybe I was flattering myself thinking that was why he chose *this* side versus the other. He rode just enough ahead that I could admire the line of his wide shoulders, my eyes moving shamelessly up and down his back, over his thighs. He must have felt the strength of my gaze, because he looked over his left shoulder and then drew on Blade's reins so the animal matched the pace of the slower-moving wagon.

I dragged my eyes away.

"Ruthie, I figure it's a sign you oughta live with Uncle Branch and me, from now on," Axton said as we rolled across the open foothill prairie, angling away from the railroad tracks which led back to some faraway eastern destination. The sun drooped low in the sky, casting all of us in a crimson glow. Ax leaned forward, driving the team with his forearms on his thighs; he looked my way as he spoke, his warm, smiling gaze flickering over Patricia. She reached and squeezed my hand in hers; her other hand remained tucked around Axton's bicep and I could sense his bursting joy over this simple fact.

Oh, Ax, I thought, with true sympathy. *First crush.*

"Ruthann's dismissal was a sign, to be sure," Patricia agreed. "Though, not exactly as you have interpreted it, Mr. Douglas. I believe fate led me to Ruthann last night. I feel certain we were meant to know one another."

"I feel the same," I admitted.

"You believe in fate?" Miles asked us and I seized this excuse to look at him. The sun gilded his body in scarlet light and for a second, a strange and horrible second, this color seemed ominous; it looked like blood. My heart stuttered in its rhythm, effectively eradicating the flicker of happiness I'd just experienced.

Stop it. It's nothing but the sun.

"Uncle Branch claims fate saved him from Federal bullets during the War, more than one time," Axton supplied.

"Fate is surely what drew our paths together," Patricia agreed.

I knew Miles wanted my response.

"I think I do," I said quietly, and then wished I could retract the comment. An eerie sense of finality hovered in the air and I knew Miles sensed something wasn't quite right; I battled the urge to lift my hands and bat away the unpleasant sensation, the same way I would a cloud of mosquitoes.

The sudden approach of galloping hooves sent Axton and Patricia craning their necks, but Miles and I did not look apart from each other.

"Hold up there, you-all!" Cole shouted, racing his horse over the prairie, bent low over the animal's head. At the same moment the wheels jounced over a large rut and I grabbed the edge of the wagon. Miles reached to steady me and without a thought I curled our fingers together.

His black mustache lifted in the half-smile to which I was growing accustomed and he squeezed my fingers before gently releasing my hand.

Patricia and Axton were both occupied watching Cole, whose horse flew past the wagon, its galloping legs a blur of frenzied motion, Cole hollering like someone headed into battle. *Show-off*, I couldn't help but think. Meanwhile, Patricia sat straighter and fussily adjusted her skirts and hair, unable to pull her gaze from him.

"Wish I had a brother to race with," Axton said.

Perhaps a quarter-mile ahead, Cole circled his mount in a wide arc and proceeded to canter back in our direction, as graceful in the saddle as Miles or Axton, men born to ride horses. Patricia's chin lifted as she watched and I could actually see the increasing pulse at the base of her throat.

Miles remarked, "You are more than welcome to a few of my brothers, young Axton. I have four, and there were plenty of days in my youth when I longed to be an only child."

"But that would be so lonely," I said.

"Peaceful," Miles amended, and caressed me with his eyes, just as I did to him. There was no denying.

Cole was upon us, his horse breathing with exertion; his eyes sought Patricia and though he greeted all of us with equal enthusiasm, he led his mount to flank the wagon on the left, closest to her.

"Ruthann, you poor girl, your day ain't been any better than your night, has it?" Cole asked. He clarified, "I heard you were asked to leave Rilla's."

"I was, but it's for the best." I prayed this was true.

"Ruthann shall remain with me," Patricia said, hooking her arm through mine.

"Or with me and Uncle Branch," Axton said. He joked, "We've got *piles* of laundry."

I leaned over Patricia to slap his thigh and connected a little too well. Axton yelped, "I was just fooling!"

"I'm sorry," I said, even though everyone was laughing. I imagined the tension of the day, all sense of fear, being carried away by the sound, like birds taking wing. I asked Cole, "What's your horse's name?"

"Charger," Cole answered, leaning to direct his smile my way. He was magnetic, even if I wasn't susceptible to it the way I could tell Patricia was; she was all but wringing her hands as she peeked from the corner of her lashes, trying not to seem too aware of him. What's more, even without having met Dredd Yancy I was certain Cole was about a hundred times more of a man; his smile gained steam as he said, "Tell me, Rawley, how'd we get so damn lucky this evening?"

Miles replied smoothly, "If by 'lucky' you mean the privilege of escorting two beautiful women to dinner, I cannot honestly explain how."

I bit my cheek to restrain a wry smile; I would be a liar if I didn't admit the compliment affected my composure.

Cole whistled through his teeth. "I couldn't have said it any better myself."

Poor Ax was way out of his league among these two; I realized Miles and Cole, as such longtime friends, had probably long ago perfected their repertoire of flattery.

"What *kind* gentlemen," Patricia said, with just a little sarcasm in her tone; she had plainly reached the same understanding, and turned her animated attention to Axton. "You said you live with your uncle, Mr. Douglas?"

"Yes, I do. Uncle Branch raised me from a sprout."

"And if I don't mistake myself, there is the old coot now," Cole said, standing in his stirrups to call hello to Branch, who was tending the cookfire, as per usual at day's end. I hadn't seen Branch in close to three days and hurried into his open arms once the wagon was halted, not waiting for anyone to help me down; I managed, awkwardly, in my two layers of skirts, and ran straight to him.

"Ruthie, I oughta be skinned alive for not watching out for you." Branch tucked me close. The smoke overpowered his body odor but I didn't care either way; I was just grateful to be held securely against his familiar, barrel-shaped chest. He was perhaps the closest I would ever get to a real father, and I loved him.

"I'm so glad to be here." I clung to his comforting bulk. "Thank you for the horse. I love her."

Branch planted a noisy kiss on the top of my head.

"Ain't nothin'. Me and the boy made up a pallet for you here, permanent-like," Branch said, and then raised his hand to the men. "Spicer, Rawley, good to see you boys again. It was a pleasure to share coffee with you this morning." He explained, "Them two was out here with the dawn, braggin' about their many adventures." Branch gestured at Patricia, still sitting beside Ax on the wagon seat. "Who have we here?"

"Uncle Branch, this is Patricia Yancy," Axton said. He shifted to help Patricia from the wagon but Cole was already there, lifting her down with both hands around her waist. And although Cole removed his proper touch the moment Patricia was on the ground, I knew it was clear to him that he'd rattled her.

I saw Branch's eyes crinkle at her surname but he said gallantly, "Welcome, my dear. Ain't I a lucky old codger, with two fine ladies at my table? But I warn you, it ain't exactly high-society dining out here."

"I couldn't be happier, truly." Patricia offered her hand. Though she was obviously a woman who could call upon her privileged upbringing and its subsequent understanding of good manners, I believed her words. Her face was wreathed in joy, cheeks blooming, blue eyes full of a light that had nothing to do with the angle of the sinking sun. Branch took her hand and politely kissed her knuckles.

Miles and Cole led the horses to the corral, tugging off their saddles and hanging them over the top-most beam, while Axton unhitched the team with me dogging his movements, anxious to claim my horse for a moment's time. I wished I was wearing trousers so I could take her for a quick ride; it was the perfect time of night. I wanted to gallop her way out into the foothills. And I wanted Miles with me.

I watched him from the corner of my eye as I patted my horse's nose, scratching beneath her forelock. He was joking with Cole; Cole shoved at his shoulder and Miles flicked his finger against Cole's hat brim so that it tipped sideways, nearly falling off. Branch was pointing out something on the western horizon to Patricia; I looked that direction and sighed in pleasure. The clouds had formed slim vertical peaks, variegated in color from cherry to magenta, an optical illusion which made it impossible to discern where earth ended and sky began. The very air seemed tinted the pink of roses. I gathered my horse's lead line and whispered, "C'mon, sweet girl."

She followed obediently, her long nose bumping along behind my shoulder. Cole made a show of opening the corral gate so I could lead her inside; there, I purposely stalled over removing her bridle because Miles was the last person within the space, where he stood with hands on hips, watching me struggle to unbuckle a strap.

He came to stand beside me. "May I?"

I managed to release the bridle and lifted it over my horse's ears, easing the bit from her mouth. "I got it, thanks."

"You are familiar with horses?"

Instead of replying I nodded, holding the bridle in one hand. My horse, though free of this last restraint, stayed near, twitching her tail and nosing my waist, maybe hoping I had an apple hidden in a pocket. The air smelled like dust and sagebrush; Miles stood facing away from the sunset and I felt blinded by both its light and my proximity to him.

"You and young Axton often ride together?"

I nodded again. A piece of stray hair tickled my face and I tucked it behind my ear with my free hand.

"Will you stay here with Branch, or return with Mrs. Yancy?"

I found my voice. "Probably with Patricia, for now." I felt like a piece of luggage no one really wanted, and were compelled by decency to claim.

His gaze unwavering, Miles said, "I ordered Aemon Turnbull from the town, though I fear he will attempt to sneak back, especially considering my absence. I am concerned for your safety. I will be at least slightly reassured if I know your whereabouts in my absence."

Confusion held me prisoner in a tight, sticky web. Miles Rawley was not mine to care about and yet here I stood, caring far more than our brief acquaintance should allow.

"Your eyes are uncommonly lovely." He spoke quietly and again I was struck by the notion that he was thinking aloud. "There is so much gold within them. The sun sets it off."

"Thank you," I whispered. We were suspended in our own private world, far from everyone else. I wanted to tell him I thought of him almost constantly but could not muster the required nerve. I cleared my throat. "I'll be all right. I don't want to you to worry. Please, don't worry about me."

"That seems at this moment like asking me not to breathe." His face was stern and imposing despite these tender words.

"When will you be back?" I slid the leather straps of the bridle between my fingers in a tense, repetitive motion. There was a note of anxiety in my tone I could not swallow away.

"Within a week. We are riding out with the dawn and will visit my brother Grantley's homestead along the way."

He studied my eyes for answers – I did the same to his, finding no satisfaction which did not involve touching him. Without thinking, the movement as instinctive as anything I'd ever done, I reached up and placed my hand on his cheek. He blinked in surprise but did not move away. My heart throbbed with hard, painful beats. I moved my palm until I cupped his jaw, stroking his skin, feeling the bristle of a day's growth of whiskers.

My spine twitched, attempting to force me forward and therefore into his full embrace. I was embarrassed to have touched him like this, with no invitation, but when he saw in my eyes that I meant to stop he covered my hand with his and turned his mouth to my palm, in effect kissing me. His mustache was very soft, his lips very warm.

"*Marshal,*" I whispered, using his title as a lawman instead of his name, and somehow this word had the effect of stabbing my heart, with such force I stifled a gasp.

He enfolded my hand within his so he could kiss my knuckles. I was breathless and afire, unsettled and confused, and so very sad. A gaping hole of sadness tore at my insides.

Oh God, I don't understand…

Miles, however, had gained a sense of ease; he kept careful hold of my hand as he invited, "I would be immeasurably relieved if you would accompany us west on the morrow. I have considered asking this of you since last night. Perhaps it is improper, but I would like very much for you to meet my brother and his wife. My sister-in-law is much in need of feminine company."

"But I…" I stumbled to think of a reason not to accept.

"Of course it seems improper," he rushed on, eyes dancing with a mix of earnestness and good humor. "But only because we are not yet well-acquainted. My mother would tell you I am the least improper of all my brothers. I must admit I am able to think of nothing but becoming familiar to you, Ruthann." He quickly backpedaled at this statement. "That sounds unseemly, which is not my intent. I wish to spend hours talking with you, 'familiar' in that sense I mean, not any other. Not that you would have assumed any other." I was fairly certain his cheeks had taken on heat. He cleared his throat and concluded, "You said you are knowledgeable regarding horses? You are able to ride?"

"I am," I whispered.

He grinned then, wide and warm, and I felt my heartbeat everywhere in my body, unable to keep from smiling in response.

"Will you consider this offer?"

"I will."

"Jesus *Christ*, Rawley, you about done fawning all over poor Ruthann?" Cole called from the far side of the corral, and Miles shot his friend a dirty look, black eyebrows pulled low, while I laughed, completely due to nerves, not humor.

"Shall we?" Miles asked, allowing me to walk first. I was still holding the bridle.

"Everyone, come sit," Branch encouraged. "I uncorked a jug of bourbon for the boys but I'm s'posing you ladies'll prefer water."

"Aw, Branch, you're a goddamn *saint*," Cole said, settling around the fire, watching Patricia as she swept her skirt to the side before claiming a spot adjacent to him. I had the sense Cole was envisioning catching her waist in his hands and hauling her onto his lap; I swore I could almost read his thoughts. Patricia studiously ignored him and instead focused her attention upon the flames.

I ducked inside the small barn, which was really more of a shed, to hang the bridle on the wooden peg intended for that purpose. Upon returning to the fire, I sat between Miles and Axton. The men were hatless now in the fine evening air, their faces sweaty, hair flattened and clothes dusty. I considered the possibility of riding west with Miles and Cole tomorrow. Of being near Miles for hours in a row. Growing familiar with him, as he had said. He sat to my right; no more than eighteen inches separated our bodies. I studied his profile from the corner of my eye and found myself hyperaware of his every movement. The heat and softness of his lips seemed emblazoned on my hand, at both points of contact.

"We got biscuits and bacon," Branch said, using his two-pronged iron fork to lift the lid from a pan on the grate over the fire, brimming with plump, golden biscuits. Bacon sizzled.

"That looks wonderful," I told Branch, who grinned.

"Delightful," agreed Patricia.

"Ladies first," Cole said, collecting two dented tin plates from the small stack near the fire, holding them out for Branch to load with food.

"*Such* a gentleman," I teased as he handed me a plate.

"Always," Cole said earnestly, inspiring snorts from both Miles and Branch.

The twilight advanced and the fire burned with a merry crackle as we dined on biscuits and rich, greasy bacon – with our fingers, since Branch owned only two spoons, no forks. The men accompanied the conversation with the passing of the whiskey jug, sipping, grimacing, backhanding their mouths, and then exhaling alcohol-scented breaths with hilarious similarity. On the first rotation I'd accepted the jug from Ax and taken a cautious sniff, which seared the hairs on the inside of my nostrils.

"Holy *shit*, what's in this?" I asked, looking up in bewilderment when everyone started laughing.

"I can't believe such a sweet little thing as you has got such a mouth on her," Cole said through his laughter, shaking his head.

"It's a Tennessee specialty, Ruthie-honey," Branch explained, wiping his greasy hands on his leather leggings, already much-stained. His accent grew more pronounced with each sip of the stuff. "Straight outta Cumberland County. Cures all that ails you, ain't that right, fellas?"

I giggled and Axton observed, "It's so good to see you happy, Ruthie."

"It does feel good to be out of Howardsville," I admitted. "I felt like a prisoner there."

"I shoulda insisted you live with us when me an' the boy first found you," Branch said. "Damn that hussy Rilla Jaymes. I shoulda knowed better. I'm so sorry, darlin' girl."

"Branch told us some about finding you," Cole said. "You have no memories of what came before?"

My shoulders hunched. Disliking being the center of sudden and rapt attention, I said only, "No."

"Me an' the boy been searchin' high an' low for answers," Branch said. "But we ain't found a soul what knows you, honey-love, I am so frightful sorry to say."

My lips felt wooden. "There isn't anyone."

"That first evening we watched the moon rise, you said you had a husband," Axton gently reminded. I clenched my teeth, the ache of those words as raw as if I'd just made the claim. I knew Axton was only trying to be helpful, not intending to cause pain.

Miles sat straighter, eyes fixed on me.

Patricia set aside her plate and leaned around Axton to rest her hand on my knee. "You have not spoken of this particular detail, dear Ruthann. We shall place an advertisement, as I said earlier. We shall do this the moment we return to Chicago."

Everyone seemed to speak at once.

Axton said, "You're going to Chicago?"

Miles asked, "When was this decided?"

Branch said adamantly, "Chicago, nothin'. You'll stay with us. I'll provide for you always, darlin', don't you worry."

"Thank you," I whispered to Branch. "I know, I really do, and I thank you. I haven't decided anything yet."

Patricia, observing my discomfort, neatly changed the subject, addressing Cole as she said, "Mr. Douglas tells us you are quite a remarkable musician, Mr. Spicer."

"He tells you true. And many thanks."

"Shall you play for us?" Patricia asked.

"Oh, I shall," Cole said, echoing her very-proper speech.

I busied myself gathering plates the second everyone finished eating, letting the conversation carry on without me. Only Miles remained quiet; I felt his gaze as I carried the stack of dirty plates into the cabin, depositing them on the table shoved beneath the window. There, in the shadow of four walls and away from direct view, I pressed the base of both hands to my face, grinding at my eye sockets, willing myself to remember.

Anything at all. Any clue to remind me who I am. Who the fuck I actually am.

I was happy once, I know it. Where did it go? I'm so scared.

This can't be all I know...

I bent forward over the table and rested my cheek against the cold, rough wood. My eyes adjusted to the dimness and I stared at the view before my nose — the edge of the table and the wall, just beyond. The chatter from outside seemed muted, distant. I couldn't move until I was certain I wasn't about to lose control; at the moment, I could hardly stand upright.

Branch entered the cabin and found me, gathering me close the same way a worried father would. "Aw, honey, c'mon back out. You's in for a real treat. The boys are gonna make music like you *never* done heard."

"No kidding?" I whispered against his chest.

"No foolin'." Branch cupped a gentle hand over the back of my head, petting my hair. "I come to fetch my fiddle for Miles. Young fool forgot his back in town."

Cole retrieved his fiddle case, which he'd strapped to Charger's back; Branch handed Miles the instrument from the cabin. Patricia and Axton remained seated around the fire while Cole stood to tune his instrument with the easy movements afforded by years of practice. Patricia shifted closer and caught my elbow, squeezing with excitement. Cole glided his bow over the strings with a couple quick skips and I shivered in anticipation. Miles brought the fiddle to his chin, plucking at the strings with his right thumb while adjusting a small peg on the neck.

Ax smoothed his knuckles between my shoulder blades; sweet, considerate Axton. He murmured, "You all right?"

I nodded.

"Are you ready to sing?"

"I don't know any of the songs." I was still watching Miles.

"You will. Songs ain't so easy to forget."

Branch settled atop an overturned tin bucket and polished a harmonica with his sleeve. The men looked to one another in the momentary lull between tuning their instruments and the first notes; even the twilight seemed to be holding an expectant breath. They all nodded the tempo almost unconsciously before Cole counted off under his breath, "A one, two, *a one two three…*"

Miles bent slightly forward, eyelids lowering in concentration. In the gathering darkness, with only the firelight to cast its flickering glow, I was emboldened and studied him without letup; his hands, with their long, capable fingers, curved around the instrument and its bow, wielding one to make the other sing. Though his mouth remained unsmiling he played with an expression of what struck me as pure rapture. It was the feeling created by the sum total of their music – Miles and Cole on the fiddles, Branch with the wailing harmonica.

I could not help but shiver, so absorbed that my shoulders jerked when Axton and Patricia began singing along. Patricia giggled at my jumpiness and I realized Axton had been right; I knew this song. I'd heard it before at some point in my past and to my amazement the melody rose in my throat, fully formed. I joined Patricia and Axton as they sang "Red River Valley." That I could recall the chorus of a song and not the names or faces of my own parents was beyond my ability to comprehend; it was maddening.

"We're good. We should go on the road," I teased my fellow singers when the song was over, the three of us applauding and cheering while Cole and Branch bowed with all the gusto of showmen; Miles simply nodded.

Axton said, "They'll be traveling the road tomorrow."

"No, I mean…" But I trailed off, uncertain exactly what I meant.

The men began the next song, another tune I recognized. An hour passed, marked by the rising silver moon; it was close to full again. They moved between fast-paced numbers and slower, sweeter ones, ballads and waltzes, as the moon climbed ever higher and tears swelled in my eyes time and again at their collective talent. The sweetness of the music dusted my skin and flowed into my ears like warm honey, inducing an almost dreamlike state; my exhausted eyelids grew heavy and at last I rested my cheek against Axton's upper arm, lulled into a state of security, tucked as I was between him and Patricia.

Axton hooked his arm around my waist, resituating so I would be more comfortable, and I tried to pretend I didn't feel the heat of Miles's gaze upon us as he continued playing, letting my eyes sink closed.

Chapter Ten

MILES, AXTON, AND COLE ESCORTED US BACK TO THE DE-
pot an hour later, beneath the light of a showy, snow-white moon.
Though Branch wanted Patricia and me to remain at the cabin for the
night, Patricia explained the necessity of returning to her train car before
morning's light, when Mrs. Mason's drug-induced stupor would presumably wear away. I realized I had to tell Patricia I'd made a decision
regarding the immediate future, and I would have to tell her tonight. But
I feared for her reaction.

It had been while Miles was returning Branch's fiddle to its proper
place that I caught him alone. Everyone else remained at the fire, laughing and complimenting the musicians, but I scurried after Miles, slipping through the door behind him, into the relative privacy afforded by
the four walls of the cabin.

"I would like to join you," I announced to his back, having reached
this conclusion while listening to the music. Probably I should have
spent more time deliberating the decision; without a doubt I should
have considered Celia and how she might feel about all of this. But my
gut instinct overrode everything else and it boiled down to one simple
fact – I hated the thought of Miles leaving town without me.

Miles hadn't realized I'd followed him inside and slowly turned,
holding the fiddle by its long neck, so he could see my face. He didn't
respond and my stomach jumped; what if he regretted asking me to accompany him? It was dim in the cabin, only the muted firelight lending
the space any illumination, gifting me with slightly more courage than I
might have possessed in a brighter setting. Twisting my hands together,

I hurried to say, "If the offer is still on the table, that is."

His teeth flashed in a wide smile and his gladness was almost palpable. "Of course it is."

"What should I bring with?" My pulse and my knees were shaking, giving me another reason to be grateful for the lack of light.

"Hat, a change of clothes, canteen, blanket. We've food aplenty. Armaments, too."

I laughed, a nervous huff of sound, and he hurried on, as if I might change my mind. "We'll leave with the dawn. Will you remain here this night, or with Mrs. Yancy in her train car? I will return for you, wherever you are."

"Most of my things are at Patricia's."

"Then I will call for you there, at first light," Miles said, and the plan was set.

Under the bright moon the wide-open landscape appeared alien; lovely and wild, for sure, but there was something about traveling in the center of what appeared endless space that made the back of my neck prickle. Axton drove the wagon, this time sitting between Patricia and me on the wagon seat, while Miles and Cole, both horseback, flanked us on either side, Miles near me and Cole near Patricia, respectively.

"Young Axton, you best thank your lucky stars," Cole said as we journeyed the few miles from the homestead to the railroad depot on the outskirts of Howardsville. He was a little drunk, I could tell; he rode Charger so close to the wagon Patricia could have reached over and touched his shoulder if she wanted to, and I had no doubt she wanted to. Cole explained, "I would give my eye teeth to be setting there in your place."

Axton laughed, both embarrassed and pleased, and because he was also pretty loaded he had the courage to say, "Not even a team of oxen could move me."

Cole gave a low whistle, two notes that suggested *uh-oh*. "Don't make me drag you off there, young fellow."

Axton muttered, "Just try," slightly too low for Cole to hear. But then in a different tone he announced, "Ruthie's been helping me learn how to talk to ladies, proper-like."

"Is that so?" Miles asked.

"Ax and I have many good talks, don't we?" I agreed, tucking my hand around his elbow.

"You're good to talk to," Axton said, using his elbow to squeeze my hand against his side, as though giving a little hug. "Nobody tells me things like you do, Ruthie."

I nudged his ribs, I hoped indicating he shouldn't get into specifics right here, but of course Cole couldn't resist and prodded, "What things? Now you got me curious."

Axton sat straighter. "Well, for one, that a lady likes it when a man – "

"*Ax*," I broke in, giggling, certain he was about to launch into our recent discussion on the marriage act. He looked my way with lifted eyebrows and I elbowed him again, insisting, "*Hush up*."

"When a man *what*?" Cole demanded, and Patricia began giggling, clinging to Axton's other arm as she waited for his response.

"I admit I'm awfully curious, myself," Miles said, and I could tell he was trying not to laugh.

"See, the thing is…" I stumbled over an explanation.

At the same moment Axton decided, "I best not tell. I don't want Ruthie mad at me."

My shoulders relaxed.

Cole whooped a laugh. "Aw, that ain't fair!"

"I shall wrest the answer from Ruthann later, once we are alone," Patricia promised, and we were all laughing then.

Miles said, "I must confess, young Axton, I am looking forward to the opportunity to talk at length with Ruthann, as well." To me, he added, "We'll collect you at first light, if that suits you."

I saw Patricia stiffen. "Whatever do you mean? Collect Ruthann?"

Shit. I'd wanted to discuss this with her in private but there was no avoiding it now. I explained lamely, "Miles asked me to ride west with them tomorrow, and I agreed." I felt terrible, and decidedly ungrateful; after all, Patricia had invited me to Chicago, asking nothing in return, with the intent of finding my family. That is, if there was a family to be found.

Patricia's eyes shone in the moonlight as she whispered, "Without me?" The hurt in her voice was apparent, though it changed quickly to determination. "Not without me. I shall join you."

"I can only just imagine the uproar that would occasion," Cole said. "Yancy's men would be on our tails, accusing us of stealing you away, before you could say 'hogwash.'"

"They shall never know. They've left town!" Patricia's resolve gained in intensity. "Please, do not leave me behind. Ruthann, *please*. Please, Cole…"

I wasn't sure if she'd ever spoken his given name in his presence. There was a tense silence before Cole said quietly, "You're a married woman."

"Please," Patricia repeated. "Please do not go without me."

"Mrs. Yancy, it would be most improper, not to mention dangerous," Miles said, in a firm tone I'd come to think of as his lawman voice. "I aim to dispute with Cole at least twice a day, just on principle, but in this case I must agree."

"*Please*," she whispered.

"I'll come along, too," Axton said, as though to ease the strain of Patricia's agonized disappointment. "I ain't seen the land farther west than here. Uncle Branch can spare me the week."

"When I get back I'll come home with you to Chicago," I assured Patricia, though something in my gut twisted at the notion. "As long as I'm not a burden to you. That's the last thing I want to be, to anyone."

"You are no burden whatsoever," Patricia said, and I realized she was swiping away tears. I reached across Axton's lap and clutched her free hand as she whispered, "I have grown very fond of you, so quickly. I cannot bear the thought of being away from you so soon. I shall die of loneliness."

"I'll be back before you know it." I considered how much I would miss her company; it seemed illogical, given the short length of our acquaintance.

The depot loomed just ahead of our advancing horses. Moonlight delineated the hard lines of Yancy train cars, their presence stark and

Williams

foreboding, somehow eerie. I saw Patricia's shoulders hunch as she beheld this unmistakable evidence of her life, her station, her marriage and all it entailed, whether she wanted it or not. She pressed the back of her left hand, the one I was not clutching, to her lips, in the manner of someone about to vomit.

Axton drew the wagon to the far side of the train cars, halting our forward progress. We were all silent now, as though to speak might crack some invisible, fragile thing that had swooped down and now hovered nearby. Miles dismounted Blade and wasted no time reaching to help me from the wagon, grasping my waist; concealed by the darkness, he did not release his hold. He wore his hat and his face was but a shadow; I clutched his wrists.

He murmured, "I will return for you at first light."

Neither of us released the other. The hair on his forearms was soft and immediate beneath my palms; my fingers moved with minds of their own, caressing his warm skin. His thumbs traced over my belly in slow, wide arcs. There was a sharp tension in the air, compressing my lungs. I fought the urge to get my arms around his neck and tuck close to the protection of his chest.

"Where will you be tonight?" I whispered.

Miles exhaled a slow breath at my question. His thumbs made another pass along my stomach; my borrowed blouse was sewn from delicate material and I felt his touch as palpably as if I wore nothing at all. I swore I heard his thoughts in that instant.

Wherever you are, he wanted to say.

His name was on the tip of my tongue but he spoke before I could gather my courage.

"We'll return to Branch's this night. I'll bring your horse with, in the morning." He glanced at the bulk of the train cars. The glow of a candle lantern shone through a solitary window in one of the red cars, both of which also boasted heavy door locks; I could sense him sizing up the security of this place where I would spend the night. I didn't want him to go but there was no logical excuse for him to stay, and we both knew it.

"Rawley, we best ride out," Cole said from horseback, his voice hoarse and tightly-wound. Axton, not about to be usurped this time around, had jumped down to help Patricia from the wagon and she stood now in silence, looking between him and Cole.

"Good-night," Patricia whispered at last, though her tone suggested *good-bye*.

Cole tipped his hat brim and whispered, "Mrs. Yancy."

Axton, rife with liquid courage, gathered Patricia's hands, bringing both to his lips and kissing her knuckles before clambering back atop the wagon seat.

Miles briefly cupped my face. He whispered, "Until tomorrow, then."

Inside one of the red train cars a minute later Patricia clung to me, both of us hearing the hoofbeats of the men riding their horses away, the wagon wheels clunking over the uneven ground. A candle in a tin holder nailed to the wall had burned almost to its last inch and cast sickly, wavering light over our bodies.

Our men were riding away from us.

I could not help but acknowledge this truth, as crazy as it was, and Patricia began sobbing. I held her close, rubbing her back and murmuring comforting nonsense, though it wasn't doing much in the way of comfort.

"Oh, Ruthann," she whispered, nose plugged, gulping between words. "I do not understand...what has come over me. Since I met him I feel I have...taken leave of my senses..."

"You haven't," I reassured, thinking of the looks exchanged between her and Cole this evening. I recognized Cole represented a kind of man to whom Patricia had never been exposed in her wealthy upbringing; he was self-assured in a way that had nothing to do with the arrogance and entitlement of wealth, and everything to do with abundant capability and magnetism. Cole was his own man; no one could buy his loyalty. Patricia was so young, and had entered into the state of marriage if not exactly against her will, then very much without the necessary life experience.

She drew away to study my eyes, as if to force me to fully comprehend the situation's gravity. "I have been able to think of nothing but Cole Spicer since first we met." She choked on a sob and I held her by the elbows, wishing I had the power to make things right – and Dredd Yancy was so not right for Patricia. But was Cole? The sight of Axton's face when he first saw Patricia, only this morning, blazed through my mind.

"Oh dear God, Dredd would murder me," she whispered, as if sensing my thoughts of her absent husband. "I shall no longer entertain such notions as I have been allowing myself. And now I have discovered *you* shall be leaving on the morrow and I feel as though I may die anyway, with misery…"

"Patricia?" called a faint voice, and we both jolted in surprise.

"She never wakes before midmorning," Patricia grumbled, swiping at her tear-streaked face. We had entered Mrs. Mason's train car rather than Patricia's in order to extinguish the candle the woman had left burning. Patricia whispered, "Let us leave her be."

I nodded silent agreement and Patricia turned to extinguish the candle; before she could manage, however, a small woman around the age Patricia's mother would have been, if still alive, poked her head from the bedroom compartment.

"I've been…so worried," this woman said, but she slurred through the words, which didn't exactly suggest a truthful statement. Her head was covered in a sleeping cap, white and ruffled like a little girl's. Two long gray braids hung over her shoulders and her eyes were glassy, like marbles, and unfocused.

"You've not been one *iota* worried," Patricia contradicted, though not as rudely as the words implied. "Melodrama does not suit you, Mrs. Mason. Now, return to bed and we shall rejoin you in the morning hours."

Instead of obeying Mrs. Mason crept into the living room and sank to the plump cushions of the loveseat, blinking up at me with mild bewilderment. She appeared high as a kite and an air of unpleasantness radiated from her. Even though she was probably harmless I battled the desire to step away. She wondered aloud, "Who in heaven's name?"

"This is Ruthann Rawley," Patricia said, with growing impatience. "I told you of her earlier this very day, which I am certain you do not recall, 'medicated' as you were. Ruthann, this is Matilda Mason. If you shall excuse us, Mrs. Mason, Ruthann and I shall take our –"

"I'm scared, Patty," Mrs. Mason whimpered. She stood on shaky legs, gripping the upholstered arm of the loveseat to retain balance. The hair on my nape skittered straight up at both her words and expression – she truly did appear scared.

Patricia rolled her eyes. "What is this absurdity? Are you able to hear yourself? Do you recall the afternoon only a month past when you believed spiders were crawling about in your teeth?" Patricia sent me a look which clearly spoke of her frustration. "And I have asked you never to call me 'Patty.' I *detest* that nickname."

Mrs. Mason seemed not to hear Patricia's words, instead peering all around the train car, leaning forward, blinking and squinting, her eyes roving into the dark corners; I felt another jolt of pure apprehension.

Patricia heaved a deep, exasperated sigh. "Mrs. Mason, you are *most* befuddled. You require rest. And not another drop of your medicine before morning, I insist."

"Please, Patty, do let me come to your car." Mrs. Mason refocused on Patricia, clutching at her elbow.

"Jesus *Christ*," I muttered. In the space of a minute I already disliked Mrs. Mason. I felt the urge to tuck Patricia behind me and therefore away from the disturbing, drugged-up woman.

Patricia smiled at my cursing, muttering, "You sound like Cole." She reached to take Mrs. Mason's shoulder and offered kindly, "If it brings you comfort, you may sleep on the wingchair in my car this night."

Outside under the moon I found my longing gaze following in the direction the men had ridden, northeast back to Branch's claim shanty; of course they had long since disappeared from sight. The prairie was empty of all but scrub brush and starlight, no sign of them or their horses in the distance. I paused, a few paces behind Patricia and Mrs. Mason, and an unbidden and unwelcome thought bounded into my mind – the memory of Miles cast in red light, the horrible notion that he was in harm's way. My gut clenched.

Miles, I thought, willing him to hear me. *Be careful. Please, be careful.*

I was abruptly furious with myself. *You are being ridiculous, Ruthann. He is a grown man. He's the marshal, for Christ's sake! He can more than take care of himself.*

We climbed the clanging metal steps to Patricia's car, Mrs. Mason stumbling to manage the task.

Patricia reached to unlock the door, fetching a long key from the pocket pouch sewn into her dress; she paused and muttered, "That's strange."

"What?" My heart clanked.

Mrs. Mason made a low sound of distress and I wanted to tell her to shut the hell up.

"It's unlocked. I swore I locked it as we left, but perhaps in my excitement..." Patricia eased open the door. The stuffy interior was black as a nightmare.

I thought, *We shouldn't be here...*

Patricia entered first and bumped against something, muttering, "Dammit." I heard her open and begin riffling through a drawer. She requested, "Allow me a moment," before locating a match, which she struck to life with a small crackling sound.

"Patricia..." I did not know how to express my growing concern.

In the sudden illumination I realized Mrs. Mason was staring at me. Unable to help it, I gasped at the sight of the woman's waxen-looking face; the expression pressed in its surface looked just this side of insane. Her ruffled nightcap and braids only added to her frightening appearance.

"They're coming for her," Mrs. Mason muttered, gaze unblinking. "He made certain of it before we left."

"What the *fuck?*" I snapped, in stun more than anger. I demanded, "Made certain of what?"

"Ouch!" The match burned low, grazing Patricia's fingertips. She blew it out, plunging us into abrupt darkness. "Ruthann, never mind her blathering. If you would help settle her there, on the wingchair just to your right, I'll light another match. Pay her no mind, she is often incoherent."

"And she's supposed to take care of you?" I nearly spit these words, disgusted by Mrs. Mason and Patricia's lack of someone to protect her. Anger and determination rose in my chest. "I won't leave you here alone this week with this woman."

I could see the image of the match flame emblazoned on the backs of my eyelids whenever I blinked; my eyes had not yet adjusted. I fumbled, feeling the wingchair near my knees, and bent to help Mrs. Mason sit; as I did so, the woman muttered, "I am so sorry…"

Before I could stand straight a chill clawed my spine, an animal's instinct that danger was near; a predator had closed in, however unexpectedly, and the coldness in the spine was the body's last-ditch effort to warn. There was a sense of movement, an outline even darker than the interior of the train car, and Patricia made a strangled sound, no more than two feet from me. I spun toward her, armed with nothing but the strength afforded by fear, and it was my sudden movement that sent a heavy object clattering to the floor.

There was a fourth body in Patricia's train car with us.

Breathing too harshly to scream I grappled to free Patricia from a brutal grasp. In the darkness the attacker was nothing more than a lumping body – no face, no identity, only an object I understood I must destroy. I heard grunting. My hands slid ineffectually over a man's taut arms and shoulders. It was like trying to cut in on two people locked in a dancing embrace. Patricia struggled furiously, her breath emerging in choking bursts. Then I felt hair, not hers. I clenched my fingers and pulled that hair by the roots, using every ounce of strength I possessed.

He issued a small yelp, releasing Patricia to punch me before I could consider this consequence, let alone attempt to avoid it. I could not make sense of Patricia falling to her knees when it was the side of my face with which his hard fist connected. I heard her scrabbling around on the floor, gasping and frantic. Stars flared across my vision and I reeled sideways, crashing into the wingchair.

"Ruth…*ann*," Patricia gasped out.

"You *fucking whore*," he growled. I found room in my panicking brain to wonder if he meant me or Patricia. He swung again, grunting with the effort, and his fist met flesh with a crunching thunk – but not mine. Someone fell hard. Someone else emitted a sudden shrill scream. Nothing made sense – we existed in a dark world of pure, stark confusion. I could not place the sounds I was hearing into any sort of context.

"*Help*," Patricia moaned.

The man lunged, knocking over a side table. There was the shattering tinkle of breaking glass. I fell over Patricia in my attempt to pull her away from him.

"Get him!" Patricia's gasping voice was in my ear.

He kicked at us with booted feet. My eyes had adjusted enough to observe that he was lying on the floor, belly-crawling toward the door, wheezing.

Shards of broken glass littered the floor.

Moonlight flooded the train car in a pie-shaped wedge as he managed to open the door. He found his feet but then tumbled down the metal steps. I heard moaning and cursing, and then the sounds of a horse.

He was getting away but there was nothing we could do.

"Oh dear God, oh Ruthann, are you harmed?" Patricia's voice was high-pitched and keen-edged with panic. Something fell from her hands and hit the floor with a dull thud.

"What...the...hell...what the...*fuck*..." I could hardly speak past the ball of screaming adrenaline in my chest.

We clung together, shaking.

"Are you hurt? Patricia, oh Jesus fucking Christ, *are you hurt?*" I demanded, "*Tell me!*"

"I don't th...I don't think so..."

"Light," I managed to say.

Patricia stammered, "There's a lot of...blood...oh d...dear, a lot of...blood..."

Panic lent me strength; I hauled Patricia to her feet and out into the night, which was ridiculously quiet, as though it could not care less for what we'd just survived. The man who'd been in the train car with us was nowhere in sight; no unfamiliar horse, no sign of the insanity which had just occurred. In the light spilled by the moon I held Patricia's shoulders and tried to determine where she was bleeding; frantic terror hazed my vision.

"Your hands," I whispered. Her hands and arms appeared black with blood, up to the elbows. Then I saw dark patches covering her skirt and started to cry, hard.

"No, it's not...*it's not*..." She struggled to gain enough control to force out the words. "It's not mine. I st...stabbed him. I stabbed his... st...stomach." Her teeth were chattering.

"You..." I choked back my sobs. "It's not your..."

"At least...I th...*think*...I did..."

"*You* stabbed *him*."

"Oh, R...Ruth...*ann* ..."

"That woman said they were *coming for you*." Anger erupted in my chest, serving to burn away some of the fear. "Who did she mean?"

"Oh dear God..." Patricia clambered up the metal steps, caught her hem on her shoe, fell, and then struggled back to her feet, all while I knelt on the ground, watching in stun.

Inside her train car she accomplished what she'd been trying to do in the first place, which was light a candle. I'd followed her by then and saw what caused her to sink to her knees, her blood-drenched skirt fanning across the floor. The interior was a wreck, evidence of the brutal battle we'd just fought for our lives. Broken glass, wet blood, and the wicked-looking, long-bladed knife surely intended for use in taking Patricia's life this very night...and among all of this, Mrs. Mason lay crumpled.

Chapter Eleven

WE WERE UNABLE TO SORT OUT EXACTLY WHAT HAD JUST happened, and were too horrified to attempt. Patricia could not stop weeping even after I led her back outside, scarcely able to remain calm enough to decide what we should do next. I knew two things. The first, that Mrs. Mason was dead; and the second, I wanted Miles Rawley. I ached from the inside out with wanting him here, right now. He would know what to do.

"She said someone *made certain.*" Patricia clenched my blouse as we stood in the chill night air, clinging to each other. "Oh, dear God. There are only two people to whom she could be referring. Thomas or Fallon."

"Your husband's family?" I clarified. My voice was dust-dry.

Patricia nodded with two jerks of her head. I could not begin to guess the implications of all of this, not right now, and squeezed her closer to my thumping heart.

I knew Miles would return with the morning's light but dawn was hours away. I was literally floundering with indecision, turning to look back at the train car, where the single lighted candle transformed the lone window into a small rectangle of gold, and where a dead woman lay on the floor. Patricia jittered, head to hem, in my arms. I tried to gather my thoughts enough to determine what we should do in the next few minutes, but they scattered like someone shaking pepper into a soup pot.

That man meant to kill Patricia. He had a knife. He was waiting for her. He would have killed her if you hadn't been there.

Oh, Jesus...

Should we walk to town?

No, there's no help there.

But Doc Turn is there.

Doc's drunk by this time of night. He's worse than no help at all.

Where is the man who did this?

What if he's out there, waiting for us?

No. Don't freak out, not now…

My mind swam to the only security it understood.

I cupped Patricia's shoulders to gain her full attention; her breathing had not slowed. "It's all right. Listen to me. Right now we have to walk a little ways. Are you able?"

She nodded slowly, seeming to understand my intent.

I helped her sit on the bottom-most step and then ventured inside the train car one last time, stomach lurching; I would not have entered the space again except that we couldn't leave Mrs. Mason exposed on the floor. I grabbed a silk throw blanket, draped over the back of a nearby loveseat, and settled it atop the woman's motionless form. I'd been the one to feel for the pulse that wasn't there, in either wrist or neck. Next I flew to Patricia's sleeping compartment and snatched the first garment I found. Back outside, nervous energy pulsing, I helped Patricia from her blood-stained clothing, which was already growing stiff in the chilly night air, and buttoned her into a clean dress, shoving the soiled one beneath the metal steps.

"Come on," I whispered, grasping her right elbow. "I'll be right beside you."

We walked swiftly away, holding fast to one another and our hems, lifting them so we could effectively move forward through the tall prairie grass.

"Am I to believe Dredd's family intended to have me killed?" She sounded like a bewildered child.

"I don't know. But things are changing, tonight." I recognized this truth, deep inside.

Under the open sky and away from the train cars, I felt better. Not as numb. Perhaps it was simple self-preservation at work, my brain grasping the realization that I wouldn't be able to accomplish what needing doing if I was disabled by fear. I kept a firm hold on Patricia as we navigated the uneven ground, stumbling along through scratchy grasses that tugged at our clothing. Twenty minutes passed, maybe more; I'd lost track of time when Patricia suddenly whispered, "I hear music."

I heard it then too, stretching across the distance to touch us, the sweet, mournful notes of two fiddles being played in harmony. I almost crumpled with relief. "Come on! We're almost there."

Within another fifty yards we spied the fire's orange flames. They'd finished the song. In the silence following the absence of music, the murmur of their low-pitched voices drifted to our ears, more reassuring than anything I'd ever heard.

"*Miles.*" His name flew from my throat. "Miles!"

Their conversation stopped mid-word.

"Ruthann?" The question in his tone grew intense with concern as he shouted, "*Ruthann!* Where are you?"

Tears flooded my face even though I wasn't actually crying. These were tears of pure, undiluted relief. I had to stop walking so I could in-hale enough breath to shout, "Out here!"

And then he was there, Cole on his heels, but I saw only Miles, who ran to me without question because I needed him.

"What has happened?" Miles gripped my shoulders.

"I…we…that is…" I babbled, unable to string together a sentence or take my eyes from his face.

Cole moved with purpose and swept Patricia into his arms, heading for the cabin. With authority, he ordered, "C'mon."

Miles looked as though he was thinking of doing the same to me but I took his elbow instead, not willing to be carried.

"What has happened?" he repeated as we followed Cole and Patricia. He implored, "Ruthann, please tell me what has happened."

"Someone…there was someone…*oh God*…" I gulped, embarrassed to be losing my cool but losing it all the same. Now that we were here and therefore safe, I could feel the shakes coming on with a vengeance.

"Was it Turnbull?" Miles stopped our forward progress to look upon my face. His eyes blazed with murderous fury. "I will *fucking tear him apart —"*

"No," I whispered. "No. At least, I don't think it was…"

"Who was it? What has been done?"

"Will you listen?" I tried to focus, clenching my muscles so they wouldn't tremble so hard. "Someone tried to kill Patricia. Just now, in her train car. Oh God, it was…we were…" Even though I'd just ordered him to listen, I wasn't in enough control to explain. My lips and teeth seemed frozen.

Without a word, Miles tucked me back against his side. My nose was near his collarbones; I caught the faint scent of bourbon on his breath. I clung to the strength of him, allowing myself this indulgence. Branch, bearing a tin lantern, hurried outside at our approach, Axton behind him.

Ax took one look at Patricia, curled in Cole's arms, and his face went stark with agony. "What's happened?"

Cole had no time for questions. "Fetch a basin of water, hurry now," he ordered, and disappeared inside with Patricia.

Axton floundered, plainly wanting to follow them; he caught sight of me, took immediate stock, and flew to my side. "Ruthie!"

Miles grasped my chin with utmost care, able to see my face in the lantern's shifting light. "You've been struck. Who did this to you?"

"Darlin', what in God's name?" Branch rooted his handkerchief from his hip pocket and passed it to my hands; I lifted the cloth to the sore spot on my temple, where a goose egg was already forming.

I forced my lungs to expand. "There was a man hiding in Patricia's train car. He meant to kill her."

Ax issued a low sound of rage and Branch urged, "Boy, you go and pump a bucket of water, quick now, like Cole done asked. Ruthie, c'mon inside." So saying, he hurried to open the door; within, Cole sat on one of the two mismatched chairs, holding Patricia on his lap, cradling her, smoothing a hand over the back of her hair, which hung in drooping tangles from the knots she had pinned up earlier this afternoon.

Cole looked up as we entered, his eyes laden with concern and rage held rigidly in check. In the glow of the lantern the bloodstains on Patricia's hands and arms appeared more gruesome than ever. Cole pressed his lips to her temple and murmured, "It's all right. It's all right now." As he spoke he worked with care, slipping the pins from her top-knots one by one, setting them on the table, stroking through her loosening hair with absolute tenderness.

Axton reappeared toting a bucket of water, which he set on the floor; his jaws clenched at the sight of Patricia clinging to Cole. But his worried gaze roved my way and he hurried to gather me in a hug. His nose against my hair, he whispered, "We shouldn't have left you alone. I'm so sorry, Ruthie."

I pressed my face to Ax's chest, unable to administer comfort, only absorb it; at last I drew back and whispered, "It's not your fault."

Miles, not about to be deterred, led me to the other chair, settling me there and then kneeling, bracing his hands on either side of my thighs, gripping the outer edges of the chair. "Tell us what happened."

I spoke haltingly, relating what I thought had occurred in the past hour, while the men listened in stunned silence. Patricia, looking younger than ever with her long hair tumbling down her back, kept her head on Cole's shoulder. Her eyes were so red and swollen she appeared to have received a beating. When I paused for a breath she whispered, "I owe you my life, dear Ruthann. I have no doubt. You knocked the knife from his hand." Her voice jerked over the words. "He yanked my head back. He meant…to slit my throat…"

Cole's face was stone as the impact of these words settled. Axton, who'd claimed the chair to my right, wore such a similar expression that for a second I could hardly tell the two men apart; the feeling was strong, almost surreal. A wave of dizzy nausea crashed over my body.

"I must go and determine what has happened." Miles spoke calmly but I imagined I could see the frenzied whirl of his thoughts, attempting to sort out the details. He clarified, "The man who attacked you and Mrs. Yancy ran away? And you believe he was wounded?"

I nodded, exhausted beyond words. I didn't want him to leave but knew I had no power to stop it.

Miles rose. "Let us go."

Axton spoke adamantly. "I'll ride with you."

Cole tucked a loose strand of hair behind Patricia's ear, his fingertips lingering on her cheek. He promised, "I'll return as soon as I am able."

Miles grabbed his hat from the hook by the door; his act of settling it over his head seemed too final, setting off a tripwire in my heart. He went outside and I jumped up and ran after him.

"Miles," I implored, and his feet stalled. It always seemed he faced away from the light, that shadows cast themselves over his stern, handsome face. I grabbed his arm with a two-handed grip. "Be careful. I'm worried. I'm so worried about you."

"I worry so for you, as well." He bracketed my face with both hands. My heart compressed and released, in swift repetition; I was mired in confusion as thick as mud.

"I don't understand this."

"It does not require understanding," he whispered. The embers of the evening's fire, just beyond us, seemed to burn my eyes. Miles rested his thumbs upon my mouth, as though imprinting it with his touch. He spoke with quiet intensity. "I will return for you, Ruthann, this I promise. I would that you rest while I am gone," and then, cradling my face, he leaned and gently kissed the lumping bruise on my temple.

I lay beside Patricia on the bear hide where Branch normally slept, the two of us covered with quilts in the far corner of the dimly-lit room. More than an hour had passed since Miles, Cole, and Axton turned their horses for Howardsville. Branch sat sentry at the fire, too restless to attempt sleeping, a long-barreled rifle braced lengthwise across his lap.

Patricia whispered, "Are you asleep?"

"No," I admitted. I lay closest to the wooden wall, one arm curved beneath my head, my other hand resting on Patricia's back; she felt so slim and delicate beneath my touch. I admonished softly, "But you should be. Don't worry, Branch is right outside and I'll be right here. I won't leave your side."

"Thank you," she breathed, and I patted her back, making small circles with the base of my palm.

"You remind me of Rosemary," she murmured a few seconds later.

"Who's that?" My hand fell still.

"Rosemary," she sighed. "My little sister. She died many years ago, when I was only a child, but I remember her as if it were yesterday."

Only minutes later she fell asleep, her breathing slowing and evening out; I kept rubbing her back, aching for her, and for what would happen now. At last I let my eyes drift shut, half-dreaming, words rolling through my mind, tugging at my consciousness.

I must have lost my ring…

My husband…

I know he's out there somewhere looking for me.

Sweetheart, can you hear me?

Oh God, where are you?

Where are you?

I jerked awake, rubbing my thumb over the bare space at the base of the third finger of my left hand. I pressed harder, using my thumbnail, creating a divot in my skin. I screamed the question across endless miles – *Where are you?*

But of course there was no answer.

I thought of what this night had revealed – the likely conclusion seemed the Yancys wished Patricia dead, their plans now thwarted. The Yancys, criminals to their core; surely the horror of this evening's events proved it unequivocally. But why? What did this mean?

What does any of this mean?

I pressed both fists to my eyes and, with determination, centered my thoughts on Miles Rawley, riding back to me.

Chapter Twelve

Jalesville, MT - February, 2014

"I DREAMED ABOUT THEM AGAIN," I WHISPERED TO CASE in the early-morning darkness of our little bedroom.

His chest was broad and warm, so wonderful a place for my cheek to be cradled. I lay with both right arm and leg latched over my husband and he stroked my back with his chording hand, his fingertips gentle as they glided up and down my spine; from time to time, he made a fist and knuckled my lower back.

"What did you dream, baby?" he murmured, kissing my forehead. I felt his breath on my eyelids, the familiar sweetness of it; he sounded drowsy, for which I was grateful. Neither of us had slept well in the past few days.

"I saw them sitting in the sunshine," I whispered. I didn't know if my subconscious was simply trying to prevent me from going crazy, therefore conjuring and providing me with a dream of my sister and Marshall appearing safe, or if it was an actual message from them.

"Tish," Case whispered, and I heard the pain in his voice. "It's good they were together. It seems like a sign. I think they would try to send us a message, if that's possible."

If that's possible.

Despite everything, I continued to grapple with the irrationality of all of this. But if what we believed was true, Marshall and my sister had *traveled* through time. Was a message contained in a dream any less plausible?

"I think it's possible," I whispered, letting myself be momentarily comforted. As a lawyer, I'd been trained to find proof, to root out the logical evidence. And everything about this situation defied all known logic. Since moving to Montana I had learned to trust my intuition and to recognize its critical importance – part of which had led me to Case. I closed my eyes and snuggled closer to his warmth, and he made a sound deep in his throat and drew my thigh tighter around his hip.

"Both mornings since they've been gone I've woken up with this horrible feeling you won't be here." He was more awake now, his voice low and hoarse. He hadn't mentioned this and I snuggled closer in response. The agony of my sister's disappearance, and of Marshall's, whom Case and I both loved like a brother, was unbearable.

Hot tears dripped from my nose and splashed onto his chest. I longed for the mornings when we lay laughing and teasing beneath the covers, wrapped in our happiness; had I dared to take our easy laughter for granted? I longed for my sister and Marshall to be returned to us. Laughter would never be the same; it would forever be colored by the loss of them, if they never returned.

Please let them come back, oh God, oh please…

Marshall thought a week, maybe two…

But what if…

I clamped down on any errant thoughts that Marshall would not succeed, that he would fail to find Ruthie. Their absence remained a mystery to most people; at first, Case and I were the only ones who understood the truth of where, and *when*, they'd gone. If Marshall and my sister did not return within the month, we'd been tasked with delivering the truth to our respective families; the very idea of such a conversation with my family sent shards of glass through my bowels. Of course I'd talked to the womenfolk in Landon – my mom and my older sister Camille, my dear Aunt Jilly, Grandma and Great-Aunt Ellen – at least twice a day since Ruthie's disappearance. The inability to speak to Ruthann had torn a hole in each of our souls.

Aunt Jilly had been the one to ask, "They've gone back, haven't they? I promise I won't tell Jo unless you want me to, Tish."

"Not yet," I'd begged, cradling the phone in the middle of the night, whispering with my beloved auntie, who had always possessed intuition far beyond an average person. "Not just yet."

"Camille knows. I can see it in her eyes."

"I know," I'd whispered to Aunt Jilly; to my mother I could only promise, "Ruthie will be back. You have to trust me."

And I was clinging to this conviction with everything in me.

Clark Rawley and his sons knew the truth; Case and I had told them yesterday evening, after much debate. Debate because Marshall thought there was a chance he and Ruthie might return before anyone even realized he was gone, therefore sparing our families additional worry. Case and I finally decided we needed to tell Clark, no matter Marshall's orders.

"Could we *all* go back there? Like, right now?" Sean had asked while we were gathered in Clark's familiar living room, the brothers crowded around us with their expressions uncharacteristically grave. Only Becky was absent from the family group, home with her and Garth's new baby. Sean had been perched on the edge of the sofa, his hands in loose fists, tense with energy. The Rawley boys all looked so much alike I could almost, from the corner of my eye, pretend Marshall was there anyway.

Except that he wasn't.

"I don't know how to explain it, exactly." I felt ill at my basic inability to help them understand; *I* didn't even understand. I was a woman who took action, who did not usually hesitate, but these circumstances rendered me helpless. I studied Clark, Marshall's father; Clark appeared haggard, the lines of his thin, craggy face exaggerated by the flickering flames in the hearth. His mouth was solemn, his thick mustache obscuring his upper lip as he looked between Case and me. Garth, the oldest brother, sat to Clark's left, bent forward over his thighs, wide shoulders hunched, fingers laced and eyebrows drawn inward. Quinn perched beside Sean on the sofa, their faces grim, while Wy, the youngest at sixteen, sat on the floor with his back resting on the edge of Clark's chair, wrists dangling over his bent knees. He hadn't removed his eyes from my face, nor had he spoken a word.

Case took up the reins. "As far as we can tell, only certain people are able to feel the pull of the past. Ruthie seemed especially susceptible. She would touch Una's letters and…"

I curled my fingers around Case's hand as he faltered; I finished for him, "And she would start to shimmer, like she was becoming invisible. We watched her disappear before our eyes, back in January. It was horrible." I gritted my teeth against the memory. "But Marsh was there that night and he…somehow he pulled her back. He *stopped* it from happening."

None of them knew how to respond; I could feel the weighty mass of their combined stun the way I would a cord of wood resting on my shoulders.

His tone begging for answers, Clark demanded quietly, "But how?"

Garth glared at us, bristling with frustration and growing anger. "Why didn't Marsh tell us? Why didn't *you* guys tell us? Why in the hell are we just hearing this now?"

I sensed more than saw the way Case's shoulders squared. Garth was like a brother to him, not to mention his longtime best friend, and so Case kept his voice calm as he answered, "Because we could hardly believe it either. Who the hell can? It seems impossible. We hid away Una's letters and thought if Ruthie never touched them again, it would be fine."

Garth stormed to his feet, plunging both hands through his thick brown hair. "But it *wasn't fine!* Where are the letters now? Why didn't Marsh tell us he planned to leave? What the fuck?"

"If you think for a second we aren't *just as horrified*…" I couldn't keep the angry tremble from my voice any more than I could the tears from my eyes.

Case squeezed my hand. "We will do whatever we can, whatever it takes, but we need your help, you guys. Believe me, I want to punch through a brick wall but it won't do any goddamn good."

Addressing Case, Clark requested, "Start at the beginning if you would, son." Clark was Case's surrogate father and the tenderness in his voice as he spoke this word to Case reassured me more than anything he could have said in that moment. Clark reached for Garth's wrist and tugged his oldest back to the couch. He murmured, "Sit, son, please.

Let's listen."

Together Case and I explained what we believed had happened since last fall, concluding at the moment in time which found us all in the Rawleys' living room with an icy winter night pressing against the wide bay windows. Ruthie's Buick had been found yesterday, lodged in a snowbank off Interstate 94, near the Montana-North Dakota border. The hood was crumpled, the seat belt still fastened, her puffy winter coat balled up on the floor of the passenger side, as though she'd been too warm while driving and shucked it. But no sign of my sister. No boot prints through the snow, no note. No cell phone call or explanatory voice message. Nothing.

"My boy loves Ruthann like I've never seen him love anyone," Clark acknowledged when Case and I finished speaking. His kind brown eyes glistened with tears. "I know if Marshall thought he could save her, he would do whatever it took. I'd do the same for my Faye, just as I know you boys would for your women." Clark's voice grew abruptly hoarse. "Marsh tried to take Arrow, didn't he?"

I was sobbing by then, no use trying to stifle it. I nodded confirmation of this fact, unable to speak, and Case drew me to his side, kissing my temple. I closed my eyes and rested my palm to his heartbeat, just to reassure myself. Arrow had appeared at the Rawleys' barn, saddled and agitated; none of the supplies Marshall attempted to bring with had accompanied him into the past. Arrow returning without his master was the catalyst for telling the Rawleys sooner than later.

"Marsh thought they'd be back soon," Case said. "He didn't want us to say anything until a week or so had passed, but we thought it was best to come and talk to all of you."

Glancing at Garth, Sean said, "This is like back when Cora's spirit visited you in the middle of the night. No one could explain it, but it was real. She was real."

Garth, hunched on the edge of the seat cushion, plunged both hands through his hair. His eyes shone with the tears none of us could contain. I hated to see them all this way, this rowdy, loving family who had been instrumental in raising Case, who loved him dearly. Once, I would have thought nothing could dampen the Rawleys' spirits.

Garth whispered, "You're right. Cora was real, I never doubted it. But this is just..."

"Crazy," Case finished for him. "I know, it's fucking crazy. But no less real."

"What about Derrick Yancy?" Quinn asked, leaning forward. "He talks like he *knows* these people from the past, right? Do you think he can travel through time, too?"

"That's a good point." I swiped impatiently at my tears. Derrick Yancy *did* speak of people and events from the nineteenth century with unusual familiarity. My mind clicked along, and after days of a stagnant and inept thought-flow, I welcomed the sensation. Maybe Derrick didn't just remember a past life, like the rest of us; maybe he'd actually *been* there.

Garth said, "The bastard was supposedly in Chicago for the holidays. Do you think he was...*back in time* instead?"

If it was true, it meant Derrick possessed the ability to return to the present; it meant return was possible, that there was a way back. I sat straighter. "Then how did he get back here, to 2014? He must have more control over it..."

"And why would he go in the first place?" Quinn wondered.

"When did the Yancys acquire their wealth?" Case asked, and I could hear the same thread of determination creeping into his voice. "When did they become the powerful family they are today? What do we actually know about their past?"

"Research," I whispered, and felt a small pinprick of purpose; I had always loved researching. "I'll start tomorrow. 1893 was when they founded the original corporation, in Chicago. Fallon Yancy is listed as the founder but I don't know much else."

"We'll see Derrick in court in Forsyth within the month," Clark said. "Now, more than ever, we have to prove this land is ours."

It had been at Thanksgiving, only months ago, that Derrick Yancy appeared at the Rawleys like a nightmare we'd collectively shared, carrying service of process documents claiming the acreage belonging to Clark, and Case's adjacent acreage, in actuality belonged to *his* family, and had been stolen after the murder of a man named Thomas Yancy in the late

nineteenth century. In my spotty attempts at researching this Yancy ancestor, I'd learned little about Thomas other than that he was the father
of two boys, Dredd and Fallon, and he'd fought in the Civil War. But
now I planned to renew researching him, with a vengeance.

"I will make it my business to find out," I declared. "Every bit of available information. Al will help me."

Al Howe was my boss at our little law firm in Jalesville and I loved
him dearly; Al would help me get to the bottom of this. He was a far
more decent man, and lawyer, than my own father, Jackson Gordon, and
I could admit this to myself at last. Despite hero-worshiping my dad,
attending his alma mater for law school and doing my damnedest to
please him, the wool had finally been ripped from my eyes; my dad was a
cheater, a liar, and quite possibly involved in dirty business dealings with
fellow Chicago lawyer Ron Turnbull; Ron was a partner at Turnbull
and Hinckley, a firm for which I'd nearly sold my soul to become an
employee.

Robbie, I thought, agony surging anew. Robbie's death in the wake
of Ruthie's disappearance was almost more than I could handle; I'd
been purposely avoiding dealing with it, and with the subsequent guilty
sadness.

Robbie Benson had been my classmate at Northwestern, a trust-
funded, privileged only child. We'd been rivals, then grudging friends,
and in the last few months, investigative partners. Robbie, newly employed at Turnbull and Hinckley in Chicago, had been quietly delving
into Ron's business dealings, keeping me posted with bi-weekly phone
calls or texts. Both of us were certain if we dug deeply enough we could
connect Ron to numerous heinous acts, including an attempt to kill
Case and me by ordering someone to set fire to our barn. Just before
Ruthie and Marsh disappeared, Robbie had sent me a message which I'd
kept on my phone; the text indicated he'd found something potentially
big. Something implicating Derrick's older brother, Franklin, and Ron's
wife, Christina.

But what?

And now Robbie was dead. An apparent overdose – a conclusion I did not for one fucking second swallow as truth. Discovered in his apartment in downtown Chicago; my father had called to tell me the news. I was stunned, devastated by Robbie's death. Since last autumn Robbie had proven he was a true friend, not just the spoiled, overbred rich kid – an image he'd played up in college, even if it was just to get laid, never mind grade favoring – everyone thought he was. Robbie showed me he could be moved to care about something other than himself, he'd discovered important information, and now he was gone.

I'm so sorry, Robbie, you could never know how sorry.

What the hell did you find?

Something dangerous. Something that scared Ron enough to go after you.

How is it fucking possible we live in this world – one in which the man I once idolized, the powerful lawyer I wanted to model myself after, is this much a monster?

Robbie, I'm so sorry and you'll never even know. It wasn't worth your life.

Now, hours after arriving home from Clark's, Case and I held each other in the dimness of our room, dawn tinting the sky with the gloomy pewter tones of winter. And something occurred to me as swiftly as a stomach cramp, a hundred times more painful. It had been gnawing at the back of my mind since we'd been at Clark's and now sprang for my heart.

"Case," I implored, and he heard the urgency in my voice and sat up immediately, clicking on the bedside lamp. I squinted in the sudden yellow glow.

"What is it? What is it, sweetheart?"

"That text…" My pupils adjusted to the light. I tried to swallow past the taste of bitter fear in my mouth. "Oh God, that text…"

"Tell me." His face was stark with concern. "What do you mean, baby?"

"I didn't think…" I gripped my temples, attempting to absorb my own stupidity. "Oh God, I didn't think…"

"*Patricia*," my husband insisted quietly.

"My phone," I whispered, gesturing at our dresser.

Case bounded from bed and brought me the phone. I scrolled to Robbie's last text, a message about finding something on Number One and that Fancy was smarter than he'd thought. 'Number One' was our code name for Franklin Yancy, while we referred to Christina Turnbull as 'Fancy.' What were the odds a reasonably intelligent individual looking for incriminating texts on Robbie's phone would decipher those nicknames? Worse yet, despite never using Ron's name, we'd used 'Hot Shot' at least two dozen times, and with plenty of contextual evidence; our final code name was 'Number Two,' which of course referred to Derrick and the huge chip on his shoulder.

"Look," I whispered, showing Case my response to Robbie's text. I'd sent it just before we found out about Ruthie's disappearance, just before Dad had called to tell me Robbie was dead; Robbie was already gone when I sent the message, which of course I hadn't known then, and his phone could very well be in the current possession of Ron Turnbull. I moaned, "Oh Jesus, *Case…*"

My reply to Robbie read, *Unless of course you actually found something!*

Dust coated my tongue. Case reread both messages. He sank to the bed beside me. "Who do you think might have Robbie's phone? Who might have read this?"

I shook my head miserably. "I don't know. I'll call Dad later this morning. He asked if we wanted to come to the funeral so I have to call him anyway. Dad said Asher and Stella – that's Robbie's parents – would like to see some of his friends from college."

Case inhaled slowly and rested his hand on my back; the simple gesture served to calm me, to let me know he was here, and would never fail to be here. My gratitude for this was overwhelming, striking at me like hail, or ocean breakers preceding a storm. I thought, *Why does life have to be so fucking precarious?*

Why did the fear of losing Case stab at my sense of security?

We'd already been down that road; again I was dragged to the nightmare I'd experienced at his bedside last August, when he'd been recovering from smoke inhalation and heart surgery, when he'd almost been taken from me. In my recurring nightmare, Case was shot in the stomach and dying before my eyes, literally on my lap, and I was able to do exactly nothing. I could scream until my throat was shredded, fight until

I fell to the ground, but nothing could stop his blood from pouring forth over my thighs.

"I have…*to throw up*…" I gagged, stumbling for the bathroom.

Case held my hair away from my damp face as I retched, gripping the toilet seat with both hands. In between bouts of puking, I apologized profusely. Case didn't try to stop either from happening; when I was finally still, and silent, he helped me to the shower, climbing in with me, stripping my lone pajama top and gathering up the new showerhead we'd had installed, one on a long extension, using it to cleanse my sweating body.

He did so with no words, the sweetness of his tender actions speaking for him, as was typical. I shuddered with quiet sobs; the warm water rippled over us as Case held me with one strong hand on the small of my back. Once I was sufficiently soaked, he replaced the showerhead and lathered me with coconut-scented soap from the pump bottle shoved in a corner of our tiny bathtub. His touch was so very gentle; the water was now blocked by his broad back, his red-gold hair damp from the overspray, droplets purling on his chest muscles. I studied his face, this man I had loved in many lifetimes. I knew not to question this truth; it just *was*. He carefully rinsed my skin, running the showerhead up and down my body. At last he bent to one knee, grasping my hips with both hands.

He rested his cheek on my belly, near my navel, and I looked down at him kneeling there, feeling like my heart might crack apart. His skin had paled with the winter months; even his wide shoulders were lightly scattered with small auburn freckles. I had spent many an hour kissing every last one. I slipped my fingers in his wet hair and held him close to my body, wishing I never had to let go, that we could stand here in the warm water, touching like this, until the earth simply turned to dust around us. There were so many fucking dangers out there; I battled an encompassing sense of vulnerability and dread. My knees nearly buckled. It was too much – this week had been too much.

"Thank you," I whispered after a time, and Case gave me his sweet smile.

"C'mon, baby, I'll make us some breakfast," he whispered.

Chapter Thirteen

I HADN'T YET TOLD MY FATHER I BELIEVED ROBBIE HAD been murdered – for one thing, it was so bizarre. And it hurt so much to consider this truth. The very notion remained sticky in my mind, coated by unreality, like something watched in a popular but disturbing television show. And secondly, I didn't think Dad could handle this theory, nor would he have any context for accepting it unless I told him far more than I currently considered prudent. Besides, Dad was too worried about Ruthie to discuss anything else; he was ready to catch the next flight to Montana.

"Your mother knows more than she's telling me," Dad said when we spoke on the phone, and he sounded as though he was barely hanging on; my heart bumped in sympathy. As angry as I was with my father of late, I acknowledged the sincerity of his pain.

"She doesn't," I said, with gentle insistence; guilty irony hammered at me, as I was the one who knew more than I was telling him. "Dad, we're all in shock but there's nothing you can do here. And there's an investigation underway." Sheriffs from both Montana and North Dakota were on the case, as we'd been informed yesterday. Of course they wouldn't find a thing; even if I shouted the truth to the mountaintops visible out my back window, no law enforcement officers would believe a word. How could they?

I realized Dad was crying and my stomach plunged. I pleaded, "Dad, it's all right."

"It's not all right!" he yelled. "My baby is missing. My baby girl is missing."

Dad gave over to weeping. He wasn't normally one for overt emotional displays and a small part of me reflected Dad really did love us; maybe the shallow, jerk-like things he routinely did, such as sleeping with married women and cheating on his wife, weren't the *real* him. I thought, *Please don't let him be involved in Ron's illegal shit. Please...*

"It all went wrong when you moved to Landon," Dad mumbled, as though thinking aloud. His nose was plugged, I could tell, and I could hardly bear to listen to him sound this way, my ultra-confident and poised father. As though I didn't know what he meant, he continued passionately, "When Joelle took you girls from me and I had no more control of your lives. Your mother set a terrible example, marrying that *goddamn criminal*, letting Camille get pregnant and you and Ruthann run wild."

"Dad!" I half-yelled. "*Stop.* This isn't Mom's fault. How can you think that? We didn't run wild. And Blythe isn't a criminal, he's a really – "

"He's an ex-convict!" Dad railed, interrupting me. I pictured him roughing up his perfect hair, standing it on end. "If not for your mother's influence, you'd be a *lawyer in Chicago* where you belong, working for a successful firm instead of wasting your life in that godforsaken cow town."

"Dad!" I yelled again, aggravated by his preposterous insults, and Case came into the bedroom from the kitchen, concerned about the level of anger in my tone. I forced myself to inhale a deep breath, holding the phone outward so my husband could hear the steady stream of Dad's frustrated rage.

It finally occurred to Dad that I wasn't listening and he demanded, "Patricia!"

I brought the phone cautiously to my ear. "I'm here." With my eyes I told Case it was all right, and he nodded and left me alone in the room.

"I'm sorry," Dad whispered after a pause. "I haven't been to work since last week. I'm a fucking mess. Are you coming to Robbie's funeral?"

"I don't know," I hedged.

"Please come," Dad said. He never pleaded and it struck me deeply. The last thing I wanted to do was venture to Chicago, let alone be in the same physical space as Ron Turnbull. Would the son of a bitch actually show up at Robbie's service? But of course he would, I reflected; Robbie had been his employee, *his acquisition*. It would be in the poorest of poor taste to avoid the funeral. If I was there maybe I could discover who was in possession of Robbie's phone. I could look into Ron's calculating eyes and judge for myself if he was capable of murder in addition to shady business deals and probably a thousand other crimes that would never be discovered.

But is it too risky? What if Ron tries to hurt you?

He can reach you in Montana just as easily. If that fucker wants to harm you or anyone you love, he can do so whether you're in Chicago or Jalesville.

My spine felt like cold, slimy jelly at this realization.

Dad whispered, "I would really like to see you. And call me if anything new happens, if anyone learns a thing."

"I will, Dad," I promised, and hung up before he could say another word.

I dialed Camille immediately after. She knew where I thought Ruthie really was and that Marshall had gone after her. I imagined my older sister, whose face and voice were an irreplaceable part of my earliest memories. Camille and I understood things that our mother, as dear and open-minded as she was, could not. Further, Camille and her husband, Mathias Carter, had plenty of proof that the past was alive, all around us, even if we were not always aware; they were certain they'd loved each other in numerous other lives. My sister picked up after the third ring and I could hear the usual activity of her busy household in the background as she answered by asking, "Any news?"

"No." I sank to the edge of the bed. "Nothing yet. I just talked to Dad."

"Shit," my sister said in response, needing no further explanation. "He keeps calling Mom and does nothing but yell at her. She couldn't stop crying yesterday. Blythe is so worried. Like he needs another reason to hate Dad! It's been so horrible the past few days."

"I miss you," I whispered. "I just want to see you."

"I know, I miss you too." In her best big-sister voice she demanded,

"Are you taking care of yourself? Getting enough rest? I called Case last night to make sure and he said you were eating and sleeping, and I don't *think* he'd lie to me..."

"He wouldn't. And I am, I promise."

"I'm so sorry about your friend in Chicago." Camille paused and in the background I could hear Lorie, her second-youngest, singing a song to the baby; the sound was one of total innocence and made my stomach cramp even worse. My sister whispered in a rush, "Tish, I'm so scared. I've been...oh God, I've been having nightmares again. I can't even tell Thias because I know he'd be too worried, and we all have too much to worry about right now." She used her special nickname for Mathias and I knew she referred to the terrible dreams that had plagued her years ago, before their wedding. Dreams in which Mathias died too early, their souls subsequently torn from one another's.

"I've been having the same kind of nightmares," I confessed. "Like everything is insubstantial, like it could all just disappear from beneath us and there's nothing we can do to stop it."

"Don't say that," Camille begged. I swore I could see her despite the distance separating us; she turned abruptly away from the peaceful wintertime scene out the window of the century-old cabin Mathias had painstakingly restored for their family. I saw the way her eyes roved desperately over their children, as clearly as if I stood beside her; Millie Jo and the twins, Brantley and Henry, would be at school, but the little ones were home with her.

And I saw the way my sister's face tightened with agony as she imagined them disappearing, her life with her true love and the family they'd made simply vanishing irretrievably, like water down a crack in the earth. She could crawl after it, scrape at the ground until her fingernails tore away, but that water would not come back in this lifetime. Camille's horror was so intense I felt it as strongly as if I'd been struck in the mouth with a closed fist.

"Milla," I said sharply, using her oldest nickname. "Listen to me. Ruthie went back for a reason we can't understand, but we have to trust it was for something important." And I was certain of this, selfishly letting it comfort me even as my heart ached for our little sister, our sweet Ruthann. What was being asked of her, wherever she was right now? I whispered, with considerable awe, "Imagine if she's meeting all of them as we speak. Cole Spicer and Grant Rawley…"

"And Malcolm," my sister whispered. "Malcolm is there too, I know he is. Oh God, she could have *spoken with him*…"

"She'll tell him how happy you are," I said. "Oh, Milla, he'll finally *know*."

I could hear her muffled weeping and pictured her pressing one hand to her mouth. She gulped and struggled for control, finally whispering, "Oh God, I pray so. I mean, you know I don't really pray, but you know what I mean."

"I do. Of course I do."

"I'm trying to accept all of this, I really am. But what if Ruthie can't get back? What if she's stuck there or Marshall doesn't find her? I've been trying so hard not to think like that, but I have that feeling again, like I did back in 2006, that something horrible is right around the bend, *right behind me*. Oh God, *Tish*…" She turned back to the frosty window in her living room, I didn't know how I knew this, but I saw her in my mind's eye as she touched her fingertips to its smooth surface, hoping the shock of the cold glass would restore her senses. I moved at once to the window that faced east, toward Minnesota, and pressed my fingertips against the pane, too. I imagined our hands making contact across the distance.

"I can feel you out there," Camille whispered. "You're touching the window, aren't you?"

I nodded, knowing she heard me even without words.

Case and I flew into O'Hare in the evening hours of Friday the twenty-first. We descended through a cloudbank that seemed a mile thick, Case with his shoulders tensed and lips clamped (he hated flying), while I sat near the tiny window and fought off sickly waves of claustrophobia. I had never been one for worrying on a flight, but each turbulent dip, however minute, seemed ominous. After much deliberation, Case had agreed to us making the trip; I felt I owed it to Robbie, even though he'd never know either way, and I wanted to see Ron Turnbull with my own eyes, wanted to get a read on his despicable face.

Fat chance. He's a goddamn lawyer.

"I can't believe I ever wanted to live here," I murmured to my husband, clutching his arm as we entered the enormous gateway where Dad and Lanny, his wife, were supposed to be waiting. O'Hare was overwhelming with noise and bustle, same as always, and even though the city was not visible through the towering glass windows I was already homesick for Jalesville and our trailer with its view of the foothills, where the sun set over the pine-studded ridge and I could journey out to the barn in the twilight, the cats at my ankles, to give Cider and Buck one last pat, one last kiss on a velvet nose, before bed.

"It makes me want to throw you over my shoulder and get us the hell out of here," Case agreed, his gaze sweeping the humming crowd. He leaned down and nuzzled my hair, murmuring, "I miss the horses already."

"I was just thinking about them."

"You sit, baby, and I'll get our bag." We were flying home on Sunday, the day after the funeral. Case had just disappeared in the direction of the baggage claim when I spied my father hurrying through the crowd.

Dad, I thought painfully.

He reached me before I managed to stand, hauling me into a hug, rocking me side to side, cupping the back of my head the way he used to when I was a little girl. I remembered the last time I'd met Dad here at the airport, last July when I'd flown from Montana to take the bar exam, when I'd been obsessively wearing Case's jean jacket, before I'd admitted my feelings for him. That particular summer day, my father had appeared his usual tasteful self, clad in meticulous designer duds and with his dark curls artfully styled. He looked terrible this evening, like maybe he hadn't showered in a couple of days, wearing faded old jeans and – I did an instant double take – ratty tennis shoes, these paired with his black Givenchy leather coat. In that instant I knew Lanny had left him.

"Tish," he said quietly. There were shadows beneath his eyes and he hadn't shaved in a week. He was almost unrecognizable. "I'm so glad you're here, hon. Where's Case?"

"He went to get our bag." I decided not to ask about Lanny just now.

"How are you feeling?" Dad asked. He rocked back on his heels and for a second I was afraid he might tumble over. I was so concerned I reached for his wrists, intending to hold him steady; he misunderstood and caught my hands in his, tears welling in his eyes.

I said, "Dad," hearing the way my voice sounded higher than usual, as if I'd suddenly reverted to a preteen pitch.

"I'm all right," he said, understanding the frightened question I'd asked with that one word, but his tone contradicted the reassurance.

Case returned, toting our suitcase, which he set to the side and reached to shake hands with Dad; the last time they'd been in each other's company was the night of the fire in our barn, when Dad had met Case for the first time. Dad surprised both of us when he disregarded Case's extended hand and hugged him instead. Dad wasn't quite as tall as my husband and I had the odd sense that Case was hugging a child rather than an adult, bestowing far more comfort than he received. It was the strangeness of the whole situation getting to me, the unreal quality of the entire trip.

"Come on, let's get you guys home." Dad drew away and passed a hand over his eyes. He tried for a little of his old self as he added, "We can order takeout if you're hungry, you two. Anywhere in the city, my treat."

"Thanks, Dad," I said, sweating in my down-filled jacket. I felt protective of him, afraid for him, and it was a horrible feeling. I lied, "I am pretty hungry."

In the cab I did my best to keep a steady stream of conversation rolling; it was otherwise too excruciating to deal with Dad when he was like this. I felt all twisted up, sick inside at what Ruthie's disappearance was doing to all of us. And Robbie weighed heavily on my mind, especially now that we were in the city where most of my memories of him were centered. I was grateful our route would not take us past the apartment

I'd once shared with my fellow Northwestern classmates Grace and Ina, just a few doors down from the bar where the three of us routinely met Robbie for drinks – Robbie, with his gigantic ego and charming, effortless smile. Robbie, with his head full of spy movies and secret codes and David-and-Goliath-like visions of grandeur.

A planet-sized sphere of despair was waiting to descend onto my shoulders but I fought it away. Despite the February chill I was sweating in triple-time now. I told Case, clinging to the security of his hand, "That's where I went to grade school, that building over there." He lifted my hand and kissed my knuckles, and I could sense him marveling anew that I had once been a part of the bright glare of this city, that I had once called it home. I shuddered at the thought; referring to the little brick elementary school in Jalesville, I said, "Blooming Rock seems a lot friendlier, doesn't it?"

Dad's condo was more of the same, but I was prepared. I battled the sharp urge to gather up his dirty dishes and begin sorting laundry; I knew he employed a cleaning service, but still. It was a ghost town inside, no sign of Lanny, but since Dad wasn't offering an explanation, I didn't ask. By the time Case and I were blessedly alone in the spare room, chill and unwelcoming with its taupe designer sheets stretched crisply taut over a king-sized bed, I was about to crack apart. I locked the door and stripped almost aggressively free of every last scrap of clothing, tossing aside my bra with especial vengeance.

"What the hell?" I muttered, cupping my breasts and massaging the red grooves left by the underwire. I swore they'd grown in circumference in the past week; I reasoned that my period was due any moment.

Case sat on the edge of the mattress and held out his arms. I melted into his embrace and he took us backward onto the bed, resting his chin on the top of my head. I pressed my nose to his neck and curved my thigh over his hip, taking pleasure in the familiar scent of his skin; he wore a threadbare t-shirt and boxer-briefs, nothing else, his typical evening attire. He curled one hand beneath my bent knee, rubbing with his thumb, and whispered, "I'm here, baby. I'm right here."

"Oh God, what if he suffered?" I heard myself blubber, my voice a rough and choking whimper. "What if they hurt him before he died?"

Case's chest expanded with a deep breath and I knew I'd caught him off guard by asking; I could tell he didn't know how to answer. He wouldn't sink to pacifying me, but neither did he want to confirm the likely truth. At last he said, "It was probably quick."

"I hope so," I whispered, banishing images of Robbie in his apartment during his last minutes, struggling with an intruder, probably a couple of intruders, who'd pinned him down and then...*and then...*

"I don't want to be here," I moaned. "I hate this place. But my dad..."

"He's in bad shape," Case agreed. "I'm so sorry, sweetheart. Do you think his wife..."

"I do," I whispered, huffing on a restrained sob. "She's long gone."

"I know he was messing around on her, but I still feel for him. Does he have friends here? Anyone he could call if he gets too depressed?"

"I don't know," I whispered. "Not many, I don't think. He's always been so busy with his job."

"No job is that important," Case said, low and adamant.

"None," I agreed, and stripped my husband of his remaining clothing, needing to feel his heart beating against mine.

Chapter Fourteen

THE FUNERAL WAS HELD IN ST. HELEN'S CHAPEL IN THE gloom of a cloudy late-afternoon and the casket was closed. I thanked God for small favors, not sure if I could have held it together if confronted with Robbie's embalmed face. I was struggling enough as it was; my breath shallow and my pulse erratic even with Case's steady arm around my waist, I stared blankly at the mass of mostly-unfamiliar faces, recognizing only Robbie's parents, both litigators at Damon and Benson. Asher, somber and immaculate in a three-piece suit, quietly greeted guests while Stella, ghostly and drawn, hovered near the coffin, supported by a woman who resembled her closely, likely a sister. Robbie had been the Bensons' only child.

Dad led us to a walnut pew on the left side of the chapel, speaking very little despite the fact he probably knew far more attendees than I did. He patted my knee once we were seated and whispered, "Doing all right?"

I nodded and tucked my hand around Case's bicep; my husband sat with a protective angle to his shoulders, solemn and imposing, as if daring anyone to send a threatening look my way. I realized, however ridiculously, that I'd never seen Case in a tie.

"I don't remember my mom's very well," Case had told me last night as we curled together in the guestroom bed; we'd been discussing the funerals of our past. He murmured, "I was eight, old enough to have it in my memory but I was so devastated I blocked it out, I think. And my dad didn't have a service, never wanted one. He was cremated after he died. Gus and I scattered his ashes up in the mountains."

"I remember my great-grandma's," I'd whispered. "Gran died the summer we moved to Landon, over ten years ago, but I still miss her. I can still see her, and hear her voice. She was a lady not to be crossed."

"Just like the woman I'm in love with," Case murmured, resting his lips against my temple.

Later he'd said, "Faye's funeral is the worst one in my past. It was like losing my mother all over again. It was so sad. I couldn't handle my own sadness, let alone anyone else's. And she died so unexpectedly. One morning she was alive and by that afternoon she'd been hit by a truck on the interstate. I know that's why Marsh was so worried about Ruthie driving alone to Minnesota. He's never gotten over his mom getting killed so sudden like that."

"I know," I whispered, resting my forehead against his jaw as we snuggled beneath the covers. "I really do. I don't blame him. I was overreacting that day, I was so scared."

"Ruthie was already out of the car before the crash, she *had* to have been," Case said. We'd discussed this already, reaching no satisfactory conclusion. We could only speculate, using the extremely limited information in our possession. Building on an earlier discussion, he added, "It was the life or death situation. I think she disappeared from her car because her life was in danger."

"Just like the man in our barn that night, last August," I murmured.

"Exactly. The seatbelt was still hooked but Ruthie wasn't in it, right? That makes me think her disappearance was just as accidental as the car losing control on the snow. As accidental as touching those letters Una Spicer wrote. And those letters were still buried in the trunk in our trailer that night. Ruthie didn't have them. The past *wanted* her to come but she didn't intend to go, not right then."

It made sense; at least more sense than anything else we had to go on at this point. I whispered, "Ruthie meant to drive to Minnesota, she was headed *to* Landon. She would never purposely hurt us, even if she was angry as hell. Oh God, what if…"

"Marshall will find her. He won't rest until he does," Case said, and I'd let the certainty in his voice comfort, if not convince, me.

Dad's quiet greeting to someone approaching our pew dragged my focus back to the here and now, sitting stiffly in this ornate Catholic chapel as a grim evening encroached on the reds and blues of the window glass. It was phantasmal; I half-expected Robbie to pull a Tom Sawyer and appear at his own funeral. He'd wait for everyone to get settled, maybe let a few people begin crying delicately into their hankies before waltzing down the long central aisle to flank his own coffin. He'd scan the crowd, then laugh and say, *Well. It's nice to see who really gives a damn about me.*

"Jackson," said an unexpected voice, one I recognized all too well; Case's attention snapped in the same direction.

My father rose, unaware of our bristling ire. Derrick Yancy, however, was well aware and did not dare to come any closer than the far end of the row, leaning to shake Dad's hand while bracing against the top of the pew with his other. Derrick was unpleasantly familiar and his gaze settled on me, as it invariably did, before flickering nervously away. And then right back. I refused to give him the satisfaction of fidgeting or appearing in any other way uncomfortable.

"Derrick," Dad acknowledged, his back to us.

If you ask him to join us I will make a scene like you've never seen, I warned my father without words.

Derrick nodded at Case and me; despite his pristine appearance and the fact that he was an expert at hiding it I could tell he'd been drinking.

"Jackie, good to see you," said another man two rows back, commandeering my father's attention. This man carried on, "Such a shame under these circumstances, though. Robert was a good boy. A fine boy. No one saw this coming."

Dad gritted his teeth, muttering, "Excuse me, I'll be right back," and stepped to the end of the row, nodding at Derrick as he slipped past him.

Derrick continued standing there like one of the stone pillars; searching my face, he said quietly, "Patricia. Are you well?"

Case all but gritted his teeth but kept his voice likewise low. "You're on my *last nerve*, Yancy."

Ignoring the menace in Case's tone, Derrick advanced a step. "I'd like to talk to you."

"You can't," I said at once, wanting only to diffuse the situation. When he appeared puzzled by my words, I elaborated, "We're engaged in court proceedings with you. It would be a conflict of interest."

Derrick's attention was snagged by someone behind us; turning, I caught sight of the Turnbulls approaching. Ron's silver hair took on the hues of the primary colors in the stained glass adorning the chapel and Christina's breasts led the way, as usual, her sleek hair smoothed to a glossy waterfall over her tanned bare shoulders. Her gown was uncharacteristically conservative and I watched as her smoky-shadowed eyes fluttered to the casket; was there a hint of sincere emotion on her flawless face? I suddenly realized that while she bore no other resemblance to my mother, her coloring was just the same – green eyes, golden-brown skin, golden hair. A wintry chill clutched at my spine; was this why Dad had been initially drawn to her?

Neither she nor Ron had seen me yet.

Immediately I sought my father, determined to gauge his reaction to Christina; she glanced his way and her composure took a noticeable nosedive. I watched heat climb her face. Her haughty expression did not alter but she was obviously flustered and I thought of Robbie saying, *It's all Jackson, all the time*, in reference to Christina. My stomach bottomed out a few more inches.

Dad was still chatting with the couple two rows back and didn't pause in his conversation; his gaze held Christina's and even if I'd had no suspicions regarding their extramarital activities until just this moment, all doubts would be erased; something was broiling between them. Dad had shaved, combed his hair, and was wearing a suit, but there were deep shadows beneath his eyes. He looked abruptly away, mouth twisting in an expression I recognized as disdain. Christina's face drained of color but I didn't know her well enough to determine if she was angry or ashamed.

I realized Ron had continued down the center aisle without his wife and paused at the end of our row.

"Ms. Gordon." Ron spoke with contrived politeness, ignoring both

Case and Derrick. "How good to see you."

I mustered my lawyer voice. "My *name* is Patricia Spicer."

"My mistake," Ron said.

You killed him, didn't you? The sensation of being cornered increased, sitting in a pew bracketed by Derrick and Ron. *Why? What did Robbie know? What dirt did he dig up on you, you fucking bastard?*

Ron's eyes bore into mine. "Pity about Benson. Smart boy. I hate to see a smart boy go so quickly downhill. Pressures of the job, I suppose."

All the air in the chapel was siphoned away. Despite the intensity of my desire to stride over to the older man and claw at his smug face, I understood that now, more than ever, I could not react. It was most certainly what Ron wanted – for me to lose my cool, to inadvertently admit I'd been part of Robbie's undercover activities at Turnbull and Hinckley. I understood right then that Ron had Robbie's phone; he'd seen the incriminating message from me. And I saw in his predatory eyes the confidence of his own authority, his unchallenged assumption of power. I was less than nothing to him, a trifling young woman, easily eliminated if the need arose.

And he was reading me right now for that very reason, searching for a need.

Christina slithered to Ron's side before I could respond. Ron's mouth lifted in a smile but his eyes were deadly. Christina did not look our way, instead tugging impatiently at her husband's elbow. I watched in silence as the Turnbulls continued to the casket to greet Asher and Stella, Ron the picture of solicitous sympathy. I felt like a pitiful little goldfish chucked into an ocean crammed with writhing eels and sleek, darting sharks; the water all around me foamed and churned with predators. Sweat beaded over my skin. The service was about to start, people shuffling to their seats. I watched the priest climbing the elevated altar, lifting the hem of his long white robe like he would an ankle-length skirt.

"I can't…" I turned desperately to Case.

He was pale, his eyebrows crooked in an expression of barely-contained horror. I didn't finish the statement but he understood, gathering our outerwear and leading me from the chapel. I didn't glance at Dad as we passed him, concentrating on nothing but getting to the door that allowed escape. Outside, I gulped deep breaths of cold February air as Case wrapped me first in my coat and then into his arms. He helped me down the front steps and then drew us to the side of the immense stone building. Sheltered against him, thick white snowflakes dusting our heads, I clung to my husband and inhaled his scent, which smelled of home. Of our dear little home in Jalesville, which we should not have left. Where we might not be safe from this point forward.

"It's all right," Case kept saying. He pressed his mouth to my hair and his body was so very warm and solid, his arms anchoring me to reality.

"It's not all right," I gasped. "Oh God, we shouldn't be here…"

"I will never let anything happen to you," Case said with quiet ferocity, lifting my chin. Even in the gloom of the snowy evening the flecks of auburn were apparent in his dear, beautiful eyes. I could see his breath in the cold air. I wanted to beg, *But what about you? Will you let anything happen to you?*

He cupped my shoulders. "Those assholes think they're above the law, but they're not. We'll prove their claim on our land is false, along with Clark."

I wanted so badly to believe what he said was possible. "But they have so much power, it scares me so much…did you see Ron's face…"

"If we think like that, we've already lost." Case stared deeply into my eyes. "You are the bravest woman I know, and the most determined. We will see this through together, I swear to you."

"But what if…"

The double doors at the top of the steps opened and Derrick appeared between them; it was obvious he was looking for us.

Case's shoulders squared. "What the hell do you want, Yancy?"

Apparently this terse question did not register; Derrick stepped all the way outside without responding, his sharp features softened by the gloaming light. Cars scrolled past on the busy four-lane, headlights beaming, wipers scraping aside the falling snow; Derrick studied the traffic as if confused. As though he wasn't sure in this moment exactly where he was; I thought of Case telling me, not too long ago, that

Derrick had no one in the world to care about him. *Arrogant, entitled, devious* – all words I would use to describe Derrick. But was he evil? Was he like Ron? Or was he truly an unloved second son, desiring so badly to get his father's attention he was willing to do anything required?

I hated myself for feeling a flicker of sympathy.

Derrick looked away from the traffic and blinked a couple of times, refocusing. He'd left the chapel without his coat or scarf and snow fell on his suit jacket, on his uncovered head. And then, sudden as a wind gust, urgency radiated from him. He descended the stone steps at a jog, peering down the sidewalk behind Case and me; I resisted the desire to look over my shoulder. One stair from the snowy ground he stopped, his breath creating a steam cloud in the cold air. He said, "You two should go."

Case met my eyes and asked without speaking, *What the hell?*

Thinking of the conversation I'd tried to initiate with Derrick last autumn, in the parking lot of The Spoke on the night of Marshall's birthday party, I responded to my husband, *Give me a second here.*

Keeping my tone neutral, I asked, "Why is that?"

Instead of answering, Derrick's eyes detoured to my stomach. Extending a solicitous hand toward me, just short of making physical contact, he whispered, "When is the baby due?"

A deep, hostile sound issued from Case's throat at the same instant a strange, powerful rush of awareness hammered at my senses. That night last autumn, Derrick had also mentioned a child.

Driven by instinct, I played along. "In November."

Derrick looked between our faces, his own pale and grim; he was on the very precipice of revelation. Despite the chill winter air, fresh sweat beaded on my skin. My heart accelerated with each breath but now was not the time to lose control. I scoured my mind for anything I could use and then it occurred to me. *Franklin doesn't exist.* Robbie's last text suggested he'd found something on Franklin. Growing desperate, I grabbed Derrick's forearm and played my ace card. "Why would you say your brother doesn't exist?"

Derrick froze, eyes becoming ice chips – but they were fixated on something down the sidewalk.

"Charles and Patricia Spicer," someone said from behind us. "Leaving so soon?"

Case and I turned to see a stranger approaching through the falling snow, tall and slender and with the sort of superficial, angular features seen on men in expensive cologne advertisements. He wore a charcoal greatcoat and matching scarf but no hat over his blond hair. His eyes were pale and penetrating. He stopped with two squares of sidewalk concrete between our bodies and I squinted in confusion, struck by the sense that I'd seen him before. He'd addressed us with barely-concealed derision.

"Who are you?" Case demanded, angling in front of me.

"Why do you ask, Charles?"

"How *the fuck* do you know my name? Answer me."

The man's repellent smile only widened.

I hardly recognized Derrick's voice as he asked, "What are you doing here?"

That was all it took for me to understand; I realized I'd once seen his picture on a brochure for their company, Capital Overland. Elusive older brother, *Number One*, the reason for Derrick's inferiority complex. It hadn't occurred to me he might appear at Robbie's funeral, but of course the Yancy home base was in Chicago. I looked for their father but no one else was in sight. Just an empty sidewalk, dusted by snow and his striding footprints. I felt the first stab of fear.

Before I could bite my tongue I whispered, "Franklin."

At the sound of his name his upper lip lifted just slightly, not quite a sneer.

Derrick hadn't moved from his perch on the steps. With more insistence in his tone he repeated, "What are you doing here?"

Franklin's eyes flicked to his brother. A bluish glow emanating from a nearby streetlight made blades of his cheekbones and his eyes were as remote as a reptile's, but he was flesh and blood, standing before us. Existing, as it were.

You two should go, Derrick had said. He'd attempted to warn us.

"Far from home, aren't you?" Franklin asked, addressing Case. "Dirt grubbers don't much like to leave their dirt, isn't that so?"

Case seemed constructed of cement; he'd shifted so that I was behind him, shoulders rigid with tension. Though every bit as mystified by this bizarre confrontation, I sensed Case's measured calculation – gauging each movement, each potential threat. He refused to dignify the question with a response.

Franklin's attention swung my way; studying me like a scientist would a lab rat, amusement gained the upper hand in his expression. He wasn't a physically imposing man; slim and fine-boned, his features almost delicate in structure – but then something stirred in the depths of his pale irises and my bowels turned to ice.

He said, "*Patricia.* You haven't changed a bit."

"Back the fuck off, *now*," Case said, but Franklin ignored this command.

My lips were stiff and cold, rendering me unable to reply. Franklin's tone oozed with both familiarity and contempt; what the hell did he mean, I hadn't changed a bit? He'd never met me before this moment.

Unless...

My brain churned through a dozen fragments of information, struggling to make a whole.

Franklin doesn't exist.

Derrick tried to warn us. He told us we should go.

He's dangerous, Derrick had said last autumn, and I thought he'd meant Ron – but maybe he was referring to Franklin. I sensed more than saw Derrick descending the final step to the sidewalk. The tension in the air grew dense, compressing my lungs. My skull seemed to be vibrating to a low-pitched frequency. But it was no time to be a coward.

Franklin doesn't exist...

I located my voice, braved Franklin's eyes, and took a chance. "What year were you born?"

A flicker of discomposure – but nothing more. A smile exposed his teeth and his tone became almost conversational. "It's the eyes, I suppose. You can always tell a whore by her eyes."

Case had Franklin in a headlock and on his knees almost before I could blink. Franklin struggled, grunting and cursing, elbows flying; his greatcoat gaped and I saw what Case was angled wrong to notice – a small black pistol in a holster strapped around his waist. The world shifted in a slow-motion phantasm; my ankles seemed chained to the ground even as a detailed image of what I must do – lunge and grab that gun before Franklin could use it – formed in my head. There was a flurry of movement from the corner of my eye, which didn't shape itself into sense until Derrick, on the same intercept course, took Franklin flat to the cold pavement. Snow lay in thick swirls and Derrick's momentum propelled their bodies a solid yard. Struck in the hip by Derrick's shoulder, Case was jerked sideways, quickly righting himself.

I cried, "No!" and grabbed for him, terrified he would return to the fight.

But he had no intention of doing that, instead grabbing me around the waist. We fled. Cars continued scrolling along the busy street, headlights beaming through the gray light; no one paid us any attention even though I could hear Derrick and Franklin shouting furiously at each other, somewhere behind us. We didn't slow down until we'd rounded a corner and dashed across two lanes. I tried to believe someone would have stopped had there been a shot fired.

"He had a gun…" My words and breath were all tangled together. I bent forward, straining to draw a lungful. I was wearing heeled boots and my ankles ached; my thoughts latched onto stupid things like my feet so they wouldn't fixate on what might have happened if Franklin Yancy had drawn his pistol.

Case, shot in the gut, dying, his blood soaking my lap…

A low, aching groan escaped my lips and I dove into Case's arms, holding him as tightly as I was able and pressing my nose to his chest, overtaken by sobs. St. Helen's chapel remained in view but we were well away, blending with those exiting shops and cafes to hail taxis. Case sheltered me, easing to the side of a brick building, keeping us out of the bright, oblong square thrown by the business's interior lighting.

"It's all right," he said. I could feel the trembling deep in his muscles but he kept his voice steady. "It's all right."

"He had a gun…"

Case waited for me to calm before getting us a taxi. Dad's condo was dark and cold on this winter's night, the vivid glitter of downtown Chicago the only illumination in the place, perfectly framed by the unadorned picture windows. I groped for a light switch. Case strode through the living room, shedding both his overcoat and suit jacket, yanking loose his tie; once in the spare bedroom, he began cramming our clothes into the travel bag. He was upset, jerking through his movements with none of his usual grace; away from immediate danger and having regained a tentative hold on my emotions, I watched in silence, not sure if offering to help would soothe him or only add fuel to the fire. I braced a hand on the leather loveseat and bent my right leg, slowly unzipping my boot; the sound seemed as loud as a buzz saw.

At last his frenzied energy propelled him to the doorway between the two rooms, where he grasped the frame on either side. Pinning me with his gaze, he rasped, "I'm so sorry."

"It's –"

"Don't tell me it's all right," he requested harshly. "Don't pacify me, oh God, I can't bear it. I'm angry at myself, not you, and I'm so goddamn sorry."

"Case, listen to me…"

"You ran into the barn after me!" His words fell like halves of a split log, husky and raw. "You ran into a burning barn to save me when I should have been the one saving *you*. Oh Jesus, sweetheart, I can't bear what could have happened. Just the thought fucking destroys me. It's my job to protect you. I love you so goddamn much, I've longed for you for so long now, even when you didn't know it, *for so many years…*"

"I'm right here," I whispered, hating how he was punishing himself. "I'm not the girl in a picture anymore and I will *never be her again*, the girl who's distant from you and who doesn't know how much you love her. I'm here with you and *I love you*. You are the love of my *lifetimes*, Case. *Come here.*" He closed the distance between us, wrapping me in the security of his arms. Tears blurred my sight as I whispered, "It's like everything around us is threatened, like everything we know could just vanish. Camille feels the same way."

"I know, I've talked to Mathias about it." Case rocked me side to side; my eyes were closed and he softly kissed each one, as he was often inclined to do. I spread one hand on his warm, lean belly, reassuring myself it was intact; no bullet hole leaking blood had appeared there. I heaved a shuddering sigh, possessively closing my fist around the material of his shirt, and he buried both hands in my hair.

"C'mere," he murmured, lifting my chin, the soft sounds of invitation rising from my throat caught between our mouths. He bracketed my jaws and tilted my head, our tongues joining and stroking. Shifting, he scooped me into his arms without breaking our kiss and carried me to the couch. I had just yanked the bottom of Case's shirt from his pants when I heard my father in the outer hallway, the keypad beeping as he engaged the code and threw open the door.

"Dad," I said lamely.

Case discreetly withdrew his right hand from beneath my long black skirt, drawing the hem safely south and resituating, keeping me on his lap but in a less intimate position.

Dad stormed to within three feet of us and demanded, "What happened? Why did you leave so suddenly?"

"I was about to have a panic attack. I'm sorry we didn't tell you before we left, Dad, I really am."

"I left as soon as I could." Dad all but collapsed into a nearby armchair. He covered his eyes with one hand. "It was terrible, all around."

He wore his overcoat, along with a scarf and matching gloves, and I was struck by a sudden memory, an old one from many years ago, of Mom sitting on Dad's lap and helping him remove his scarf, unwinding it in a way I now realized was seductive, one slow loop at a time; it had been a winter's evening and they thought Camille and I were sleeping. Camille had been dutifully snoozing but I'd crept from our room at the sound of the front door, which meant Dad was finally home, and spied my parents kissing. Dad took the scarf from Mom's hands and draped it around her like a shawl, tugging her closer.

I'd felt so safe back then, reassured that my parents loved each other and always would. And now, sitting near my father, whose poor choices had led to him being alone, I felt a pang of stinging sympathy.

Did you pick Christina Turnbull because she looks like Mom?

I was dying to ask but couldn't bear to hear the answer.

Dad indicated the spare room. "Are you leaving?"

"By tomorrow, remember?" I said. "We want to get home."

I sensed Dad's restraint; he wanted to ask us to stay, knowing he could not. He narrowed his eyes but not in an angry way; it was an attempt to glean from my tone and posture what was really going on, just as any well-trained lawyer would.

It was now or never. "Dammit, Dad, I know about you and Christina."

Dad blinked twice. Then he stood and stalked to the kitchen, disappearing around the corner and slamming a cupboard, then the freezer door; I heard ice rattling into a glass.

"Don't walk away from me!" I leaped to my feet, stumbling over my long skirt.

Case steadied me with one hand around my hip; his eyes said, *Maybe now isn't the time...*

It has to be, I said back.

Dad reappeared, clutching a scotch. "That is none of your business!"

"It *is* my business! Don't treat me like a child. You cheated on another wife, Dad, how low can you possibly – "

Dad pointed a finger at my nose. "I am your father and you will not – "

"What does she know?" I interrupted, changing tactics, fists on hips. Case moved his hand to my lower back, patting gently; I forced a calmer tone. "What has she told you?"

"What would Christina have to tell me?" Dad spoke with a deceptively level tone, almost as if he wanted me to start listing things so he could determine what I knew. I refused to believe Dad would conceal something of magnitude, even if his mistress requested it.

Misgivings growing by the second, I whispered, "Maybe I should ask what *you* have to tell me," and sank back to the couch cushions. Case waited for Dad's reaction in complete silence; I was afraid if Dad said the wrong thing, if he'd somehow jeopardized us, I could not be responsible for my husband's actions.

"Christina and I have been seeing each other, yes," Dad admitted, cupping the nape of his neck in an ages-old gesture of defeat. He directed his gaze at the carpet. "We've been in a relationship for over a year. We're discreet. We never mention Ron. But it's over now, unequivocally."

"*Jesus Christ*, Dad. Where's Lanny? When did she leave?"

Dad closed his eyes. "Three days ago."

"Did Ron order him killed?" Unable to stop, my heart pounding like a hammer on a stubborn nail, I faced off with my father. My throat was dry and tasted metallic. "Tell me, Dad. Tell me if he ordered Robbie killed."

Dad gaped at me with genuine shock. His mouth opened and closed, then opened again as he rasped, "I hope you know if I believed that to be true, Ron couldn't hide from what I would do to him."

"Like what?" I insisted. "What the fuck would you do?"

"I'd kill him," he said tightly. "You're my daughter. For Christ's sake, Patricia, I once hoped you'd work for the man. Do you think I'd have let you work for someone I believed capable of such things?"

"You agreed he was a criminal," Case said. I could hear in his tone he believed Dad's words. He elaborated, "Last summer, in Jalesville, you told Tish that. What did you mean?"

"Ron turns a blind eye when funds are misappropriated. He's an embezzler, not a murderer." Dad sounded like he was on the witness stand.

"Does he pay you off?" I gasped.

"Of *course* not." Dad was terse, on the defensive.

"Because you're fucking his wife and don't want his suspicion directed your way!" A small, more rational part of my brain registered bald shock that I would dare speak to my father in such a manner.

Dad's eyes blazed and I tensed, ready to face his wrath. But then he deflated, sinking to his armchair and draining his scotch before asking, with quiet intensity, "What reason would Ron have to kill Robbie?"

"Because Robbie knew something." Spurred by the insanity of this entire trip, by the horrible sensation of time running out, I gripped one of the plushy arms on Dad's chair, leaning toward him. "Robbie was having an affair with her too, Dad. Did you know that?"

Dad's eyes darted between mine, *right, left, right, left,* in obvious shock.

"Do you think Ron found out about them?" I pressed. But Robbie's news, his final text, hadn't been about Ron; it had referred to Christina… and Franklin Yancy.

Dad's shock was morphing to outright horror. He rasped, "No. It can't be true. I would have known."

"How? Like either of them were planning to tell you?" I bit back the urge to really lash into him, imagining what my great-grandmother would have to say just now; Gran had never been fond of Dad. I knelt beside his chair so our faces were at the same level. "We saw Franklin Yancy tonight, at the funeral. What do you know about him? Who the hell is he, really? Why would Derrick be afraid of him?"

Dad was pale, the lines bracketing his mouth and creating grooves in his forehead appearing deep and heavily drawn. I floundered; despite my outburst of questions I wasn't sure how to proceed. Did I mention outright there was a chance the man everyone believed to be Franklin Yancy was an imposter? Which begged the question – who the hell was he? *What* was he? Someone not restricted by the usual limitations of time?

Just like Ruthann…

Without intending it, I began to weep. Dad dropped his drink, ice fanning the carpet, and leaned over the chair to hug me.

"*Ruthie,*" I sobbed, overpowered by the force of my sadness. What if we never saw her again? What if Franklin had drawn his gun and fired on Case? How did he know us well enough for such hatred?

It's because we're all connected. The answer is right in front of you.

You have to see, you have to understand…

Dad was crying too, low and devastating. "Oh God, my sweet Ruthann, my baby girl. I can't bear not knowing where she is, or if she's alive…"

Case knelt beside me, resting a hand between my shoulder blades. I swiped at my leaking eyes, overheated with agony, and met my husband's gaze. At his unspoken question, I nodded with two small bobs of my head.

And then I whispered, "Dad, we have to tell you something."

Chapter Fifteen

Montana Territory - 1881

"WE SHOULD BE THERE WITHIN THE HOUR," MILES SAID, and there was an unmistakable note of anticipation in his voice. As though he understood his master's words, Blade nickered and shook his mane. Miles patted his horse's silver neck, stroking him with the knuckle of a bent thumb. I had grown familiar with the mannerisms of both horse and rider during our journey west from Howardsville; I'd even settled on a name for my sweet little dun mare, and now called her Flickertail.

"Is that a species of moth?" Miles had asked. "Or bird?"

"Not one I've ever heard of," I said. "I just like how it sounds."

"I've never seen anything like these rock formations." I indicated southward, where a gorgeous T-shaped configuration soared out of the ground. I pictured imaginary roots, like those upholding a tree, sunk deep into the earth, anchoring it for centuries to come. The farther west we traveled the more varied the landscape, rocks stacked atop one another as though a giant playing with its toys had arranged them. The sharp scent of sagebrush hung suspended in the hot, motionless air; small pink flowers with five blossoms, which Miles told me were bitterroot, grew in thick patches along the uneven ground.

"They are quite awe-inspiring," he agreed, removing his cigar to respond. He smoked all the time; I had grown accustomed to the scent of tobacco. I'd requested a drag last night around the fire, to everyone's mild shock, and my subsequent coughing fit justified their surprise and gave us all something to laugh about. Miles continued, "That rock, in particular. I've always had an urge to camp beneath it, though Grant's homestead is so near there's no reason. Yonder," and he nodded to indicate, "is where Henry Spicer intends to stake his claim. There's some five hundred acres adjacent to Grant's land."

"You haven't thought of claiming it for yourself?" I was wearing the same clothes I'd left Branch's claim shanty in – Axton's trousers, belted with a length of rope, one of my own blouses with the sleeves rolled to elbows, my corset (which I detested with a red-hot passion, but *not* wearing it was out of the question), and a hat Branch had lent me, with a wide brim which kept my face shaded. I felt at ease as I rode, my blouse unbuttoned to just between my breasts, which might have been one button too far but I was so hot, my skin slick with sweat beneath my clothes; besides, no one out here cared about those kinds of rules.

Miles was also sweating under the glare of the sun, black hair tied at the nape of his neck, his shirt likewise unbuttoned and with sleeves rolled back. "I haven't yet considered claiming my own land, to be honest."

"Honesty is good." I teased him a little, trying to coax a smile. His default expression was often a frown, eyebrows pulled low, even though I knew there was a sense of humor in him. But he was ultimately possessed of a very serious nature.

At last he offered me the half-grin I'd hoped for. He rode with effortless grace; I was no good at guile and therefore acknowledged the fact I was attracted to him. *A lot* attracted to him. Not that I would breathe this fact to a soul. I had no idea what exactly existed between Miles Rawley and me; I only knew I wanted to be around him. I craved his company and tried not to question it any further, at least for now. And, as he had hoped, I'd grown more familiar with him during our ride; we'd been at one another's side since dawn.

"I meant, I haven't thought of settling down in one place in the fashion of my brother," Miles explained. "If Grant hadn't been injured four years past, I believe he would not have considered such either. Though, married life suits him well."

Grant, the oldest Rawley brother, had ridden with Miles, Cole, and

Malcolm Carter in what Miles referred to as their 'outlaw days,' though he insisted they weren't truly outlaws, only fancied themselves as such, back then. Grant currently raised cattle and made a good living selling beef to eastern cities. Now that the railroads stretched so far into the Territories, ranching had become a profitable business, according to Miles, and a respectable one. Miles had only related a small fraction of their former adventures, and I felt sure he downplayed much of it, but it seemed he, Grant, Cole, and Malcolm had been involved in no small amount of danger and trouble.

"What will your brother and his wife think of all this? They won't be upset that you're arriving with three strangers?" I asked as we rode Blade and Flickertail out of view of the T-shaped rock. Not that anything could be done about it at this point; Grant and Birdie were getting unexpected visitors within the hour, whether they wanted it or not. Around last night's fire, Miles had explained he would relate the entire story to his brother once we'd settled in, but instructed Patricia to shed her married surname for the time being.

Miles arched his back, stretching. "Grant is a reasonable man, not easily shaken. And dear Birdie will be so pleased we've brought her feminine company. Not to imply that she won't be curious and concerned, both. However, I am certain she will adore you at once."

"What makes you so certain?" I pestered.

"Just a feeling," he hedged.

Patricia, Axton, and Cole trailed perhaps a mile behind us; Axton drove the wagon with Patricia sequestered in the back while Cole flanked them, riding Charger. I'd unhitched Flickertail from the wagon in order to ride with Miles this morning.

"There is not a soul back east who cares for me," Patricia had whispered as we walked across the prairie the night we'd fled the depot. Her voice was tinged with iron as she vowed, "I shall never again return there."

Miles, Cole, and Axton found the man Patricia had stabbed no more than a mile east of town and within an hour of the attack; he'd presumably fallen from his horse and lay supine in the moonlight. Cause of death was the gashes opened across his lower abdomen. Miles told me later it was one of the worst knife wounds he'd ever beheld. They did not recognize him, speculating before the discovery that it might be Vole, but the dead man was unknown and carried no identifying items.

"Mrs. Yancy is a tougher woman than I would have given her credit," Miles told me.

I couldn't agree more; despite her small stature and the delicate way she carried herself, I'd witnessed her determination and strength, in spades. Though I'd inadvertently knocked the knife from the attacker's hand, it had been Patricia whose quick thinking saved us that night. If she hadn't grabbed the knife from the floor and applied it to his gut, likely he would have strangled us to death, killing us one way or another. It seemed unreal, my mind having blocked out most of what had occurred. I remembered it the way I would the memory of a bad dream, in disturbing, disjointed images.

"The Yancys will come looking for you," Cole said the morning after the attack, all of us gathered around Branch's sunrise cookfire, benign yellow light streaking the horizon; Patricia and I had no intent of venturing from Branch's property until we managed to formulate a plan. Even a scrap of a plan. The men had returned in the night hours with Patricia's bloody clothing and both bodies in tow, Mrs. Mason's and the attacker's; the dead were now wrapped in blankets and tucked into the wagon, which had been stowed in the barn until we – meaning Miles, I gathered – decided what to do. He was banking on the assumption that no one in town knew what had occurred at the train cars.

"Yancy's men only just left Howardsville on their scouting mission," Branch said, whittling a stick as he sat on a hewn log, unable to remain still. "They ain't gonna be back this way for days."

"Dredd had naught to do with this," Patricia said, with certainty. She was exhausted, her lovely face wan and drawn. Plum-colored shadows edged her eyes. A faint breeze lifted the ends of her long, waving hair, which she had not pinned up, and she appeared younger than ever. She whispered, "I shall adhere to the belief that my husband was kept out of any decision made to kill me. He has long been Fallon's fool, but I am not."

"He's a dead man if I see him. If I see any of the goddamn Yancys," Cole said, with stern conviction not one of us doubted; he sat to Patricia's right, holding one of her hands between both of his. I saw how Axton gauged the amount of intimacy between Cole and Patricia, obviously longing to be the one who dared to make such promises to her.

Miles sighed and was about to speak, but Patricia broke in, imploring, "You mustn't say such things." Her blue eyes shone with sincerity. "Please understand. I have already endangered all of you beyond measure. I shall take my leave from this place this very day."

"*No*," Axton whispered.

Cole brought their linked hands to his lips and kissed Patricia's knuckles. "You *shall not*. Not if I have a thing to say about it. The Yancys will have to get through me to get to you."

At his words I felt something inside me shift and vibrate, as if responding to a distant signal. My teeth went on edge; I resisted the urge to cup my temples and apply pressure.

Branch said somberly, "Then you must get your stories in line, you-all."

Miles, seated on the opposite side of the breakfast fire, met and held my gaze. He was worried as hell, I could tell even with no words and very little movement from him. But ultimately I agreed with Cole; we couldn't let Patricia return to people who'd tried to have her killed.

"You have to know we won't let you leave." I leaned to curl a hand around her knee.

Patricia opened her eyes; her smile was a weak, pale version of its usual self. "I cannot stay. It is not possible."

"Dammit!" Cole spoke with increasing fervor. "Didn't you hear a thing I just said?" She bent her head, lips compressing, and he whispered, "Well, didn't you?"

Miles asked, "Mrs. Yancy, can you think of any reason your husband's family would wish you harm? What purpose would it serve them?"

Patricia lifted her face. "I must presume it is my father's fortune which motivated these actions. Thomas is well aware I am my father's sole heir and while my dowry was substantial, I alone remain in control of Father's former estate in Boston and a small but profitable silver mine in the former Colorado Territory. Remove me from the equation and Dredd would have immediate control over both properties and their subsequent incomes. More than enough to launch Thomas's latest business endeavors, whatever those may currently be." She concluded grimly, "But he shall not have his wish to be rid of me, not just yet."

I could almost see Miles's thoughts galloping like a runaway team. He asked, "Does Mrs. Mason have kin, back east?"

"She does not."

He paused, looking toward the sky as he considered. At last he returned his serious gaze to the fire, directing it at each of us in turn. "I cannot leave this matter unresolved. If we are in agreement, and if I have your collective trust, then I will officially conclude the following – a man attempted to rob the Yancys' train car last night, met trouble with Mrs. Mason, struck and killed her, fled the scene, and drunkenly fell on his own knife."

Cole sat straighter, listening with growing hope. "Yes, that's the way of it."

"But what of me?" Patricia watched Miles, recognizing him as the one to determine our fates.

Again I could nearly read his thoughts. Before he could speak I did, addressing Patricia as I said, "You were killed, too. It's the only way."

My words sank in, earning an eerie silence.

Miles said, "It was my first thought as well, but I am skeptical of the success of such a plan."

Branch piped up in immediate agreement. "And right you are! That's a mountain of risk, young'uns. It's too dangerous. Think of the stink this'll raise in town. The young wife kilt while her husband's men were away? The Yancys won't stand for it! They'll bring hell down upon the town."

"Uncle Branch, it's what they wanted, don't you see?" Axton leaned forward earnestly. "Even if they raise any kind of trouble, it won't last long. It would be all for show."

I nodded, in agreement. "If we let them believe Patricia is dead then their plan *worked*, at least in their minds. Eventually, probably sooner than later, they'll let it go."

Miles studied Patricia. "You cannot imagine the far-reaching consequences of such a decision. Are you willing to release your claim on everything your former life entailed? Life as you knew it, forever out of reach?"

A fledgling sun ray cleared the eastern horizon and cast Patricia's forehead in golden gilt, tinting her irises a dazzling, otherworldly blue. I shivered almost violently, connected to her in a way I could not have explained, even if tortured for answers; our fates were linked on a level beyond my comprehension.

"My life has already been irrevocably altered," she whispered, resting the fingertips of her free hand upon her neck; it was her left and the glittering ring placed there by Dredd Yancy seemed to mock her passionate words. "The life I knew vanished with my father's death."

Miles pulled no punches but I recognized the logic of his questions. "What of their desire to receive a body for burial in Chicago? Will they not expect such?"

Cole said sharply, "*Miles.*"

"But he's right," I said. "A funeral would be expected." My thoughts whirled through possibilities. "What if we left it unconfirmed? What if the conclusion is that Patricia simply disappeared and is presumed dead? There's no one to say otherwise."

"Thomas or Fallon shall investigate the matter if my death is unconfirmed," she said, with a note of real fear. "It's no use. I must return to Chicago or risk endangering all of you."

"And let them kill you there?" I cried. "Patricia, *no.*"

"Out of the question," Cole agreed.

Miles's thoughts were leaping ahead; he asked Branch, "Have you the canvas covering for the flatbed?"

"I do, indeed."

"Had we left before dawn, on horseback we'd arrive at Grant's homestead by mid-afternoon. With the wagon and the delay, it'll be after dark." Miles glanced at the rising sun. "I will spend the day in Howardsville tying up loose ends. Cole, I would that you –"

Axton sat straight and interrupted. "I can do it, Marshal Rawley. I can drive the wagon."

"I'll drive the wagon, young fellow," Cole said decisively. He didn't speak the words but his tone suggested Axton wasn't up to the task.

Axton was not to be deterred. "You planned to leave town with the marshal today, everyone in Howardsville knows. Won't it look strange if you're suddenly up and gone while he's still about, investigating a disappearance?"

Branch clamped his lips to keep from outright forbidding Axton to go but his eyes were troubled as he watched his nephew's face.

"He's got a point," Miles said to Cole; as he spoke, he snapped a kindling twig into pieces.

"You trust a boy to protect the women?" Cole demanded, jaws squaring as he faced off with his old friend.

"Axton is no boy," I said before Miles could reply, irritated by Cole's attitude; more heat than I'd intended crackled in my voice. "He and I can take turns driving the team while Patricia hides in the back. Isn't that why you asked about the canvas covering?"

Miles nodded; I couldn't read the exact expression which had overtaken his features, somewhere between speculation and unease.

"I can do it," Axton repeated, refusing to look at Cole, who was visibly close to losing his cool. Axton, meanwhile, appeared as calm as a windless morning and I was proud of him, though I wouldn't embarrass him by admitting it just now.

"Cole, you and I will remain in town today," Miles said, with growing determination. "Gauge the reaction, get a sense of the response." He fixed his gaze next on Axton. "Head northwest, follow the trail. I don't have cause to think you'll need it but I'll give you the double-barrel and you keep it in reach. Make camp at dusk on Dry Run Creek. There's a small valley sheltered from the main trail, you can't miss it." His eyes locked on mine. "We'll find you there by evening."

"Stay, you-all," Branch implored, unable to keep quiet. "There ain't no reason you can't hide out here."

"It's too close to town," Miles said, low and respectful. "There's not enough room. Besides, seeking refuge with Grant is temporary, at best."

"We'll be all right," I told Branch, loving him and wishing I was as sure as I sounded. "We'll be back this way before too long."

He nodded reluctant acceptance but there was little else to do – we had no choice but to move forward.

Though our plan was tentative at best and uncertainties hovered like iron weights over our heads, I was grateful to leave the threat of the town behind. The wagon was creaky and cumbersome but its slow pace allowed for each detail of the foothills to be imbibed. Sitting on the wagon seat alongside Axton I inhaled the rich scents of masses of blooming wildflowers and tall prairie grasses, their heavy, nodding tassels rustling like dry leaves. Even the bright sunshine seemed to permeate my nostrils with each breath; sunlight possessed a sweet, clean smell, often caught in the folds of the laundry I'd hung out to dry.

The sky was as blue as Patricia's eyes, laced over with gauzy, fair-weather clouds. But for Ranger and Flickertail, pulling the wagon, and birds and butterflies by the dozens, the three of us had no company but each other. We traveled toward blue-smudged mountain peaks across an enormous circle of undulating land, grasses rippling like waves on yellow-green water. Rock formations jutted from the earth in every direction.

"You all right?" I asked Axton once the prairie had swallowed us from view of the cabin.

My voice seemed intrusive; we traveled the first mile in complete silence, as if to speak would go against Miles's instructions. How I'd hated to ride away from him; I looked back at the last minute, finding him watching, growing ever smaller as the grinding wheels increased the distance between us. He, Cole, and Branch stood in a grim line near the shanty cabin, Miles and Cole on their mounts while Branch, iron cooking tool in hand, observed as we disappeared. Axton kept the shotgun within reach, as promised, while Patricia, bundled in a quilt, lay hidden in the wagon bed, its canvas covering tied in place over the arch of wooden ribs.

"I am," Axton said in response, releasing a slow exhale with the words.

He and I sat close enough that I could tuck my hand around his elbow, first making sure this wouldn't impede his hold on the reins; I craved the warmth and security of another person's touch. I'd slept no more than twenty minutes last night, disturbing thoughts poking my eyes every time they tried to close. And when I did succeed in dozing off, I dreamed of fleeing from men mounted on black horses, stumbling barefoot over rocky ground to escape, dragging Patricia with me, knowing we had no chance.

"Ruthann?" she whispered from behind us, and Axton and I almost clocked foreheads turning to look at her.

She rolled to her knees. Tears streamed over her cheeks and her voice shook as she repeated my name.

"Come up here with us," Axton said, somewhere between an order and a plea.

I scooted to make room and she clambered between us on the narrow wooden seat, weeping, hiding her face in both hands. Her hair hung loose, falling over her shoulders in soft disarray; a good scrubbing had not fully removed the bloodstains from her slender fingers. Protectiveness surged and I held her tightly. Axton wrapped his right arm around both of us and Patricia collapsed against his chest. Her shoulders shook as she muffled her sobs behind her hands.

"I'm so sorry," she choked out, again and again. "I am so very sorry."

"You've nothing to be sorry for," Axton murmured. "Not one thing."

"It's all right, let it out," I encouraged. Tears burned my eyes at the sound of her despair. "We're here, Patricia, we're not going anywhere. Don't worry."

"I am…ever so grateful…" she gasped. "For both of you."

She finally calmed, sobs subsiding as she swiped at her wet face. She was pale as a snowdrift, violet shadows swelling beneath her eyes; her lips appeared likewise puffy. A strand of hair was caught in the corner of her mouth and my heart ached with sympathy and concern to observe as Axton, with tender movements, tucked it behind her ear. Closer to her than he'd ever been, his pining gaze tracked every detail of her face; he swallowed hard and withdrew his arm, sitting straight and refocusing on the horses.

"You have to know we would never let you go back to them," I said.

"I am selfish beyond compare," she whispered, rancor in her tone, gaze fixed on the far horizon. She wrapped both arms around her own midsection, in the manner of someone about to vomit. "You are in harm's way for helping me and I cannot forgive myself."

"*Patricia*. That's not true." I reached and shook her knee, for emphasis.

"If harm comes our way, I aim to stop it," Axton said; his tone vowed, *I would do anything for you.*

"You need rest," I said, concerned anew, for both of them. I couldn't exactly initiate a talk with Axton, especially since the main topic of the conversation was in such close proximity. Infusing my voice with decisiveness, I added, "Come on, I'll try to sleep, too. Ax, you all right for a while?"

"Course, Ruthie," he murmured, looking my way.

I held his gaze for a heartbeat and he crinkled his brows, sensing I was trying to communicate something to him, unsure what.

Later, I told him. *We'll talk later.*

To my surprise, Patricia and I slept for hours in a row and the day passed uneventfully. Axton pushed on until the sun began its long, melting descent toward the west; I woke before Patricia and cautiously skirted her sleeping form as I rejoined Ax on the wagon seat, squinting against the low, bright glare of afternoon. I'd slept without dreaming and my head was somewhat clearer; by contrast, my mouth tasted like rust and my hair was a mess of tangles. Miles had mentioned a creek by which to set up camp and I intended to bathe no matter how cold the water. The air was pleasantly mild, the sun warm and languid on my face. I leaned around the edge of the wagon to survey the land behind us, longing for a glimpse of Blade cantering our way.

But there was nothing but empty miles.

"You feeling better?" Axton whispered.

"I am. How's your back? You've been hunched over those reins all day." I briskly applied my thumbs between his shoulder blades and along his nape, and he issued a low, appreciative groan. Keeping my voice at a whisper, I implored, "Ax. I don't know how to say this…"

I had his full attention and pressed on before losing my courage; it was Axton, for heaven's sake, with whom I'd discussed many an intimate topic in the past two months. But this was different. Words failed me as I studied his familiar face; the deep green of his eyes shone with traces of gold in the sun. His lips were slightly parted, as if poised to ask me what in the hell I was so worried about saying. Of course he wouldn't think of interrupting me; it was not his way.

"I'm so proud of you," I blurted. "I think the way you stood up to Cole this morning was really impressive."

His brows lifted in two perfect arches of surprised pleasure.

"I like Cole, I really do, but he's…he's just…" I faltered, hating the way I was messing up this chance to talk to him about Patricia. What was my exact intent, anyway?

"He's what, Ruthie?" Ax prompted. His shoulders had squared, as if I was about to relate something truly dreadful.

"He's cocky," I whispered in a rush, peeking over my shoulder to ensure Patricia was still sleeping. "And vain. She's infatuated by him, I can tell…"

As if alerted by the tension in my voice, Patricia stirred and I gritted my teeth. I wanted to tell Axton I thought he was a better man all around – but then again, who was I to make such a determination? I hardly knew Cole; I was using my limited impression of him to make judgments, which was unfair. Besides, Patricia remained a married woman; it was not something she could simply wish away.

Axton continued to study me, his eyes serious and full of questions.

"We'll talk more tonight," I promised.

He nodded understanding and then murmured, "There's the creek, yonder."

Chapter Sixteen

THE TRAIL WOUND DOWNWARD IN A MEANDERING FASHION, taking us into a small valley sheltered by cottonwoods and a worn ridge of rock slabs, a sort of rough natural fence. The creek was shallow and not much wider across than I could chuck a heavy stone, but I supposed we were lucky to find any liquid in a waterway called Dry Run. Clouds were stacked on the western horizon, painted a luxurious mauve by the setting sun. Axton jumped to the ground and helped us down before leading Ranger and Flickertail to the creek; the horses snorted and stomped, plunging their long noses into the wetness for a long drink.

I rubbed Flickertail's warm neck, bent low over the water source. "You're a good girl. What a good girl."

My legs were as stiff as wooden planks but I strode a few yards away and crouched, splashing my face, wetting my blouse, and it was there, kneeling at the water's edge, inhaling its cool, earthy scent, that a chill seized my spine. A sense, *a knowing*, of a place with blue water. A large, glistening expanse of blue water, crystalline and beckoning. My eyes flew open but there was nothing more than the meager little creek upon whose bank I knelt – nothing like the picture in my mind.

Was that a memory? Did you just remember something from your past?

I stood in a rush, darting my gaze over the water, attempting to provoke the same sensation. A memory had stirred, I was certain, and my heart increased in speed.

"There is a peculiarity to the air here, is there not?" Patricia asked, coming to stand beside me and guessing the direction of my thoughts, at least to some extent. "It is like nothing I have known before now. I feel alive here, truly."

Her loose hair hung to her shoulder blades, rippled and windblown. Resting her forearms atop her head, clutching her wrists in either hand, she regarded the scene before us. Upon her face was a hesitant, fleeting sense of peace.

"It is beautiful. And it smells good out here," I muttered, rubbing my eyes. Lukewarm water dripped toward my elbows but I didn't care; the vision of blue water had faded. I elaborated, "In town, no one bathes."

"Well, it *is* a rather process to fill and heat a tub," Patricia said, and I was relieved to see a tentative smile move across her lips.

"I meant to wash up in the creek but now I'm not so sure. I can't let my clothes get wet since I don't have any others."

"And it would be unseemly to disrobe out of doors," she added. "Though, I am certain you could trust Axton to spare you a few minutes to bathe." Her gaze followed in the direction he'd disappeared, about fifty yards down the creek bank, seeking a moment's privacy.

I watched carefully for her response as I said, "He's the kindest man I've ever known, other than Branch."

Patricia's throat bobbed as she swallowed, arms lowering to her sides. She whispered, "He is, indeed."

I was tempted to go swimming, unconcerned about wet clothes or nudity for a few reckless seconds, but considering that Miles and Cole might soon be joining us, I decided against it; instead, Patricia and I shared a soap cake, washing our faces, hands, and forearms. She settled me in the shade provided by the wagon to finger-comb my hair and had just begun braiding its length when Axton returned, his shirt collar and shirtsleeves damp. He smiled to see us, the last of the sun washing red-gold over his handsome, guileless features, glinting in his beautiful hair. He radiated a sense of accomplishment; he'd gotten us this far without mishap.

I love you so, I thought, with a sharp, passionate jolt of emotion. *You are a better choice for Patricia all around, Ax, I know this to be true.*

"Any sign of Miles and Cole?" I asked him.

"They thought not until after dark," Axton replied, moving to unhitch the team. He rested a hand briefly on my shoulder as he brought them to graze, leading Flickertail first. "Don't worry, Ruthie, they can look after themselves."

I nodded, trying not to consider all the ways our plan could swiftly go wrong. I knew Miles was more than capable, I *knew* this, and still I prayed with an evangelical level of intensity that Yancy's men would not return before Miles and Cole rode out of Howardsville; it seemed unlikely they would, but *what if…*

"In the meantime, let's get a fire going," Ax said.

He angled the wagon north-south and settled us on its west side, allowing for a view of the spectacular sunset afterglow, the horizon awash with orange and gold. Next he used a trowel to clear a patch of ground, making a rough oval of dirt over which to build the fire. Patricia still appeared depleted and settled quietly on a blanket, watching as we roved in a wide half-circle, collecting anything we could use for kindling.

"Ruthie…" Axton spoke from a few feet away, both of us bent over the ground and with armloads of twigs.

"What?"

He looked my way. "It's exciting to see this land, to be away from home, and I feel guilty for saying so."

"You shouldn't feel guilty, sweetheart," I said, and he smiled a little at my use of the endearment.

"But I do. Uncle Branch was sad to see us go," Axton acknowledged, straightening to his full height. "I miss him already. He's the only daddy I've ever known."

"Hey. Come here." I stood so I could hug him with my free arm, resting my cheek against his chest. "You can tell me whatever you want, you know that." I stood on tiptoe to kiss his jaw, finding it prickly with a day's growth of stubble. "I love you dearly, Ax. And Branch is the only father I can remember at this point, too."

"I love you too, Ruthie."

"I don't know if I've ever had a brother, but I'd want him to be just like you."

"Same here," Axton murmured, squeezing me extra tightly before drawing away. Stealthy gloaming light began leaching color from the landscape, tinting objects with grays and pewters. He spoke with quiet wistfulness. "I always wanted a big family, with plenty of brothers and sisters."

"I bet you'll have at least ten kids someday," I mused, with an unexpected glimmer of premonition. A vague and blurry picture formed itself into sudden, fleeting crispness – of Ax laughing and roughhousing with a rowdy band of little redheads.

"You think?" he whispered in a tone of bashful awe, unable to keep his longing gaze from crossing the distance between him and Patricia.

Returning to the task of gathering twigs, I murmured sincerely, "It would be a crying shame, if not."

"Hallo the wagon!" hollered a familiar voice and my heart blazed like a firecracker; I dropped the entire bundle of kindling I'd gathered as Axton and I turned to spy Miles and Cole riding near, their horses cantering elegantly in the direction of our camp.

"Thank God," I breathed, nearly going to my knees with relief, able to draw a full breath for the first time since early this morning.

"You care for the marshal, don't you?" Axton murmured, watching me watch Miles, and I nodded without speaking.

Miles heeled Blade to a gallop and arrived ahead of Cole, bringing Blade close to where I stood.

"I'm so glad you're here," I said, unable to hold my tongue, the welcome heat of reassurance swamping my body. "I've been so worried all day. You don't even know."

"As have I," Miles said, and my heart hurtled against my ribs as he offered a genuine, full-fledged grin. "I could not ride swiftly enough. *You* do not even know."

"Do you think we need to worry about snakes?" Patricia asked after we'd eaten dinner and intended to retire to the pallet of quilts in the wagon bed, with no small amount of anxiety. Miles, Ax, and Cole stood at the edge of the creek many yards away as she posed this question, hidden by the darkness, the three of them laughing about something with their backs to us, probably standing down there peeing. I almost giggled at the thought, giddy with relief that Miles was finally here.

"Snakes?" I repeated, looking up at Patricia, who'd stood to shake out her skirts.

"Yes, in our bedding. Suppose one crawls inside while we are sleeping."

"We'll ask them when they get back up here," I promised. I remained sitting, arms wrapped around my bent knees – a position I would have avoided were I wearing a skirt instead of Axton's trousers – in no hurry to retreat to the wagon.

"They shall poke fun at us, for worrying."

"They won't," I whispered, even though they probably would. "Here they come."

The tripod of wood arranged for the fire had tumbled as it burned, creating a muted red glow, much less brilliant than the blazing orange of its earlier, higher flame. By this scant light I watched the men approach from the creek, seeking Miles. Instead of reclaiming their spots around the fire all three stood in a momentary lull, as though Patricia and I were guests at a fancy dinner party and awaited their assistance.

To fill the awkward gap, I hurried to say, "We were just headed to bed."

"Will you two be warm enough in that wagon?" Cole asked. I sensed his sincerity; I also recognized he was no more than a step away from offering to join us. Patricia ducked her chin to hide her fluster.

"We will." I spoke firmly.

"Will it be a bother to you if we sit for a spell before retiring?" Miles asked.

"No, of course not," I said. I wished they could play their fiddles, but of course they hadn't toted along the instruments on this journey.

Without another word Miles stepped around the fire and reached to help me to my feet. He released my hands as I stood but our gazes seemed ensnared.

"We'll be right here," he murmured, then added hastily, "Should you require anything. Either of you."

Thank you. My lips moved but no sound accompanied the words.

"You are more than welcome."

Before I lost my nerve I said, "Wait! What about snakes in the wagon?"

Patricia murmured, "Or other…undesirable creatures?"

"Snakes are not particularly common out here in the open, as I've ever noticed," Miles said. "They tend to prefer caves."

Axton gathered up a lantern and offered the most practical solution. "C'mon, I'll check the wagon for you."

Once the wagon was deemed critter-free, Cole sidestepped Axton to help Patricia climb the tailgate to enter its confines. Miles and I remained at the fire a few yards away; when it was apparent I had no further excuse to linger, I said, "I better join her."

Miles nodded, resting his fingertips briefly upon my arm. "Goodnight, Ruthann."

I matched his courteous tone. "Good-night, marshal."

"I would that you call me by my given name," he requested.

I steadied my voice and whispered, "Good-night, Miles."

The men reclaimed their places and proceeded to smoke and talk in low, quiet tones, their combined voices as comforting as anything I'd ever known. Once in the wagon, I snuggled beneath the quilt with Patricia, both of us too exhausted to whisper. I lay facing the arch of canvas lit by the fire's dull-red glow, imagining the foothills beneath the half moon, a wild expanse stretching much farther than my eyes could perceive; the back of my neck prickled at the thought of all that dark emptiness but I scooted closer to Patricia, effectively eradicating the feeling. I turned my thoughts instead to what Miles and Cole had related earlier, as we ate dinner around the fire.

A reasonable stir had been caused by the death of Mrs. Mason and her unknown attacker. Miles and Cole had delivered the bodies to the undertaker and saw to it that both were secured in proper coffins; burial in the local cemetery, situated on a hill outside town, was arranged and paid for. Miles proceeded to spread the word that young Mrs. Dredd Yancy was also presumed dead. He gave orders that the train cars were to be locked until Thomas Yancy's men returned from their scouting mission and further investigation could be conducted. Miles left word he would return to Howardsville in a month's time, when his route permitted, and could be contacted then; his deputy, Alvin Furlough, was to be sought in the meantime in the event of any additional inquiries.

Of course we all knew this was only the beginning; the road ahead was one of danger and uncertainty, but no one said otherwise – at least not for this evening.

"I wish they could play their fiddles," Patricia murmured, the last thing I heard before drifting to a state of fretful dozing.

Time passed in fits and starts; at some point I began to dream.

Ruthann.

His familiar voice flared to life in my sleeping mind. I knew it was him, *my husband*, and in the dream I flew to my feet, peering outward at the gloom of the midnight prairie.

I'm here, I'm right here! I cried in frantic response, scanning the emptiness. *Where are you? Why can't I see you?!*

He spoke again in the voice I knew all the way to my dark, secret center, urgent with insistence. *I am coming for you, angel. I will find you, I swear to you.*

I need you, oh God, I need you. I am dying without you...

I will find you. Do you hear me?

I hear you – I need you – I need you – I screamed these words, repeatedly screamed my husband's name.

My arms and legs jerked in a violent attempt to give chase, ripping me from any sense of him and casting me back to my reality. I sat so quickly blood drained from my skull and I reeled sideways, ending on hands and knees. It took long, shuddering moments to acknowledge my surroundings, to accept that I remembered nothing. The ache of sadness assaulted. I wrapped both arms around my head, hollow with pain. The air was chill, the fire a mass of glowing coals. I heard people and horses nearby, breathing with the slow, even cadence of sleep.

I was sweaty beneath my clothes, skin rippling with goosebumps, and slid from beneath the quilts, taking care to avoid waking Patricia. I was too restless to remain still, supercharged with frustrated agony. I wanted to flee into the cold darkness and run until my blood was pounding and I found what I was looking for, as senseless as this was; I couldn't remember a goddamn thing. I also needed to go to the bathroom, which allowed for a legitimate trek away from our camp. I eased to my knees, letting my head hang as I tried to collect my thoughts; my temple hurt where I'd been struck only a night ago, in the train car.

Why can't I remember?

Oh God, let me remember. Please. I'll do anything…

I climbed down and then skulked away from the wagon, intending to find somewhere to crouch, figuring the best place for privacy was near the creek. I angled that direction, both arms wrapped around my jittery ribcage. Damp sweat evaporated quickly away from the warmth of Patricia and the quilts, leaving me chilled. I was barefoot, which was really stupid; the ground was prickly and uneven, and probably over-populated by biting creatures, so I slowed my pace.

If you step on a snake, you have no one but yourself to blame.

I hadn't walked more than a dozen yards when I sensed someone be-hind me; before I could think of spinning around to confront him, hands clutched my upper arms. I gulped on a scream as he demanded in a low voice, "Where are you going?"

"The bathroom!" I hissed, yanking at his iron hold. Irrationally an-gry at being detained, I assumed for the moment he didn't realize how strong his grip was. "Let go!"

Miles turned me around and with the light of the moon at his back he appeared a featureless silhouette, his face obscured in shadows. He was close enough I could smell his breath and skin, and found them fa-miliar; how in the hell this was possible, I didn't know. It was like a rock dropped into the deep well of sadness in my heart.

"I apologize," he said after seconds of tense silence ticked away between us. "You were experiencing a nightmare, only minutes ago. I am terribly concerned for you." His voice was hardly a whisper as he speculated, "It is surely the trauma of what you've endured which causes you to cry out."

"Cry out?"

"You were…" Miles broke off the explanation and shifted position, as if uncertain how to proceed. I felt the moon was unfairly spotlighting my face, leaving his in specter-like dimness. At last he concluded, "You were repeating the word 'marshal,' which led me to believe you were calling for me."

I could not make out his irises in the darkness. I admitted in a whisper, "I don't remember what I was dreaming."

"It is unsafe to roam out here, where I…" He cut short these authoritative words and amended, "Where no one is able to see you."

Instead of arguing with him, as was my first instinct, I conceded, "I know."

"I will wait for you," he decided, but did not turn around or offer any other privacy.

"You don't have to wait. I'll be right back."

"Back from where?"

This was getting ridiculous. "I am not going to pee *in front of you!*"

He was rendered momentarily silent.

"Did you hear me?" I demanded.

"How could I fail to hear you? We are but a foot apart!"

I lowered my voice, stunned by how quickly Miles roused my temper. "I know you were just worried. It's all right." He didn't move and so I hinted, "Can I have just a second?"

"Of course," he muttered stiffly, and proceeded to turn his back and cross his arms. His posture was so rigid he appeared carved of wood.

I sighed; there was no winning this one, and so I hurried to the creek bank without further comment. When I returned he offered his arm, which I interpreted as an apology, and together we walked back to the fire. Axton and Cole lay snoring, the last of the embers glowing like rubies. Miles led me to the wagon where we stalled, facing one another in the darkness; Miles released my arm.

"I'm sorry I woke you," I whispered at last.

"Do not apologize." Stars rioted across the backdrop of sky behind him, creating the illusion of swirling motion. The air was cold and damp.

I realized I'd failed to do something important and so whispered, "Thank you for doing this, Miles." A beat passed between us; I'd spoken his name for the second time tonight. "We're all indebted to you."

"I only pray we are successful. Of course you are aware Cole is very much besotted by Mrs. Yancy. He is set on his course. I know him well enough to recognize his stubbornness."

"It's no secret," I whispered, touched nonetheless that he'd confided in me. "Axton is crazy about her too, in case you hadn't noticed."

I sensed him nod. "I have, and so has Cole. He was much aggrieved this morning after you took your leave. It was a long day all around." He paused. "For you as well, and I am keeping you from sleep. We should arrive at Grant's before noon if we set out at daybreak."

"Right," I whispered, sensitized and restless, thinking of how he'd gripped my waist last night, the way his thumbs had caressed my belly. Before he could help me up, I hurried to climb over the tailgate, thwacking my shin on the way, stifling a groan. I whispered over my shoulder, "See you in the morning."

"In the morning," he repeated softly, and returned to the fire.

But the damage was done; I didn't sleep the remainder of the night, lying in silence beside Patricia, flat on my back and both hands resting on my chest – like I was dead in a coffin, I realized, with an unpleasant shiver – watching the canvas grow lighter by degrees as dawn advanced. It was palest silver when I finally left the quilts and crawled to the oval opening; the fire pit was in view, all three men stretched around a pile of spent coals. I could see my breath in the air and my gaze landed upon and clung to Miles, his back to me, a lone blanket drawn haphazardly to his waist.

He'd untied the twine holding back his long hair and his pistol remained strapped to his hip; he lay with an arm curled beneath his head. Studying him sent an insistent pulse beating in my belly, then lower, an escalating desire to hurry over there and let our hair tangle together as I wrapped my arms and legs around him. The fire was low – he must have been freezing. I definitely was and I'd been buried beneath two heavy quilts.

I'll warm you, I thought. *Oh Miles, let me warm you…*

Jesus Christ, Ruthann.

I was shocked at my thoughts; I hardly knew Miles Rawley.

Go to him…

Aching, but resolute, I turned away and wrapped into my own arms.

Chapter Seventeen

A MAN ON HORSEBACK RODE OUT TO MEET OUR SMALL PAR-
ty as we approached the homestead of Grant and Birdie Rawley, late
the following morning. I was impressed with the appearance of their
sprawling ranch, including a two-story, wood-framed house and numerous outbuildings, all of solid-looking construction, with a large corral
ringing the south side of an enormous barn. At least a dozen horses
milled about inside the enclosure. There were blue mountain peaks along
the western horizon and I felt a spurt of pure appreciation for the rugged
beauty of this place.

"There he is!" the man called, spurring his horse and riding straight
to Miles. The moment his feet touched the ground, Miles was wrapped
in a bear hug. I dismounted more slowly from Flickertail, touched to
witness the affection between the two brothers. Grant Rawley's resemblance to Miles was immediately obvious – the tall, wide-shouldered
stance, the long nose and clean-lined face, though Grant's hair and eyes
were a lighter brown and he wore a full beard in addition to a mustache.

"It's been too damn long," Miles said as he embraced Grant.

"You can say that again," said Grant, thumping Miles's back with
both fists. He drew away and assessed the group before him with an air
of good cheer. Hands widespread, he inquired, "Who have we here?"

"Ruthann Rawley." I stepped forward and offered my right hand,
which Grant accepted and kissed. His eyebrows became steep arches
at my words; he sent Miles a quick, sharp look which melted to a grin.

Jubilation in his tone, Grant cried, "You've taken a wife, brother! I
wondered at the womenfolk. My Birdie will be beside herself with joy."

I stumbled, "I'm not…"

Miles touched my elbow, as though to apologize for the misunderstanding. "Regrettably, Ruthann is not my wife."

Cole, leading Charger, interrupted all of us. "It's a long story, Grantley, one which we'll account for soon enough."

Indicating the wagon, Miles added, "This is Miss Patricia Biddeford and Axton Douglas. You'll recall Branch Douglas from the old days," and Grant nodded.

"And I am Grantley Rawley, at your service, ladies," he said, recovering his self-possession. "My Birdie will be overjoyed at your presence. Please make yourselves in every way at home here." So saying, Grant offered me his arm. Over his shoulder, he told Miles, "Little bro, if you'd lead Gunpowder, I'd be much obliged."

"Always was a ladies' man," Cole grumbled, while Miles proceeded to walk both his own horse and Grant's, a high-stepping mare.

Birdie Rawley hurried outside the second we were in her dooryard, one child on her hip and another clinging to her skirts. She wore her golden hair in a smooth bun and dimples flashed in both cheeks as she smiled, surveying this group of people who'd arrived mostly uninvited at her house.

Grant said, "This is my wife, Roberta Rawley."

"I declare. *Company!* I haven't been so glad since I don't know when. Please, call me Birdie. Grantley, take your son so I can offer a proper welcome." She passed the baby to her husband and hugged us each in turn. The toddler lost hold of Birdie's skirt and began fussing but Cole picked him up and tossed him in the air. Miles took care to introduce Patricia, Axton, and me to Birdie before she could assume the same thing Grant had.

Even though I could tell she was dying of curiosity as her eyes danced between us, Birdie didn't press for questions. She invited, "Do come inside. I have lemon tarts, imagine that! Though, it is the last of the lemons dear Fannie sent." She planted her hands on her hips. "Cole Spicer, you handsome devil, you haven't changed a bit. It's that hair, is it not? No one with red hair could ever be *completely* good, could they, girls?" She turned her teasing gaze to Axton and inquired, "Might the same be said of you, young fellow?"

Axton flushed and pressed his hat, which he'd politely removed, tighter to his chest.

"My wife is very free with her opinions, aren't you, honey?" Grant said, winking at her. I thought suddenly of what Miles had told me the night he threw Aemon Turnbull in jail, the night he'd cleaned the wound on my forehead, about his father teaching him two things – one of which was to marry a woman for love. It was clear each of the Rawley boys had been given the same advice.

"I most certainly am," Birdie agreed, fluttering her lashes at Grant. "I'm so very glad to have womenfolk for company that I am quite beside myself."

Referring to the baby in his arms, Grant said to Miles, "Little brother, meet your newest nephew, Isaac Charles."

"Might I hold the child?" Patricia asked.

"Of course," said Birdie, and Grant passed his son, who was perhaps six months old, into Patricia's arms. Her face bloomed as she gently bounced him, earning a gurgling laugh from the baby.

Birdie said, "You may hold him for the duration of your visit, Miss Biddeford. He is only satisfied when being held and another pair of arms is *most* welcome."

Patricia had shed her married surname, as Miles had requested, and I wished it was as easy to likewise shed her marriage. I wanted to will away the lingering sense of doom, which dripped inside my heart like a leaking pump, a constant reminder that things were not right.

But try as I might, I could not.

Dinner was to be served outside since the weather was so lovely, the sun slowly disappearing behind the mountain range on the horizon. Clouds had banked behind the peaks, lending the sunset a burning violet glow. Patricia and I were given a room to share in the main house, while Miles, Ax, and Cole claimed beds in the bunkhouse, where Grant's ranch hands lived; another man, a cook, had his own shanty cabin with a stovepipe poking through the roof.

Patricia and I stripped from our dirty traveling clothes and took turns washing our faces and armpits – in that order – in the basin Birdie made certain was waiting in our room. We were situated on the second floor, in a cramped room with a bare wooden floor and a low, slanted ceiling, but it had four solid walls and a bed complete with a feather tick and down-filled pillows, and so neither of us breathed a word of complaint. Sunlight trickled through the rippled glass of the single window in the room. Birdie, taking stock of our limited supplies, had also provided undergarments and dresses for us, the material fresh and crisp and wonderfully clean.

"How soon do you think Cole and Miles will tell them the truth?" Patricia asked, as I sat on the bed and let her brush through my curls. I wore nothing but an underskirt, Patricia clad in a loose-fitting chemise, as comfortable around one another as actual sisters; I'd spent a long time scratching at the red grooves my corset cut into my skin and was very reluctant to replace it; to avoid this, I sat with my knees bent against my bare breasts, both hands cupped over my toes. I rested my chin on my right knee and shivered at the gentle passage of the brush over my scalp.

"I think Miles and his brother keep very little from each other," I said. "But Grant and Birdie don't seem unreasonable. I think they'll listen. They trust Miles's judgement." At least, so I hoped.

Patricia rested her palm on the back of my head, lost in thought for a spell. At last she whispered, "I recognize the indecorous nature of such topics, but I…that is, I…"

Recognizing her discomposure, I hurried to tell her, "There's nothing you could say that would shock me, I promise."

Her eyes closed and she sank to sit beside me on the mattress, the bed neatly made up with an embroidered quilt of pristine white. Holding the hairbrush to her breasts, she breathed, "I have only once in my life… made love."

Of everything she could have said right then, I'd expected this probably the least. She opened her eyes and searched mine.

"But what about…"

"That is not entirely correct," she interrupted, speaking quickly now, like someone confessing a wrongdoing. "The phrase, I mean, 'making love.' I have never made love with anyone. What occurred on my wedding night was most certainly not that. It was a perfunctory duty Dredd felt he must perform. It was over in minutes and he never touched me in any fashion, after that first night." She shuddered while I absorbed this troubling – but perhaps not all that surprising – news. She whispered, "I am a fool, Ruthann. A fool of monstrous proportions. I have indulgently let myself believe in a future free from my former obligations."

I kept quiet; we both knew there was no easy solution.

Patricia inhaled a soft breath, resting a closed fist upon her forehead. "Cole is…" Her cheeks took on heat as she reframed her words. "I am quite unused to such feelings, to say the least. I do not believe I would be disappointed if he and I…that is, if we…" Her voice dropped another confessional notch. "Oh, dear God, I am a fool."

"Hey. Stop it. It's not wrong to feel this way. Your only experience has been with someone like Dredd. And it sounds like that experience was awful, right?"

"You don't think me wanton?" Her tone was inundated with apprehension.

"Wanton? Of course not!" No matter what my impression of Cole, I could not let her believe her emotions were wrong. Even so, I felt like I was betraying Axton as I said, "You're too hard on yourself. Desire is a natural part of life. Cole is a good-looking man, of course you've noticed him. He's certainly noticed you. And he's tough. He would stand up for you, fight for you. Would Dredd do the same?"

Patricia released a small huff of a laugh, pressing her fingertips to her closed eyes. "Heavens, no."

"We can't know what the future holds. But whatever it does, I hope you know I am here for you, I promise. No matter what."

Her tense posture relaxed and she rested her forehead upon my bare shoulder. "Thank you. In return I promise the same. I cannot fathom a time when I did not know you, as unreasonable as that may seem." She studied me in silence for a long moment. "You are quite beautiful, within as well as without, which is *most* uncommon. I have the sense you do not realize your beauty, though another member of our party has noticed, quite absolutely." This close to her, I could see the way the blue in her irises was variegated; darker indigo spokes radiated outward from her pupils. Her lashes were thick and black, in contrast to the pale honey of her eyebrows. She persisted, "Have you no idea to whom I refer?"

I looked at my feet, feigning preoccupation.

Patricia smoothed her palm over my hair, the mattress sighing as she stood and continued wielding the brush. She murmured, "The marshal's eyes are for you, sweet Ruthann, whether you shall acknowledge it or not. Cole said he has never before seen Miles smitten."

I wanted to ask, *Haven't you noticed the way Axton watches you? Talk about smitten.*

But I didn't want to hurt her – and besides, I knew she had noticed.

"There is a woman in Howardsville pregnant with Miles's baby," I blurted without thinking, tears blurring the sight of my bare toes. I hated myself for choking up at this statement.

"The plump woman from the saloon, is it not?" Patricia asked. "The woman who requested I look out for you?"

"Yes," I whispered.

"Shall he claim the child?"

"Likely not." I knuckled my eyes to prevent the tears from falling, but no such luck. "Celia plans to send the baby to be raised back east."

"It is the best decision, for all involved," Patricia said, with somber certainty.

"But it's not. It's his *baby*. It's a cousin to Grant and Birdie's little boys, a part of this family. Miles has a responsibility to Celia and their child."

"Bastard children are difficult to acknowledge in the best of circumstances." Patricia's tone was gently matter-of-fact. "Though, I cannot imagine the 'right' circumstances for such a thing."

I used the underskirt to swipe away my rolling tears, sniffling pathetically. Patricia tipped her forehead to my hair and whispered, "Take each day as it comes. I remember my mama speaking the same to Rosemary and me, long ago. I have very few memories of Mama and Rosemary, either one, but I treasure each."

"Thank you," I whispered. "I am so grateful for you, you have no idea."

She kissed my cheek and ordered softly, "Come, we shall soon be called to dine and we cannot under any circumstances appear below dressed as such."

I glanced down at my bare breasts and snorted a small laugh, muttering, "Yeah, I think you might be right."

Patricia walked past the four-paned window en route to replace the brush, but her feet stalled and she dropped to an instant crouch, grasping the windowsill and muffling a strange little sound. To say I was alarmed was a serious understatement; I flew from the bed, disregarding my topless state, and raced to her side.

"Is it the Yancys?" I demanded breathlessly, one of my many horrible fears. Realizing I was naked from the waist up, I crouched beside her, only to realize she was laughing, wagging her head side to side.

"No, no…"

"Then what?" I cried.

"Down in the yard, near the hand pump…" This mystifying explanation was followed by Patricia proceeding to peek as cautiously as possible over the bottom ledge of the window, as though a gunman waited outside, poised to take aim at anyone appearing in the glass rectangles. She breathed, "*Oh, my goodness…*"

I lifted my head just enough to peer down at the yard below. This particular bedroom faced south, toward the hand pump and the ranch hands' bunkhouse…

…And Miles and Cole, washing up for dinner, just as Patricia and I had been only a little while ago.

Both of them were shirtless, splashing water over their strong torsos with as little concern as any men, laughing together about something. Miles's black hair hung loose and damp, falling nearly to his shoulder blades. Cole's hair was also wet; he scrubbed his hands through it, biceps bulging, and Patricia uttered a small, soft sound. I shivered hard, watching Miles, my nipples round and firm as pearls. His shoulders were so wide, his arms long and his muscles leanly sculpted, belly flat as the blade of a knife. Thick black hair covered his chest. He was so handsome and tempting, and had no idea I was watching him from afar, radiating with desire. As we continued shamelessly observing, they finished their ministrations and began toweling off.

"Oh…" I whispered weakly.

Cole made a half-turn, almost like he was about to look up at the window and spy us spying on *them*, and Patricia and I dropped to all fours and out of sight. Patricia hung her head, both of us overcome by breathless laughter.

"I'm naked!" I gasped.

"I'm *nearly* naked!" she responded.

A light knock on the closed door sent us scurrying like mice across the floor to the side of the bed farthest from the sound, curling over our bent legs as though this would prevent anyone from seeing us.

"What if…what if…it's *them*…" Patricia could hardly speak, overtaken in mirth.

"Patricia? Ruthann?" It was Birdie. "Is there anything you require before dinner, my dears?"

I managed to respond, "No, thank you!"

After Birdie's footsteps retreated, Patricia elbowed my waist and whispered, "There *is* something I require…"

"What's that?"

She collapsed, rolling to her back on the wooden floorboards, covering her eyes with both forearms, her breasts plainly visible through the thin material of the chemise. "I am utterly shocked by my own thoughts. I fear my answer would only shock you."

I poked her ribs with my toes and she curled up, giggling.

"I think I can guess."

"No, surely you are too much a lady. As I said, I am shocked…"

I opened my mouth to respond when new footsteps sounded in the hallway and a familiar male voice at the door inquired, "Ladies? Can I escort you to dinner?"

"Of course!" I called, but unfortunately Axton took this as an invitation to come right in, which he did. Though not one prone to drama, I shrieked as the bedroom door swung inward, dropping flat to my naked front side, while Patricia nearly died with laughter. Maybe it was simple stress relief, but it seemed we could not laugh enough to satisfy the urge.

She flipped to her belly, the chemise hiking up around her bare thighs.

"What in the world?" Axton sounded truly confounded; before we could blink he took the three steps into the room required to see us, huddled on the far side of the bed. He immediately said, "*Oh –* " in a strangled voice, and then retreated, stepping backward and proceeding to stumble over a low footstool, landing with a wall-rattling thunk, arms flailing and boots widespread.

Patricia laughed so hard she cried.

More boots then, pounding up the wooden steps. Miles appeared in the doorway, I could see the top third of him from my position on the floor. I buried my burning face against the backs of my hands, arms bent like someone sunbathing. His expression, based on the brief glimpse I caught of it, was of complete stun, black eyebrows lofted high. He wore a clean shirt, his damp hair hanging loose.

"I swear…" Axton tried to say but by now he was also laughing, supine on the floor.

"Ruthann…is…*naked*," Patricia wheezed.

"I am *not*," I retorted, daring to lift my face to contradict this statement, keeping my chest against the floorboards. My skin prickled with goosebumps, my hair falling across my back and shoulders. Miles looked as though he couldn't decide whether to be shocked or amused, though amusement was winning the upper hand. He held my gaze with his dark eyes, which crinkled at the outside corners as a slow grin spread over his mouth.

"Near enough," he teased, his deep voice with a hint of heat, the first he'd ever allowed when speaking to me; his gaze flickered in the direction of my breasts as though he could not help it and I saw his chest expand with an indrawn breath.

My heart thrust violently.

"I swear I only asked if I could escort them to dinner, I didn't know anyone was *naked* in here," Axton said, almost choking on the word. "And then I tripped…"

Patricia gained enough control to confirm, "This unfortunate situation is simply a misunderstanding," but then Cole, also clad in a clean shirt, filled the doorway and she fell to laughing again.

Cole took one look at the scene before him and said, "*Dang*, you-all."

I hid my face for the second time, feeling a flush expand from my ears straight down to the soles of my feet.

"Out, all of you scoundrels!" Birdie suddenly appeared behind Cole, peering under his arm, which he'd braced on the doorframe. She demanded, "What is the matter with you men? Haven't you the courtesy to leave the presence of unclothed women?!"

But even I had to laugh at this ridiculous question, keeping my face to the floor, not daring to insult Birdie.

Cole said innocently, "Birdie-honey, life just wouldn't be worth living if we were forced to *leave* the presence of unclothed women, and I know Grant feels similarly regarding this matter…"

Birdie smacked Cole's arm just as Axton asked, sounding truly perplexed, "But what were the two of you *doing* over there, in the first place? Unclothed, that is?"

Miles turned from Birdie to hide his grin, reaching to haul Axton to his feet, and Cole grabbed the quilt from the bed, draping it over Patricia and me with the air of a showman. Just before the whiteness settled over us I caught Miles's gaze and he winked, still grinning.

Needless to say, Patricia and I were late to dinner.

Miles, Cole, Grant, and another man named Stadlar, who was employed as Grant's foreman, made music that night until the moon was high in the sky. Grant dug out fiddles for both Miles and Cole while Stadlar played a tin whistle; the music was haunting and mournful, jubilant and uplifting, by turns. Their combined talent sent repeated shivers climbing the individual bones of my spine. I snuggled under a blanket with Patricia; Axton, who'd apologized three times for his earlier blunder, sat on Patricia's far side. Patricia could not tear her eyes from Cole any more than I could tear mine from Miles.

"I love watching them play," Patricia whispered. "The intensity of their joy is truly astounding."

She was right and I found myself reflecting on the abundant joy found in the making of music; it was something that carried over from generation to generation, from one life to the next, in essence never dying, lasting through all time…

Time…

A shiver unrelated to my love of their music clutched at my gut.

The leaping bonfire was surrounded by every person who lived on the ranch – Birdie and her boys, the young men who worked for Grant as cattle hands, the cook, and the cook's son, a boy about five years old. There didn't seem to be a mother, but I didn't ask. The men passed a jug that reminded me of the one Branch used for whiskey, which I studiously avoided. The mood grew rowdier as the booze made the rounds, the musicians imbibing as much as everyone else.

The Spoke's bumping tonight, I heard someone say in my head, and then blinked at the strangeness of the thought.

Birdie held her youngest in her arms while her older son roved from lap to lap; Patricia and I took turns cuddling him. Even Ax held him for a spell while the men played a ballad, resting his chin on the boy's soft curls; he would be such a good father, just as I'd sensed on the journey here. I thought of how Celia once said I should marry Axton. Dear Celia, who meant to help me just as I meant to help her; and yet Celia was the one carrying Miles's baby, left behind in a saloon many dozens of miles east while I sat at a fire within a few yards of him, entertaining thoughts of us making love until dawn. At least Celia had been given that privilege, repeatedly.

Punishing myself, I recalled the night I'd first learned of her pregnancy.

I was half in love with him, Celia had said, and I hated myself for the possessive jealousy burning in my chest at the remembrance.

You selfish bitch, Ruthann. You complete hypocrite. Of course Celia meant she was totally in love with him and still is. Don't pretend you don't know it.

I had always known this truth, even if it was the last thing I wanted to acknowledge. Pride had motivated Celia's decision to order Miles to leave her alone, and her continued work as a prostitute was based on pure survival; she intended to send her illegitimate child east to a better life, with no pleading, no hope of keeping her baby. Celia was a thousand times stronger and nobler than me.

I deserved to be slapped across the face.

The song ended, its mournful notes falling into stillness, and Axton murmured, "That was pretty, weren't it?" to Birdie's little boy, who nodded and shifted his head, resting it against Axton's chest.

"Daddy ain't played my favorite song yet," the boy said, drumming his heels on the ground.

"What's your favorite song?" Patricia asked gamely, smiling at the boy. Her merry eyes lifted to Axton's and he was careful not to study her too intently – but I saw his expression in the glow of the fire and would have known then, if I hadn't already, just how strongly he felt for her. He swallowed, throat bobbing, and tore his gaze away as Patricia continued chatting with the little boy on his lap.

A movement caught my eye and I looked up to spy Miles headed our way, a cigar between his teeth, carrying a borrowed fiddle by its long neck. He came to a halt near my bent knees, grinning down at me in the firelight; my heart was all jacked up, my blood humming, unable to keep from responding to him no matter how badly I wished it otherwise. I felt like a lowdown, dirty traitor. Celia deserved so much better.

"Are you enjoying the music?" he asked, removing the cigar. "I came to see if perhaps you had a request."

"I love all of it," I replied truthfully, unable to look away. Even what sounded like a minor commotion on the opposite side of the fire did not pull our gazes from each other.

"However, Ruthann only just mentioned she particularly enjoys the waltzes," Patricia said, nudging me with her shoulder.

"Then we will kindly oblige." Miles appeared downright naughty, there was no denying, as if he were entertaining a number of impure thoughts; my suspicions were confirmed when he asked, with feigned innocence, "You didn't get any splinters, did you? Earlier, that is…"

"Are you teasing me?" I fired back. "Was that a joke?"

"I am only concerned for your wellbeing," Miles said calmly, shifting the fiddle to the opposite hand, balancing the cigar between forefinger and thumb and then tucking a stray strand of hair behind his ear; in the night, it was black as an ink spill. He had not tied back its length as he usually did; combined with his mustache and the scruff on his unshaven jaws, he looked like a pirate. He murmured, "That would be a painful place for a splinter."

Axton snorted restraining laughter.

Matching Miles's nonchalant tone, I agreed, "Yes, and digging it out with a needle would be *especially* painful."

"Well, if I am able to be of any – and I mean *any* – assistance…" Miles let his voice trail to silence. His wide, wicked grin sent shockwaves of heat straight to the juncture of my thighs. I shifted position, blazing with arousal and guilt, in almost equal measures.

Axton and Patricia were laughing, Patricia rocking sideways and taking the edge of the blanket with her.

"You just let me know," Miles finished.

"How about you play me a waltz and we'll call it good?" It was loud enough around the fire that my breathlessness was not obvious.

"*Smitten*," Patricia exhaled in my ear, as Miles rejoined Cole and Grant.

Eventually the late hour began to take casualties. Birdie kissed her husband, bade us all good-night, collected her boys, and headed indoors. Some of the men stretched out near the fire, intending to sleep there, and because Birdie, the only other woman present, had retired, Patricia and I decided to do the same. Grant and Stadlar continued playing, a slow, wistful tune in keeping with the quieting night. Miles and Cole excused themselves and skirted the fire on the opposite side when they saw Patricia and me preparing to go inside.

"Good-night, Ax." I bent to hug him around the neck, from behind. I planted a kiss on his cheek, which was rough with stubble.

"G'night," he murmured, catching my forearms in his hands and squeezing, in this way reciprocating my hug.

When I straightened, Miles was there to offer his arm.

"Did you enjoy the waltz?"

"I loved it." I tucked my hand around his hard, warm bicep and could not help but picture how he'd looked washing up at the pump; undiluted lust had flooded me at the sight of him, I could not deny. And yet to define my feelings for him as simple lust was indescribably wrong – there was so much more than that boiling inside me. We walked to the house, well away from the fire. The pure, sweet notes of the fiddle reminded me of a tinkling music box. Miles paused and turned to face me.

"It brings me great pleasure to make music for you." He studied me in the dimness. "Sleep well, sweet Ruthann."

I was desperate to keep him a moment longer, even as thoughts of Celia loomed in the back of my mind, armed with sharp claws. "Thank you for bringing me here to this place with you. Your family is wonderful. It's such a gift."

"I would give you many gifts, were I able," he said, and my heart ached at his sincerity.

"I know you would," I whispered. I'd stepped closer to him, or maybe he'd drawn me closer. "You have been so good to me, Miles."

"Nothing has ever felt more natural." He touched my hair with his free hand, stroking with great care, as if afraid I might bolt; when I did not, his touch grew bolder, long fingers twining into my curls. "I have treasured this time with you. It is a gift just to be near you."

Tears welled and I was glad it was too dark for him to notice. I could hardly bear such a heartfelt compliment. "Thank you, Miles. I don't deserve that…"

"That is untrue. You deserve so much more. So much more than I could give you." He cupped my jaw and traced my lower lip with his thumb. I struggled to breathe. He was so near and I hurt so badly; the sadness inside of me threatened to crest like a wave that would take us both under. I wanted Miles to kiss me and yet I was terrified he would, all at once. He was no more than a few inches away and I was about to explode with keen-edged, desirous tension.

"Ruthann," he whispered intently, cradling my face, leaning closer… our mouths were a breath apart when I turned coward and broke away.

"Good-night," I stammered, and retreated inside before he could say another word.

In the darkness of our room, Patricia and I lay beneath our quilt, backs touching as we snuggled together for warmth and comfort. She whispered and I tried to listen, curled with knees to chest, trembling, plagued by the sweet words Miles had spoken to me. He would have kissed me if I hadn't fled. Guilt wrapped heavy fingers around my heart; I couldn't even admit to Patricia how much I wanted him.

Oh God, Miles…

I finally realized Patricia lay in silence.

"I'm sorry," I whispered. Outside, the music had ceased. A few men remained around the fire; their low, murmuring voices drifted through the window glass to our ears.

"Whatever for?" she asked softly, and I felt the mattress shift as she turned toward me, smoothing a hand over my hair, spread across the pillow.

"I wasn't listening."

"You are lost in thought." She paused. "You believe you were married before now, do you not, before your loss of memory?"

I pressed the base of both palms to my closed eyes and nodded. The pain banding my center was so terrible I felt attacked.

"And that you may still be married?"

"I want to believe he's out there, looking for me…"

My voice seized and Patricia scooted closer, slipping an arm about my waist and squeezing. "Then you cannot give up hope, dear Ruthann."

"But what if…"

"Hush," she soothed as I began weeping, assaulted by choking sobs. I tried to speak but could not; I was too depleted.

I know he's out there.

But what if he doesn't come for me?

What if there's no one and I really am crazy?

And what about poor Celia and the baby?

Oh God, please let me remember who I am…

"We shall not speak of it again this night," Patricia said firmly.

I reached to lace together our fingers and brought our joined hands to my heart.

Chapter Eighteen

Between Birdie and Patricia, I'd learned to stitch a hem, attach a sleeve to a shirt, churn butter, and mix up bread dough, skills I did not remember ever learning. Birdie had been horrified by our overall lack of proper clothing; I possessed little enough to begin with and Patricia's expensive belongings were, by necessity, left behind in the train car, so Birdie took it upon herself to make us each a new dress and two new underskirts, and was currently knitting woolen shawls. I helped with the weekly laundry, glad I had at least one household skill to put to use. My time at Rilla's seemed like a fading nightmare – I clung only to thoughts of Celia, who was always at the back of my remorseful mind. Nightly I prayed she was doing well, that she was caring for herself and the unborn child as best she could.

I could never hope to repay Birdie's dear, welcoming kindness. Patricia and I had been guests at the homestead for nearly a month; there was a chill in the air not present when we'd arrived in early September, and a heavy new quilt on our bed. Miles had spent the evening following our arrival explaining to his brother and Birdie the events leading up to our flight from Howardsville; overcome by anxiety, I'd feared the worst – that they would summarily insist we be removed from their home. But the trust between Miles and Grant ran deeper than I'd understood, and no orders to seek refuge elsewhere were issued. Miles took care to relate the details of the conversation to Cole, Patricia, Axton, and me later that same night.

"I must continue my circuit no later than tomorrow," Miles said, looking at me as he spoke; my heart began sinking. "I have no wish to leave but I am already delayed, due in Billings."

We surrounded the table in the quiet, lantern-lit kitchen. Grant and Birdie had retired to bed, allowing momentary privacy. Miles sat at the head, hands folded and demeanor steady, Cole at the foot, both forearms resting on the table's surface; Axton claimed the chair across from Patricia and me, close enough we could have reached mere inches and touched his hands. Patricia, to my right, could not seem to keep her somber gaze from roaming to Axton, who sat with wide shoulders slightly hunched, his hair curling along the back of his neck. I remembered thinking, months ago in Howardsville, that Axton had no idea how appealing he really was – and as he sat there across from Patricia, taking pains to remain focused on Miles rather than her, he appeared unusually aloof and almost achingly handsome.

And I felt, more strongly than ever, a sense of the connection binding the five of us. I studied Miles in the apricot tint of the lantern, sitting with forced calm when inside my head a distant roar grew louder by the second.

If you would just understand…

Miles was unfinished issuing orders. "Ruthann, Patricia, you will remain here for the time being. We are dozens of miles from town and no one rides up on the homestead undetected. You will be safe here. Cole, I would appreciate your accompaniment to Billings. Axton, you've done good work, young fellow. You delivered the women safely here and now I have another favor to ask of you."

Axton waited in silence but I could sense his pride at the compliment.

"I would that you return to Howardsville within the week. The men sent to scout for Yancy will have returned to town by then and I am counting on you to get a read on the situation in my absence. Gauge the mood and return here to Grant's with the information you gather, by month's end. Cole and I will have returned by that time. What say you?"

Axton's shoulders squared. When he spoke, his voice was gruff with responsibility. "Of course, marshal."

And though she scarcely shifted position and spoke not a word, I sensed the regret gathering inside Patricia.

To say I had missed Miles in the past month would be an unspeakable understatement. My eyes roved the northwestern horizon dozens of times a day, watching for any sign of Blade's galloping return. Patricia and I spent almost every waking moment together, more often than not in Birdie's company; I could barely remember a time when Patricia hadn't been part of my life. I loved her dearly and had come to care deeply for Grant, Birdie, and their boys, a loving family fortunate enough to remain intact.

More than a hundred times I'd debated telling Birdie about Celia, but Patricia continually reminded me it was not my place to do so. It was easy to talk to Birdie, who'd been starved for the company of other women; I was so tempted to confess what I knew. Birdie's sense of humor bordered on naughty and she seemed never to tire of conversing, or discussing the newspaper articles and monthly periodicals she received in the mail courtesy of Grant and Miles's mother, Fannie Rawley. Most importantly, I knew if I dared to trust her with the knowledge that another Rawley was due to enter the world, she would take charge. She would see that Miles's baby was not sent away.

Patricia and I continued to share the small upstairs bedroom, lying awake long after everyone else fell asleep, sometimes laughing so hard we smothered the sound with our pillows but more often discussing topics of a serious nature. One such conversation took place the night Axton had saddled Ranger, three days after Miles and Cole departed for Billings, and set out on the return journey to Howardsville.

"Ruthie, I must tell you something." Patricia's usual sleeping position was her right side, knees bent, but she lay now facing the ceiling, fingertips resting on her eyelids. My pupils had long since adjusted to the dimness and I rolled to face her, seeing the gray line of her profile silhouetted against the pale wall. My eyes were sore and grainy; I'd been so sad to bid farewell to Axton it manifested as physical, weeping pain. I hadn't been apart from him for more than a few days since my arrival in Howardsville. Patricia and I kept nothing from each other but her tone carried weight – much the same as it had when she'd first mentioned her terrible wedding night.

"I'm right here," I whispered.

When she spoke at last, her voice emerged with a vulnerable note I'd never before heard. "I've done something unforgiveable."

I lifted to an elbow, about to contradict her, but she kept speaking, pressing harder and harder against her eyes.

"Axton kissed me last night. We took a walk together after dinner, to the creek beyond the main house, as you know…"

I had known, but this particular detail came as something of a shock. It explained the gravity of Axton's demeanor before he'd left this morning, and Patricia's reticence and immediate disappearance after he rode out. I'd found her curled on our bed, feigning sleep. Now, many hours later, her torture had grown to immense proportions.

Feeling I owed it to both of them, I talked straight. "Axton's in love with you. I've known since the day I introduced you to him."

She choked back a sob, squeezing her temples as though holding them in place. "Oh, Ruthie, I've known the same. I'm hardly blind. I recognized his infatuation and was flattered by the attention. I certainly never imagined I would see him beyond that first evening, when Branch invited us to dinner."

"What did he say, yesterday?" I whispered, reaching to gently remove her rigid grasp, fearful she would bruise her own face.

"He is so very sincere, Ruthie, and perceptive, it hurts me like a fist to the chest." Tears rolled down her temples as she fought another wave of weeping, determined to speak. "He told me to keep safe, for he would never forgive himself if something were to happen to me in his absence. He said he meant no disrespect, and it was clear I cared for Cole, but he could not ride away without telling me how he felt. He said…he said he knew I was the woman for him the second he saw my eyes *that morning in Howardsville*…" She gulped and her chest heaved; her throat sounded like someone had applied a razor to its length.

"Oh, Patricia," I breathed, hurting for both of them. I thought, *Axton, sweetheart, that was so very brave.*

"My arms were around him before I knew I had moved, Ruthie. Since we first met I have thought of little but Cole, this is true, but when Axton touched me there was only *him*. Oh, dear God, he kissed me and I...oh Ruthie, I lay here now recalling the feel of him in my arms, the taste of his mouth, and my legs are weak. The simple act of speaking his name aloud causes my stomach to become hollow...*Axton*..."

I couldn't help but feel a surge of triumph – were Ax still sleeping in the bunkhouse this night, as he had since our arrival, I would have dashed out there and congratulated his boldness.

"What did you think when you kissed Cole?" I felt it was only fair to ask.

"I haven't," she whispered. "We were never able to steal a moment's time. You shall recall when he and Miles left we were in the company of the entire household." She issued a low, growling sound of frustration. "I am a vain, fickle woman. What I have done is unforgiveable. The night Cole carried me to Branch's cabin I wondered how I could ever wish for anything more. I wanted to beg him to stay, to hold me through all the hours of the night. How might I harbor feelings for more than one man? For this is the plain truth – my feelings for both of them are undeniable. What in God's name is the matter with me? I know the word you are surely thinking...and you are justified for thinking it..."

"Tish, enough! Don't make me smother you! Stop punishing yourself."

There was a moment of complete silence before she whispered, "'Tish?'"

"What..." I blinked in slow motion, a beat of awareness pulsing between us. My mind rolled like a long, low wave headed toward its demise upon the shore. I admitted, "I don't know where that came from."

"How peculiar, Ruthie. How could you have known? That was Rosemary's nickname for me, when she was very small."

I felt cold and hollow. I fought the urge to throw off the quilts and flee.

I don't belong here. Oh God, I don't belong in this place.

I felt it more strongly than ever before.

"Ruthie?" Patricia sat up, concern lacing the word.

"I'm fine," I whispered, but it was a lie. I regrouped, with effort, but my breath was shallow. "You haven't done anything wrong, do you hear me? You are entitled to care about whomever you want."

"I care for them both. I *want* them both. Is that not the very definition of shamelessness?"

I could handle no more and gathered her hands. "Nothing needs to be decided tonight. It's all right."

"I love you, Ruthie, thank you for being here. I do not know what I would do without you."

"I love you too, Patricia," I whispered honestly.

Tish…

"Wolves, they think, based on his wounds? Or perhaps a catamount?" Birdie asked Grant the first week of October. It was an hour after dawn, the promise of a clear, bright day on the horizon. Grant, who had eaten before daybreak with his men, now stood sipping coffee, leaning against the woodbox and watching Birdie as she boiled oats for their boys. Birdie's cheeks were flushed and her golden hair hung in a long braid; she wore a hastily-tied apron. She was the type of person unable to still for long but her work never slowed her chatter. She peered over her shoulder at her husband, awaiting his response. I sat at the table rolling biscuit dough; I did my best to rise early to help Birdie in the kitchen, usually leaving Patricia in bed, snoring.

Grant nodded. "I'd put my money on a wolf, likely a weakened stray from a pack. A confrontation with a mountain lion would have left the fellow dead."

"Might be that they'll need my help," Birdie mused, stirring vigorously. "If Amos thinks he won't recover. Do the wounds need stitching? What was Henrietta's opinion?"

"Wolves attacked someone?" I asked. Despite numerous anxieties, I hadn't yet been given reason to fear wild animals.

"I apologize, Ruthie, we are speaking of a neighbor, Amos Howe, a dozen miles west of here," Birdie said. "Amos found a man badly injured on his property a day ago. The poor fellow was unconscious and blood-ied. Amos recognized an animal was responsible, not a human, and rode over to warn us. Wolves will pick off cattle if we are not careful. But we've no reason to fear, dearest. Attacks by animals are few and far be-tween, even out here in the Territories."

"The man isn't someone Amos recognized from around these parts," Grant said, and though his tone roused no cause for alarm, my hands stalled over their task. "No horse, but his mount likely spooked and ran. No supplies, no pocket watch or bible inscribed with a name. I admit I'm damn curious. I've been wondering about it since Amos rode over to tell the news. Amos said Henrietta was worried if that answers your question, Birdie-honey."

"Has he come to? Been able to tell them anything?" she asked.

"Not as of yet. He's fevered and ailing but of course Henrietta is do-ing her best to revive him." Grant slowly shook his head, holding his cof-fee mug a few inches from his chin. "Amos was hopeful for his recovery, said he's a young man and seems strong. Amos said the fellow opened his eyes for a moment and it gave him a start, gray as smoke they were."

I jerked as if stabbed between two ribs. My mouth went dry.

"Ruthie?" Birdie paused, moving to my side, resting a comforting hand on my shoulder. "Whatever is the matter, dear? You've gone pale as a bedsheet."

"I'm all right," I whispered, but it was far from true.

What's wrong, what's wrong…oh God, what's wrong…

But there was no answer.

Miles and Cole returned that very night, well after the moon climbed past its zenith and began a slow descent, the sound of their horses draw-ing me from bed. Allowing Patricia to continue sleeping, I hurried to button a skirt over the chemise I used as pajamas and wrapped my new shawl around my shoulders. Grant, Stadlar, and several other ranch hands were already outside to greet them but I paid no mind to any-one else, running barefoot across the cold and prickling ground. Miles caught sight of me and heeled Blade, dismounting with the graceful movements I knew well. I gathered my shawl tighter and stayed put even though my heart leaped toward him.

He paused just within arms' reach and said with quiet gladness, "Ruthann. Are you well?"

I hadn't seen him in over a month and my voice trembled. "I've missed you."

The desire to move the mere inches it would take to come together drove at both of us, I knew, but we remained apart.

"And I have missed you. I am very happy to see you. Words cannot express."

"How was your trip?" I sounded so bland and stupid. The words I wanted to say, but could not manage, broiled just beneath the surface.

"I was glad for Cole's company, for more than one reason. But we can discuss this tomorrow, when you have not been rudely pulled from sleep. You are chilled."

"I'm not," I insisted. I was clutching the shawl so tightly for other reasons, such as holding back my heart from jumping through my ribcage. I rushed on, "Birdie has been so kind. She's made winter clothes for Patricia and me."

"I told you she would adore you at once." Behind him, Blade snorted a loud breath, nudging Miles in the spine, and he shifted to avoid his horse's questing nose. "We will talk first thing in the morning. You return to the warmth of your bed…"

His voice was hoarse and my blood burned; I didn't move. Instead, I spoke his name and just that one word was temptation enough for him to touch my face. He cupped my cheek and passed his thumb over my mouth.

He whispered, "I like hearing my name on your lips. I like it very much."

Within the house, baby Isaac began to cry.

I reached up and clutched Miles's wrist. A soft rush of air escaped my throat. It was all the invitation he required; my hands slipped over his collarbones, seeking to hold him in a full embrace at last, my murmur of welcome caught between our mouths. I dug my fingers in his loose, thick hair. He released Blade's lead line to wrap me in his arms. When Miles lifted his head, we were both short of breath. I flushed from hairline to toes as he studied me with mild amazement; his black hat was slightly askew.

"I'm glad you're home," I whispered, my palms resting on his chest. I could feel his heart thrusting against my breasts.

"I don't know when I've ever been gladder to *be* home," he whispered back and wasted no time reclaiming my mouth. I angled beneath his hat brim, returning his kisses with increasing abandon, punishing myself – I knew the feel of this man, I knew his taste, and yet he wasn't…

Oh God, he wasn't…

I broke away, a roaring in my ears, as wide-open and aching as if torn apart mid-body.

"Your horse is stealing off, Rawley!" Cole called from somewhere distant.

Miles kept me anchored flush against his chest; he stole one last, soft kiss before whispering, "Until tomorrow, sweet woman."

"Might do to keep a few more men out in the evenings," Miles told Grant at breakfast.

There had been rustling activity across the Territory, in all directions, and Miles did not believe there was such a thing as being too cautious. Though he did not come right out and admit it was the responsibility of Bill Little's gang, more specifically the man called Vole, I could tell this was what he believed. I intended to ask him privately, when we had a chance to talk alone, rather than in front of everyone at the breakfast table; it turned out I had the perfect opportunity later that afternoon.

"Who exactly is Vole?" I asked.

Even though the air was cold and the wind held a bite, the sky was cloudless. We had saddled Blade and Flickertail and now rode alongside one another, toward the mountain range guarding the western horizon. Its upper ridges were blunted rather than pointed peaks, but majestic nonetheless, a smudgy blue-gray in color and frosted with snow. I borrowed Miles's jacket, the one Cole had draped over my shoulders back in the jailhouse in Howardsville, and wore the trousers Axton had once lent me.

Miles said, "It is a long and complicated story. To be honest, I have tried in these intervening years to forget some parts of it, as Malcolm Carter is one of the dearest friends I have ever been fortunate enough to have, and he will never overcome the loss of Cora, his woman. You will meet him, in time, as he ventures this way now and again. He does not wish to attempt overcoming the loss, and I never fully understood that before." His chest expanded with a breath and his gaze skittered out toward the mountains. "I've never known Vole's given name, or if he even possesses one. Malcolm and Cole first came across him back when Vole rode with Bill Little in the spring of 'seventy-four. They were all working the railroad that year, and Bill was obsessed with Cora."

"Did Bill Little kill her?" I whispered, already dreading the answer.

"Malcolm believed so, though when we had the bastard pinned down and on death's door…" Miles cut short his words. "I do not wish to offend you."

"I'm not offended. I feel like you trust me when you tell me these things."

"I wish to speak freely to you, at all times. And I wish the same of you, in return."

I nodded agreement.

He continued, "Malcolm, Cole, Grant and I met up again later that summer. Grant and I had not seen Cole for over a year, and Malcolm for nearly eight years, at that point. For a time, Cora rode with us and she and Malcolm were so happy. They intended to marry. We…" His voice grew rough. "We made the worst mistake of our lives in leaving her behind that night. Malcolm will never forgive himself. He ripped himself inside-out with the torture of it. We thought he would take his own life. He scarcely spoke to any of us for over a year. Searched the countryside for months without let-up. His name amongst the Cheyenne is One Who Hurts. Or Wandering One. And he never found her."

"No one ever found her? That's so horrible…"

"Bill claimed with his last breath Cora disappeared from him, that he did *not* kill her. Malcolm killed him, and three of the bastards who rode with him, but Vole got away. I have come across a fair amount of wretched men in my time as marshal, men I would as soon see in a noose before sunrise, Aemon Turnbull included, but Vole remains one of the worst specimens yet, nearly as bad as Fallon Yancy. I wouldn't let a dog I liked venture near either man without my protection."

"And you think Vole is riding in the Territory again?" I curbed the odd urge to look over my shoulder. In my imagination Vole resembled a furtive, oversized rat, whiskers and all. I drew Flickertail closer to Blade.

"My instincts suggest he is, as much as I hate to admit it. Cole and I talked to ranchers across the Territory on our circuit. Vole isn't choosy about inflicting harm, but he's borne a black-dark grudge against the four of us for years, me in particular. My shot took him in the cheek. I only wish I would have split his infernal skull. If he appeared just now I wouldn't waste time speaking, I would open fire on him."

"I'm not shocked, in case you were worried."

Miles looked my way, his eyes in the shadow of his hat brim. His hair was tied back, as usual, his lips solemn and his hips moving with the rhythm of the horse beneath him. I felt another burst of rampant desire, unchecked and insistent, thinking of kissing him last night.

"The killings east of here, out Yankton way, speak of his work. Men shot in the back, their guts sliced open. I hate to speak of such. And Vole has long been associated with the Yancys, at least from a distance."

"Guts sliced out? That's so brutal."

"Cole was correct in his statement that we should have ridden the bastard to the ground and killed him, four years ago. Do you see now why I wished for you to accompany me here to my family's home, where there is ample protection, where I know you are safe?"

"I do," I whispered. "And I am so grateful for it."

We spoke next of Axton; Miles was of the opinion that he should have returned by now. Patricia and I had harbored the same troubling thought for days; we spoke of it every night.

"Do you think the Yancys will come looking for her?" I wanted Miles's opinion. "I worry about it all the time."

"It all depends whether or not they believe she is dead. I knew both Dredd and Fallon as boys, as you know. Dredd was…perhaps 'hesitant' is the best word. Not one for action, and Fallon bullied him terribly. If either comes looking for her in Howardsville it's my hope they will find no solid leads. No one other than Branch and Axton knows her location."

"How much longer will we remain here?" This was yet another subject Patricia and I whispered about at night, but neither of us wanted to ask for fear of the answer.

Miles hesitated a long while. In the distance, I heard the low moaning of many cattle; 'lowing' was what Grant called the noise. And then the air shifted and the distant sounds were no longer audible. He finally spoke.

"Ruthann, I cannot bear the thought of taking you back to Howardsville, where you would be unsafe when I ride my route. I would that you remain here, with my family, under their protection and care, until I return. I intend to return to Howardsville within the week and from there I will wire the federal offices in Washington. I intend to request a position with a smaller range, so that I might…"

I gulped. My palms slipped over Flickertail's reins.

He continued, with determination, "So I might settle and therefore be able to take a wife."

"Miles…"

"I know this is improper, I truly do, and hardly romantic. *Christ*, I am doing this all wrong…"

I tugged Flickertail to an abrupt halt.

He drew on Blade's reins and made a half-turn, so we faced each other. His features were stark with sincerity as he removed his hat, held it to his chest, and spoke quickly and solemnly, as if I might heel Flickertail and ride away before he could finish. "I am asking you to become my wife. I have never known something as absolutely as I know I am to be with you. You have my heart, Ruthann Rawley, and already my name, as inexplicable as it may be. But I would make you mine, in all ways."

My heart seemed to plummet, landing with a dull thud between Flickertail's hooves, and I imagined my horse kicking it up into the air to sail far away. Because surely I was about to break Miles's heart; I couldn't bear it.

"I…" My tongue seemed swollen, unable to bring forth the necessary words.

Miles studied me with an expression of near-torture, already anticipating I would deny him. He whispered, "Is it…"

I found an ounce of strength. "Miles, I care deeply for you." My voice broke but I forged ahead. "The truth is you deserve better than me. I don't even know who I am. I can't remember a thing beyond last summer, when Branch and Axton found me near the creek bed." I started to cry and was both ashamed and embarrassed.

Blade snorted at my agitation, tossing his beautiful silver head; Miles kept him expertly in line. "I know who you are, to me. I only care that it hurts you not to know. I cannot imagine my life without you in it, Ruthann, please know this."

The beauty and sincerity of these words only served to further gouge my heart, releasing a sharp burst of anger – I could not survive this pain if I allowed myself to feel it and so I welcomed the anger, letting it flood my senses. "We're living here in some kind of sick denial, *all of us*. Celia is pregnant with *your baby*, back at Rilla's! You can't keep ignoring this fact, Miles. And Patricia *refuses* to accept that she is still married. She believes she's in love with both Axton *and* Cole, did you know that?" My voice emerged in breathless huffs, as if someone was punching me with white-knuckled fists. I cried, "Don't you understand? Patricia told me she'd help me find my husband. He's out there, looking for me, I *know it…*"

Miles flinched, his jaws tightening, but he was honorable enough to say, "Then I will do everything in my power to help you. I wish to bring you happiness. I have never wanted anything more."

Sobs clawed at my throat; I slid down from Flickertail and tugged at Miles's right leg, wordless, wracked by weeping. But he understood, dismounting at once, holding Blade's lead line in one hand and catching me against his chest with his other arm. I pressed my face to him, shocked at the depth of relief his body offered, inhaling his scent like someone coming up for the third time. Someone headed for certain drowning. My hat fell off and he bracketed the nape of my neck, kissing my forehead, my temples, murmuring soft sounds of comfort. I soaked his shirt with my tears but he didn't release his hold.

"Sweet Ruthann, don't cry." I didn't know how much time passed as we stood embracing. The sun seemed to be in a different place in the sky. "I will help you, I swear to you. And I will speak again with Celia, I promise you this as well."

I rubbed miserably at my wet face, muttering, "I'm so sorry…"

"Do not apologize," Miles said. "I aim to make you happy. You know this, do you not?"

My heart was bruised black and blue, swollen beyond repair. I stood on tiptoe to put my arms around his neck and hugged him with all my strength. He crushed me close; Blade and Flickertail hemmed us in, one on either side.

"Thank you," I whispered, and then drew away.

Miles bent and collected my hat, which he handed to me. "You are most welcome."

"I'm sorry I freaked out." Sometimes my words popped out differently than everyone else's; I was used to the way people's expressions reflected this momentary lapse in the flow of conversation, while they sorted out what they thought I meant.

"You've nothing to be sorry for." Miles replaced the hat on my head, stroking my jaw with his fingertips. "Not one thing."

But that's where he was wrong.

Chapter Nineteen

BY THE TIME MILES AND I RETURNED TO THE RANCH, IT was late afternoon. Patricia was waiting on the front porch to speak to me. I found myself thinking her eyes had never looked bluer. She caught my elbow as I came near, snuggling against me as she was prone to do, and I squeezed her close.

"What is it?"

"I've something to tell you. Might we walk, just us two?"

"Of course." I linked our arms. I wore Miles's dark jacket and Patricia was bundled in her shawl, though it wasn't especially chilly; the vivid sun had warmed the day. We walked out beyond the house, toward the mountains, in companionable silence. It wasn't until we were well past the yard that Patricia stopped our forward progress, turning to face me and catching my hands. I studied this woman I loved dearly, who was as much a sister to me as any I could imagine. She squeezed my fingers as she whispered, "Cole has asked me to be his wife."

A shifting in the gut, a change in the wind, a distant, wailing cry –

"Is that what you want?" It was growing stronger, the sensation of hurtling out of control, of events about to sweep us away from solid footing and into the fray. How was it I already knew there wasn't a goddamn thing we could do to prevent it?

No, I thought. *Please, no…*

"Cole wishes for us to winter in Iowa, with his family, and return here in the spring to make our permanent home." When I couldn't find words to reply Patricia implored, "Have you any news for me?"

My forehead crinkled; I wasn't sure what news she thought I might possess.

"Miles proposed to you this very day, did he not? He spoke of it with Cole last night." Patricia searched my face as if for clues. "Did he not?"

I located my voice. "He did."

Her voice flowed like water over smooth rocks long ago sunk to the river bottom; I heard the desperation beneath those slick, wet stones. "You and Miles could accompany us on the journey east. Miles has not returned home to Iowa in over two years. We could winter there together. We would not have to part, Ruthie, *don't you see…*"

Misgivings swarmed my skull. I knew she saw it in my eyes.

I'm so scared. Something is so wrong.

I tried to believe what she suggested could happen –

We could spend the winter together in Iowa and return here in the spring. I could become Mrs. Miles Rawley.

Oh, dear God…

Tears bloomed in Patricia's eyes and overspilled; her voice shook. "Something is dreadfully wrong."

"I know," I whispered, numb with certainty.

Her grip on my hands became almost feral. "*Axton…*"

"He's all right. He *has* to be." I could not think otherwise.

"Promise me," she begged, almost childlike in her intensity to believe in my words.

But I could not promise anything.

As the autumn weather was so fine the men made music well into the evening. I sat at the fire in the company of many with a bristling spike planted in my heart, oblivious to the surrounding merriment. The firelight flickered over Cole, Grant, and Stadlar as they played. And Miles. My dear, honorable Miles, who had told me today, in so many words, that he loved me. I watched him without ceasing, studying his face, his body, his long-fingered hands which cradled a fiddle with such ease, such grace and tenderness, the same way he touched everything he cared for. When the men struck up a waltz, Cole took a break from fiddling and asked Patricia to dance; I saw the way his arms locked about her, I saw how he studied her face.

When the whiskey jug made the rounds, I damned it all and took a cautious nip, unable to keep from gasping as the alcohol seared the interior of my mouth. But after the initial burning shock the whiskey built a small, comforting blaze in my belly. By the jug's fourth round the booze had allowed my limbs to relax and I stole another long glug, backhanding droplets from my lips. The men were fiddling a waltz, one I recognized and loved, one Miles and Cole had played around the fire that night at Branch's. Tears made my face all sticky. The alcohol in my blood lent everything an amber tint. My bones felt rubbery and my thoughts were slow, struggling across my mind like tiny tadpoles through syrup.

One of the ranch hands, a man named Jem, sat nearby. I leaned way over to tug his sleeve, wondering aloud, "Don't they know any Bon Jovi?"

Jem crinkled his eyebrows. "How's that, Miss Ruthann?"

I forgot what I'd asked, instead mumbling, "I have to puke…"

Jem must have read my lips because he lurched to his feet and hauled me away from the fire. I was peripherally aware of Miles handing off his instrument and following us; Jem relinquished me to Miles's arms about halfway to the house.

"*I'm sorry,*" I gasped as another round of vomiting doubled me over.

"She's liquored," Jem explained needlessly; this fact was obvious.

Miles held me while I threw up all the whiskey I'd consumed. When it was apparent I had nothing more to heave, Miles led me inside the house and up the steps to the room I shared with Patricia; within the familiar space he helped me sit on the bed and then lit a candle.

"I'm so sorry," I moaned, cradling my head.

Miles knelt before me, grasping my hands and kissing the back of each one. "There is nothing to apologize for."

I groaned as another wave of nausea struck but this time I had nothing left to expel.

Without another word Miles bent to unlace my shoes, setting them on the floor near the foot of the bed. "Lie down. I will bring a cloth for your face."

The room spun when I attempted to lie flat so I shifted to the side, drawing up my knees and concentrating on the sphere of light cast by the lantern. Miles was absent only moments before he returned with a cup of water and a dampened linen cloth, which he folded over my forehead. The mattress sagged as he sat near my hip. I held out my hand and he enfolded it, face again in shadow while the candle seemed to strike me in the eyes. "Rest. I won't leave your side."

"You are so good to me," I whispered.

"I am in love with you," he said somberly, and the despair that overtook me was so forceful I thought I might be split in two. I shook with it, the gashes reopened along my heart. I wanted Miles – but not exactly him. I couldn't explain it any better than this. I only knew something deep inside me understood the disparity and perceived the depth of my need. I wanted my man, wherever he was; I needed him with all my heart. I had once been loved so completely and passionately even the echo of its memory was unbearable, now that it was gone. For whatever reason it was gone and I could not accept it.

"I want…I want…" I was repeating myself like a child, like a fucking idiot drunk. I sobbed, "I want…*him*. Oh God…oh God…*where is he?*"

"Ruthann." Miles's voice was husky with compassion. "Come here."

He removed his pistol from its holster and placed it on the nightstand before collecting me in his arms, cupping the back of my head, drawing it to his chest. I clutched the material of his shirt, choking on sobs; his collar was soon soaked with my tears, for the second time today. He stroked my hair; his heart beat against mine. After a long time I fell silent, exhausted and spent, and Miles whispered, "I wish more than anything in this world I could give you what you want. Do you speak of your husband?"

A sighing shudder wracked my body as I nodded.

"Had I the power, I would return him to you, I swear this." He pressed his lips to my forehead; his mustache was soft against my skin, his lips warm. "But I fear he is gone."

No, I wailed, without sound. Deep inside, I could not accept this as truth.

"You sleep, sweet angel, I will hold you."

I froze. "What did you say?"

He cupped my jaws and with utmost gentleness kissed my lips, which were wet with salty tears. "I said I will hold you. Trust me. I wish for you to trust me."

I whispered honestly, "I do trust you, Miles."

"For now, that is enough," he whispered against my hair, and held me close to his heart.

Later I was to wonder what might have happened after that night, had fate taken a different direction. I was human, after all. Images replayed, rapid-fire, through my mind. I saw Miles as he appeared the first afternoon we'd met, astride Blade and smoking a cigar; I saw him gently administering a cloth to my bleeding forehead; playing his fiddle with all of his devoted love; lying near a banked fire along the trail while I contemplated crawling to his side and holding him and never letting go.

Oh Ruthann, oh God, you should have gone to him.

Why didn't you?

Why...

Hours passed, carrying us into the deep black bowels of night. The music had long since ceased, the men on night rounds saddling up; Patricia had not appeared in our bedroom, leading me to believe she and Cole were somewhere together. Miles kept me close, my arms folded against his chest, his even breathing indicating he slept. When I jerked awake there seemed no apparent reason. I lay motionless and stiff, stretching out with my senses to recognize what had ripped me from sleep. At first I could hear nothing but the creaks of a house at rest; there wasn't a breath of wind outside. Something was terribly wrong.

"Miles," I whispered urgently, sitting up.

Miles rose, swift and soundless as a striking hawk, collecting his pistol in one smooth motion.

"What's wrong?" I whispered, my heart sounding off like a gong.

He moved to the window, peering into the yard below from the edge of the glass. He murmured, "I'm not certain, but you woke me from a bad dream, I'll not deny it. Something isn't right."

I slipped into my shoes, head aching and vision wavering, but determined to stay at his side. Miles's posture changed, becoming threatening as he zeroed in upon something outside. I dropped to a crouch, terror sizzling through my center.

"Rider," he said. With rapid, efficient movements, he grasped my arm. "Come."

We clattered down the wooden steps.

Miles yelled, "Grant!"

Grant met us in the kitchen, tugging suspenders in place, pistol in hand. Both children were crying; I heard Birdie shushing them. The back door burst wide open, emitting Cole and Patricia. Grant tossed a shotgun from its wall hanger straight to Cole, who caught it and chambered a round. All three men gathered in the front yard, arranging themselves in a semi-circle and aiming their firearms at the approaching rider.

Cole lowered the shotgun. "It's Axton!"

With those words Patricia flew from the house, me on her heels.

Axton slid from Ranger's back almost before the horse was at a halt. He held his ribs and walked with a hitching gait; my heart lurched. Miles holstered his pistol and ran to catch Axton before he fell. Patricia raced to Axton's other side but didn't dare touch him, not knowing the extent of his wounds.

"Get him inside," Grant instructed. "Birdie! We got a wounded man!"

Birdie, wrapped in a quilted robe, her hair in its customary nighttime braid, hurried to light two lanterns, sweeping the cloth from the table and bundling it in a corner. The boys were still crying from the direction of her bedroom but she paid them no mind.

Taking immediate stock of the situation, Birdie ordered, "I need a basin."

Patricia flew for the hand pump in the kitchen.

"Axton," I breathed, hovering at Miles's elbow as he helped him atop the table. My innards seized; there was blood all along Axton's right side.

Birdie rolled up her sleeves and brought one of the lanterns closer.

Flat on his back, allowing Birdie to unbutton his shirt, Axton whispered, "I got here as fast as I could."

Miles rested a hand on Ax's upper arm and kept his voice calm. "What's happening?"

Axton grimaced as Birdie removed his shirt and eased down the waist of his trousers, all of us gaping at him like he was some sort of science experiment. Axton's lean torso was wet with sweat and rusty-red blood had crusted along his ribs and over a deep wound near his right hip. The last I'd seen him he'd been riding east, waving farewell, bound for Howardsville. He focused on me and I clutched his outstretched hand.

"What is it, Ax? What's happened?"

"They killed Uncle Branch." He sounded like a stranger, his voice hoarse and rough.

"Who?" Grant demanded.

I understood plainly it was no time for sympathy but my heart shredded at Axton's words. I clung to his hand. Patricia returned with the basin, her face as white as bare bone, terrified eyes tracking all over Axton, absorbing every detail.

"Men rode into town and killed Deputy Furlough just before sundown," Axton said in the stranger's voice. "Killed him and tore up the jailhouse. Set fire to it next."

Miles was up and pacing.

I shifted to the side so Birdie could better examine the extent of the damage; she ordered, "Hold the lantern near," and inspected him with knowledgeable eyes. "I see two wounds. This one on your hip needs cleaning and stitching. There's no time to waste."

Cole demanded, "What men?"

Axton's eyes roved from face to face; he reminded me of a spooked horse. I cupped his cheek, cold against my palm. "Sweetheart, listen to me, it's all right. You're all right. What men are you talking about?"

Standing near his hip, Birdie bunched a damp cloth and began dabbing away dried blood. With determination, I kept focused on his eyes.

"Axton," I implored.

He drew a shallow breath. "We were in town because Ruby threw a shoe. We heard the shots from Lyle's," and I knew he meant the blacksmith's barn, adjacent to the livery stable. "And there was Deputy Furlough in the street, bent over his gut…"

"Then what?" I whispered.

"Two men were on horses and they were yelling. One was Aemon Turnbull." My heart plummeted at this name. "They wanted to know where the marshal was. They shot up the jailhouse windows."

Miles stopped pacing; his distressed gaze found and held mine.

Axton clenched his jaws as Birdie continued her ministrations; he sought Patricia's attention, already fixed upon him, and whispered her name.

"I'm here," she breathed, moving as close as she dared, smoothing hair from his sweating forehead.

Axton reached and gently clasped her wrist. "The Yancys' train cars came back late this afternoon. I've kept watch since they left, weeks back, but now they've returned."

Patricia faltered. Cole was there at once, wrapping a possessive arm around her waist.

Oh Jesus, she said with no sound.

"They're coming for me," she choked, her voice so thin and reedy it hardly sounded like her own. Her hands flew to her face, fingertips making divots in her skin. "They do not believe me dead. Of course they would make certain for themselves."

"You are *not theirs*," Cole said heatedly.

Patricia stood immobile, mired in a nightmare.

Cole spoke again, more adamantly. "Patricia!"

Miles asked Axton, "Did anyone follow you?"

Ax tore his eyes from Patricia. "No, I swear, no."

"We can't take chances. We have to assume they did," Grant said.

Axton tried to sit. "Marshal, Uncle Branch knew the other man riding with Turnbull. It was the one called Vole."

Chapter Twenty

"JESUS CHRIST," GRANT MUTTERED. "JESUS *fucking Christ.*"

Only Miles retained a shred of calm. "What happened next, Axton? How was Branch killed?" I'd never heard him sound so serious. "You said they were asking after me?"

"Uncle Branch has been carrying his pistol again. When he saw what was happening, he didn't hesitate. He shot at them. He hit one of the bastards but they fired back." Axton's mouth twisted. "Uncle Branch was hit near a half-dozen times before they rode away. He was just gone, marshal. *Gone.* It was so quick. I couldn't do a goddamn thing. I dragged him inside the livery and rode out here as fast as I could push Ranger – I didn't know I'd been hit 'til I was miles from town."

Miles inhaled hard through his nose, his eyes steady with purpose as his mind clicked along, taking into account every possibility. "You did the right thing, Axton, but we must presume someone followed you. I need for everyone to listen to me, right now."

Even Birdie, working over Axton with all the determination of a field nurse, paused to look at Miles. She appeared ghostly in the lantern glow. Grant understood without further instruction, immediately pulling rifles from the rack near the door and boxes of bullets from the drawer of the hutch.

"I'll sweep the yard. I want all of you to stay indoors and away from any windows." Miles watched me as he spoke. "Birdie, you know your way around a firearm. Keep the Henry near you at all times."

I skirted the table to confront him. "What are you going to do?"

"I'll let Grant's men know what's happening. We'll stay here and lie low, for now," Miles said, and I heard the way he meant to offer reassurance. His black hair hung loose, his collar unbuttoned. I thought of how I'd been safe in his arms only fifteen minutes ago.

I am in love with you, he'd said.

There were so many things I should have said in return. The heart-smashing agony of it is we very seldom know that the last time we speak to a person is actually the last time.

Celia, I thought, with sudden horror.

Branch and Axton weren't the only ones who knew we'd fled Howardsville. Celia knew where we'd gone...

What if they'd somehow gotten to her?

Miles saw the play of terrorized thoughts over my face. His eyebrows drew inward, asking, *What is it?*

But I shook my head, unwilling to add fuel to the fire of his worry.

"Cole, help me," Birdie instructed, and together they half-carried Axton to the pantry beyond the kitchen, a narrow space with no windows, where Birdie hurried to drag aside the butter churn and spread a quilt on the floor. She ordered briskly, "Fetch the stitching thread, my largest needle, linens, the basin and the whiskey. Hurry now!" and Patricia and I leaped to do her bidding.

Miles, pistol at ready, slipped outside; to my relief, he returned within minutes, letting us know, "Yard's clear." He'd gathered up the ranch hands not on duty with the cattle and men clustered around the table, loading rifles and pistols, talking all at once. The cook left his young son with us, the boy sleepy-eyed and bewildered. Birdie worked to heap blankets and pillows in the far corner of her bedroom, away from the activity; I heard her tell the boys to stay put before she rejoined us.

Just outside the pantry, in the darkness of the hall, Patricia caught Birdie's arm and whispered, "Might I use the necessary? The yard is clear, Miles said, and I shall not be long..."

Birdie, distracted, nodded at this request. "Hurry back."

I should have known right then but I was so unfocused, torn up over Branch, distraught over Celia's wellbeing, and terrified to assist in what amounted to surgery here on the dirty pantry floor. I called after Patricia,

"Do you want me to come with you?"

She did not look back as she said, "No, I shall return directly," and disappeared around the corner, toward the door at the back of the house, the one which led to the hand pump and the outhouse. I heard the soft thump of the outer door as Patricia slipped from view.

Birdie's face hardened with determination as she swept aside her skirts and knelt beside Axton. The men spoke loudly in the other room, crowding the table as they planned for imminent attack, their voices rising over one another's. Birdie shut them out and held my gaze. "I'll need your help, Ruthie."

I nodded with as much confidence as I could muster. One of the lanterns had been positioned on the floor to light our work.

Birdie gently traced the side of Axton's face. "You'll be all right. It will hurt but I'll work as quickly as I am able. I have stitched many a wound."

Axton jerked his head in a quick nod.

"I'll be right here," I promised, threading our fingers. "Right here, Ax."

It took perhaps twenty minutes. I lost track of time. Blood smeared Birdie's fingers, wrists, and forearms. Axton grunted, muffling cries as she cleansed the wounds with generous pours of pure whiskey. I held his hand, letting him grip as tightly as he needed, bracing my knees against his thighs to keep him in position so Birdie could work. Based on the evidence, Axton had taken two bullets to his right front side; one had gouged a shallow trench of flesh just below his pectoral muscle while the second, more damaging shot had passed through the side of his waist, tearing a ragged hole above his hip. Small black flecks, which Birdie identified as gunpowder residue, speckled the skin of his torso.

Birdie washed both wounds, concentrating on the hip shot; despite the terrible, ragged appearance of its exit point on Axton's lower back, Birdie insisted it needed only cleaning and stitching. She said, "Thank God it did not penetrate the bone. I am ever so glad I needn't first dig out bullet fragments," and I knew she spoke from experience.

Before plying the heavy stitching needle she murmured, "Hold still as you are able," and without further ado, fell to work. Cold sweat leaked over Axton's temples; he clenched my hand.

"You're doing great," I repeated again and again, until the words became nonsensical.

The noise in the kitchen faded away, Miles having issued brusque orders to the men to take up positions in the nearby hillside, where they knew the lay of the land and could keep watch for anyone riding near; he joined us in the pantry toward the end of the ordeal, resting a hand on my shoulder.

Miles murmured to Birdie, "Good work."

Though Birdie stitched with admirable skill, the sewing together of Axton's flesh stretched over an agony of long minutes. Without intending it I suddenly gagged, burying my face against my shoulder, embarrassed for appearing weak when Axton was the one whose bloody, wounded skin was being pierced.

"It's done. You did well, Axton," Birdie said, with notes of satisfaction, tying off the final thread.

"Thank you," he whispered on an exhale, eyes closed.

"Rest now," I whispered, and bent to kiss his forehead, taking care to avoid jostling him.

Birdie wiped her bloody hands on a cloth. "You were good help, Ruthann."

Miles lifted me to my feet, leaning close to inquire, "Might I steal a moment's time?"

In the dimness of the kitchen I collapsed against his chest and let him hold me. I clung, absorbing his strength.

"It's all right," he murmured, burying his face in my hair, stroking it with both hands, letting my curls twine around his fingers.

I pressed my cheek to his heartbeat. "What's happening?"

"I don't know what to think," he admitted. "I don't believe for a second Vole is stupid enough to ride up on a well-defended position but I don't aim to take any chances. I'm damned upset about Branch. And Furlough. Can't say I was overly fond of my deputy but he didn't deserve to be shot like a dog on the street. Jesus Christ."

"Axton said they wanted you." Fear and anger twisted together in my throat. The lack of light cast him in tones of gray but I knew his face well enough to fill in the tint of his skin, the dark intensity of his eyes.

"Vole wants me most, the piece of horseshit. I should have pursued and shot him dead four years ago, I knew it then. He must have met Turnbull outside of Howardsville. Nothing like one angry idiot to rouse another to violence."

"I'm so scared. What if Patricia's husband is in town…"

"Don't be scared, sweetheart. I'm right here. I will never let anything happen to you."

Agitation burned my skin; I was sick with fear despite his sincere reassurance, my heart beating too fast. Miles continued, "What we spoke of remains true. You will stay with my family until I am able to return. I will leave with the dawn and see what is to be done about the damage to Howardsville. I'll wire for a transfer of route, as I said. And I will come straight back to you."

"But what about…" I trailed to silence, knowing with all my heart that I didn't want him riding away from me. The air in the room seemed supercharged, the way it felt before a thunderstorm broke and came at you across the surface of a wide blue lake…

"What about what?" he whispered, hands widespread on my back. I felt impossibly fragile, vulnerable in spite of his capable strength.

"Are you able to wire your family, in Iowa?" He nodded and I would forever after be glad I spoke the next words. My voice shook only a little. "Because I want you to tell them…I want you to tell them you'll be bringing a wife when you return there next."

Miles stood motionless as my words registered meaning, his face with its typical stern expression.

My heart pulsed. "If the offer is still on the table, that is."

He whispered, "Of course it is," and grasped my jaws, claiming my mouth for a kiss that spoke of his relief, his abounding joy. I had accepted his proposal of marriage; my breath was caught somewhere between promise and surrender. I slipped my arms around his neck and our kiss deepened. He took my lower lip between his teeth, then my chin, kissing my neck, tilting my head as he willed it in order to taste my skin.

"*Miles…*"

He exhaled in a rush, resting his forehead to mine, grasping my waist. "You must believe me when I say, despite the terrible circumstances, I have never been happier." He punctuated these words with another kiss, parting my lips with his tongue and hauling my hips flush against his; he was harder than any fencepost and my knees almost buckled. He whispered, "I must go. I despise leaving you here but I'll be close by, just outside. I cannot slack in my duties because I wish to make passionate love to my fiancé atop the table." There was subtle humor in his tone.

"I'll be here," I promised, hating to relent to the necessity of letting him go. I caught his face in both hands and tugged him back; a sharp, possessive thrill shot across my belly at the sight of his grin before our lips met, more urgently than before. I released my hold on his jaws only to commandeer his wrists and bring his hands to my breasts, arousal swelling like a living thing, beating through my blood.

He groaned, low and soft, cradling my breasts, tracing my distended nipples with his thumbs, his tongue circling the inside of my mouth. I lifted into the heat of his touch, running one hand down the front of his trousers, desirous and unashamed; we'd lost so much time already. I was determined we would lose no more.

"*Woman*," he gasped. "Oh Jesus…we have to stop…"

I knew he was right; I rested my forehead against his neck. Miles cupped my shoulder blades. His pulse thundered against my sweating skin. He drew back, eyes steady on mine, and whispered, "I love you, Ruthann Rawley."

Without another word he disappeared into the night.

And I was ashamed, horrified to the core of my soul – it was not until then, alone in the dark kitchen, that I thought, *Patricia*.

The recognition of her overdue reappearance in the house overtook all other concerns, inspiring a secondary beat of fear. My gaze darted around the room, empty but for me. I heard Birdie in the bedroom, soothing her boys; I flew to the pantry to find Axton lying on his un-injured side, a small pillow tucked under his head. At the sight of my terrified face, Ax lifted to one elbow.

"What is it, Ruthie?"

"*Patricia*," I moaned, and the floorboards seemed to tilt as I stumbled to the back door, flinging it open and peering at the yard, as ominous as a graveyard. Of course she was nowhere to be seen. I ran to the bedroom, where Birdie sat on the floor nursing Isaac, the other boys crowding her skirts. She looked up as I gasped, "Patricia is missing!"

Birdie's lips dropped open. "Oh, dear God…"

Axton had staggered to his feet, gripping the doorframe to remain upright. His eyes held mine and I saw that he understood. Agony distorted his expression. He said, "She can't be more than an hour ahead. I can overtake her."

"Maybe she's just upstairs," I babbled, ridiculous though it was, and raced to the room we shared, calling for her, riddled by guilt; of course she was not there. I closed my eyes, imagining I could see her fleeing eastward even now, doing her best to intercept what was coming before it reached the rest of us. My thoughts took desperate wing. Roughly an hour head start; she left the house claiming she would be right back while the rest of us were crowded inside, the men around the table and Birdie and me around Axton. Had she dared to lead a horse from the corral?

Of course, I figured, stumbling as I descended the steps at a clip. It would only make sense. On foot, there was no chance she would reach the men riding this way before one of us caught up with her. And Patricia was nothing if not compassionate, and determined. She loved us. She would not allow us to be endangered again because of her.

Patricia…

What do we do, oh God, what do we do now?

Axton was bleeding again, redness staining his tattered shirt as he rummaged for bullets in the drawer; Branch's pistol lay on the table. With single-minded stubbornness, he announced, "I'm going after her."

I grabbed for his elbow, intending to stop him, but before I could speak a cry rose from my throat and it was Miles's name on my lips right then. Birdie called for me from the bedroom, a high, panicked note. Baby Isaac's crying seemed to fill the entire house. A black cape of dread swept down, smothering me in its confines. I could not move fast enough across the floorboards to the outer door. Just as I reached it a single gunshot cracked the night. I jerked as though electrocuted. The knob slipped in my sweating grasp but I wrenched open the door.

And then I saw.

Heedless of all else I ran, falling to both knees and scrabbling to Miles, protecting his head with my torso, hearing only an endless wail that tore my throat from the inside out. The ground flew in chunks as additional rounds struck the dirt. Someone was running at us. Someone else yanked me backward by the armpits. As though watching from a distance, my senses operating remotely, I observed my body as Axton half-dragged it through the open doorway. I heard men's voices roaring in outrage. Cole returned fire as Grant ran for the house with Miles in his arms.

"Oh God oh God oh God…" My voice spilled and jerked as I dogged Grant's steps. Miles's head hung back, exposing his throat. There was a gaping wound near his sternum, spouting dark blood against the ivory of his shirt.

"Get them out of here," Grant said roughly, referring to the little boys, and Birdie, still clutching Isaac, obeyed without question. Grant deposited his brother upon the bed with absolute tenderness, cupping a hand around Miles's forehead. It must have been near dawn; pale gray light stained the room.

"*Miles,*" Grant whispered. Anguish cut a trench across his bearded face.

The yard outside was ablaze with shouting voices, with gunshots and buzzing chaos, and Miles rolled to one elbow, reaching for his brother's hand. Gripping it, Miles whispered, "Go."

I could see what it cost Grant to obey this command but he did, kissing Miles on the forehead – "I love you, my brother" – before leaving the room at a run.

I yanked free from my underskirt and folded the material over the blood flowing from Miles's body, frantic with the desire to save him.

"Would you have married me?" he whispered, slick with sweat, white as death. With both hands I pressed the underskirt against the wound killing him before my eyes. His blood was liquid heat against my palms. The mayhem outside grew distant, as though the volume had been lowered – I heard only Miles.

"*Yes*," I said, a half-moaning gasp, and the air around us shimmered with urgency, begging me to understand. I fought the sensation that I was about to be cleaved down the center, my heart forever after in two separate pieces.

"Come closer," he whispered and I did at once, climbing beside him on the bed. He was dying. I was as certain of this as I'd ever been of anything and my heart ached, the blade slicing deep. "Stay with me."

"I will," I gasped, choking back harsh sobs. "I'm here, sweetheart, I'm here. I won't leave your side."

"I love you so." His voice was low and rough. "I loved you the moment I first saw you, Ruthann, riding your horse with no saddle."

There was nothing I could do to stop the blood pouring from between his ribs. I heard myself beg, "Don't leave me, Marshall. Oh God oh God, don't leave me, please, *I'll do anything…*"

I felt tricked by a cruel, indifferent fate. Disoriented memories flapped like moths at the edges of my mind. A shrill screeching filled my skull more with each passing second, the chaotic sound of clocks out of sync, and I was at once struck by the impact of a memory – that of a car flying toward mounds of banked snow on the side of a wintertime road. My body shuddered, anticipating the crushing blow of that exact moment.

Oh Jesus, oh my God –

And just like that, it all rushed back.

My eyes slammed shut and in my mind I jolted forward with tremendous force, my car, my old Buick, careening out of control, the tires screaming over the packed snow on I-94 in February of 2014, the afternoon I'd been driving to Landon from Jalesville through a prairie blizzard, *over one hundred and thirty years from now –*

My desperate eyes flew open, seeking the man before me.

Marshall. Oh, dear God, Marshall –

I finally understood.

Marshall's soul was inside this man.

Marshall's soul was in Miles.

I crawled on top of him, clutching his face, bracketing his hips with my thighs. I put no weight upon his frame; I only knew I must touch him this way. He made a low sound of joy and gripped my waist, dark eyes burning with the last of his life.

"*I love you*, I don't want to hurt you…" I kissed his face, his temples and cheeks, his eyes and lips. His blood was everywhere and I wanted to die with him in this moment. At least our souls could be together then.

"You aren't hurting me. Oh God, Ruthann, let me touch you."

I brought his weakened hands to my face. He couldn't begin to know how much I loved him. Tears gushed as I imagined that Marshall, my Marshall Augustus Rawley, could somehow hear me speaking the words. "I love you with all my heart and I promise we will find each other again."

His thumbs brushed the length of my cheekbones. "Your beautiful angel face."

"I swear to you I will find you, in time we will find each other again. Remember that, oh God, remember that. *Promise me*."

"I promise." He was pale as a skeleton. I was panicking, wheezing and sobbing.

"*Miles…*"

"Don't cry, angel…" His eyes slid slowly to one side.

I clung as death robbed him of all warmth, the bullets that had killed him staked out in his body. I held him and sobbed brokenly.

Miles was dead and Patricia was gone. The adjacent hillside and acreage, anywhere a person armed with a long-barreled distance rifle may have hidden, was crawling with Grant's men, but there was no trace of the man whose shots had killed Miles. One of the ranch hands, a man named Hanson, was found with his throat slit, stuffed in the scrub brush on the rise across from the house, exactly where the shooter would have been positioned before scurrying away. Outside in the yard under the hot morning sun, I stumbled to the corner of the house and dry-heaved. I clung to the ground on all fours, vision pinwheeling. I could hear Cole's panic-stricken rage through the wooden walls; he and Axton yelled ferociously at each other.

Thoughts and memories crashed inside my head, fighting for

attention. I knew exactly who I was, and where I'd come from, for the first time in many agonizing months.

Marshall... Tish... Case...

How long have I been gone?

What do they think happened? Oh Jesus, they must think I'm dead.

Miles is dead. Oh dear God, Miles is dead.

Patricia is Tish, my sister. Oh God, how did I not see?

What do I tell them? How do I get back?

Grant was suddenly there, hovering between my hunched body and the glare of the sun; without a word, he lifted me into his arms. Grant, the man I knew in 2014 as Garth Rawley, carried me back to the house. Tears rolled down his face and dripped from his bearded jaws.

I begged, "Let me see him."

Grant honored this wish, placing me atop the bed where Miles lay in stillness, hands limp; his eyes with a slit of white showing where the upper and lower lids would not quite meet. I curled around his body.

Grant sat on the other side of his brother and bent his forehead to Miles's shoulder, weeping unashamedly. "I should have gone first. I'm eldest. I should have gone first."

Miles's soul had already fled to the place souls go after death, wherever that may be; I thought of a conversation with Marshall, back in Jalesville in 2013, warm and safe in the guest bedroom at his house, in which we'd just made repeated love.

What if I died early? And you lived to the end of your natural life?

I could not clamp hold of my escalating panic.

What if this changes everything? What if I never get back to Marshall?

Gasping breaths heaved at my chest and I rested my forehead against Miles's neck.

"I am eldest," Grant whispered again; his sobs were quiet and devastating.

"I loved him," I whispered, and Grant reached to take my hand.

"I never saw him love anyone the way he loved you, Ruthie."

You have to go, I understood. *You have to go now.*

Chapter Twenty-One

HOWARDSVILLE APPEARED DECEPTIVELY QUIET FROM A half-mile out, lit by the violet threads of an early sunset. I eased on Blade's reins, bringing him to a halt, cautious now, after hours of hard riding to get here. Astride Charger, just to my left, Cole lifted the spyglass and peered in the direction of the depot. To my right, Axton sat the saddle in tense silence; he was bleeding again but I knew better than to mention it. His agonized fury had burned itself into something slightly more manageable since last night. Between the two men existed a tightly-wound tension held only precariously in check; our collective desire to find Patricia overpowered all else, forcing them to work together rather than attempt to kill one another for a second time.

Cole's nose was swollen, appearing slightly off-kilter, and his lower lip was split, discolored by an engorged magenta bruise; Axton had thrown punches without mercy, knocking Cole straight to the floorboards, unfairly blaming him for Patricia's disappearance. It had taken all Grant's considerable strength to restrain Ax and keep Cole from attacking. Birdie had been the one to restore order, weeping as she begged them to stop – Miles had not been dead fifteen minutes at that point. The agony in the household was thicker than blood. But no amount of threat or persuasion could stop both men from going after Patricia.

I hadn't explained to anyone what I'd remembered, and had no plans to explain in the near future; for one thing, I knew they would be hard-pressed to believe a word. I'd barely had a chance to grapple with the sudden knowledge of past and present, of why I was *here* rather than home. Just now there were more pressing concerns.

But Marshall had not left my thoughts, not for a second.

Marshall, sweetheart, I have to believe you can hear me. I know you didn't mean what you said that night. I know you didn't want me to go, you were just worried. Oh God, I love you. My heart aches with loving you. I will get back to you or die trying.

I missed him so much that iron nails seemed lodged in my lungs with each new breath. Had time passed similarly in 2014? If so, I'd been gone for many months. Marshall, Tish, our families; all of them would be terrorized with worry, only amplified by the lack of evidence for my disappearance. I clamped down on a fresh wave of panic, remembering every detail of the fight between Marshall and me before I'd left Jalesville that February night. He'd been so jealous and afraid, and masking it with anger.

I'd stormed from our apartment, self-righteously furious, intending to drive straight through to Minnesota; partly because the trip was necessary but mostly, I could admit now, to punish Marshall for what I considered his lack of trust. I closed my eyes, recalling the sequence of events after I left – standing in the parking lot of our little apartment in downtown Jalesville, just a few blocks from The Spoke, scraping snow from the Buick's windows with angry slashes of my forearm, jamming the keys in the ignition and driving away with hot tears blurring my vision.

Maybe fifty or sixty miles I'd driven that night, along snowy I-94. It was hard to know for sure. I recalled passing the road sign for Miles City but hadn't yet crossed the state border into North Dakota. The winter weather grew more severe with each revolution of the tires. Even slapping at full speed, my windshield wipers could not keep up with the abundance of flying snowflakes. I appeared to be driving in a vortex of whirling white. I knew if I possessed any hope of returning home, I needed to remember the moments just before the accident, when I'd lost control of the big, heavy car on the unplowed interstate somewhere east of Jalesville. I scoured my memory, lifting thoughts as I would rocks on a lakeshore, examining each for a clue as to what had happened in that instant to send me to 1881.

Una Spicer's letters were back in Jalesville, at Tish and Case's house. It was always because I touched the letters that I felt like I was disappearing...

And the night Marshall and I rode to the site of the old homestead…

I thought, for the countless time, of Aunt Jilly saying there was something from the past we had to understand.

I understood plenty now.

Aunt Jilly, hear me. If anyone can hear me, it's you. Tell the womenfolk I'm all right. I'm here for a reason…

And that reason was Celia Baker. I meant to find Patricia, but I also intended to find Celia and force her to seek refuge with Birdie and Grant. I was adamant that Miles's child be raised with his relatives; I'd told Birdie everything about Celia's pregnancy and she said in no uncertain terms, "Bring her to us. I will raise the child as one of ours if she does not wish to keep him."

The notion had occurred to me within minutes of Miles's death – Marshall's family believed Grant Rawley was their direct ancestor, but maybe he was not. Maybe the family I knew and loved in 2014 descended from Miles Rawley's illegitimate child. It was the closest I could come to an explanation for my presence here in the nineteenth century; if I hadn't discovered the truth of his paternity, Miles's son would have been sent away, the Rawleys would never have known, and the chain of descendants which eventually led to Marshall would not have existed. And maybe I would never know for sure, but I did not plan to take any chances.

Snapping my attention back to the present, Cole murmured, "The black train cars are there on the side track. Four, this time. No red cars."

"Do you see anyone near them?"

We were west of town, momentarily stalled; despite the urgent flight from Grant's homestead we'd taken care to plan our next moves. I knew Cole and Axton both longed to ride down there and violently remove anyone in their paths to get to Patricia, but I'd reminded them with all the persuasive force I could muster they would likely be killed in the attempt, thereby accomplishing nothing. Besides, it was possible Patricia wasn't being kept within those train cars; I refused to voice my fear that we would come across her body on the route to Howardsville but there had been no sign of her, for better or worse.

"No one near the cars just now." Cole continued to peer through the spyglass, his words distorted by his injured lip.

I flattened one hand against my chest, praying this might ease the gouging pain centered in my heart; I hadn't yet begun to deal with the loss of Miles. Of course he and I had been drawn to each other – his soul was a part of Marshall's, a connection deeper than perhaps all else. They also shared a bloodline, which made more sense the longer I considered the evidence; wouldn't a soul, seeking the comfort of familiarity, the presence of souls it had known in other lives, return to a particular family? Wouldn't the same souls, and therefore families, be drawn together, craving additional lifetimes in one another's company?

"She's only hours ahead," Axton had said as we'd ridden from Grant's at midmorning. I left Flickertail behind in favor of Blade, a stronger animal all around and one better prepared for hard riding. I'd braided my hair and tucked it under my hat, dressed in Axton's trousers and Miles's heavy jacket, which still retained his scent. We pressed hard for Howardsville, knowing the window of time was swiftly closing; Patricia may very well have been a prisoner within an eastbound train car as we spoke.

Cole vowed, "I aim to kill the bastard who got Miles, I swear on my life. But I can't think on that now. Not until Patricia is safe."

"She left to save *us*, you know this." I glared at the horizon with sore, gritty eyes, hating myself all over again for not realizing her intentions last night. If Axton should have aimed punches at anyone, it was me; I'd watched Patricia leave the house. I'd been the one in a position to recognize what she was about to do, and to stop her.

Cole cleared his throat with a harsh, grating noise. "I know it. If we don't find her you might as well shoot me dead, because I don't aim to go on."

"If anything happened to her, *I'll* shoot you dead," Axton muttered grimly.

"Stop it!" I'd screamed, startling them both; I clung to self-control by only the thinnest wisp of thread. "Not another fucking word! We'll find her. We *have* to."

They had immediately obliged; talking soon became impossible as our horses galloped east. Later, when we slowed the pace to give the horses a respite, Cole dared to speak again, no room for debate in his tone. "You should know Patricia and I are to be married. She accepted my proposal."

Axton's jaws and shoulders squared like one preparing to enter battle. Without glancing toward Cole, he said, "I should like to hear it from her."

"You don't understand," Cole had said, and I'd looked his way at once, hearing something beneath his words, recognizing information of which I had not been made aware. I raced through last night's events – Patricia and I had spoken on our walk yesterday afternoon, but the remainder of the evening we'd found no time alone. Miles had helped me to bed last night, but Patricia hadn't returned to our room…

"It'll be full dark in less than an hour," Cole said now, retracting the spyglass, stowing it in his saddlebag.

"You have to let me ride in alone," I reminded them. As per our plan, they would wait at Branch's empty cabin until I could determine what had happened in Howardsville since Aemon Turnbull and the man called Vole shot up the jailhouse and killed Branch; I prayed Ax and Cole would not inflict bodily harm upon one another before my return. "I'll go first to Celia, like we talked about. Maybe she's heard something. I can sneak into Rilla's the back way and get to Celia's room without anyone ever knowing." I was dying to know if she and the baby were unharmed.

Cole said, "I aim to keep an eye on the train cars while you go down there."

"What if someone sees you?" I argued, shifting on the saddle. Blade snorted and stamped his front hooves, one after the other. "You two need to get to Branch's, like we talked about."

"Ruthie…" Axton began. He was pale and drawn, in no shape to be up and about, let alone for hard riding. But his eyes burned with purpose.

I mustered my sternest stare, fixing it on Axton. "There's no time to argue. Give me fifteen minutes. I'll meet you and we can decide what to do next. *Case!*" I hissed when he didn't respond, and then all but stuttered to correct myself. "Ax! Please, listen to me."

"I am listening, I swear."

I didn't bother telling him he was bleeding again; he already knew.

Cole pinned me with his intense gaze and insisted, "You got your rifle, Ruthie? You ready to use it?"

Miles's rifle was secured in a leather scabbard on Blade's saddle. I felt better for having this armament, not that I would be much good at using the huge, cumbersome thing. Cole had given me rudimentary instructions while we rode. I figured I could blow a hole in the side of a building, at least.

Aim for the chest, dead center, not the head, Cole had instructed at least five times.

"Yes, to both. I will see you soon." I curbed the urge to worry over Axton's ashen appearance, heeling Blade's flanks and insisting, "At Branch's!"

My last sight was of Cole nodding in terse, tight-lipped agreement.

I took a side street to Rilla's, eyeing the familiar sights of Howardsville by lantern light. As I neared the saloon I saw the remains of the jailhouse, only a block away, burned to its foundation, the listing iron cell bars the only pieces of the interior yet upright.

If I see a hair on your head, Aemon Turnbull, you are fucking dead. I will shoot you square in the chest or straight in the spine and I will not hesitate for a fucking second. I will kill you like you killed Miles Rawley.

I realized Vole could be just as responsible for shooting Miles. I had no idea what Vole looked like and would not recognize him on sight, but that played to my advantage, too; he didn't know me, either. I wanted Vole and Aemon dead, both of them, bloodthirsty in ways I'd never known myself capable.

Rilla's main floor was lively with music, as always. Her windows glowed copper and I could see my breath on the chill night air as I approached the back porch, with slow-paced caution, the place where I'd so often sat with Axton and Branch during my early days at Rilla's; I remembered the night Axton and I admired the full July moon, my very first evening in Howardsville. The rocking chairs were empty and ghostlike this night, the moon absent from the sky, lending better cover.

I'd intended to tether Blade to the iron hitching post at Rilla's but thought better of it and tied him two saloons down the block before backtracking and creeping inside, listening as hard as I could. All activity was happening at the front of the saloon, as usual; the kitchen remained unoccupied. Just ahead was the narrow, enclosed staircase I'd climbed many times while living here and I climbed it now, taking care not to let my bootheels thump on the wooden risers.

The upstairs hall seemed vacant but I waited out of sight, a few risers from the landing, to make sure, stretching out with my senses. Familiar noises met my ears, bed frames thumping, sighs and grunts and moans. I cringed at the memory of all the nights I'd listened to those sounds, recalling nothing more about myself than my name. And then, catching me off guard because there were so many other things I needed to be thinking about just now, life or death things, I thought of making love with Marshall, my sweet, passionate Marshall. It was like a lightning bolt from a clear sky sizzling into my deepest center, so forceful I bent forward and pressed both hands to my belly.

I miss you so much. Marsh, oh God, I would give anything to hear your voice, to feel you touch me. Do you know this? Probably they found my car and you think I'm dead. Oh Marsh, believe I'm alive out there. Please, believe that.

"Ruth?" A harsh whisper, but I recognized Celia's voice and it returned me abruptly to the here and now, hiding out in a whorehouse in 1881. She edged closer, advancing to the top of the staircase, and I flew up the last three steps to embrace her. Her plump arms enfolded me, knocking the hat from my head. I could feel her rapid heartbeat and the fullness of her belly. She murmured, "I knew I heard someone creeping about back here. Come along, grab your hat and be quick!"

Celia toted me to her room; she shut and latched the door, and then asked softly, "What did I tell you?"

But she wasn't speaking to me.

"Oh God!" I cried before I could lower my voice. I raced to the bedside, falling to both knees, my hands hovering like birds, afraid to touch her because it might hurt her even worse.

They'd beaten her brutally. Tears washed my dusty cheeks as I babbled and cried at the same time, trying to tell her it was all right now, and to find out who'd done this heinous thing to her. Engorged purple blotches and angry red welts marred nearly every inch of her pale face; her right eye was swollen shut. She lay on her side on Celia's bed but at my sudden appearance she struggled to one elbow and reached for me.

The words distorted by her bruised lips, she whispered, "I am...ever so sorry."

I gathered her cold hands, resting my forehead on her knuckles. "You're here, we've been so scared, *oh my God...*"

Patricia intertwined our fingers. Her voice shook. "He killed him... didn't he?"

I couldn't sort out if she meant Miles, or if she thought Axton was dead. I clamped hold of my wits and drew a deep breath, knowing I must explain. Celia, wrapped in her gray silk shawl, perched on the edge of the bed. She put her hand on my spine, rubbing with gentle circular motions. I knew my words would hurt Celia, even if she claimed to have no more feelings for Miles, and so I looked between both women as I whispered, "Miles was shot from a distance. He's...gone."

I could hardly speak the word. I refused to say *dead*. Celia's face tightened into an abrupt mask of pain. She gritted her teeth and smoothed her free hand over the bulk of her pregnant belly; tears leaked from beneath her long lashes as she whispered, "Miles. *Goddammit.*"

Patricia moaned, "Oh, no. *No, no...*"

I reached to rest my palms on Celia, as lightly as if touching a soap bubble. She covered my hands and I felt Miles's son shifting within her. The shock of it beat at me; what if I was touching Marshall's many-times great-grandfather? Would Marshall and his family – dear Clark, Garth and Sean, Quinn and Wy – suddenly cease to exist if I did not save this baby? My desperate eyes flew to Celia's – her beautiful, thickly-lashed gray eyes, *Marshall's eyes* – and I said, with passionate certainty, "This child is a boy. He is kin to the Rawleys and the only child Miles will ever father. Please, *I beg of you*, go to his brother, Grant Rawley. Grant and his wife Birdie will care for you. Birdie will raise this baby, she has sworn to me. I will help find someone to escort you to them. Their homestead is due west of Howardsville."

Celia's dark eyebrows knit in consternation. "I aim to send the child east, as we discussed. Rilla's allowing me three nights off, each week, under this condition."

"Celia," I pleaded. "So much more depends on this child than you could ever know, please, *I beg of you.*"

I knew she couldn't possibly comprehend the situation – and who could blame her – but she did perceive my sincerity and cupped one soft palm against my cheek, which was wet with tears.

"They won't turn me away?" she whispered, and for the first time I glimpsed hope in her eyes.

"Of course they won't. I told them everything." I rested my temple upon her bulging stomach, not caring if this seemed crazy to her and Patricia; the baby pushed a foot or an elbow against the gentle pressure of my touch. I thought fervently, *Be safe, little baby. Stay safe. I need you. Your descendent is my true love and even if I never find him again I need to know that Marshall Rawley will exist somewhere in time.*

"Little Ruthie," Celia murmured, petting my hair as she would a cat nuzzling her belly. "You are a strange one, I ain't gonna lie, but I don't doubt you mean what you say."

"Then you'll go to them?" I rejoiced, and a phantom of a smile touched Celia's full lips. She nodded with two slow bobs of her head.

Patricia touched my shoulder and implored hoarsely, "Is Axton all right? What of Cole?"

New fear ravaged her expression. I scrubbed tears from my face and hurried to tell her, "They are both here with me, waiting for us at Branch's. I'll take you there."

But to my surprise, she insisted heatedly, "*No.*"

"What do you mean? Tell me what's happened! Why are you here?"

"Celia found me." Patricia clung to my hands as she related what she'd been through since she disappeared, speaking carefully through her beaten mouth. "I would rather have died than leave with no word, but I could not risk losing my resolve. The moment Axton spoke of the train cars I knew what I must do, that all of you were increasingly endangered by my continued presence. I had perhaps a quarter-hour's head start, at most, and prayed it would be sufficient."

"Who beat you?"

Once outside, she had slipped to the corral and found a horse still tacked, leading the animal by its halter until out of sight of the house; then, heart quaking, she climbed atop the mare, clumsy in her skirts, and cantered east.

"I thought to divert them."

And she had, intercepting a group of five mounted men, none of whom she recognized in the confusion of darkness and terror. Even so, she explained who she was and offered to return to Howardsville in their company, with no trouble. She had made herself so vulnerable, been at such mercy, and it was almost more than I could bear.

"None of those men were the Yancys?"

"None directly. They were, however, hired by Thomas, this much I was able to discern. And once I was able to focus upon their faces, I recognized Aemon Turnbull, the beast who attacked you in Howardsville. And another…"

"Tell me," I implored. "Another, what?"

Patricia winced, lips compressing.

Celia answered instead. "Another of them bastards demanded to know Miles's exact whereabouts. Patricia claimed not to know but the bastard beat her into telling him."

Flashes of heated sickness pulsed in my gut. Patricia seemed to be choking and I climbed beside her on the bed, aligning our bodies exactly the way we'd slept in our shared bed. Cuddling her close, this woman whose soul I believed would one day inhabit my sister Tish, I said, "It's not your fault. It's *not*. You tried to save us."

Patricia wept, clinging to my forearms, pressing her bruised face to my neck though it must have caused her pain. She gulped, "I thought if I didn't tell him…he would kill me."

She was referring to the man called Vole, I would have bet almost anything. Patricia explained that after he'd dragged her from her horse and punched her repeatedly, he demanded again to know if Miles was hiding at the Rawley homestead. Half-senseless with pain, Patricia nodded and the man threw her to the ground and mounted his horse, cantering west without further ado. The remaining four men debated for a time whether they should accompany their companion, finally concluding that rather than risk their skins in a gunfight, they could return to Howardsville with the Yancy bride and claim their monetary prize.

Thomas Yancy had offered them gold in return for the safe delivery of his daughter-in-law; though, as Patricia learned, the Yancys had made no public announcement of her disappearance, preferring to keep the matter secret and involving others on a strictly need-to-know basis. They couldn't contain the gossip in Howardsville but the remote railroad town was a far cry from Chicago. Celia, keeping an ear open for news of us since we'd left town, heard talk earlier this afternoon she didn't at first believe, that of a woman brought to town under the cover of darkness. Alert for any sign of information, she recognized Aemon Turnbull's horse at the hitching rail at Rilla's, his old favorite haunt. It hadn't been too difficult to guess that Turnbull was enjoying the services offered upstairs.

"I thought the little bastard might have you captive, Ruthie," Celia explained. "I caught Turnbull in Lucy's room, pants around his goddamn ankles. I should have brained him on the spot. I told him I knew he had a woman somewhere and he would tell me where or I'd separate him from his favorite body parts, forthwith." A small, wry smile stretched her lips. "It wouldn't have been much of a difficulty, seeing how his wrists was tied to Lucy's bedposts at the time."

Turnbull admitted to Celia the men he'd ridden into town with had been hired by Thomas Yancy to find Yancy's daughter-in-law. Turnbull claimed he wanted no trouble, said they'd found the girl during the night and deposited her at the train cars just as ordered, and there she remained.

"No longer his problem, Turnbull said, and I headed for the depot before the bastard could blink," Celia explained. "No plan, no idea what I might say. Ain't but two hours ago, this was. I knocked on that railroad car door 'til my fist was near bleeding before a fella answered. Two men sat in there playing cards, drunk on cheap whiskey, but I came up with a story while I was waiting, thank God, and said I'd been hired to clean up young Mrs. Yancy for the journey back east. Told them to get her in the wagon and haul her to Rilla's or it would be their sorry hides. And I brought her straightaway here."

"But now I must return," Patricia whispered.

"Are you kidding me?" I cried. "You aren't leaving my sight! Case would never forgive me, for one thing."

"Case?" Patricia whispered hesitantly.

"Cole. I mean Cole," I said hastily; I had to take better care not to slip up like that. "Shit, it's been more than fifteen minutes, hasn't it? We have to meet him and Axton at Branch's. They'll flip out if I take any longer." I hesitated for less than a second; now was not the time to worry about the animosity between Ax and Cole, and how it would unfold once Patricia was in sight.

Patricia sat straighter, knotted with tension. "No. Thomas's men would kill them without a moment's hesitation. There must be no interference. I must return with no struggle." Her eyes grew wild with fear. "Ruthann, please heed my words."

"I won't let you go back to men who beat you. You aren't safe!"

"None of the hired men shall lay a hand upon me," she insisted. "They shall return to collect me before full dark and I *must* be here."

"And then what?" I demanded, heart clubbing.

"I shall return to Chicago and face my husband." Her stubborn will faltered a little, even if she didn't want me to notice, and she lifted her chin with admirable fortitude. "It must be this way, there is no other, do you not see? I cannot imagine what they would do to Axton or Cole." Tears poured down her swollen face. She swallowed hard, whispering past a massive bulge in her throat, "Dredd is easily convinced of anything I say as long as Thomas and Fallon are away."

"*No*," I interrupted. "I won't let you. Ax and Cole will only follow after, no matter where you go, you know this is true."

I could sense curious questions rising in Celia's throat but she said nothing.

Patricia shook her head, fiercely.

"I'll carry you if I have to!" I yelled.

"Please understand, Ruthie…"

"There's no fucking way I'm leaving you here!"

There was a sudden commotion below, on the main floor. Celia lifted an index finger, indicating silence; she went to the door, opening it and stepping into the hallway. Shouting male voices, the sounds of an escalating argument. The music stopped with a screech of fiddle strings. And then someone threw a heavy piece of furniture, maybe a barstool. I raced to Celia's side, peering around her as if I had a hope of seeing what was going on downstairs; the absence of fiddle and piano was so strange that other doors began popping open, everyone inquisitive. Above the cacophony of raised voices we heard Rilla's scornful demand, "What gives you the right?"

Someone fired a gun, the noise sending us jerking in startled fright.

"You two must go, *now*," Celia hissed, shaking my elbow. "Get away from here as quick as you can!"

"But what about—"

"I'll be right as rain, don't you worry," Celia insisted. "I'll get to the Rawleys' place, I swear to you I will. Now go! Patricia, you too!"

I threw my arms around Celia and kissed her round cheek. "Be safe."

We might have made it. I hooked an arm about Patricia's waist and together we crept down the back steps and through the pantry; there was screaming from the bar, and additional gunshots. The twilit night was just beyond the screen door, our freedom only steps away. I knew I could get us to Blade. Our footsteps clattered over the porch boards.

"Leaving so soon, Patricia?" asked a man as he strode around the side of Rilla's building, detouring through the alley.

Patricia faltered, issuing a short, high-pitched cry – a rabbit in the jaws of a steel trap. I stared between her and this tall, slender stranger effectively blocking our flight.

"Fallon," she whispered.

Chapter Twenty-Two

HIS MOVEMENTS WERE RAPID AND BRUTAL. BEFORE I could react he grabbed my shirtfront, yanking me the rest of the way down the porch steps, flinging me so hard to the ground I sprawled sideways, struggling for breath. Patricia flew to my side but two additional men converged on her from the alley. Fallon's voice was lethal. He ordered, "Get that dumb cunt *out of here*."

The two men hauled Patricia away, each one clutching an arm. I lay hunched on my left side but at the sight of her disappearing with them I rolled to hands and knees and tried to scramble after her. Fallon planted a foot on my stomach and stomped me to the hard-packed dirt. My fingers slipped over the smooth leather of his boot as I tried to shove it away.

"Who the fuck are you?" he asked, bending lower, increasing the pressure on my ribs. My eyes had adjusted to the dusky gloom and I saw him at close range. He was fair and blond, his face carved on an angular plane, almost angelic; no hint of what he really was etched upon the smooth surface. I couldn't answer, even if I'd wanted to; I was afraid I'd lose consciousness before I could inhale a lungful past his crushing boot. But then he changed tactics, removing his boot and crouching beside me, using the gun in his right hand to swipe hair from my forehead. The metal was cold and unyielding on my sweating skin. He spoke lightly but the threat was unmistakable. "Tell me who you are, right now."

I managed a partial inhalation, racing through what I knew about the Yancys, both past and present; and then, like the sharp, painful tip of an arrow shot from another time, I remembered something. A key piece in an intricate puzzle clicked suddenly into place.

"Franklin doesn't exist." My lips were so numb with what I'd just realized I barely managed to articulate the words. Immediately I recognized my mistake. Though it was swift, and concealed at once, I saw stun pass over his features.

He backhanded me with one smooth, economical motion; I didn't even see his hand twitch before it made contact. Gripping my jaws, fingertips anchored against my teeth, he hissed, "What did you say?"

A bright flash, lightning over the lake, had burst across my vision; hazed with pain and fear, for seconds I saw nothing but a blurry watercolor version of his face. His breath fanned my forehead; I was sure his next move would be to kill me and my mind presented and clung to an image of Marshall, waiting for me somewhere out there. And so I was afforded the courage to whisper, "You're Franklin Yancy."

Fallon's face seemed carved of ice, frozen in an expressionless mask as he processed what this meant. Then he jammed the gun barrel against my forehead hard enough to dent the bone; his pale eyes were ablaze. "Who *the fuck* are you?"

I clamped down on my violent fear. It was far from true, but I choked out, "I know everything about you. *I know when you die.*"

I braced for quick retribution. But something unexpected replaced the fury on his face. He looked almost...satisfied.

"You're her sister, aren't you?" He spoke softly, regaining his composure inch by inch as he reached this conclusion. "That lawyer bitch who married Case Spicer, the one Derrick thinks he's in love with. You're her sister who disappeared, not just a past counterpart. Son of a *bitch*." Fallon eased back a few inches. "Derrick refused to kill her, the useless fuck. He's as useless as Dredd is, here."

There were many things I could have said in that moment but I heard myself beg, "Tell me the way back."

An increase in the volley of noise from the front of Rilla's saloon refocused his attention. He rose without a word, yanking me up by an elbow. As he stalked around the side of the building he kept the gun tight against my ribs and murmured in my ear, "I intended to split your skull right here but I've changed my mind. Keep your mouth shut and I'll let you live another day."

Our wrists were tethered with short lengths of rope, handcuff-like, before three men with pistols escorted Patricia and me, the two of us riding double on one of their horses, toward the Yancy train cars under Fallon's curt order. I felt like I'd been hit by a Mack truck, my mind muddy with all the information I'd been asked to absorb since Miles died; one thought, however, leapfrogged all the others, taking immediate precedence.

Fallon Yancy can jump through time. He must have at least some control over it. Holy fucking shit. Tish and I should have known – all the clues were right there.

The passenger cars had been reattached to the main engine, ready to transport us eastward. I took frantic stock of the area as Patricia and I were summarily hauled in the direction of the depot, terrified that Ax and Cole were watching everything from a distance. Of course they were – far more than fifteen minutes had passed and they would realize something was wrong. I prayed they wouldn't dare to act, outnumbered and outgunned; I sent a desperate plea to them with all my strength.

Stay put. Please, stay put. You'll be killed and that would finish Patricia.

The saloon was in ruin behind us. Someone had shot Rilla; I caught a glimpse of her heavy body sprawled across the floor, with Lucy and several of the other girls surrounding her, crying and calling for Doc Turn. I was dizzy with unreality, attached to my physical body by only a tattered thread. Of course a group of criminals could waltz in the front door and shoot to kill; there was no law left in Howardsville. I held fast to Patricia as our horse was led through town; her head drooped against my shoulder, her face decorated afresh with blood. I'd seen one of the men strike her when she fought to struggle away from him. I kept a tight lid on my fury, leaning closer to her to whisper, "It'll be all right."

It was an outright lie and I knew she knew it, but she said nothing. Fallon Yancy, a dust-colored hat settled low on his head, rode just behind Patricia and me, using us as cover. Fallon surely assumed I had an accomplice and recognized that this person was somewhere out there, watching; therefore he wasn't taking any chances. Fallon was no one's fool; he knew no shooter would dare to take a bead on him, not when Patricia and I were in the same line of fire. It was all I could do not to peer over my shoulder at Fallon; I could feel his incinerating gaze centered on my nape as he debated what I knew and how to extricate this knowledge from me as swiftly as possible. I swept the horizon once more, sensing Ax out there.

Don't try anything. Oh God, please. If you die on us now, I'll kill you, Axton Douglas!

Celia, I thought, with equal desperation. I prayed she would get to Birdie and Grant, as she'd promised. And then, my mind rotating like an out-of-control carousel, I thought, *Blade! He's still tethered at a hitching post, waiting for me.*

An almost-full moon had risen to glow over the town. I stared at it like a crazy person, my sense of reality floundering between past and present. I saw my oldest sister Camille, her golden-green eyes darkened with sorrow as she stood on the dock, resting her cheek on our mother's shoulder. I saw Mom's beautiful face, pale with strain as she stared across Flickertail Lake, Grandma and Aunt Ellen close by, all of them dying a little more each day that I was gone with no word. I saw Aunt Jilly pressing her fingers to her temples, trying with everything in her to establish a connection. I saw Tish, curled against Case's chest as she cried for me; my family, the women who loved me, unwilling to give up hope. And Marshall. The strength of my love for him superseded all else. I refused to believe he would somehow cease to exist in the future, that the Rawleys would simply vanish into vapor. I would die before letting that happen.

A single shot fired from a rifle jerked our spines and sent everyone scrambling for cover. My heart dropped like a falling stone. We were no more than a block from the depot, on the outskirts of town, and blood bloomed, thick and red, between the shoulder blades of the man riding in the lead. He fell from his saddle and struck the ground with a solid thud; his horse quickstepped, crow-hopping to avoid tripping over the body.

"*Stop!*" I screamed.

Fallon's men returned furious fire and high-pitched ringing filled my ear canals. I battled the fantasy of heeling the horse and doing my best to get us to the safety of Axton and Cole. But safety was only an illusion – we'd be caught in the crossfire.

Fallon yanked the horse's lead line from my hands, bringing the animal against his own mount, so close our knees brushed.

"How many?" he demanded.

Before I could blink, let alone answer, Axton and Ranger appeared from the north, Axton riding without holding the reins, a rifle braced on his shoulder.

"NO!" I screamed, my voice muted by discharging guns.

Axton fired, dropping another of our captors, and then wheeled Ranger to the side, seeking cover to reload – I saw Cole positioned at a right angle, firing the shotgun, covering Axton's advance while Fallon's men raced for the shelter of the train cars. Instead of following, Fallon halted his horse, and therefore ours, with a brisk, vicious movement.

Time became a slow-motion sequence, a surreal step-by-step.

Calm as a summer afternoon and just beyond my reach, Fallon leaned to the right and aimed square at Axton's midsection.

Patricia was screaming Axton's name, struggling against my hold.

I lunged toward Fallon but I was too late. The last thing I saw before hitting the dusty ground was Axton flying backward, unseated from Ranger – being skinned alive would have hurt me less than the sight. I rolled to avoid stomping hooves, my bound wrists inhibiting all movement. Fallon dismounted in a hurry, dragging Patricia from the saddle; having taken quick stock of the situation, he abandoned both horses and used us as cover instead, the gun held to Patricia's head. Awkward, stumbling with our wrists tethered, Fallon all but dragged us the remaining yards to the train cars. There, he herded us like animals into the second-to-last car, a dark and stuffy space; our exit was cut off by the muffled thump of a slammed door.

Patricia flew for the window, ripping the shade from its moorings. Dark blood had flowed from her nostrils, painting her lower face in an obscene pattern of stripes.

"*Axton,*" she sobbed, hands spread like starfish against the small glass rectangle. I joined her at the window, sick with panic, but could see nothing but chaos. No sign of Axton, Cole, or their horses.

"Oh God," I whispered, trembling, tears blurring my sight. I could not bear to acknowledge what was probably true – that Axton had just been killed before our eyes. "Oh God, *please no.*"

"*He's right outside…*" she moaned, tripping over her skirts to reach the door, yanking at the handle. She slammed her fists on its surface, clawing at the impenetrable iron. Both of us lurched forward as the train chugged to sudden motion. The cars inched at first, gaining steady momentum along with Patricia's hysterical screaming. Terrified she would hurt herself I clutched one of her arms and held fast, cursing my bound wrists.

The whistle on the engine issued an elongated moan and before we knew it, Howardsville was behind us.

The train sailed through the night with a clickety-clacking rhythm. Once I'd managed to calm Patricia, settling her on the bed in the sleeping compartment, I located a box of matches in the drawer of the nightstand, refusing to think of being in a similar train car the night Mrs. Mason was killed. With the light of several subsequent, fumbling strikes, I found a candle, lit its wick, and then proceeded to search for any sort of food. There was none, and no water; our wrists were bound with rope and I had to go the bathroom. But these seemed like trivial concerns in the face of everything else. I finally returned to the sleeping compartment at the sound of Patricia's quiet weeping. I joined her on the bed and we grasped hands, our bodies rumbling along with the rapid tempo of the steel wheels.

"He's still alive," she breathed. "I can feel it."

I tucked my chin over Patricia's soft, loose hair and whispered, "I believe so, too."

Oh Axton, sweet Ax, please be alive out there. Oh God, please be alive. I can't bear it.

Time, and many miles, passed before I finally said, "Patricia, I need to know everything you do about Fallon."

She issued a shuddering sigh. In the dimness the uninjured parts of her face were few and far between; blood and bruises bloomed in dark patches across her skin. The rope around my wrists scraped as I lifted both hands and touched her hair.

"Please, tell me. I have to know everything."

"He is a beast," she said, grit and steel uniting forces in her tone. "I wish to kill him with my own hands. I wish to cause him colossal pain before he departs this earth."

"I couldn't agree more but I need you to focus." I rallied my determination. "Please, Patricia, it's more important than you know."

I felt her shoulders lift with an indrawn breath. "He is the sort to send others to conduct his criminal enterprises. I am stunned by his appearance here in the Territory." She sounded at least partially in control but then choked on a sudden harsh moan. "Ruthie…what if –"

"Stop," I commanded; now, more than ever, I had to be strong. "I know it's hard but we can't think like that."

She nodded, gulping back a sob.

"When and where was Fallon born?" I pressed. "Do you know?"

"October of 1853, in Lancaster, Pennsylvania."

I had no idea how to frame a question that asked what I needed to know – if the Fallon Yancy who'd appeared in Howardsville tonight was the same person born that October. Was he an original part of this timeline, or another altogether? Franklin Yancy didn't exist, but did Fallon? Who was he, really?

"Have you ever been given reason to believe Fallon was lying about his birthdate?"

"Ruthie, what is it? Please, I beg of you to tell me."

"Would you know if…"

"If what?" she insisted when I trailed to a halt; she'd gained a slim margin of control over her emotions. "Please explain. Please trust me with your questions."

"I do trust you." I paused, absorbing the warmth of her fingers locked around mine. "It's just that…I don't know if you can believe what I would tell you."

"I shall believe anything you tell me. How could you think otherwise?"

I thought of Tish, who never hesitated, who always spoke her mind. Gathering all my courage, I whispered, "I remembered everything about my past the night Miles was shot." Hot tears welled, blurring the outline of Patricia's earnest face. "You see, I was born in Chicago, in the month of January…in 1991."

There was a moment of silence as I sensed Patricia grappling with this statement.

I rushed to explain. "I'm not crazy. I know it seems that way, but I promise you I'm not. My entire family is there, in the future. I haven't seen them in all these months. I haven't seen Marshall since that night…" And just like that my composure plummeted, deteriorating fast, my voice breaking like dead branches. "I left him in our apartment…in the middle of winter. We had such a bad fight…he thought I believed *he wanted me to go…*"

How could I have been so selfish? How could I have disregarded his concern? I knew very well he'd been jealous of my ex-boyfriend, Liam, but that didn't mean Marshall lacked trust in me. I'd let my pride blind me, refusing to see what truly motivated his anger was simple fear. Faye Rawley, his beloved mother, had died in a car accident the autumn of Marshall's eighteenth birthday, creating a jagged hole of vulnerability within him. And even knowing this, I'd left our apartment without a final word, without even saying good-bye, propelled by self-righteous anger, when I should have turned around and run back inside, straight to his arms.

Remembrance stormed my senses – the sound of his warm, husky voice, the love in his eyes, the scent of his skin and passionate strength of his embrace. Our wedding was supposed to have been last June and I pressed my thumb to the bare spot on my ring finger, imagining the engagement ring Marsh had given me the night he proposed, a family heirloom diamond he'd had set with garnets, my birthstone. I remembered making love with him, the immediacy of him wrapped between my legs, the easy, teasing way we'd always had, the endless, heated hunger he never failed to rouse. How had I gone so long without him? How would I continue?

"*Marshall*," I wept, repeating his name, ambushed by despair.

At long last I fell silent, rendered hollow and withered. Patricia had not released her tender hold on my hands. When she spoke my body twitched, even though she whispered her question.

"Dear Ruthann, you mean to tell me you've not yet been born?"

"You don't believe me," I whispered miserably.

"I believe you, I promise. I am attempting to reconcile your explanation with what I formerly understood about the laws of the universe. What I mean is, how is it possible you were born in the twentieth century but exist now in the nineteenth?"

I wagged my head side to side, exhausted and aching. "I wish I could tell you how it happened. The first time I felt pulled by the past, I'd touched letters that were written by Cole's mother, Una Spicer."

"Letters? What letters? When were they penned?"

"1882," I whispered. "Una wrote them from Montana Territory, in 1882." I sat up and so did Patricia, facing me on the narrow bed. "I want to tell you everything but I don't know where to start. There's so much."

"Then we are fortunate it is a long way to Chicago," she whispered, squeezing my hands.

Chapter Twenty-Three

"I DREAMED THE SUN WAS OUT," I MURMURED, PERCHING on the edge of Patricia's cot. There were no windows in our room but we were allowed to roam once a day in the small patch of garden allotted for us to take the air, where we came into contact with no one but Sister Beatrice and, very occasionally, Sister Marguerite. Though, Marguerite had taken studious care to avoid us since our last conversation; her kindness did not extend beyond her fear of the Mother Superior. The rest of the nuns seemed to prefer keeping watch from a slight distance, rarely condescending to speak to us. It was after dawn and Sister Beatrice was due any second to escort us to the chapel.

Patricia lay on her right side, the only position she could comfortably manage these days; her belly was so bulky in contrast to her small frame it had become a struggle for her to walk during the last two months. Without opening her eyes, she murmured, "Good morning, Ruthie."

Months ago we'd named the unborn baby Cole Montgomery Spicer, after his father, but referred to him almost exclusively as Junior. Or Monty, if I was trying to coax a smile from Patricia. He was past due, as best we figured with our less-than-scientific way of keeping track of passing time. Patricia felt from the first she was carrying a boy, undoubtedly conceived the evening of the last day she'd seen Cole, when they made love in the empty bunkhouse after his marriage proposal. I knew the intent of the nuns here at the Immaculate Heart of Mary was to separate Patricia and her child the moment the boy emerged from her womb. Of course I would die before letting that happen. Just *how* I would prevent this from happening plagued me on a nightly basis, ever-increasing now that his birth was imminent.

"He could use a little sunshine and so could you, Mama," I said. Patricia wagged her head side to side but I insisted, "Come on. Sister Bitch-face will be here any minute. I'll help you walk."

And I earned the smile, however small, I'd been hoping for, using our nickname for the grim-faced, stubbornly silent woman who walked us without fail to our morning and evening prayers, and had since day one in this hellhole of a convent where we existed in only slightly better conditions than convicts.

Patricia wore a loose, bulky black dress, the only color the nuns allowed us to wear. All of the clothes we'd arrived with had been disposed of; to be fair, and I tried my best to be fair so I would not go entirely insane, the majority of the nuns treated us with a sort of bland apathy. Pity and slight revulsion at our sinful ways, sure, but no one was outright hostile; we'd not been physically abused. When we first arrived at the convent, just after Thanksgiving, when Patricia had no longer been able to hide her pregnancy from Dredd, the nuns were stricter, more uncompromising. They'd forced Patricia to kneel and pray almost without end, which she had endured even with her incapacitating morning sickness.

Posing as her lady's maid, I'd knelt dutifully at her side, spreading my shawl beneath her knees to provide a layer between her and the stone floor of the small chapel, doing our best to help each other's mental state from complete unraveling; when we did pray, it was always for Axton. Eventually the nuns grew accustomed to our presence, or at least learned to tolerate us, and the rigor of endless prayer decreased to twice daily, morning and evening. In what was surely a case of Stockholm Syndrome, in addition to the balm of advancing springtime, I'd even grown fond of the adjacent chapel where we were escorted to repent, a narrow, vine-covered stone building located away from the main structure of the convent, its own separate, peaceful place.

By this point in our friendship Patricia knew everything about me, and vice versa. Without television, radio, or cell phones, magazines, books, or board games, not so much as an ink pen, we'd spent the weeks and then months – hidden away far more effectively than we would have been in a maximum-security prison – talking, singing, and dancing. I'd taught her every song and dance move I could remember, and until growing too large and cumbersome, she danced every single one with me, including the Macarena, the Grapevine, and the Electric Slide. I told her about airplanes, cars, television, the Internet, and refrigeration. She entertained me with stories of her childhood, in turn teaching me how to waltz and dance the Mazurka.

She knew all about Landon, Flickertail Lake, and Shore Leave, Jalesville and The Spoke, and could have named each and every person in my family tree, including grandparents, nieces, nephews, and the entire Rawley and Spicer families. She knew my theory about souls remaining in family groups, and how I thought she and Tish shared a soul, as well as Marshall and Miles; the verdict was still out on whether Case was Axton or Cole. We talked to stave off the horror of what lay ahead, for both of us. We spoke nightly of our plan to escape this place, a small Catholic convent we assumed was somewhere in Illinois; it had taken us, along with our armed escorts, roughly half a night to reach it after leaving the Yancy estate in Chicago.

There seemed limited hope of making contact with the outside world; there was no paper trail, no hint of where we'd been taken, and even if Cole or Axton – we chose to believe he was still alive – dared to breach the security of the Yancys' home, they would find zero trace of us. The past winter proved long and harsh, punctuated by endless blizzards. Oddly, Patricia and I remained together due to the efforts of none other than Dredd Yancy. He'd arranged for Patricia, whom he believed to be the victim of rape, to spend the duration of her pregnancy at the convent where his mother's younger sister had once been sent to serve as a nun; later, while a resident, the poor girl grew ill and died. Once delivered, Patricia's illegitimate child would "disappear" into an orphanage and Patricia, miraculously recovered from an unspecified ailment, would return to Chicago to reclaim her status as Mrs. Dredd Yancy.

Fallon's words, spoken back in Howardsville, made more sense the longer I was acquainted with the younger Yancy brother. Dredd – slim and dark-haired, with a delicate, almost pretty, facial structure – wasn't exactly useless, but he held no actual job and rarely ventured from the luxury of the family estate on Lake Michigan. The sprawling mansion was located just outside Chicago, which even in 1881 seemed to me like a huge and teeming city. Thomas Yancy maintained a second home in Boston, where he resided during the winter months, only returning to the lakefront estate to escape the broiling summer heat. As far as everyone knew, Fallon traveled extensively, both in the States and abroad, orchestrating the family's business interests while Dredd was a compliant rule-follower.

We had further learned that even when Fallon was absent he was everywhere, at least as far as Dredd was concerned; Fallon's orders were not to be questioned, let alone disobeyed.

Patricia and I were separated within an hour that night on the train, when we'd been forced to flee Howardsville along with Fallon; he recognized his blunder in allowing us the chance to speak privately. The train had slowed in the empty darkness, alerting us to danger as it ground to a halt. Peering out the single window in the sitting compartment we beheld nothing but featureless black night pressing against the windowpane. Patricia's breathing grew shallow; I tried to comfort her even though my heart felt about thirty seconds from a full-blown attack. We heard boots clanging on the steel steps. Clutching each other's hands we could do nothing but wait as bolts were unlocked from the outside and the heavy door swung open.

I was pulled from the train by a man who led me along the tracks to the passenger car directly behind the engine. I was dirty, reeking, and blood-smeared; my wrists were raw beneath the rope binding and hindered my ascent into what could only be Fallon's personal chamber. He sat smoking a cigar, the scent of which brought Miles to mind and offered fleeting comfort. The red tip of the ember glowed as Fallon inhaled; his order emerged along with a lungful of smoke. "Leave her and go."

I stood as far from him as the length of the room permitted. Behind me the door thumped shut, leaving us in smoky dimness. Fallon sat in a wingback chair with one ankle atop the opposite knee, shirt collar undone and sleeves rolled back. A bandage had been tied around his upper arm on the left side; I saw traces of blood. I hoped the wound beneath it hurt. I hoped he felt it with every breath. Try as I might to keep a neutral expression, hatred welled in my eyes. My knuckles became ridges of peaks as I fisted both hands. I'd never been so close to someone I despised so desperately. He'd killed countless people, including perhaps Axton.

"Tell me how you got here," he said.

"Tell me the way back," I whispered.

"How long have you been in the nineteenth century?" he continued, as though I hadn't asked a question of my own. "How much did you tell that little whore of my brother's?"

"I won't tell you anything unless you promise to keep Patricia safe." I squared my shoulders. I had everything to lose but it was no time for weakness.

Fallon moved so swiftly the muted cry barely cleared my lips. He fisted a hand around my hair, bending my head to an unnatural angle, and poised his cigar an inch from my right pupil. Ashes dusted my cheek. His eyes were so frightening, reflecting the red ember-point in twin bursts of burning color, I could almost believe he was less a human than the embodiment of a true monster, the one right behind you, the one hiding in your closet, keeping silent watch until it's too late.

"You will tell me whatever I want to know or I will blind you. You think you're at liberty to fuck with me, is that it?" He spoke softly but I knew he meant every word.

No. My lips moved but only a whimper emerged.

He released my hair and retreated one pace. My knees were so limp I folded straight to the carpet, listing sideways because my hands remained bound together. Fallon crouched beside my prone body and drew again on his cigar. He smiled as I struggled to one elbow, bending my knees toward my chest.

"Miles Rawley was a shitless coward. I knew him from boyhood, did you know?" His voice now conveyed a conversational tone. He flicked ash on my waist and resettled his forearms on his narrow thighs. "Dredd and I lived with the Rawleys after our mother's death in 1864. I buried her alongside the hired hand she was fucking at the time. My father was away fighting the Rebels that summer. I figured he would have done the same, had he been home."

I blinked, fighting off waves of intense panic, seeking anything in the vicinity I could use as a weapon – not that there was much. I spied a long iron poker, the sort Branch had used to poke at his cookfire, propped near a small brazier, but its current distance from me might as well have been a thousand miles. I would have been forced to belly-crawl at least a dozen feet to grasp it; Fallon would be on top of me long before I could get my hands around its iron length. He went on talking; despite every-thing, I had the odd sense he wanted to impress me.

"The first time I leaped it was utterly inadvertent, only a week into the future. It took me some time to realize *when* I was, of course. The why of it I did not attempt to understand, at least not back then. Over time I came to realize it was a gift, the universe's way of acknowledging my superiority. It was 1869 and I was a month shy of sixteen. Father and Dredd and me, poor as shit, panning for ore in the miserable foothills behind us. And then one night I leaped over a week and discovered a thick silver vein had been unearthed in the foothills a few minutes' ride from our shanty. I was allowed roughly four hours during that first leap, just enough time to ensure the location of the silver vein. When I returned to the past, the *present* as Father and Dredd knew it, I said I'd had a dream.

"Father demanded to know where I'd vanished to earlier in the af-ternoon, told me I'd scared him half to death. But wasn't he surprised when my 'dream' proved fruitful. Eventually, once we began to accumu-late wealth, I learned to better manage the explanations for my disap-pearances. To this day, Father and Dredd aren't entirely aware of all the details. But I've made us unimaginably rich and so they don't question. They allow me a wide berth."

Momentarily abandoning thoughts of reaching the iron poker, I stared at his angular face as if transfixed – and in a way, I truly was. He was detailing for me the story of his abilities, studying the air a few feet above my head, witnessing things I could not begin to imagine. Somewhere in the back of my mind I realized this outpouring of information, a confessional of sorts, would only be made before someone who would never live to tell another soul.

Keep him talking, I thought.

It took willpower to dredge up my voice. "Do you always...go forward?"

His head twitched as his eyes sought mine, reminding me of a snake. "My full potential is restrained because my leaps are arbitrary. I've tried for over a decade to manage them, all without success. Often I'm allowed only a few hours before being returned here, to what I perceive as my original timeline. Thus far I have only been allowed to leap into the future from a fixed point. Never the past." He paused for a terrifying beat, holding my gaze. "Which brings me to you. The only thing keeping you alive is this fact. I want to know how you travel backward rather than forward."

My next words must be chosen with extreme care; I debated lying but recognized the futility.

"I came here accidentally," I whispered through a dry, rasping throat. "I don't have...any control over it."

"You've never been displaced prior?"

I shook my head.

"How did you know I was Franklin?"

"There was a text...saying Franklin didn't exist."

"Explain."

"Someone texted my sister's friend, Robbie Benson, with those words."

Franklin leaned back to direct a huff of laughter at the ceiling. "How poetic. I saw your sister and her dirt-grubber husband at Benson's funeral on my last leap."

"Robbie's dead?" I gaped at him, unable to restrain my shock. Oh dear God, what else had I missed? What had happened in my absence?

Fallon shrugged. "He saw me leap. I appeared in Christina's bedchamber and he was there, rooting through her things. I knew he was fucking that high-priced whore, along with a truckload of others including myself, but it wasn't about that. He saw me." He shrugged, reflectively. "It was almost the last thing he saw."

I squeezed my thighs with both hands, seeking my center. I could not allow him to drag me down this dark, warped path. A dozen questions surged to existence in my head, swirling like laundry in a boiling kettle, sheets streaked with the bodily fluids of dozens of male customers…

Bile surged in my esophagus; I choked it back. "It was *you* in the barn that night."

He cocked his head, again reptilian-like. "What do you mean?"

"In Case's barn that night. It was you. You disappeared because the dogs were about to attack."

He didn't respond and in a flash I realized it hadn't yet happened to him. He hadn't yet *been there*.

"Your…leaps aren't chronological?" I whispered. My jaws felt wooden but I was dying to pry answers from him. *It's probably how you* will *die*, something in my head whispered.

"They are not. Derrick wouldn't admit to it, but he set fire to that barn in hopes of scaring your sister away from Jalesville for good. Ron Turnbull wanted her dead, too smart for her own good he said, and I can't say I wouldn't have enjoyed hearing about a Spicer roasted like a hog in the hearth, but Derrick wouldn't burn their home. I haven't the same control over him as I do Dredd, you see. I am only a tentative figure in that timeline, despite my existence as Franklin."

"Why Jalesville?"

"It's simple, really. It's where I first leaped from, my own personal lightning rod. I'm drawn to the land there and exercise a modicum of control over my leaps from that starting point. That's the main reason for buying up the otherwise useless town. Very few people in the twenty-first century know of my abilities. Ron Turnbull, Derrick, and Derrick's father, T.K. They've maintained a façade for me, an identity as T.K.s elder son, Franklin." He took a moment to puff his cigar. "It's quite fascinating that those I know in this time have counterparts in later centuries. The Yancys are my blood, of course. They keep my secret because I increase their wealth." He smiled, exhaling a thin stream of bluish smoke. "And because I know things they couldn't imagine. Take Miles Rawley's damnable mother, for instance. Or rather her future counterpart, Faye Rawley."

Ice water seemed to replace my internal organs.

"What…"

Fallon knew he'd struck a nerve, had flayed open every fucking nerve in my body. His smile widened. "In 2004 she suspected the power plant near her home of illegal waste dumping. T.K. Yancy owned the plant at that time and wasn't complying with environmental regulations. It was a trifling thing, easily dealt with, but a local law-dog teamed up with her and the investigation got out of hand. Stirred up national media attention. T.K. was on track to end up in federal prison. This little shit town, everyone so proud of taking down a wealthy outsider whose business holdings trickled into their turf. The goddamn public *loved* Faye Rawley. She was a fucking folk hero."

"What did…" I couldn't bear to finish the question, pressing my folded hands as hard as I could against my heart.

"She was a dead woman, as far as I was concerned. I killed her the very next time I leaped to a timeframe before the investigation had happened. Small cars are no match for trailer-trucks, especially on highways. Problem solved, for a time. No threat of federal prison for T.K on my next leap to 2004, and Faye Rawley was buried beneath a tree in her backyard."

Hot, vicious fury seared away any trace of logic. I lunged with no other thought than causing Fallon Yancy as much harm as I was able.

"You fucker, you fucking son of a bitch…"

He was in a crouch and ill-prepared to dodge. I crashed against his front side, taking him to the carpet, the cigar flying from his grasp. I scrabbled over his body, seizing what little advantage I could, gripping his hair with both hands. I would have bitten and torn free any part of him I could reach if he hadn't jabbed a closed fist and connected with my solar plexus. Wheezing, gasping, I rolled to the side and he was on me at once, pinning me flat to the carpet. His face was red, teeth bared. My breath was too short to struggle; I smelled his sweat with each attempt at an inhalation, so scared of him my sense of reality zizzed in and out like a lightbulb in its dying flickers.

Focus, Ruthann!

The iron poker was now less than three feet from my right side.

He stretched one leg across my thighs and put his mouth against my ear. "I should kill you right here. I want to kill you. But I also want to fuck you."

"I'll rip off your...*fucking testicles*..."

"I will do whatever I want with you, you stubborn little bitch. You think you're brave but you're not. I know what you love. I know you loved Miles Rawley and that you love his family in the twenty-first century." Confidence was so dense in Fallon's voice it spread over my skin like syrup. Keeping me pinned, he promised, "And I will *kill them all* the next time I leap, I swear this to you, do you hear me?"

Rage burst through my blood, gurgling in my ear canals. It took only a slight shift to knee his balls with every ounce of strength I possessed; I was still wearing trousers and hit him so squarely he collapsed to the side, wheezing too hard to groan. Crying and gasping I scrambled across the floor like an injured beetle – my fingers closed around the solid hardness of the poker. Gripping it like a baseball bat I surged to my feet, remembering Blythe teaching Tish and me how to place a hit in order to best disable an attacker.

Fallon hunched on hands and knees and I swung for his head. He lifted an arm either in an attempt to shield his face or catch the weapon mid-swing and his forearm took the blow. He yelped like an animal – I heard a horrible, sickening crunch – but I swung again, determined to take him out, raising the poker above my head like an executioner's axe. It whistled through the air and then, before my eyes, Fallon vanished. I fell forward with my enraged momentum and the poker gouged a big chunk from the plush carpet, instead.

Patricia and I sat together on our favorite bench, one of lichen-covered stone beneath an intricately-carved grape arbor. Even in the dark heart of winter we'd found time to sit on it, scraping aside snow and speculating what the garden would look like in warmer weather. The mid-morning June sun bloomed brightly over us for the first time in what seemed like years, dusting our eyelids with pale gold. Other than her bulging pregnancy, Patricia was so slim that she appeared waifish, as though every nutrient she absorbed went straight to the baby. Violet-gray shadows decorated the fragile skin beneath her eyes.

I told her, "You look beautiful."

She shook her head. "Did I not ask you to cut the shit?"

In the span of months we'd been imprisoned together Patricia had adopted many of my expressions. I smiled at these words paired with her naturally formal tone and admitted, "You did, yes. But you really do look beautiful."

And she did, I was not just attempting to keep her spirits up.

"Well, then I suppose I should thank you," she whispered, but no sooner had she spoken than she uttered a soft groan. She grabbed my hand and directed it to the tiny foot or elbow pressing outward.

I thought of touching Celia's belly in a similar fashion as I whispered, "Hi, Monty."

Patricia murmured, "That's your Aunt Ruthann, love."

I wondered constantly about Miles's son, praying multiple times a day that Celia had reached Grant and Birdie, and remained with them. Her baby would have been born over five months ago and I prayed just as often that he'd arrived in the world under Birdie's care. What had Celia named him? Had Celia kept him, or trusted him to Birdie and returned to Howardsville? Not knowing was yet another sharp shovel carving holes in my soul. What if I never discovered the baby's fate? It seemed as though Patricia and I had been prisoners at the convent for decades; at times, I felt certain we would die here.

Fear was a constant force at the back of my mind, strung like a sticky spider web; I'd forgotten a time when I was without its presence. Despite the fact that he'd not reappeared since the night in the train car when I'd tried to kill him, Fallon's words trailed me like demons – he'd kill them all, he said of my family, and I did not doubt his capability to do just that

– but were the words truth, or threats calculated to force my hand? And where the hell had he gone? Was Fallon in the twenty-first century even now, preying on them? My helplessness was infuriating; how could I hope to get a message to my sisters or the Rawleys, to *any* of them, when I remained trapped in both the convent and 1882? I couldn't even get a message to anyone in *this* goddamn century.

And I thought, as I did in various versions every hour or so, *Please hear me, Marshall. Aunt Jilly, Tish, please hear me. Please be careful. You have to recognize the danger. He's more dangerous than anything I've ever known.*

Of course I told no one other than Patricia what actually happened in Fallon's train car that night, but according to Dredd his elder brother often left for weeks at a time, and always quite suddenly. Dredd was clueless regarding most of his family's activities; fortunately for Patricia and me, he was also reasonable, soft-spoken, and kind. For a brief span of time last autumn, before Patricia realized her period was late, she and I lived in relative peace in our small corner of the Lake Michigan mansion; Dredd allowed us to remain in the same bedroom, only requesting Patricia dine with him in the evenings. I'd tried twice to escape the grounds but both times was escorted back inside by male servants, less kindly the second time, to our second-floor suite.

Mr. Yancy's orders, ma'am, I was informed, underscoring yet again that Fallon's directives were not to be disobeyed. And here, stashed away at the Immaculate Heart of Mary, Patricia and I were trapped even more completely than we'd been in Chicago. I joked that the nuns seemed to be expecting a full-scale assault, as their garden walls were constructed of stacked stones, easily six feet high and tipped with wrought-iron spikes. Even if the nuns weren't lurking everywhere, insidious spies wearing wimples, Patricia was in no condition to be shimmying over walls and traversing the prairie on foot to reach the nearest city, especially not during the winter months.

Sister Marguerite, who appeared younger than the other nuns and wore a differently-styled wimple, had dared to speak with us a handful of occasions. Once she'd actually touched Patricia instead of shying away from her like the rest of the sisters; I wanted to tell them they weren't in any jeopardy of getting pregnant by association. Marguerite had whispered, "May I?" and at Patricia's nod, reverently rested her palms on the firm curve of Patricia's belly. It was during our second conversation with Sister Marguerite we'd finally learned exactly where we were; Illinois, but only two miles east of the Iowa border, on the outskirts of a little town called Beaufort. Later that same night, Patricia had been wild with the knowledge we were so close to Iowa, where the Rawley and Spicer families both homesteaded.

"Cole could be only miles away," she'd moaned, overcome with sobbing. "But he doesn't know we're here!"

"His parents intend to head west in the spring," I'd reminded her. "Remember, Cole said that? And so did Una's letters."

I had tried my best to recall every line of Una Spicer's letters, scouring for clues; I was certain the Spicers had been in Montana Territory by 1882. And then there was the letter written by Malcolm Carter which had once fallen from a Jalesville High yearbook and into my hands. In this letter, Cole was missing and Malcolm wrote of Miles's death. *They are yet unhealed at Miles's passing* Malcolm had written, referring to Miles's parents sometime in May of this year, 1882. Had Grant taken Miles's body home to Iowa? Was Malcolm Carter searching even now for Cole, while Cole searched for Patricia and me? And what of Axton? Lying in the narrow bed, huddled against Patricia's warmth through the long winter, I found my thoughts often turning to Miles. *I am yet unhealed, too. I know you loved me, Miles Rawley, and I will never forget that.*

Patricia tipped her wan face to the June sunlight and whispered, "I'm so scared."

Usually we only spoke of these things at night, in the dark of our tomblike little room.

As I had many times before, I vowed, "I won't leave your side."

"It's soon, Ruthie, the baby is coming soon. I can feel it." New desperation colored her voice.

"Are you having contractions?" I demanded in a whisper, half-rising from the bench.

"I have been since early this morning," she confessed breathlessly, catching at my wrist, and my heart contracted. She closed her eyes, exhaling through her nose. "I didn't want to say anything yet, but they're getting stronger. Oh Jesus, Ruthie, *they'll take him from me.*"

I cupped her belly, as much to keep my own fears in line as to alleviate hers. Only too well could I picture the nuns with their vulture-like black robes, crowded around the bed, hunched and ready to snatch the baby the second he emerged. I opened my mouth to respond when something drew our gazes abruptly to the left, in pure disbelief, as it was a sound neither of us had heard in a very long time. Other than creepy, beak-nosed Father Doherty, who preached on Sunday mornings, there was a decided lack of men at the Immaculate Heart of Mary.

But this voice was most certainly male.

Low and urgent, he called a second time, "Ruthie! *Patricia!*"

I froze. Then I blinked.

It was Axton.

He was alive. Alive and standing near the lilac border only twenty feet from us, wearing a gray wool jacket and a battered straw hat, carrying a hedge clipper. I thought maybe I was hallucinating – maybe I'd lost my mind at last. Patricia whimpered, every bit as disbelieving, her face suffused with shocked heat as she stared. She tried to stand but I caught her wrist, terrified she would run to him and ruin his cover.

Axton lifted one hand, indicating not to advance. I read the caution on his face as plainly as the extremity of his relief. He advanced casually closer, boots crunching over the crushed rock of the garden path; I couldn't take my eyes from him, terrified he would disappear in the fashion of a mirage. Once he was no more than ten feet away, he whispered fervently, "Holy *Christ*, am I glad to see you two."

"Axton," I breathed, gripping the stone bench with one hand and Patricia's wrist with the other, hanging on for dear life. It was all I could do to remain sitting when I wanted to tackle him and cover his familiar face with kisses.

"Listen," he said, speaking quickly. "The nuns think I'm a gardener sent to replace their old one. I been sleeping in the little shed, yonder. I got in here two days ago but I haven't been able to get close to you until now. Where do they keep you? What part of this place?"

I indicated by pointing. "We're in a small chamber room at the back of the main building. North side, last door on the right. They lock us in and there are no windows."

Axton declared, with quiet vehemence, "We're getting you out of here, this evening when they take you to pray. Can you be ready?"

"How?" I demanded. "Who's 'we?'"

Axton looked hard into my eyes and I could sense his blazing desire to tell me something, but his self-control was extremely admirable. He only insisted, "Just be ready. This evening, at prayer, you hear me?" His gaze clung to Patricia, caressing and holding her just as his hands and arms would have; he vowed, "I'll get you out of here, *I swear to you*."

"Axton," Patricia whispered, and at the sound of his name on her lips, determined fire burned anew in his eyes. She said as though caught in a dream, "You're here."

I repeated, "But how?"

There came the soft rise and fall of other voices, serene and female.

Ax said only, "Be ready," and then walked away, out toward the brick courtyard where Patricia and I weren't allowed to venture.

"Did I just…did we just…" I pressed a hand to my thudding heart.

Patricia's skin was mottled with a brilliant flush that suddenly, alarmingly, drained away. I was afraid she was about to faint and hooked my arms around her shoulders. Tears washed over her cheeks.

"It's all right, it's all right." I cupped the back of her head. "Did you hear Axton? Did you see him? He's alive!"

She clenched the material of my shawl and struggled to draw a full breath.

I repeated, "It's all right. Shhh, honey, it's all right."

At last Patricia nodded, to my great relief, swiping at her running nose with her knuckles. She whispered, "We shall be ready."

My heart was already ticking like a time bomb. I just prayed it wouldn't go off before this evening and give us away.

Chapter Twenty-Four

THE DAYS HAD GROWN LONGER WITH SPRING, WHICH would have been a welcome thing if we weren't waiting so desperately for this evening's prayer time to arrive. Neither of us was able to eat lunch and I couldn't stop pacing our tiny room as the day drifted into late afternoon. I tried to make Patricia nap, to no avail. Her contractions remained steady and I prayed without ceasing, to every entity possibly listening, that the baby stay put until we were away from this place. I bundled our extra dresses and underskirts just like I would have a pair of sleeping bags, including the binding cloths I had been given to use during my period. We each had one pair of shoes and we were both wearing them. Far too restless to sit still, I braided Patricia's hair and pinned it up for her.

Maybe seventy thousand times since his appearance, Patricia had said, "Axton is alive. He came for us."

I shelved all worry over the fact that she was in love with Axton and carrying Cole's baby; it was a trifling concern just now. I replied, "Of course he did. And Cole must be with him. And maybe Grant? Malcolm Carter? Or one of the other Rawley brothers?"

"What will I say to Cole? What will he think…"

"He'll be so grateful to see you he won't be anything but overjoyed. I promise."

"But…"

"Patricia, I love you dearly but I can't deal with what Cole is thinking. At this moment I couldn't give less of a fuck!" My anxiety had morphed to irritation.

"Ruthann!"

"I'm sorry."

Patricia indicated the clothing I'd tied into travel bundles. "How shall we carry our belongings with us when we are simply attending prayer? Shall that not appear suspicious?"

"Maybe *you* have a better idea?"

She rolled her eyes, reminding me more than ever of Tish. "It was a sincere effort, nonetheless."

"Thanks," I muttered.

At long last the evening bells resounded, our only indicator of passing time since we couldn't see the sun from our room.

"I'm going to explode," I groaned. I felt like I'd spent the day running uphill, exhausted and drained, even though my only physical exertion had been pacing. My chest grew alternately hot, then cold. Patricia lay on her side on the cot, watching me expectantly, and I prayed yet again, *Please, Monty, stay put. Stay put until we can get the hell out of this place.*

She whispered, "Axton was here, wasn't he? Or did I simply dream that?"

I stopped my feverish pacing and knelt beside her. I felt terrible for my earlier bad mood. "He was here. He said they're getting us out of here." I tried for a smile. "If anyone can convincingly lie to a bunch of nuns, it's Ax."

"Thank God for him," Patricia whispered, her eyes wet with tears as she clutched my hands. "My sweet Axton. He is completely without guile. Of course they shall believe every word he speaks."

I felt hysterical laughter pushing upward from my ribcage; I recognized the desire to lose control, whether through laughter or wild sobbing. *Hold it together. Now more than ever, you have to hold it together.*

"You make him sound like a little boy. He's older than you are."

She whispered, "But you and I have each gained a year in this place." She meant our birthdays, as we'd each celebrated one – though 'celebrate' was definitely the wrong word. Patricia turned nineteen in April and I'd turned twenty-four in January.

"Yes, we're getting ancient," I said.

Patricia's face went suddenly blank. My horrified gaze flew to her belly, which changed shape before my eyes, visibly tightening in an unmistakable sign of progressing labor. She released a half-moaning gasp and tried to sit. "That one was strong…"

Fuck, I thought. *Fucking shit.*

But I said, "I'm right here."

Patricia groaned and then sucked a sharp breath.

I gripped her shoulders. "Not now. Oh Jesus Christ, not now. Oh Patricia, oh *fuck*…"

She gritted her teeth, face ashen and her eyes inward-looking, drawn into wordless communication with the baby.

"Honey, we can't let them know you're in labor."

"I know," she half-whispered, half-grunted. "I know. I shall die before letting them see my son is coming."

No sooner had she spoken than a light knock sounded on our door, as it always did at this time of day, when Sister Beatrice (Bitch-face) came to unlock our room and walk us to the chapel, where she would wait while we "prayed." I'd long wondered if the sister was being punished, maybe doing some sort of penance, because she was not allowed to join the others at breakfast or dinner until after accomplishing this twice-daily duty.

Of course Patricia and I were only allowed to eat in the secrecy of our room. Sister Beatrice drove me crazy, never speaking, hardly acknowledging we were human. I wanted to shove her nose backward into her expressionless face, if for no other reason than to cause a reaction in her, but I stifled this cruel urge as I heard the familiar sound of locks being disengaged. I wondered in which pocket of her black robe she hid the keys.

"*Patricia*," I hissed.

"I am well," she insisted, composing her face. Sweat created a glistening sheen on her forehead and upper lip, but she lifted her chin and smoothed her hair. When the door swung inward, revealing Sister Beatrice, Patricia met the sister's bland expression with one of her own.

I thought I might be experiencing the first stages of a heart attack as

I tucked Patricia's arm in the crook of mine and helped her stand. She kept her face neutral as we followed Sister Beatrice down the dim stone corridor and then outside, where the evening air embraced us like an old friend. A thin layer of fleecy clouds scattered the gold of the lowering sun and with extreme effort I kept my gaze ahead, rather than relenting to the desperate urge to scan the courtyard for signs of Axton.

What if we imagined him?

What if –

Sister Beatrice held the chapel door for us. Patricia gripped my arm and I could hear the slight strain of her breathing, but she walked without a hint of discomfort. The nun took up her usual place beside the door, letting it close behind us. Once relatively alone, encased in the quiet peace of the chapel, Patricia stalled and bent forward. She was sweating hard now, trickles slipping over her temples.

I whispered, "I'm so sorry. Hang on, we'll get you out of here."

"I'm all wet," she moaned. "Oh dear God, my legs are wet!"

"Soon," I promised, jittering with nerves. I would carry her out of this place; I would knock out that stupid nun and carry Patricia to safety. "Ax will be here soon."

"Is it blood?" she whimpered, and I could tell she was about to lose her cool like nobody's business.

I helped her lift her skirts and was relieved to see only clear wetness, no hint of the telltale red of blood. "Your water broke, like we talked about might happen, remember?"

"But that means he's coming right now!" She started to cry.

Axton! I prayed. *There's no time like the present!*

There was a small scuffle just outside the door. I couldn't release my hold on Patricia to see what was happening but a second later the door opened and emitted Axton, holding Sister Beatrice backward against his chest, one hand over her mouth. The sister's frantic eyes darted between Patricia and me.

"Thank God," I gasped, almost going to my knees with relief.

"Help me, Ruthie, there's rope just outside the door."

Patricia sank to a nearby pew as I helped Ax knot a handkerchief around Sister Beatrice's mouth before securing her to a pew.

"Please keep quiet," I begged the nun, and the first essence of emotion I'd ever observed shone through as she glared like a kicked badger. I couldn't resist whispering, "You're a *saint.*"

The moment his hands were free Axton hugged me, rocking us side to side. He whispered against my hair, "I'm so glad to see you, Ruthie, I can't tell you."

But the woman he truly needed was only steps away; he released me and flew to Patricia's side, falling to his knees before her. Gasping and crying, she threw her arms around him while he clasped her to his chest, burying his face against her neck. Patricia heaved with sobs, digging her fingers in his hair.

"You're alive, *you came for me...*"

"Of course I did, sweetheart..."

"I've been so scared...we thought you were dead." She held his face in both hands, studying him with the desperation of the damned. "I love you, Axton, I love you so. I'm sorry...*I'm so sorry...*"

He kissed her forehead, her eyelids, her cheeks and chin. She tugged his mouth to hers and a burst of agony ricocheted through me – I was witnessing something I should not, I realized, a moment of intimacy and surrender. I thought of Cole, who was by far my second choice for Patricia but who deserved better than this; the child was his, after all. There was no other choice for her but Cole, not anymore. I bit my lower lip as Axton drew away. I couldn't see Patricia's face, only Axton's, which was overcome with his aching love for her as he breathed her name. "I've been so worried. Are you hurting, sweetheart?"

It was up to me to put a stop to this; I said firmly, "She's in labor, Ax, of course she's hurting! Come on, you two, let's go!"

Ax gained immediate control, nodding his understanding. "C'mon, I got the gardener's wagon yonder in the courtyard."

He carried Patricia, looking both ways before navigating the expanse of brick; I followed close behind them, my heart lodged somewhere near my voice box. The nuns were at dinner but at any moment someone could spy us, Mother Superior and her lackeys could stop us –

The gardener's wagon, a ramshackle cart with a boxy bed and no canvas cover, was parked in the gathering gloom with its tailgate down. Ranger was hitched to it and Axton jogged the last few yards, setting Patricia on the wooden bed with as much care as he could manage. "Lie down, sweetheart, quick now. I'm so sorry I have to haul you two like this."

I understood his intent at once, climbing in beside Patricia and a number of barrels lined up on one edge. Patricia scooted as close to the barrels as she could manage and I squeezed beside her. She was breathing hard; there were large damp patches on her skirts.

"Hold on," I begged.

Axton drew several empty cloth bags nearer to us, creating a less human-like outline, and then spread a dirty canvas tarp over us, probably the one that usually made an umbrella over the wagon bed. He murmured, "No one's stirring yet. We have to clear the gate now. Be as quiet as you can."

We heard him climb on the wagon seat and command, "*Gidd-up,*" to Ranger. The halter chains jingled and we bumped forward, the wooden wheels creaking over the bricks. Our scant covering was translucent. I tipped my forehead against Patricia's and we grasped hands.

Axton murmured, "Here comes the gate now, just ahead."

I didn't dare breathe. Patricia closed her eyes as Axton halted Ranger and we heard a man's voice; I hadn't realized there was another man besides Father Doherty on the property.

But of course they'd have a man watching the gate, I thought. Again I felt an imminent heart attack, my pulse firing so hard my veins hurt. *What if he asks to check the wagon? What if this is one of Fallon's men? Oh Jesus...*

But this man sounded ancient as he greeted Axton. My gaze clung to the canvas covering a few inches from my nose as I listened, wild with fear. Patricia's hands were damp and trembling. I enfolded them more securely within mine.

Axton said, "Fine evening, ain't it?"

He sounds natural.

The man responded by asking, "You headed to town, young feller?"

Go with it, I tried to tell Axton. *Go with that.*

Ax said, "Surely am," and I pictured his winsome smile. "I'll return before full dark."

There was a pause and I figured we were done for. Patricia's shaking increased. But then came the sound of clinking iron and Axton's calm, "Thank you, sir. Good evening!"

And the wagon resumed motion, carrying us from the Immaculate Heart of Mary for the first time since last autumn.

We traveled over extremely bumpy ground. After maybe a mile and a half, when we were probably at last out of sight of the convent, Axton said, "We're away!"

I shoved aside the canvas like someone surfacing from a river, overcome by relief that I was not about to drown. We were traveling west and the evening sky arched above us, smooth as velvet and painted with warm lavender hues. I inhaled great gulps of air, tears streaking my cheeks. The open prairie stretched to all sides around us, as beautiful as freedom.

I cupped Patricia's face and exulted, "We're away!"

She managed to nod acknowledgment, breathing harshly, clutching her belly, and Axton halted Ranger and jumped to the ground, racing to the back of the wagon where he reached for Patricia, letting her grip his hands. I realized he'd lost all traces of boyishness since I'd last seen him. He moved now without hesitation.

"It's all right," I assured Patricia, kneeling beside her in the wagon bed. I looked to Ax. "Where are we going? Is it safe in town?"

He held my somber gaze. "No, we've been avoiding the town. They'll be half-crazy with worry by now. I've not been able to talk to them since I made the trip to town *yesterday* evening and they don't know that I've talked to you."

"Is Cole with you?" I asked.

Axton's eyes were almost unreadable but I knew him well enough to perceive the depth of agony; he nodded.

"Does he know, Ax?"

Before he could respond something west of us caught his attention. He lifted his left arm, waving in wide arcs, and hollered "I got them!"

I spied the outline of a horse and rider silhouetted against the sunset, the horse at a full-out gallop. My breath twisted and caught. I thought wildly, *Miles?*

"Who…" I whispered.

I heard a voice, shouting my name. A deep, husky voice, one I knew way down deep in my bones. Disbelief became instant, blazing recognition. And then I gathered my skirts and leaped from the wagon, heedless of nothing else but getting to him.

"*Ruthann!*"

He drew on the reins, dismounting before the horse had halted, but nothing could stop him now. Joy exploded within me, hot and swift and potent as he rushed to me.

And then I was wrapped in his arms.

I heard choking sobs and harsh, exerted breathing, both mine and his. We were in perpetual motion, trying to defy all known physics and crawl at once into each other's skin. The force of our embrace took us to the ground, where we continued to tangle around each other, struggling to become one entity rather than two. I stared at him as one tortured and deprived, at the man I had once known better than anyone else in my life. He took my face between his hands, tears streaming over his cheeks.

"It's you, it's you, oh Marshall, *it's you…*"

He fell into my eyes, studying me as if unable to believe we were touching, alive in the same space together at last, hearts beating and blood flowing. He pressed his lips to my forehead, crushing my body to his and shuddering with silent sobs, rolling us again, so that I was cradled to his chest.

"I'm sorry, I'm so sorry," he moaned, his voice raw, unimaginably pained. "*Ruthann.* Oh Jesus Christ, you're here. You're alive. *I love you…* you know I love you, don't you? *Tell me you know…*"

"I do know, Marshall, I do, come here," I begged, shifting to wrap my arms around his neck. "I have never stopped loving you. Not ever. I knew you didn't mean what you said that night…" It seemed so long ago now, in another life we might never again be allowed to inhabit.

"I can never forgive myself for speaking to you that way. I can only pray you'll forgive me. I was sure I cursed myself by saying those things to you. And then you…" He choked on a sob before finishing in a hoarse whisper, "You disappeared. And I haven't seen you since, until this moment."

"You're here. You're here with me. I've never been so happy," and even though I was weeping, within my chest cavity there was a sense of repair – of my heart being made again whole.

He kissed my face and neck, soft and honoring kisses, breathing against my skin, my hips anchored between his bent legs. He said passionately, "You've been restored to me and I will never ask for another thing in this life. You are everything I need, my beautiful angel-woman. Is it really you?"

"It's me," I whispered, my fingers curled around strands of his hair, which was loose and tangled and hung well below his shoulders. "It's me, sweetheart. I've been going by Ruthann Rawley here, from the first. That's how I think of myself."

His eyes flashed with a deep and yet cautious joy as he studied me at close range in the sunset light, for the first time in so long. I drank in the sight of his familiar handsome face, seeing for the first time the evidence of his heritage – his beautiful gray eyes with their secondary spokes of color, just like Celia's, unchanged except for the pain, which would take time to fully dissipate. He had not experienced any lightness of spirit in far too long. His nose – long and knife-edged, just like Miles's – and his wide, sensual mouth, jaws peppered with thick black stubble; his dark hair was longer than I'd ever seen it, streaked with a few threads of silver, giving him a distinctly more mature aura.

"That's how I always think of you, my darling, my sweet darling. Will you let me kiss you?" He spoke with such longing, a haunted remembrance of pain. He held my face, gently thumbing away my tears.

In response I lifted my mouth, exhaling softly against his lips before pressing near. Marshall groaned and drew me immediately closer. My body had never forgotten his kisses and responded instinctively. I opened my lips, flooded with memories of all our past kissing, all our lovemaking, the beauty and joy of it; the dam in my mind broke, after so long, and I moaned as our tongues joined, sleek and hot, tasting him and letting myself remember everything.

Low, wordless sounds of love lifted from my throat, meshing with the same sounds from Marshall's. The taste of him was so familiar, and so good, his taste I had not allowed myself to think about, in order to survive…the feel of his tongue stroking my skin, the way his lips played over mine and how our mouths fit so perfectly, molded for each other alone. I held his head with both hands, feeling his jaws moving as we kissed. Marshall ran his hands without ceasing over my body, shoulders and ribs and hips, down and back up again before anchoring possessively around me. I rubbed my cheek on the stubble of his beard as he released a shuddering breath against the side of my neck.

At least partially sated upon one another, he whispered, "There's so much to tell you. Oh Jesus, have you been hurt? Oh God, you're so vulnerable here…"

"I haven't been hurt, not how you're thinking," I assured him, and his eyes closed in temporary relief.

"Come with me, we're on the ground for the love of all that's holy." Marshall rolled to his knees and then his feet, lifting me with, keeping me close to his heart. It wasn't until then I remembered we were not alone, and saw two other horses and riders near the wagon, along with Blade, who Marshall had been riding. Marshall tucked me to his side and together we hurried back to everyone else. Axton had relinquished Patricia to Cole; Cole was holding both her hands, speaking in low tones. Ax stood yards away, watching Marshall and me approach. A man I didn't at first recognize sat astride a tall chestnut horse, observing with curious dark eyes.

Ax said quietly to Marshall, "Well, I guess you *do* know Ruthie."

Marshall lifted my chin and kissed me flush on the lips, smiling into my eyes; I refused to release my hold on him. His voice was huskier than normal as he said, "Ruthann is my heart and my soul. I told you I'm not much good without either."

"I know it ain't the time to bring up particulars but I'm Malcolm Carter, ma'am," said the man on horseback, tipping his hat brim.

Why, it's Mathias, I realized, punched anew in the gut. *Mathias, my sister Camille's husband.*

Marshall knew exactly what I was thinking. He nuzzled my hair and acknowledged the strangeness of it all, whispering, "I know."

Without thinking I cried, "Aces! Your horse! Why, he's beautiful." I recognized the animal from the old picture Camille kept on her nightstand. I could only just imagine my sister's joy to know I was meeting them.

Malcolm nodded, obviously pleased; he patted his horse's neck with pure affection. "We're both pleased to meet you, Miss Ruthann."

And then from the back of the wagon Cole said urgently, "My son is about to enter this world, you-all, can we hold off on the introductions?!"

Chapter Twenty-Five

COLE MONTGOMERY SPICER, JUNIOR, WAS BORN SO QUICK-
ly there was still the afterglow of sunset in the sky as he entered the
world. At my rapid-fire orders (as I was the only one of us who'd ever
actually attended a birth), Axton climbed into the wagon bed and braced
Patricia from behind, bolstering her with his chest against her spine,
while I hurried to help her scoot closer to the end of the tailgate and
lifted her heavy black skirts; we'd never been given underwear at the
convent, other than the binding cloths I'd needed for my periods. None
of us was concerned about anything but helping Patricia; there was no
embarrassment, no awkwardness at her partial nudity.

I tried to keep blatant alarm from my voice as I beheld the sight of
her parted thighs. "He's crowning. Oh wow, he's crowning *right now.*"

The delicate skin between Patricia's legs bulged unimaginably far to
accommodate the blood-smeared oval of the baby's head. Cole's face
went slack with amazement before he gathered himself and moved closer, gripping her knees in his strong hands.

I told Cole, "That's good, you keep holding her knees. When she
pushes him out, we'll both be ready."

Patricia, braced against Ax in a half-reclining position, was trying her
best to look brave, I could tell. Her belly clamped with continuous contractions, her face pale as a moonlit rock. Just observing the clenching of
her muscles made my own stomach hurt. She groaned and sweat beaded
on her upper lip but she studied my face for instructions.

"He's almost ready to be born. When I say so, I want you to push,"
I said, and she rallied, chewing her bottom lip and nodding with vigor.

Axton cupped his hands about her elbows. He also watched my face for orders and I felt a tremble ripple through my limbs.

"You can do this, Ruthie." Marshall bolstered me from the left side, kissing my temple. He said to Patricia, "We'll all help, don't worry."

She tried to smile. And then she gritted her teeth as muscle spasms shuddered over her. I cringed in sympathy – simply observing was painful. I thought of the night my niece Millie Jo was born, back home in Landon; I'd been twelve years old and slightly horrified by the messy process, honored to be there, sure, but it was terrible watching Camille go through what seemed like the worst physical pain of her life. At least that night there had been an entire hospital staff available if anything went wrong.

Cole kept firm hold of Patricia's knees, making circles with his thumbs; he gritted his teeth with each low, groaning cry that emerged from Patricia's throat, hating to see her in such pain.

"Hold her hand," I instructed Malcolm Carter, who'd dismounted and hurried to assist. "And Marsh, you take her other hand. Let her grip you."

The men obeyed my orders without question. Despite the danger looming literally just over the horizon – Sister Beatrice and our absence from the convent had surely been discovered by now – there was a blazing beacon of joy inside me as I beheld Marshall, only a few feet away, here in the nineteenth century. *He had come for me.* Of course he had, and my heart soared with the realization. He and Malcolm each took one of Patricia's hands, letting her squeeze them as she would.

Buoyed by sudden optimism, I ordered, "All right, Patricia, I want you to push! Push hard! He's right here!"

She bore down, closing her eyes, tipping her chin to her chest and grunting. Her arms and legs shook, hips lifting from the tailgate.

"Good work," Cole encouraged. I'd wanted him positioned here rather than behind her so he could watch the birth as it happened.

Axton held her with unconditional tenderness, tucking loose strands of hair to the side so they weren't in Patricia's face. I heard him murmur, "You're all right. It's all right."

I cried, "Another, come on! Don't give up now!"

Patricia obeyed, grinding her teeth. She panted and groaned, pushing again. Her face and neck grew mottled with the strain but the baby wasn't cooperating. There was more than a trickle of blood now, redness staining the wagon bed; I could tell Cole was ready to go ballistic, holding it together only by a thin thread.

"Tish, try breathing like this." Marshall jiggled her right hand and demonstrated the breathing technique by pursing his lips.

"Everyone!" I encouraged. "Come on, push!"

Patricia, between gasps, laughed at how stupid we all looked, breathing in pants with our lips puffed out like fish. She moaned, "I can't...*it hurts so fucking much*..."

"You can!" I rested my palms on her belly and applied pressure. "He's almost here! You'll hold your son!"

She tried again, straining for all she was worth. Her hairline was wet with sweat; more streaked her face as she emitted a low, guttural moan and the baby's head emerged, facedown.

"There he is!" I shrieked. "Cole, get your hands ready!"

Cole cupped his palms, stun etched across his features as his bloody, wriggling son was delivered into his wide palms. Patricia's head fell back against Axton's chest; her ribs heaved.

"He's here!" I cried triumphantly, wiping tears on my shoulder.

Cole kept repeating like he couldn't quite believe it, "My son. *My boy*."

"Let me see him," Patricia whispered, beaming at the baby in the manner of radiant sunshine breaking through a cloud bank. Her eyes glowed true-blue in the last of the light.

"Put him on her belly," I told Cole, who did so, with utmost care. The baby was splotchy and red, tiny hands curled in snail-shell fists, crinkly face streaked with blood and pinched with the rigor of being born. A thin, pulsing, blue-white cord connected him to his mother. I explained, "It's all right, some blood is all right. She's got to deliver the afterbirth." I told Ax, "Help her lie back a little."

Cole murmured to Patricia, "I love you. And I will never let you go again."

I avoided looking at Axton.

Malcolm cupped Cole's shoulder. "Congratulations, old friend." To Patricia he praised, "You done a fine job, dear lady."

I leaned so I could kiss Patricia's forehead. "You did so well. There's just a little more and then you can rest."

At my further instructions, Patricia delivered the placenta. It was really messy, it was a little repulsive to handle, but I loved Patricia and I was not about to let her see I felt that way. Marshall bolstered me with an arm around my waist, understanding I was ready to collapse. The wagon bed, already crowded with barrels and flotsam, was now even dirtier, grime mixed with blood and other indefinable wetness; I felt terrible Patricia had been forced to give birth like this. But then, as my gaze swept to the gorgeous expanse of evening sky, I thought, *No, this is right. We could have been in the Immaculate Heart of Mary, think of that.*

"Wow, so that's a placenta," Marshall marveled.

"I need a knife," I said, a little desperately. My fingers were slick with blood and I needed to cut the umbilical cord. The front of my skirt was smeared with more blood.

"I got one," Malcolm said immediately, producing a pocketknife, which he politely wiped clean on his thigh before handing it over.

"About here, do you think?" I wondered, indicating two inches above the baby's belly button, or what would become his belly button once the end of the cord fell off. He was fussing, working himself into a tiny temper, which I knew was a good sign. I said to the baby, "Hello there, little man." And then I smiled wider. "He's a redhead."

"He's so beautiful," Patricia murmured, cupping his head and caressing his face. He remained curled on her belly. Cole bent and pressed his lips to the baby's fuzzy hair.

"I'm trying to remember what Wy's belly button looked like when he came home from the hospital. It had a safety-pin thing on it," Marsh said, his hands wrapped around my waist; he bent down so he could kiss the side of my neck. We were unable to stop touching each other. He speculated, "We should tie it off first, with twine or something like that. Will he have an outie or an in-y belly button? Isn't that based on how the cord is cut? That's a lot of pressure, Ruthie."

I giggled, lifting my face so I could kiss him, never minding that now probably wasn't the time – I simply had to feel his mouth on mine. Marsh grinned and pulled me closer. He was giddy with relief and delight, same as me; I could feel it flowing from him like whitecaps over a lake. Marshall touched our foreheads together and squeezed my waist. He whispered, "Holy God, I'm almost afraid to blink, angel."

"That is most certainly Marshall Rawley," I heard Patricia murmur.

Malcolm eyed the heavens. "I hate to say so but we oughta move before too long. It's a terrible thing to ask of a new mama but we ain't in a good place out here."

Within minutes we were westward bound, where the sky gleamed with a faint yellow stripe, seeming to guide our way. I'd successfully cut and tied off the umbilical cord, and as I scrubbed clean with water from Marshall's canteen, was rather proud of myself. Axton drove while Cole lay in the wagon bed with Patricia and the baby, cradling both of them in his arms. Malcolm rode alongside, talking quietly with Ax, while Marshall and I rode double on Blade, as we had so many times back at home in Jalesville, on Arrow, lagging in the wake of everyone else. Marshall's thighs were tight against mine, his arms locked around my waist, and he felt so good behind me I was lightheaded. I wanted to flip around and straddle him, to take him into my body in a thousand different ways.

Reading my thoughts loudly and clearly, cloaked in the deepening darkness, Marsh swept aside my hair and bit the side of my neck, then my earlobe, cradling my left breast with his free hand, finding the rounded swell of my nipple with his thumb and letting his heated words play over my skin as he murmured, "I know this isn't the time and I'm being completely honest when I say it is heaven above just to hold you, but *I need to be inside of you*. I need it like I need water or oxygen. I can't think of anything but feeling your beautiful, delicious nakedness pressed against me. Oh Jesus God, woman…"

I shivered and clutched his thighs, tilting my head to kiss his neck and take his chin between my teeth. He groaned as I closed my teeth over his lower lip, reaching back to stroke him through his trousers.

"That's gonna poke you in the back all the way there, I'm sorry," he whispered against my mouth and I giggled, even though I was breathless with need for him.

"You don't sound very sorry…"

"Oh God, I'm not sorry, I admit it. That feels so good, angel, *don't stop*…"

Tears flowed even though I didn't want to cry anymore; emotions stormed through me, beyond my control. His easy way of teasing me was so familiar, so right, something else I had forced myself not to think about in his absence. Before my throat closed off I whispered, "*I've missed you so much*…"

Marsh drew on the reins, bringing Blade to a halt to enfold me in both arms. "I missed you so much I thought I would die. Every second we've been apart I hurt like someone beat me senseless." He pressed his lips to my temple. "I've been living like a dead man without you. I've only held on day to day because I knew I would find you. I couldn't rest until I did."

"When did…*how did*…"

"I went after you the very next day, back in 2014, as soon as Tish and I figured it out. I was crazy with worry, honey, you can't imagine. And I got here, to 1881, last September," he explained. "I was mauled the first half hour I was here. Here I am, this naturalist, this *outdoorsman*, and I blunder into a goddamn stray wolf. I thought I was dead right there. I didn't come to for a good three days after Amos found me. I was lucky as hell he did. I was just miles from Grant and Birdie's place."

"You were right there?" I whispered. I increased my grip, as though he might just disintegrate. "You've met Grant and Birdie? Oh Marsh, sweetheart, there's so much to tell you…"

"I know, angel, I really do. I met them all, and the Spicers. It's so crazy to see Garth here as another version of himself, and Becky, I can't get over it. And their house and our land…" He drew a deep, shaky breath. "And to see everyone we know in the people here, like Case and Tish, and Mathias. I don't know what to think. I don't have any context for what I think."

"Marshall," I whispered, not certain how to begin what I wanted to say. Tears fell over my face, wetting my jaws, dripping to my breasts. I clutched his forearms. "I met *you* here. Did they…did they tell you…"

I felt him nod. He said, with quiet reverence, "I met his little boy. And Celia asked me to give you her love, first thing."

"Oh, thank God," I breathed, choked up all over again. "She brought the baby to Birdie…*thank God*."

"He was born around Thanksgiving. She named him Jacob Miles Rawley. Birdie and Celia told me everything they could about you, and about Miles. He's buried along the creek near the homestead, angel."

A sob pushed at my breastbone. I didn't want Marshall to feel guilty, or jealous, but I had to tell him what had happened. "Miles was *you*, Marsh, I knew he was you…*and he loved me*…"

"Of course he did," Marshall whispered, and tears tracked over his cheeks in the moonlight. There was nothing but sincerity in his voice. "He was *me*. Of course he loved you. There's never been a time when I haven't loved you."

I cried and Marshall held me as we traveled across the nighttime prairie, intending to make swift tracks from Illinois. We talked almost without let-up, speaking over the top of each other, interrupting as we'd always done.

"You'd disappeared with Patricia only *six days* before I arrived at Grant's," Marshall said. "Can you imagine? I've never felt so helpless. I slept all winter in the room you'd been using, angel, and the pillows in there smelled like you. I wouldn't let Birdie wash those sheets for anything. I can't believe they managed to live with me all those months, when I was ready to tear apart the walls. And then it snowed, *and snowed*, and covered the train tracks. We couldn't hope to travel, even by horseback, and I was like a crazy man. We didn't discover exactly where the Yancys secreted you and Patricia, or if you were even still with her, until just two weeks ago. I've never been so insane with worry as these past months of searching and waiting."

"Did you…was Fallon…"

"No, we got all our information from a servant in the Chicago estate, Dredd's butler. 'Footman' is what he called himself and he told us that Mr. Thomas Yancy and Mr. Fallon Yancy were 'away.' He didn't know where."

So Fallon hadn't yet returned from wherever he'd disappeared before I struck him while in his train car; at least, he hadn't returned to Chicago. I recognized the need to tell Marshall everything about Fallon, including what I'd learned about Faye – I was so sick over what Fallon had revealed that night I could hardly hold it in my mind, let alone consider the pain it would cause Marshall. And the question remained, begging to be answered – where had Fallon existed these past months? What if he was roaming the twenty-first century at this very moment, targeting our families? We had to get word to them, somehow. There had to be a way.

Marsh was saying, "Axton is about the best spy you could imagine. He seems so innocent that people don't suspect him of anything. I mean, he really is a good guy. I feel like he could be my little brother. And does he ever love you. I'd be jealous as hell except I couldn't hate anyone who cares for you and it's so obvious he's in love with Tish. Or Patricia, I mean. Cole knows it, too, and his tolerance is pretty goddamn low, but even he can't deny how much Axton helped us find you two. He helped us even knowing Patricia was pregnant with another man's baby. *That's* devotion."

"How did you find out about the convent?"

"Dredd's footman was in a relationship with the maid who cleaned the room where you and Patricia were kept until you vanished last November. This woman said one of you was pregnant – and I'm not gonna lie, angel, I just about fucking died thinking it might be you – but her next words were it was 'young Mrs. Yancy.' Thank God she was willing to dig into the matter a little deeper. Between her and the footman, we finally found out where Dredd had sent you."

"We were sure we were goners." I shuddered violently. "The nuns meant to take the baby, Marsh. Patricia and I have been planning an escape for months now but I think both of us knew there was nothing we could really do."

Marshall tightened his grip on me "I will always come for you, angel, no matter what. I admit I cut it pretty close this time, but I will always come for you."

Later he explained, "I'm a marshal now, can you believe it? A lawman. I took over for Miles since there was no one else available, or willing, in Howardsville. Axton volunteered, but he's too young."

Cold terror gripped me at this information. "No. Marsh, *no way*. Absolutely not. It's so dangerous." As I spoke, a lightbulb seemed to crackle to existence above my head; I could almost see it in the air. I whispered, "Wait a second, *you're* the marshal. The marshal from Una's letters! When I read those for the first time in 2013 that's why I was so worried about him – because he's *you*. Una mentioned Miles's 'passing.' I knew about Miles dying before I even got here. Oh, my God…"

I felt Marshall shiver; the same tremor passed from him to me as the realization spread through us both.

"It makes sense now," he murmured. "The letters make sense."

My mind was muddy with lack of sleep, with everything I was trying to contemplate. "There's so much we don't know yet…"

Marshall rested his chin on the top of my head. "Sleep, angel. You're exhausted. And I found you. Nothing else matters."

At last I slept, held fast in Marshall's arms; when I woke, hours later, a bright dawn spilled across the eastern sky, clouds rippling in a succession of narrow little waves with gold-gilt edges. The air was chill with night; the first sun beams shone a fiery orange. We didn't stop for breakfast and I was well aware of the quiet, intense conversation taking place among the men while I took a turn riding in the wagon with Patricia, even as I tried to tune it out; they were discussing the immediate future. It seemed the nearby Cedar River was the point where we would be forced to venture in separate directions.

Patricia was as comfortable as our meager supplies allowed, bundled in a shawl, her son in her arms while Cole handled the team; he sat with shoulders hunched and I would have paid a fair amount to know what was in his mind just now. I couldn't begin to guess. Axton rode only a few yards away, his spine straight as a soldier's, keeping his eyes from the wagon with all his effort. I lay beside Patricia and the baby, smoothing my fingertips over the baby's soft scalp, trying not to think about how quickly I would be separated from this woman I loved as much as my real sisters. I knew Tish and Camille would understand; they wouldn't begrudge me this love for Patricia, here in 1882. I'd spent the past ten months in her almost-constant company and to say I would miss her was a grievous understatement.

"You did so well," I told Patricia for the hundredth time, kissing the baby's forehead. The back of the wagon was hard and bumpy but the jostling didn't seem to bother him.

"I could not have done so without you."

"Hi, Monty," I murmured, caressing his silky cheek. "I think 'Monty' suits you."

"You know, I rather like it," Patricia said. "And it would be less confusing that way."

"It would," I agreed.

Studying my eyes, she acknowledged, "You have found your Marshall."

Tears blurred my vision. "I have."

"I could not be happier for you, sweet Ruthann." Patricia reached to tuck loose hair behind my ear, both of us determined to keep the mood light. "You are glowing this morning, from within. He is a *very* striking man, if you do not mind my observation. What is it Aunt Jillian would say about him?"

I giggled, thinking of all our candid conversations. "A fox."

"Yes, that's the way of it." Patricia smiled. "A *total* fox."

Marshall looked my way; neither of us could keep our eyes from the other for very long. He grinned and my blood rushed accordingly. I couldn't help but wonder, despite all the pressing matters crowding for top attention in my mind, when he and I would be allowed a moment alone. Right now I would be content with fifteen minutes. Five, even. And I shivered with pure, surging anticipation.

"You warm enough, angel?" Marsh called over.

"I am. I'm snuggling with the baby." But my eyes told him the real reason I'd shivered and his grin turned wicked. He blew me a slow, sweet kiss.

"We haven't long, do we?" Patricia murmured a little later, her head braced on her bent arm and her eyes closed.

"No," I admitted, watching the rising sun play over her lovely face. Despite her joy over Monty I sensed the anguish pulsing just beneath her skin; I could not help but notice the amount of times her eyes sought and held Axton. The shadows beneath them were deep, her honey hair loose and tangled. I felt a sharp pang at the thought that someone should brush it for her – and that someone had been me, for so long now. I'd cared for her as I would a beloved little sister and now I had to entrust her care to Cole. And there was no chance to discuss weighty matters with Patricia, such as how she felt about her inevitable future with Cole; I witnessed the same desperate agony stemming from Axton even though his face was currently impassive.

"We shall spend one night at the homestead of Charles and Fannie Rawley, no more," Patricia whispered. "We can't endanger them that way."

I wanted badly to accompany them, to meet Miles's parents and his remaining brothers, but I knew there was no way; there wasn't time.

"Do you think Dredd knows we're not at the convent anymore?" I kept my voice low. Neither of us wanted to mention the man we feared most, as if to give voice to Fallon Yancy's name was to conjure him. The minute he resurfaced in Chicago Fallon would discover our last known whereabouts; and try as he might both Patricia and I knew Dredd wouldn't refuse his brother information.

"We must assume they both do." Her soft voice was heavy with the burden of this knowledge. "And they shall come looking. Last night I told Cole of Fallon's bizarre disappearance, and what you and I believe about him, that he is perhaps able to jump through time. I'm sure you are aware that Marshall has shared the truth with Cole and Axton…" Her voice broke over his name and she cleared her throat, glancing toward the wagon seat where Cole sat. But Cole was listening to Malcolm, not paying attention to my conversation with Patricia. She continued, "They know when he and you are from. Cole confessed that at first he was uncertain what to believe as truth, but he has come to trust your Marshall quite implicitly."

"Marsh told me the same thing. I'm so glad they trust each other." I paused for a beat. "You have to go to the last place Fallon would ever look."

"Does such a place exist?" she whispered.

Malcolm halted Aces, indicating the horizon ahead. "Cedar River, due west."

My heart sank; Patricia curled her fingers through mine. We had but minutes now.

"Ruthie…" she whispered, rife with quiet desperation.

I squeezed her hand. "I'll watch out for him, I promise you."

She clenched her jaws, restraining tears with herculean effort; she could not stop her gaze from seeking Axton one last time. He'd drawn Ranger to a halt, flanking the wagon on the left and subsequently out of Cole's sight, and allowed himself this last moment to look Patricia's way. Axton's face was cast in auburn light and divulged no errant emotion – but his eyes betrayed him, burning with everything he realized he could not say, with what he was giving up, however unwillingly. Their gazes locked for an eternal instant before Axton broke it, looking westward instead. I felt the trembling in Patricia's body.

She brought her knuckles to her mouth as she whispered, "Good-bye."

We parted ways on the banks of the Cedar River. The decision had been made for Cole and Malcolm to take Patricia and the baby north into Minnesota, while Marshall, Axton, and I would push west, toward Howardsville. Despite having discussed nearly everything else during the night hours, Marsh and I had not spoken of one crucial topic – the probability of our successful return to the future. The six of us stood now in a tight cluster near a rushing river brimming with springtime thaw. We were all overtired, and wired as a result; it would not sink in until much later this day that we were actually parting ways, possibly forever.

"You'll be in Landon," I marveled, hugging Patricia with all of my strength, for about the tenth time. I gushed, "You'll see Flickertail Lake and White Oaks Lodge! Of course Shore Leave hasn't been built yet, but I can almost believe Mom and Camille and everyone will be waiting there for you." I was babbling at this point, tears in my grainy eyes.

Malcolm stood near my right elbow as I spoke, which he touched, requesting with quiet intensity, "My Cora. Tell me of her. Marshall has spoken of her…"

Given the nature of our abrupt introductions, I'd not yet been allowed a chance to really speak with Malcolm, though Marshall explained last night that Malcolm wanted badly to ask me about Camille – that is, *Cora*, as he had known her. I studied Malcolm Carter in the morning light; he was lean and wiry, broad-shouldered and dark-haired, his eyes the deep, rich brown of pecans. His mouth was full and soft, his nose with a sprinkling of freckles which lent a boyish sweetness to his handsome face. His eyes stung me, though – the sadness in their depths was devastating and irreparable. Even though he did not exactly resemble Mathias, I sensed my brother-in-law within him just as strongly as ever.

"I believe her soul is in my sister, Camille," I said softly. I wanted to tell Malcolm everything I could, to ease even a fraction of the ache in his eyes, but circumstance and the press of time were forcing us apart. I bit down my regret and hurried to say, "She is married to Mathias Carter and she knew you in Mathias, from the first." Malcolm drew a slow breath. "She is happy, then?"

"So happy," I said, and Malcolm engulfed me in a hug. I felt the wetness of tears on his face as his cheek briefly rested against my temple. I held him tightly. "Camille knows of you. She has your picture and she loved you from the moment she first saw it. She keeps it near her at all times."

Malcolm nodded, unable to reply. His chest heaved, only once, but roughly.

"She never stopped loving you. And she forgave you a long time ago, you must know that. If she knew I was speaking to you, she would be overjoyed."

"She is a mother?" He drew back to search my eyes.

"Many times over," I said, joy in revealing these truths to him intermixed with his pain.

"It's what we always wanted," Malcolm whispered. "Will you…speak to her, of me?"

"Nothing would make her happier. I will tell her all about you."

Next I hugged Cole. "Take care of them. Swear to me."

"I will, Ruthie. Thank you for caring for her these many months." Cole drew back and regarded Axton, with grudging respect. "And you, Axton Douglas. I owe you more than I could ever repay."

Axton nodded, his lips compressed in a grim line. He was pale beneath his tanned skin, doing his best to keep his haunted eyes from Patricia.

Axton, Patricia tried to say, her lips forming the single word though no sound emerged, and Ax relented and hugged her, though quickly, almost stiffly, a far cry from the way he'd held and kissed her yesterday in the chapel – but that would remain our secret. It was the least I could do for him. I saw what it cost him to draw away and know that Patricia was exiting his life, perhaps for the final time.

But he kept his expression in check.

Marshall passed the baby back to Patricia's arms. He said emotionally, "Thank you for being there for my Ruthie."

Patricia stood on tiptoe to kiss his cheek. "Promise to bring her back to me, soon."

The air between us was fragile, tense with all the things we wished to express in this limited moment, and sharp with those we couldn't bear to acknowledge. Dangers lurked everywhere, around every bend. Thousands of dangers and the maddening pulse of the unknown. And beneath this was the fact that if it was possible, Marshall and I planned to return to the future we'd once known, far removed from this place and time, to reclaim the life we'd once lived.

"I love you," I whispered, holding Patricia one last time.

"I know it. I could not love you more," Patricia whispered. "Dear Ruthann. Be safe. Please, be safe."

"We'll send word," Cole said. "As soon as we've arrived in Landon."

"Look for word by July," Malcolm said. "If all goes well, we'll reunite by next summer."

Marshall nodded and panicky breaths pushed at my chest. But I said steadily, "Yes."

I looked back until they were out of sight.

Chapter Twenty-Six

WE RODE HARD, NOT STOPPING UNTIL ADVANCING EVENING forced us to slow. The wagon had been left behind, as of course Patricia could not sit horseback to travel, and even with Marsh and I riding double on Blade we covered dozens of miles, stopping for the night somewhere in north-central Iowa. Marshall and Axton, who were well supplied from the days of planning their "assault" on the convent, determined we would have food enough to get at least to the edge of South Dakota. Or what would become South Dakota in the future; right now it remained a territory.

"If the weather keeps fair we can get back to Howardsville in about two weeks," Marshall had explained, though he was quick to clarify, "As long as it isn't too rough on you, angel."

I assured him it was not. Marshall's presence, the gift of being restored to each other, overshadowed all else. As long as he was beside me, I felt we could face anything.

He was in the process of building a fire near a small copse of cottonwoods, a lively stream burbling in the background. Ax was down by the creek watering Ranger while I cared for Blade, who had been recovered in Howardsville back in October. I situated Blade's heavy saddle on a low-hanging branch and rubbed his silvery hide with the bristle brush, murmuring soft endearments, occasionally resting my forehead on his flank; I could not help but think of Miles. Miles, whose soul was right here within Marshall and fulfilling his promise to me, I had no doubt. I looked over my shoulder at my man, crouched beside a bundle of kindling and about to strike a second match, and my heart felt incapable of holding so much emotion, of containing so much love – the strength of it would tear me at the seams.

Marshall felt the heat of my gaze and looked up from where he knelt by the fire, its growing flames flickering in his gray eyes, and then he was advancing without a word, without a sound, drawn to me as an arrow released upon a target. I dropped the brush and he seized me in his arms, claiming my mouth with no restraint, an untamed force that would no longer be denied. His lips opened over mine, tongue stroking and plunging, tasting me from the inside out; I moaned and clutched his shoulders, grinding my hips against him in a fever of need. I was still wearing the long black dress from the convent, stained and dirty and probably beyond repair – but beneath it, I was completely and blessedly naked.

We struggled in a wild whirlwind of motion, bunching the heavy layers of skirt up past my thighs, my fingers flying over the fastenings on Marshall's pants – the incredible hardness of him in my grasp as I stroked his familiar length, up and down. I dropped to my knees and brought him into my mouth, swirling my tongue, taking him deep, tasting how he had already come a little, as he gasped, low and harsh, and clutched the back of my head. We forgot our proximity to Axton, forgot the fading sun continuing to lend its light to the evening, disregarded Blade and the humming mosquitoes and the chill air. I stood, breathless and aching for him, and Marshall groaned as he cupped my bare flesh at long last, kissing me so forcefully my head bowed backward. He clamped a firm hold on my hips, my legs threading his waist as he backed me roughly against the trunk of a nearby cottonwood and slid fully home.

"*Ruthann*," he gasped, as I quivered violently and came all over him with his first thrust. I muffled my moaning cries against the hard curve of his shoulder, clamping my teeth, holding fast with arms and legs as he pounded into me, just exactly as I needed.

"*Yes*," I begged, rocking against him. The outside world ceased to exist. There was only Marshall, the onrushing force of him overtaking my senses as he plundered my body and sated our souls. "Oh God, Marshall, *yes*…"

"*Oh holy Jesus*," he groaned, shuddering as he came in a hot rush, suckling my lower lip and gripping my hips hard enough to leave fingerprints.

I kept my legs clenched about his hips, possessive, ravenous for more, breathing as though I'd just sprinted two miles; I peppered his neck and chin with wet little kisses, holding his jaws with both hands. I knew – I really did – that we had to restrain this need; Axton would return with Ranger in tow at any second, but I could not make myself stop.

"You feel so goddamn good," Marsh whispered hoarsely, as our bodies stayed joined and he stayed hard. His eyes blazed gray fire.

Reality inserted itself in the steady sound of approaching footsteps and I became slowly aware of our surroundings, smelling campfire smoke and the tang of green leaves; the whisper of flowing water reached my ears. I blinked and threw my arms around Marshall's neck, hugging him with all my strength; he exhaled against my temple, kissing my ear and whispering, "Thank you, angel. I needed that so much. Oh God, my knees are shaky now."

"Same here. In case you couldn't tell."

As we whispered, Marsh lowered me back to the earth, simultaneously helping to resituate my tumbled skirts and hauling his pants into place. Once we were safely clothed he grinned, so handsome, his eyes full of love as he smoothed tangled curls from my hot, perspiring face. He kissed me flush on the lips just as Axton appeared from down by the creek, leading Ranger. Ax was pale and drawn, his eyes grim even as he attempted a smile for us; probably it was obvious what we'd just been doing – the air surrounding us was almost visibly steaming – but Ax made no comment and simply tethered Ranger near Blade.

Marshall caught my hand and led me to the fire; beneath the heavy skirt my bare thighs were slippery with the aftermath of lovemaking but my concern was at once directed at Axton, who was hurting way down deep in his bones. He'd risked himself to save Patricia and me in an act of utter selflessness; he loved me and was in love with Patricia, and yet neither of us could give him the love he desired in return. He'd saved us because he was a good and decent man, because it was the right thing to do, only to turn us over to other men. Axton sat to my left, wordless, bracing his forearms over his bent knees.

And then he closed his eyes and, without drama, lowered his head.

"Ax," I whispered, kneeling beside him, wrapping an arm across his wide shoulders. "Oh, *Axton*..."

"*Don't*. Please don't tell me it's all right. I can't...bear it." He spoke as though a fist gripped his Adam's apple. His shoulders heaved and I looked up at Marsh, telling him with my eyes I needed his help; Marshall's shirt was askew, his dark hair disheveled from my questing fingers, and a large, cherry-red hickey adorned the side of his neck to match the raspy stubble-burns his scruff had left on mine. His brows crooked in concern as he looked from me to Axton and I sensed his desire to say something, anything at all, to help ease Axton's despair. But Marsh knew as well as me there was nothing to say. Instead of speaking, he crouched on Axton's other side and added the comfort of his touch along with mine. He gripped the younger man's shoulder and squeezed.

Axton covered his face with both hands.

"I am so sorry," I whispered, rubbing a gentle circle on his spine, mid-back. I knew it would do less than no good to say stupid things like, *You'll get over this. You'll find a woman you love just as much.*

His words emerged low-pitched with grief, punctuated by harsh breaths. "My heart is torn up, Ruthie, oh Jesus, *it hurts so much*, and now she's gone again and I don't know if she's safe..."

Over Axton's bent head, Marshall's pained gaze held mine.

Why does love have to be so punishing? I wondered, understanding that Marshall could very well be in Axton's place; if life had conspired to keep us separated, the gouging anguish would be exactly the same, for both of us.

"Cole will keep her safe," I whispered against my better judgment, not sure if it was the right time to remind him. But I had to say something.

Axton lifted his face and his expression cut at me. He gritted his teeth, nostrils flaring. "I know. And I know she...has to be with him. And I know I am a *goddamn fool* but I can't stop loving her. How can I live the rest of my life without her? How, Ruthie? It isn't possible." His beautiful green eyes were steeped in dark certainty. "Since I met her in Howardsville that morning I knew I was hers, and that she was for me. It's the strongest thing I've ever felt. How can it be wrong?"

"Loving someone is never wrong," Marsh said, and his tone was gentle.

"Isn't it? What if you'd found Ruthie only to discover she'd already married Miles Rawley?" Axton suddenly demanded, catching me off guard as swiftly as a white-knuckled fist to the gut. Ashes seemed to coat my tongue as I observed this question strike similarly at Marshall's composure.

Marshall said with quiet certainty, "Then my heart would have turned to dust, Axton." Though he directed his words at Ax, I knew he was really speaking to me. "Even knowing what I do about Miles, even understanding how he felt about Ruthann, I would have been finished, for good. There wouldn't be a place I could ride, no place on this earth far enough to outrun that kind of heartbreak."

Axton whispered, "Then you understand." There was a beat of complete silence before he stood. "I'll be back before morning."

"Where are you going?" I cried, stricken by his unexpected mention of Miles but unwilling to let him do something desperate.

"I aim to ride a spell, that's all," Ax said, his tone softening. "Don't worry, Ruthie. I don't want you to worry, not over me."

I stood and hugged him. "I love you, you know I do. And you saved us. I will never forget that. There is someone out there for you, I swear to you, Ax."

"Thank you," he whispered, even though I knew he was unwilling to accept that last bit. He gently set me aside, unwinding the lead line and gracefully climbing atop Ranger, who he had not yet unsaddled. He angled his horse northward and heeled Ranger into a trot.

I turned to Marshall to find his speculative gaze following after Axton, man and horse rapidly erased by the dusk. Marsh said, "I swear he reminds me so much of –"

"Case," I said at once, and Marshall nodded affirmation.

"But if *Cole* is Case, then who…" Marsh cocked his head, still in a crouch beside the fire, forearms braced on his thighs.

"I would have come to you," I said then, the fire dancing over my face as I spoke. Axton was out of sight. I began unbuttoning the front of my dress, with controlled urgency, holding Marshall's somber gaze. "I would have come to you, *no matter what*. You know this."

Marshall slowly stood to his full height. I slipped my arms from the long sleeves, one at a time, heart throbbing. His strong hands encircled my waist, bringing me against his body.

"I know," he whispered. "I've never known anything more."

Much later, wrapped around each other in the shelter of two heavy blankets positioned near the scarlet glow of the embers, he murmured, "I miss the strangest things. Like Twinkies. You know I don't even like the stupid things and yet I find myself craving one."

"Chili fries," I said, and giggled as he groaned. "Like your Aunt Julie made at The Spoke."

"Hell *yes*, and what about Chinese takeout…"

"*Mmm*. Egg rolls, fried shrimp….oh God, chocolate-covered peanuts…"

"You do love those. You had them in our coffee canister, instead of coffee."

"Pizza," I said, giggling more, my cheek against his chest in this languid moment between bouts of lovemaking. "Maybe we could try to make one. Has pizza been invented yet?"

Marshall laughed, burying the sound against the top of my head; I could almost pretend we were in our old queen-sized bed in our little apartment in Jalesville, once upon a long time ago, over a century into the future. He whispered, "Imagine the sound when you pop the top on a beer can."

"What about a toilet flushing?"

"Or a radio."

"Car engines."

"My hands sometimes twitch to feel a steering wheel when I'm riding a horse."

"Mine too, that's funny."

"I've dreamed I'm playing my drums, a couple of times."

"Oh, honey…"

"It's funny the stuff you practically forget you knew."

"Remember when we had sex in your dad's basement while you were playing your old drum set?"

"Of course. You didn't think I'd forget that, did you?"

"The cymbals kept pinging."

"*You* kept pinging," Marshall teased, and we scuffled, the blanket on top of us sliding free and exposing my bare legs to the chilly air. He was quick to tuck it back around us, tenderly kissing my neck, using one hand to latch my right leg more securely around his hip. "Stay in here, angel, it's cold out there."

"Only because you make me ping so hard," I said as he shifted our positions, tucking me underneath him. Enfolded in his delicious heat, I snuggled closer.

"Nothing brings me more pleasure," he murmured, licking a teasing, ticklish path upward between my breasts. I could smell my scent all over him, just as his inundated my skin and hair and tongue. We'd sweat and come all over each other so many times in the past few hours, as the stars rotated above us, that I'd lost count. We hadn't slept, too preoccupied with one another.

"Are you hungry?" I worried, hearing his stomach growl, pressing my palm there.

The teasing expression on his face dissipated. "Yes, but the sight of your face is all the sustenance I need." He used his index finger to outline my lips, then traced a soft path down my neck and a gentle circle around each nipple, at last resting his palm over my heartbeat. His voice was a husky murmur. "And this. Feeling you beside me, the warm softness of you, seeing the love in your eyes. I don't know how I've gone on day to day without that."

Our bare limbs were intertwined; Marshall had come in me probably a dozen times already. The flesh between my legs was decidedly tender but still I craved the feeling of him inside me again, where I could hold him as close as humanly possible and know for those moments we could not be forced apart.

"I've thought so many times about the first night I ever touched you," he whispered, curling his fingers through mine and bringing my knuckles to his lips. "August eleventh, 2013, the most incredible night of my life, to that point. I will never forget the perfect beauty of that, when you let me touch you for the first time. Ruthie, I have thought of nothing but you, for so long…"

"I shouldn't have left," I whispered, and tears blurred my vision. It struck me that I hadn't apologized for the winter afternoon I'd fled our apartment. I cupped his face with my free hand and finally said, "I know I hurt you in so many ways and I am so sorry. I know you were just worried about me."

His eyes were wet with tears as he studied me. "I would lie awake and think of what I would say to you if I had the power to rewind time. How I would beg your forgiveness. What I would feel to have you back in my arms. I was so jealous, and so stupid. I let my anger get the best of me… can you forgive me?" His throat was raw with emotion.

"Marshall Augustus," I whispered. I traced my thumb over his cheekbone, caressing the contours of his face as I had always done. "I forgave you a long time ago. We're together again and it's all that matters."

He held me close to his heart.

I confessed, "I'm scared to sleep, for fear when I wake up this will have been nothing more than a dream. I've dreamed of you so many times."

He brought his forehead to mine, our eyes an inch apart. "I will never let you go again. Not ever. This I vow."

My thighs curved again around him. "I was so scared. That was my worst fear, that I wouldn't see you again."

He gently tongued my lips, sinking deeper into my body as I moaned and arched upward. He whispered, "I have begged all the powers that be for you to be returned to me, angel, begged all the stars in the sky, prayed every prayer I've ever known, day and evening and night…"

I dug my fingers in his hair. "I need you, *I need you so much*…"

His expression was almost stern with the passionate intensity of what our love created – the strength and joy of what bound us.

"You are mine," he said intently, between open-mouthed kisses. "You have always been mine, Ruthann."

"Yes," I breathed, clinging with arms and legs as he surged fully inside. "*Yes*. And you are mine…*I love you*…"

He took me once again beyond any words, to the sweet, hot, sacred place I knew only because of him. The place that rose up and swirled about us, wrapped us in our own private world, let us linger there for long, trembling moments, the place that heard my gasping moans and his husky, throaty cries of release, and where we at last sank together and were allowed a moment's respite from the outside world. And where our souls clung just as intently as our bodies, at long last reunited.

Axton and Ranger had returned with the morning light. Marsh and I slept for a few hours before dawn, braided together; I woke to the sight of a bleak, cloudy sky, safe and warm against Marshall's hairy chest. Axton was crouched with his back to us, tending the fire. As I stirred, Marshall opened one eye and whispered, "Morning, darlin'."

"Morning," I whispered, kissing his neck, doubly grateful for the heavy blanket, as I was completely naked.

Axton murmured, "Good morning, you two."

Marshall, also naked, was experiencing what we'd always called the 'alarm cock,' stiff as a tree trunk beneath the shelter of the blanket. His lips curved with a half-grin and he smoothed a warm hand over my ass, squeezing lightly, acknowledging what he wanted us to do but what we most assuredly could *not*, at least just now. His scruff was at the point it was nearly a beard, a sexy, menacing, pirate-type beard.

"We forgot to put our clothes back on," Marsh groaned. "Axton, I hope you aren't easily offended."

"I ain't," Axton said, still facing away, and to my relief I detected the slightest hint of amusement in his voice. "I'm sorry I can't give you more privacy."

"Axton Douglas," I reprimanded. "You don't have to be sorry for a thing." I paused. "What's your middle name? I just realized I don't know."

"It's Ethan. You told me yours one time. Marie, right?"

"That's right. Well, Axton Ethan Douglas," I said formally. "What are you cooking? It smells delicious."

"I shot a couple of prairie hens." Ax dared to look over his shoulder. He was exhausted; there were dark smudges beneath his eyes but his familiar face broke into a smile. "I've never seen you look as beautiful as you do right now, Ruthie, and it makes me happy."

There were numerous ways this could have been taken out of context; after all, I lay naked and sleep-tousled in Marshall's arms no more than a few feet away from Axton as he made this observation. But it was Ax, whose sincerity and ingenuousness could never be doubted; I knew he loved me and was truly glad to see me in a state of happiness. Marshall was also touched, I could tell even without a word. I lay sprawled over his chest beneath the blanket and he tucked loose hair behind my ears with both hands, just as Miles had once done, with the same adept tenderness. Tears splashed down my cheeks as I whispered, "Thank you. Both of you."

"And I agree, wholeheartedly," Marsh said, his fingers lingering in my curls, brushing away my tears with his long thumbs.

"We've got miles to travel before nightfall," Axton said, turning back to the iron stakes braced over the fire, rotating the meat. "I thought it might be nice to have a hearty breakfast."

"You thought right," I said. There were so many things I wanted to ask – so many things we needed to discover, and so many to fear. But under this pewter sunrise, a sky thick with clouds that appeared to have been shaded by heavy pencil strokes, tucked close to Marshall, I was limp with relief. I was well aware of the dangers all around us. *Vole. Aemon Turnbull.* And far worse, Fallon Yancy waited somewhere out there, stealthy as a predatory animal, one that stalked its victims to certain death.

But just at this second my mind could hold no other emotions than love and gratitude. And determination. Marshall and I would figure out what was required of us here in the nineteenth century. We would ensure the safety of the Rawley family as best we could – surely that was why we'd been drawn to this time, to ensure their lineage continued onward. And even if Marshall and I couldn't physically return to the future, I was still determined to get a message to my family and the Rawleys, a message they could find in the twenty-first century – they had to be made aware of Fallon. We had to find a way to reach them, even if we remained here.

The way back, I thought, holding the promise of these words in my mind. *If return is possible, if there is a way back, we'll find it.*

Chapter Twenty-Seven

In Between

I KILLED MY MOTHER IN 1864.

She was the first person I ever killed. She'd been fucking a hired hand in my father's barn while my father was away fighting the Rebs and I slit her throat with my fishing knife, utilizing the darkness and plain surprise to my advantage. I was a few months from my eleventh year, slightly built for my age, and no one suspected I could use a knife so well. The hired hand, no older than a score or so, younger than Mother by a good decade, could not react fast enough. My blade slipped between his ribs and he fell back on top of Mother, but differently than he'd been on top of her earlier, while I'd spied from the haymow.

Dredd never guessed the truth. I told him Mother was sick and died in her sleep. I'd buried her under the oak tree out beyond the house by the time Dredd woke that humid morning, a precursor to a sweltering July day. I wanted to tell him what I'd really done, how I'd killed two people without either of them uttering a sound, how I'd hauled their wilted bodies in the wheelbarrow in which our father hauled dead pigs, depositing them into the ground in one hole it had taken me almost until dawn to dig. How the pit was deep but not quite long enough, and the bodies made shapes like the letter C once I'd rolled them in it. How I'd said, *Sleep tight*, before I'd shoveled the earth back over them.

But of course I wasn't stupid enough to let the pride of my accomplishment override basic common sense. Instead, I told Dredd to make a wooden cross for Mother. With the War on, no one made a fuss over one more grave. No one would ever know two bodies filled it, unless I allowed them to know. Fannie Rawley did not discover Mother was dead until she rode over in the flatbed wagon, along with Grant and Miles, to visit, the Wednesday next.

She said, *For the love of all that's holy, why did you not ride to us with the news, Fallon? You poor boys. Oh, you poor little boys.* And she forced us back to the Rawleys' homestead with her for the remainder of that summer.

Ma was sick, Dredd kept saying. *She was fevered.*

Dredd believed everything I ever told him.

The first time I leaped it was utterly inadvertent, and I woke with the skin peeling from my face under the blazing midmorning sun. I leaped only a week into the future that time, though it took time to make sense of where I was. Of *when* I was. The *why* of it I did not attempt to understand, at least not back then.

It's because you're special, was my first thought. *More capable, more intelligent, more powerful than others.*

I had tried for over a decade to manage my leaps, all without success. At times I was only allowed a few minutes before being whisked back to the past. The most I'd been allowed was a full three days in Chicago in 2013, which I used to my extreme advantage. I kept words and numbers and facts catalogued in my mind, the only storage facility I trusted. I made it my sole purpose in life to ensure the Yancy family continued to increase its wealth and subsequent power. I was determined we would never again know the humiliation we'd faced after my father's public disgrace in 1868.

But still, I could not leap if I *tried* to leap, which aggravated me into murderous states of rage. The leaping happened spontaneously and there was no pattern other than that I seemed drawn to the early decades of the twenty-first century. The first time I'd leaped so far through time I'd gaped like a halfwit, overwhelmed by the dazzle of a world far removed from the nineteenth century in which I'd been raised in near-poverty. I would do anything, I understood, to remain in the twenty-first century indeterminately. But it seemed my true purpose was to work at securing my family's holdings in the place I returned faithfully after every leap, the timeline to which I'd been born in 1853, and where I spent most of my days.

And I was wildly successful. I learned in my leaps of railroad stocks, gold bonds, silver bonds. Land. Real estate. Stock market dabbling. I retained tidbits from each and every leap, returning with new information every time, aided in part by my descendants. Derrick Yancy was T.K.'s only child. I officially met him in 1993, when I founded Capital Overland as 'Franklin Yancy.' Derrick was nine years old then and I was already well-acquainted with his father, T.K., who had learned quickly to trust me, mainly because I knew everything about him and everything which had led to his vast fortune. Together we'd created *Franklin*, passing him off as an older brother, a son T.K. had fathered before his first marriage. To Derrick I was like a magician, appearing intermittently and at a variety of ages, a man his own father called 'son.'

Through T.K., I formed a remote business relationship with Ronald Turnbull; the alliance between our families was old and valuable. Very occasionally I fucked Ron's whore wife, Christina, a woman addicted to the thrill of power, which I could appreciate. Despite her willingness to spread her skilled legs I was not anxious to see her again, as during my last visit I had disappeared from her private bathroom, still reeking of her perfume; explaining this would be an annoyance, and would require precision. Though she knew everything her husband did, illegal or otherwise, Christina had never guessed the truth about my abilities and I meant to keep it that way. It became quickly obvious why I'd been dragged from the luxury of her downtown condo and deposited back into the nineteenth century.

Dredd's cunt wife had gone missing, and though I despised the sharp-eyed bitch, Patricia Biddeford remained necessary to my plans, in that her presence was required in order to produce an heir. Dredd's purpose was linked to this, of course; he would father this heir and continue the family line. Retrieving Dredd's wife involved a journey to Howardsville – and how I fucking hated being reduced to travel by horseback when I carried the knowledge of cars and jets – even so, I had never dared passage in an aircraft, uncertain whether I would survive an inadvertent leap while my body was suspended miles above the earth.

And as it turned out, this latest leap had been my last since the woman named Ruthann Rawley, a woman whose surname I'd understood to be Davis, fractured my arm in my passenger car. If she had been lying about knowing my time of death, she bore impressive skills; I could not determine if the statement was false, an unplanned act of desperation, or not – she had caught me off guard, a singular rarity. Something in her eyes led me to believe she was serious, and I trusted my own instincts above all else. I recognized she was both misplaced in time and had information I required – which was why I'd let her live.

But she's dead now. The moment you force answers from her, she's fucking dead, I reassured myself, up and pacing for the countless time, keeping my broken arm close to my ribs. It hurt, but I'd borne worse injury; the last man who'd physically harmed me later died in agony, at my hands. Ruthann meant to kill me that night; the intent was unmistakable in her eyes, and it was this act which sent me to Between.

Several times my leaps led to Between and each of those times occurred when my life was endangered. *Between* was the name I'd assigned it, a place perhaps best likened to a Catholic's idea of purgatory, as time seemed not to exist in any form here, a hollow space cloaked in vague shadows. It was like trying to see objects through a fogged window; the more closely I looked, the denser the murk. Sounds were muffled as though plugs dammed up my ears, even that of my own voice. Indeed, all my senses were muted in Between.

When I returned from what seemed mere minutes in Between, weeks or even months might have passed in the real world – the world outside Between, that is, as I had no idea where Between actually existed. I could walk for miles here and go nowhere; my footfalls made no sound. I had never encountered another person, nor as much as another object. It seemed to be a holding place and I disliked admitting to any weakness – but Between was a disarming void, a prison of sorts. And yet, it offered protection. While in Between, I planned. I paced and I planned, and minutes would tick past on the stopwatch within my head. Departure was unfailingly abrupt and I was anticipating departure at any second.

Ruthann Rawley was first on my list of people who needed killing. The goddamn Rawley family had worked against mine for too long now; no more would I allow this to happen. I would see to it that Dredd impregnated his wife, Patricia – I *had* seen this, during a leap – and I would see that Ruthann Davis Rawley met her end. Even better, that those she loved met theirs first, so she could witness what her attempts to thwart me had caused. After all, to my understanding there was no more chance for pain once a person was dead. And I intended to cause her pain, this woman connected with far too many people who worked against my plans – Malcolm Carter and Cole Spicer, both names bitter on my tongue; the goddamn Rawleys.

Once I took care of her family I would go after her lover. Once I'd calmed, once I'd searched my memory, I realized I had seen Ruthann during a leap to 1882; a brief leap, in which I was present at a hanging, and her lover was one of those about to be hung. Another Rawley, of course.

Soon, I promised myself.

And as the thought crossed my mind a small rush of air stirred the hairs on my body, a feeling I had come to anticipate, one that meant I was about to depart Between. I crouched in preparation and was simultaneously struck with an odd childhood memory, of hiding in the tall prairie grass near the shanty in which I'd been raised, hearing my brother's voice as he counted to ten in a singsong rhythm. In my head, Dredd shouted triumphantly, *Ready or not, here I come!*

I smiled, repeating the words as Between faded away and I was allowed to leap.

I am coming for you, Ruthann.

Ready or not.

Printed in the United States
by Baker & Taylor Publisher Services